JOHN THE BELOVED

Deborah Osborne Wyatt

ELM HILL

A Division of
HarperCollins Christian Publishing

www.elmhillbooks.com

John the Beloved

Published in Nashville, Tennessee, by Elm Hill, an imprint of Thomas Nelson. Elm Hill and Thomas Nelson are registered trademarks of HarperCollins Christian Publishing, Inc.

Elm Hill titles may be purchased in bulk for educational, business, fund-raising, or sales promotional use. For information, please e-mail SpecialMarkets@ ThomasNelson.com.

All Scripture quotations, unless otherwise indicated, are taken from the King James Version. Public domain.

Library of Congress Cataloging-in-Publication Data

Library of Congress Control Number: 2019909192

ISBN 978-1-400326440 (Paperback)
ISBN 978-1-400326457 (Hardbound)
ISBN 978-1-400326464 (eBook)

To my beloved husband, Jeffrey without whom this book would never have been written or published. You are the one that my heart longs for and our love is my favorite and the most beautiful symphony. To paraphrase Song of Solomon: your mouth is most sweet! You are altogether lovely. You are my beloved. You are my life. You are my love. You are my friend. I love you forever.

TABLE OF CONTENTS

Prologue

His name is John. Other than this and the fact that his music resonates within my soul, I know nothing about him; nothing except that I am falling in love with him. Who is this man? Why is he more than any other? To understand, you must listen to his music. It is unlike any sound you have heard before and it is as unique to him as his fingerprint. The way he arranges the notes on a scale is unorthodox yet it is genius and his talent is unrivaled. I wonder: Why does he shy away from the world? Why does he choose to share his music only with me? And why does he not wish to meet face to face? I have no answer to these questions but I am grateful to him. His music saved my life. The song that is our story began four months ago on a summer evening in August in Indiana.

CHAPTER ONE

The day was turning into evening. As the shadows lengthened upon the fields, the heat began to dissipate and the sun faded into a warm, golden glow instead of a harsh yellow blaze. I needed some time to myself, so after supper I went for a walk. Eventually, I found myself in the cornfield. August is one of my favorite times that God has created. The corn is high and green and when the summer breezes blow through the stalks, it creates the most beautiful sound. Combine that with the surrounding sounds of nature and you have the most glorious symphony of praise from the creation to the Creator.

I was five when I realized that where I hear music, others hear only sound. It was a day much like this one. I was working in the field with my Daett. We had paused to wipe our brows clean of sweat and to drink water deeply. As Daett drank, I closed my eyes and listened to the orchestra.

"Isn't it beautiful?" I asked Daett.

"Nothing is more beautiful than working hard to ensure a bountiful harvest," Daett agreed.

"No, Daett," I replied. "I mean, yes the harvest is beautiful, but I was talking about the music the wind makes as it blows through the cornstalks."

Daett looked at me curiously as if I was not known to him.

"John, that is fanciful talk and it is not fitting for you to talk in such a way," Daett said firmly as he pulled on his beard.

1

Even at five, I knew that Daett pulling on his beard meant he was distressed. I knew that I should not upset him any further and that there would be consequences if I did, but this question of sound versus music so perplexed my young mind that I had to ask him.

"What do you hear, Daett?"

"Wind," he snorted and glared down at me as if in warning. I heeded his warning and silently went back to work, but the questions kept coming into my mind.

Now a grown man of twenty-two, I'm standing in the same field and smiled sadly at the memory. It was unfortunate to think that others could not hear the music that I do. I wondered how much happier Daett could be if only he could hear music like me instead of only sound.

I shook my head as if to shake Daett out of my mind if only for a little while. I was determined to enjoy the symphony while I still could. Being a man, it was time for me to cease being childish. Turning off the music was proving to be more difficult than I could have ever imagined, and it was delaying my progression into manhood.

I tilted my head back and closed my eyes, allowing the final sunbeams of the day to warm my face, and I waited silently. My patience was rewarded shortly. The breeze began softly then grew stronger before waning again. Just when I thought the song was over, the wind regained strength and began to crescendo, ultimately reaching fortissimo. In my mind, I began to see the notes arranging themselves upon the measures. I found myself wishing I had brought a piece of paper and a pencil with me; then I remembered I had promised myself composing music would stop. I was a farmer not a composer, and I need to start thinking like the former and not the latter.

Just as I was turning to head back towards the house, the sound of beautiful music reached my ears. Captivated by the beauty of the music, I began walking towards the sound. It drew me to the edge of the cornfield and to the end of my Daett's property and there I stopped. The lights glowed from within the house that was now visible to me. Through the open window, the music came dancing out towards me, pulling on me like a harness on a horse, both constraining and guiding me towards the source of the beauty that filled my ears and created an odd and desperate longing within my heart.

A young woman sat at a grand piano playing a piece of music. Her body swayed slightly and gracefully to the tempo. She was completely immersed in the song. I was captivated. Unconsciously, I stepped forward almost out of the field and onto the lawn. Then I caught myself and took a step backwards. I did not want her to see me. I was afraid that if she did, she would stop and I did not want the music to cease. She was just as lovely as the notes she played. As I watched her, a desire within me that I thought I had purged myself of long ago began to burn within my heart stronger than ever before. I wanted to hear my music played aloud.

♫

Music is my refuge and solace. From the time I was three, I have been playing the piano. The notes and keys are more familiar to me than the words of the English language. Indeed, I find it easier to communicate with my fingers through music than with my vocal cords. Since I have spent more hours a day playing the piano than anything else, my friendships are almost nonexistent, but the amount of songs I can play is extensive, many of them from memory. Tonight, I was in the mood for Liszt. "Liebestraum" swept me away as always and, for the duration of the stanzas, my mind was filled with the joy that beautiful music always brings.

Sadly, the song always ends and reality does not. The long suppressed tears now broke free. I slid off the piano bench and onto the floor and since I was all alone, I allowed myself to cry. I cried because of the pain and the fear, but mostly I cried over the loss and waste. It was a true cliché: life is not fair.

The music had stopped. I had been lying on my back staring at the night sky as I had listened to the lovely music when the music ended abruptly and the sound of harsh sobbing rang out into the night. I sat up and looked through the window. She was lying on the floor crying. My heart broke with compassion at the sight of such sorrow and although I didn't know her, I longed to comfort her.

Later while trying to sleep, I could not stop thinking about her. I wondered what caused her such pain and wished that there was a way to bring her solace. Then an idea began to form inside my mind. I crept out of bed and went out to the barn. Ben, my longtime horse and friend, protested when I made him move so that I could get to the floor beneath him. I pried up the floorboards to reveal my hiding place. The metal box was just where I had left it. I had placed the box here nearly three months ago and I was so convinced then that I would never need to retrieve it that I had nailed the floorboards down. Had I deceived myself or if I had never heard the music tonight, would they have stayed buried and eventually forgotten? Perhaps the fact that I had placed my music into the box and hidden it instead of burning it suggested that deep inside, I was unwilling or unable to give my music up completely. I stared at the box in inner turmoil. I closed my eyes and attempted to pray, but my mind was too clouded and confused. The wind blew gently through the barn, rustling the straw melding with the sound of the horses sleeping and occasionally snorting. From the direction of the front porch, I could hear the tinkling of my Mamm's wind chimes. Across the barn, one of the cows mooed quietly as if he was talking in his sleep. Without conscious thought, the sounds began to layer themselves and form notes on stanzas in my mind. My right hand raised and fell in tempo with the song that I could see and hear in my mind. Abruptly, my hand dropped and the song stopped. I stared down at the metal box. The decision had been made: there was no turning back. The orchestra was tuned and poised, ready to play at my bidding. Perhaps if I let them play this one last sonata, I could retire them to silence forever. I retrieved the box, replaced the floorboards and the hay, and patted Ben on the rump, letting him know he could reclaim his spot. Quickly and quietly, I went back into the house and up to my room, relieved that no one had heard me.

Being the eldest son allowed me the joy of having my own room, small as it might be. Tonight, I was especially glad. I looked through the sheets of music from the box. Strangely, it was like seeing the smiling faces of old friends. I felt guilty at how wonderful it was to hold them in my hands and to hear the sounds of them in my mind. All of them were like my children but I had to pick just the right one. Finally, I was able to choose. Satisfied, I closed the box and hid it away. Then after I wrote a quick note, I went back to bed. Finally, sleep overtook me and gave my mind peace.

From the upstairs window, John's Daett, Abram, watched as his son entered the barn. He waited until his son came back out of the barn and into the house before he withdrew from the window. He sat down in the rocking chair heavy in spirit. He listened as John quietly crept back into his room. What was his son hiding from him? He looked at his wife's sleeping face. He was thankful that she was unaware that he was worried about John. Truth be known, he had never understood the boy. Though he tried to be a good Daett and to raise John right, there was always a part of John that he had not been able to understand or reach. He prayed God would be able to deal with that part of John that was foreign to his Daett. He would have faith and leave John in God's hands.

CHAPTER TWO

In sunlight, the fears of the night seemed ridiculous and far away, and hope seemed possible. I went downstairs to the kitchen in search of coffee. Cup in hand, I stared out the big window next to the table and marveled at the beauty of the cornfield shrouded in mist. Briefly I thought about breakfast, but a wave of nausea washed over me just at the thought of toast.

Thank God, I can still drink coffee, I thought with a wry smile. I was a nonfunctioning zombie without my morning pot of coffee.

Looking around at the homey kitchen, I noted countless reminders of my grandparents, Nana and Poppy, everywhere: the framed cross-stitch picture of a quilt draped over fence made by my grandmother, a picture of the two of them smiling into each other's eyes, and the salt-and-pepper shakers that my grandfather had fashioned out of recycled glass chili pepper jars. The hooks on the back of the kitchen door still held Nana's apron and the hat Poppy always wore, as if at any moment they would enter the room and use them. I liked having them there. They comforted me. Even though my grandparents were gone, it was like having a part of them with me every day. Indeed, living in their home during this difficult period of my life gave me a safe haven. As I had no close living relatives except my mother, it was the nearest thing to being with family that I could obtain. On impulse, I crossed over to the door and took down Poppy's hat, brought it up to my nose, and smelled the interior of the hat.

I could faintly smell the scent of Poppy's hair oil. Tears pricked my eyes as I rehung the hat almost reverently.

Having finished my first cup of coffee, I felt more alert. I poured a second cup and headed to the living room. This morning, I was in the mood for Bach. I had just sat down on the piano bench when I noticed a manila envelope lying on the floor in front of the door. Intrigued, I got up, walked over to it, and picked up the envelope. There was no address or writing of any sort on the outside of the envelope. I looked out the front windows but saw no one. I was positive it had not been there the night before. The only assumption I could reach was that someone had slid it under the door either late last night or early this morning. How very odd. From whom could it be? I opened up the envelope and pulled out some papers. The first page was a short note.

Thank you for the beautiful music you played yesterday. I could not help but hear your lovely piano playing through your open window. If it would not be a bother, please play the enclosed music. It will not be up to the standard of which you are accustomed, but I hope it brings you enjoyment. Thank you.

Respectfully,
John

How intriguing and somewhat disconcerting! The view from every window in the house was cornfields, soybean fields, wheat fields, and the road; there wasn't another house within eyesight or earshot. I wondered how someone had heard me playing. Perhaps someone out for an evening stroll? The thought of being spied on was uncomfortable. Still, the tone of the note was pleasant enough. Even with a cursory glance at the sheet music which appeared to be hand-drawn and penned, the arrangement appeared to be very interesting. Without hesitation I went over to the piano, placed the sheet music on the stand, and began to play the music.

It was … beautiful and unlike anything I had heard or played before.

The piece was entitled "Spring Morning" and, as my fingers moved across the keys, I was transported to an April morning. I could almost feel a fresh spring breeze blowing across my face. When the music came to an end, I looked out the window almost expecting to see tulips and daffodils in the lawn instead of roses and daylilies. For the first time in months, I felt happy even if just for a moment.

Unsure of when or even if the lady would play the music, I prayed that I would be in the field when she did, so that I could hear her play my song. I should have asked her to play the piece at a specific time, but that would have been presumptuous and I had already imposed upon her enough. God heard my prayers. Daett had suggested that I check the field to see how the corn was progressing and I had happily complied. I had just pulled back the husks on an ear of corn, looked it over, smelled it, and put a fingernail into one of the kernels to see what the texture was like, when the sound of "Spring Morning" came flowing towards me. Mesmerized, I walked through the field, cornstalks brushing against me until I reached the edge of the field. She was at the piano just like last night. Her long blond hair gleamed in the sunlight. Embarrassed and ashamed to be staring at her unbound hair, I closed my eyes. It did not help. The image of her beauty was burnt into my mind. As the music climaxed, I was overwhelmed with emotion. It brought me unspeakable joy to hear my song played aloud. The notes in reality were even more beautiful than I had imagined.

I had thought that hearing her play one of my songs would have sated this unreasonable desire within me. Instead, I found that the smoldering fire of desire within me to hear her play more of my music was now in full blaze. Dear God, what was I to do? The image of her last night— broken, tearful—came to my mind. I opened my eyes and looked at her through the window. She was looking out towards the lawn and she was smiling. If my music brought her joy in the midst of her sadness, then perhaps it would be all right to bring her another song or two.

♫

The music was over but it played on in my heart. It gave me the strength to face the day. I wondered about John. Who was he? Would he be back? I hoped he would bring me more music. I thought of one of my favorite professors and long-term friend, Dr. Gregory Lewis. He was always complaining that modern composers lacked "originality." I picked up the cell phone and called him. It went straight to voicemail.

"Hi, Gregory, it's Elise. A new piece of music has quite literally landed on my doorstep that I think you will find very intriguing. I know nothing about the composer except his first name. I will fax the music over to you. Call me back and let me know what you think. Talk to you later. Goodbye."

After faxing the music over to Dr. Lewis, I headed upstairs to get ready. It was going to be a long and grueling day.

♫

When your mind is otherwise occupied, it is difficult to focus on your daily tasks. My Daett kept looking at me with that wondering look in his eyes. Did he suspect anything? Conversation had never been easy between us. Discussing my love of music with him would not be possible; he would not understand or approve. All he knew was farming and serving God, and that was what he expected for my life as well. Many times, I had thought about talking about music with my Mamm. Then I quickly dismissed the notion. She would feel obligated to tell my Daett.

"John, is anything troubling you?" asked Daett. "Seems to me maybe your mind is not here in the fields with me today."

"I am all right, Daett. Just a little tired."

He let it go but I could tell he was worried and I hated that. However, the alternative would bring him even more stress so I said nothing.

Somehow I made it through the day and evening. That night when my family was asleep, I looked through my music with a critical eye. Which one would she like? Were any of them good enough for her to play? After much thought, I finally made my choice.

Later, I came back home and went to bed satisfied. In sleep, I dreamed of the beautiful lady playing my songs on the piano, her long blond hair swaying in time to the music. When I woke up, I lay there for a few minutes wishing that I could go back to dreaming.

Conscious that my Daett's eyes were closely watching me, I did not dare stray to the edge of the cornfield for the rest of the week. The suspense was unbearable. I constantly wondered about the beautiful lady; I wondered if she had played my music and if she had liked it. I also found that I was worried about her and hoped she had not been crying. Sunday came and as our family joined others in worship, I had difficulty keeping my mind on the service. My thoughts kept straying to the beautiful young lady, her golden hair, and the sound of my music being played by her. Due to a guilty conscience, I felt as if someone was watching me. I looked around almost expecting to see God Himself looking at me with condemnation in His eyes, but instead my eyes met the gaze of a young lady named Leah. She wasn't beautiful like the lady, but she was pretty in a quiet way and she had a nice, friendly manner. She was a couple of years younger than me and was friends with my sister, Rachel. We had known one another our entire lives but over the past few months, I had become cognizant of the fact that when she was around me, I would often catch her looking at me with admiration shining in her eyes. She had not been shy in letting me know that she liked me in ways that were not forward. Life could be easy with Leah. Certainly my parents would be joyous at such a union; it would be what was expected of me, what was wanted for me. She was one of us; she shared my faith and our way of life. It would be easy to find myself married to Leah and it would not be an unpleasant life. However, once someone has glimpsed the sun, how can they be expected to live in the dark? I smiled at Leah, not wanting to be rude, and then I quickly looked away.

After the long church service, I was eating my lunch when I felt someone tap my shoulder. I turned my head and found myself looking into Leah's brown eyes.

"John, would you like a piece of my strawberry pie? Rachel told me it is your favorite," she said, smiling sweetly at me.

"How nice of my little sister," I replied with a smile. "I would love a piece of your pie, but I can go get it for myself in a little while. You do not have to wait on me."

Leah blushed and smiled. She nervously smoothed back a stray lock of her brown hair back into her cap. "I don't mind, John," she said. "I would like to bring it to you."

I watched her as she walked away towards the dessert table. I noticed then that other ladies were waiting on their menfolk, bringing them plates of food with smiles. It is the way of our people so it wasn't unusual for a young lady to bring a young man food, but yet it made me slightly uncomfortable because it seemed to be her quiet way of letting other young ladies know that she was staking her claim on me.

Leah brought me a generous portion of pie and I accepted it with gratitude. She didn't leave me yet and I realized that she was waiting for me to taste the pie. She watched me eagerly as I took a bite, waiting for my reaction. I smiled at her and told her it was delicious. She blushed and bobbed as if to say thanks and then to my relief, she left. The sound of giggling captured my attention and I looked over to see Rachel and a group of her friends avidly watching the transaction between myself and Leah. They couldn't know the turmoil within my heart. Innocence is bliss. Why could I not joyfully become what I was expected to be?

The morning after the first piece of music came; it took everything within me to make it out of bed. It was midmorning before I was able to set up in bed and, as soon as I did, a wave of nausea and fatigue washed over me like a tidal wave. I just wanted to climb back in bed and try to sleep through the sickness. Then the thought occurred to me: what if another piece of music had come? So compelling and intriguing was this idea that I got out of bed and went downstairs. My efforts were rewarded. With trembling hands, I picked up the brown envelope.

Dear Lady,

Thank you so much for playing my song. Words cannot express what it meant to me. To hear my music played aloud was more than I had ever dared to hope for. Your talent is truly amazing: a gift from God. I hope it is okay with you that I brought you another song. This one came to me during a time of great difficulty and gave me the strength I needed to see me through. May it bring you comfort.

Sincerely,
John

Exhausted just from the effort of climbing down the stairs, I did not have the energy to play the song. I went over to the couch, lay down, and looked at the sheet music. This song was also transcribed by hand. It was entitled "A Song in the Night." I fell asleep looking at the notes and hearing the hauntingly beautiful music in my head.

The ringing of the telephone awakened me.

"Hello."

"Hello, Elise, this is Gregory. How are you, love?"

"Weak but all right," I replied.

I hate awkward silence. It always makes me want to do something utterly ridiculous or to say something inappropriate just to alleviate the moment. Why do people ask questions they don't really want to know the answers to about subject matters they clearly do not want to discuss? I kept my decorum and let Gregory off the hook.

"So how are things with you and Gloria?"

"Wonderful!" he exclaimed; the relief in his voice over the change in subject was almost palpable. "I received your fax, Elise. I found the piece of music extraordinarily unique. I hope you don't mind but I played it for a few friends that we had over for dinner last night. One guest, a friend of yours actually, Donovan Shane, was exceptionally intrigued. He is interested in helping this composer publish his music and would even like to have his orchestra perform the piece. It is quite an honor for an unknown composer!"

I felt as if someone had thrown a bucket of ice-cold water on me, but I somehow managed to utter an agreement.

"Donovan is going to be in Indianapolis next week for a performance and he said he would like to see you and hopefully have the opportunity to meet this composer friend of yours. You can expect him to call you soon. I gave him your new telephone number. I knew you wouldn't mind."

"No, not at all," I lied.

"Wonderful! It has been nice talking with you, Elise. Thank you so much for sharing John's music with me. Gloria and I wish you a full and speedy recovery."

"Thank you, Gregory. Goodbye."

"Goodbye, love."

I hung up the phone and lay back down on the couch. If I had the energy, I would have smashed something, but since I didn't, I cried. If I had known Gregory would share the song with Donovan, I would never have faxed him John's song. Fate is a cruel and twisted thing. Anger gave me the energy to get up off the couch and onto the piano. As I played the piece, I was again amazed at the amount of emotion infused into John's music. Ironically, it was as if John had looked into my heart and placed my feelings into song. I wanted to meet him. After some thought, I went over to my desk and wrote a letter to John. Then, I placed it on the front porch mat and secured it with a rock.

Days went by and the letter remained in place. I felt nervous like a schoolgirl preparing for her first date which was ridiculous since I didn't even know John. Through his music, I felt as if I did know him on some level. Certainly, I felt connected to him. However, once Friday came, all thoughts of anything but making it through the nausea and fatigue were driven from my mind. The letter remained on my porch forgotten.

It had seemed as if the day would never end. Finally the sun had been replaced by the moon, and the noise of the day muted to the soft whispers of the night. Stating I wanted some fresh air, I went off for a walk alone. Without conscious thought, my feet took me in the direction of the farmhouse. I knew that I had missed the playing of "A Song in the Night." Perhaps that was as it should be. She may have needed to experience the song alone. Still I needed to go to her home and to be close to her. Besides, I had another song for her.

The house was dark and quiet. She had gone to bed early. I was disappointed but not distracted from the task at hand. I was just about to slide the package under the door when I noticed an envelope weighed down by a rock on the front mat. My name was written on the front! I eagerly picked up the letter and slid the other under the door. I could not wait to read what she had written to me.

The barn has always been a safe haven for me so that was where I went. By the light of a gas lantern, I read the letter. The letter was written on beautiful floral stationery that had a slight scent of lavender.

Dear John,

Thank you so much for sharing your music with me. Your songs are amazing and they have come to me during a time when I need music. I would enjoy meeting you face to face so we can discuss your music. You have a talent that needs to be shared with the world, not just with one pianist. Also, I could introduce you to people who could help you should you be interested in having your music published. Again, thank you for the music.

Sincerely,
Elise

Elise. What a beautiful name! The notion of talking to her face to face was tempting but I knew this was not an option for me. I had never looked into her eyes or heard the sound of her voice. I knew nothing about her life or her people, but still I felt connected to her in a way that I had never felt before. Logically I knew I should withdraw from her life now, but I did not want to, not yet. Lying back against a bale of hay, my thoughts went to Elise with the beautiful blond hair.

A song began in my heart, soft at first then gradually building to a full swell. Pencil and paper in hand, half the night was gone by before I even realized it. I looked back over the pages. It was beautiful; probably the best work I had ever done but it was not yet complete. I gently placed it in the metal box and hid it from view; as I did, I wondered how the song would end.

The letter was gone and another envelope took its place. I raced inside eager to play the new piece of music John had brought me, but before I could even take the sheet music out of the envelope, the telephone rang, interrupting me. Annoyed, I answered the phone.

"Hello."

"Hello," he replied.

Donovan Shane; who else could have that deep, melodic voice? It used to bring me to my knees with delight; now, it simply brought me pain.

"Donovan," I said, trying to keep my voice steady. "Gregory said you would be calling."

"Yes, I am relatively close to your hometown. I am in Indianapolis for the weekend. I wondered if you would want to come to one of my concerts?"

"It sounds lovely, Donovan, but unfortunately my doctor has forbidden me to be around large groups of people right now."

Awkward silence is really loud. I had thought about not even mentioning my illness while talking to Donovan. I could have made up many plausible excuses all while ignoring the elephant in the room. Then, I decided not to out of sheer spite. The elephant was the reason Donovan Shane had discarded me like a piece of trash and I was not going to let him off that easy. No, I preferred to make him squirm a little. Why should I try to make this any easier for him? It certainly wasn't easy on me.

"Ah, yes," he said, clearly uncomfortable. "I hadn't considered that possibility. I just assumed you would be able to come. I am sorry, Elise."

He did sound genuinely compassionate, just not enough to want to include me in his life anymore. Then, I remembered my favorite Barbie as a child. My mother had bought her for me on my seventh birthday. She was a birthday Barbie. I played with her daily. One day, I was posing her just as I had many times before, only this time when her leg made that popping sound, much like knuckle cracking, it had a harder tone to it. When I attempted to straighten her leg back out, it refused to go back in place and stayed permanently bent. I took it to my father, crying. Daddy could fix anything but he told me he couldn't fix this.

"It is okay, Elise," he said as he kissed the top of my head. "She is still a pretty doll even though her leg is bent a little. You can still play with her."

But I didn't want to play with the broken doll. Instead, I shoved her to the back of the box that held my Barbies and covered her up with other dolls so I didn't have to look at her anymore. After that, I would see her in the box as I rummaged through it and a pang of regret that I scarcely understood would course through me. Sometimes, I would even pick her up and look at her and remember how much fun I used to have playing with her, but I never played with her again.

I realized that to Donovan Shane, I was just like that broken Barbie. He didn't want to be associated with imperfection; it did not compute with his image. I didn't know whom this made me angrier with: him for feeling this way, or me for allowing it to affect me. Then I thought about John's music and how truly special it is. It didn't seem fair to keep his music all to myself. I couldn't punish John to spare my feelings. I remembered his words: how he wanted, desired to hear his music played out loud. And I knew that I couldn't deprive John of that joy.

"If you have time before your flight, you would be welcome to come to my home," I said, finally breaking the silence. "It is an hour from Indy so if you don't have time in your schedule for it, I understand."

"Actually, I have all of Sunday," he said. "My flight doesn't leave until early Monday morning. I would be delighted to see you. Thank you."

"Okay, I will see you soon."

"Wonderful," he said warmly. "Goodbye for now, Elise."

After giving him my home address for his GPS, I hung up the phone with trembling hands. I was angry at the realization that I felt excited about an upcoming visit with Donovan. He was only coming because he had heard about John's music from Gregory. Still, a part of me hoped that he was also coming to see me and I felt betrayed by those feelings.

Needing to settle my nerves, I went to the piano, John's music in hand. I pulled it from the envelope and placed it on the stand. Ironically enough, this piece was entitled "Old Friends." I began to play the piece. How did he do it? How could he make music speak this way? The notes and chords were like a conversation between two very close friends: gentle, easy, comradery. Then without warning, an outside element was introduced and it caused division and discord between the two friends. Just when the conflict was at its height, a calming melody was introduced and played between the two melodies until harmony was once again achieved. By the end of the piece, I was smiling. His song had told an old and familiar story, one we all experience in our lives many times. I was glad this one had ended happily with the friendship still intact. I could not say the same would be true for me and Donovan.

It was Friday evening, a time for singing and laughter with my friends. Leah was there and kept smiling at me. This made me intensely uncomfortable. She wanted something from me that I did not have to give her. A part of me wished that I could forge a relationship with her. It would be a familiar and peaceful life inextricably intertwined with our families and community. Yet the question remained: would I be truly happy if I turned off the music? Now, I wasn't even sure if I could. I also wondered if Elise was not haunting my waking and sleeping thoughts, would I feel differently towards Leah?

"It is a lovely night," signed my friend with a smile.

"Yes, although it is hot," I agreed.

"Perhaps you are hot and sweaty not just because it is August but because of a certain young lady," he teased.

I pretended not to understand and went back to singing.

"Does your silence mean something, John?" Samuel teased after he elbowed me to get my attention. "Maybe you are keeping secrets from your best friend; secrets about a beautiful young girl?"

The image of Elise playing the piano flooded unbidden into my mind. I shook my head as if to shake it out.

"No?" asked Samuel, misinterpreting my head, shaking. "I'm not sure I believe you! But if you are not, you should be thinking about it. In case you haven't noticed, Leah is interested in you. She would make a good wife."

"Who are you? My Mamm? I am not ready to get married yet but when I am, you will be the first to know. Besides, you know that I am not eligible for marriage yet."

"I know," he replied, looking injured. "We've been friends since we were babies. We have done everything together up until now."

I knew what he was talking about, what everyone was talking about and wondering: why was I not taking the eighteen-week classes so that I could be presented as a candidate for baptism this fall? Just a few weeks ago, I thought I would be ready to take that step in the spring and then I heard Elise playing the piano and, much to the anger and disappointment of my parents, I decided not to take that next, natural step in my life.

"I know and I am sorry, Samuel," I said as I placed a hand on his shoulder. "I wish I could explain but I can't."

"Why not?" he asked. "What have you done so terrible that keeps you from what you know is right? What is it that you are not sharing with me?"

"It is nothing like that. I haven't done anything wrong," I lied because I knew the bishop and my Daett would not agree with me. "I am just not ready."

"When will you be ready? You are twenty-two, John. It is time for us to become men and to marry beautiful women and have many children."

"All you ever think about is beautiful women," I said with a smile.

"Yes, that is because I am also twenty-two and ready to be a man! Look over there next to Leah. That is Miriam Miller. She just moved here from Ohio and I am going to make her acquaintance. Who knows? Perhaps she will let me give her a ride home!"

"Good luck."

"I don't need luck. I have my good looks and charm to rely on!"

"What if she doesn't know sign language?"

"Everyone can understand this," he signed and then pointed to his face as a big smile spread across his face. "Besides, if I need to, I have my paper and pencil."

He sauntered away confident and assured in his choices for his life. I longed to be like him. He knew what he wanted and wasn't plagued with doubt and worry. I watched as he talked to Miriam. Fortunately for him, just as he reached Miriam, her cousin Leah joined them and she was able to interpret for him. Samuel was right, though: Miriam had no trouble understanding his smile and she returned his smile with a sweet smile of her own. He must have felt my eyes upon him because, after several minutes, he turned and gestured for me to join them.

"John, this is Miriam."

"Hello, Miriam," I said as I nodded my head in greeting. "It is nice to meet you."

"Hello," she said shyly, her face flaming red and her eyes unable to meet my gaze.

"Miriam has been kind enough to let me take her home tonight. She is worried because it leaves Leah in an uncomfortable situation. You see, Leah came with her older brother, Eli, and he is also giving a young lady a ride home."

"I see," I said. And I certainly did. Tomorrow I would tell Samuel how unhappy I was with him putting me in this situation, but in the presence of young ladies, I could not. I did the only thing that could be done: I offered Leah a ride home. The eagerness in her voice and delight in her eyes as she accepted my offer caused my stomach to feel as if someone had placed a very cold and heavy rock inside me. What I offered as a polite gesture was perceived by her heart as something much more. I had given her hope and there would be no turning back without causing her pain.

CHAPTER THREE

The week passed quickly and I awoke on Sunday morning to the sound of rain hammering down on my tin roof. The fact that it was raining only dampened my mood further. In a few hours, Donovan would be here. Everything had been cleaned and polished; everything but my heart. I had been sixteen when I met Donovan. Having travelled the world playing music, I felt mature beyond my years until I met him; he made me feel gauche. His handsome face and smooth manners turned me into a giggling schoolgirl, stirring emotions inside of me that I had not yet known existed. The first time that I heard him play the violin, I was completely captivated and he knew it. For years he toyed with my emotions, being careful not to make any promises or cross any line of impropriety but still managing to give me hope of a future relationship. On my eighteenth birthday, Donovan asked if he could take me out to dinner in celebration. Since her divorce from my father, my mother had been interested in only one thing and since I wasn't in a bottle, I was no longer of interest to her except as a source of income. It came as no surprise that she let me go out on a date with a man ten years my senior. I felt like Cinderella preparing for the ball. Mother even let me borrow some of her jewelry. By the end of the night, Donovan Shane held my heart completely in his power. I wondered if we would still be together if I hadn't become ill.

Shakespeare came to my mind. Love that is altered by circumstances is not love. Perhaps our relationship hadn't been love, but for me the pain of his rejection had been very real. Still I couldn't be angry with Donovan; not really. When I told him of my diagnosis, he had behaved sweetly to me but I could instantly feel him pull away not with actions or words but with his heart. When I calmly accepted his decision to end our relationship, he could not control the look of relief that flooded his eyes, although he kept control of the expression on his face. I suppose I had foolishly hoped that he would argue with me and try to change my mind but he had not. He had let me go. He watched without protest as I took a sabbatical from my professional career and a permanent leave from his life. My last day at the symphony, they had thrown me a party. I watched as Donovan laughed and flirted with the newest member of our orchestra, a nineteen-year-old violinist with silky dark hair and a perfect flawless body. She was the unbroken Barbie.

As I heard the car pull into the driveway, I took one last look in the mirror. With vampires being so popular, maybe the pale skin, sunken eyes, gothic look was in.

He looked amazing. I had forgotten just how handsome he was. He smiled at me shyly, melting my heart.

"Hello, Elise," he said in his melodic, deep voice. "It is so good to see you. I have missed you."

He reached for me and it felt as naturally as breathing to be in his arms once again. He smelled wonderful. The feeling of being in his arms so strong and safe almost made me weep. Quickly regaining my composure, I pulled away from him and reluctantly left his embrace. I invited him inside my home.

"I couldn't picture you on a farm, Elise," he said with a smile. "You, the city hopping, globetrotting pianist settling down in the country seemed unbelievable. But seeing you here in this peaceful, beautiful place, I realize this is the best place for you right now. It is charming."

"It was my grandparents'," I found myself explaining. "I used to love coming here to visit them as a child. My mother hated it but for me it has always been home. I actually inherited it a few years ago but you probably already knew that."

"Perhaps," he replied airily, "But if I did, I had forgotten."

Naturally, I thought dryly. *The great Donovan Shane isn't going to remember something that doesn't involve himself!*

"How is your mother?" I heard him asking and I forced myself to focus.

"I don't know," I said quietly. "I haven't seen her since I came here two months ago. The last time I heard from her, she was in Paris with her latest boyfriend."

"Sorry, Elle. I know that must be tough for you, especially since you need her right now."

"Some people don't do well with sickness," I said with venom in my voice. "Besides, I am used to my mother focusing only on herself and ignoring me. Anyway, you didn't drive all this way to talk about me or my mother. Let me show you the music."

Donovan took the pages eagerly and scanned them with his expert eyes. I felt like a fourth grader at the science fair waiting to be judged.

"Well?"

"Extraordinary," he said slowly. "The composer is certainly untrained and unorthodox but still, he possesses sheer, raw genius. Play a piece for me."

At his request, I sat down at the piano and began to play. When I was finished, I turned to Donovan. I recognized that gleam in his eye. It isn't anything that can be put into words but it is the look that all musicians, true lovers of music, get when they experience a piece of music that speaks to their soul.

"It is beautiful!" he exclaimed. "Just a moment; let me go and get my violin from the car. We can play it together and start to get the idea of how it might sound if played by an orchestra."

As he went for his violin, I turned the pages back one by one until I had reached the beginning. It was wonderful to share the beauty of John's music with someone who could appreciate it, but it also saddened me. It was no longer just ours.

The morning worship service seemed extraordinarily long and arduous to me. Watching my friends as they worshipped God knowing that in the fall they would renounce the devil and the world, commit to Christ and to accept the Ordnung, made me feel isolated and separated not just from my community but also from God. After service, I told Mamm I did not feel well and walked home alone. I couldn't bear the thought of looking into Leah's hopeful eyes. I walked through the wet fields so I wouldn't encounter anyone on the road. I wanted to avoid polite conversation with anyone. The only thing I did want was to hear music even if only to justify to myself my choices.

I was halfway through the cornfield to her house when I heard her playing one of my songs on the piano. I walked to the edge of the cornfield and sat down in the wet field, not caring that my clothes were getting soaked. I set my umbrella aside, I closed my eyes and tilted my face up towards the sky, allowing the rain to pelt my face as I listened to her play. If ever beauty could be put into sound, this was she. Then the song stopped and the music ended. I waited, sure that more would come. A few minutes passed before the song began again, but this time it was a duet: a piano and a violin. It was … beautiful. Captivated and curious, I rose to my feet and looked towards her house.

I first saw her seated at the piano. Then I saw the violinist. He was a tall, well-built man; I knew my sisters would call him handsome. The man was her perfect complement in both looks and talent. I looked down at my plain clothing and work-worn hands; how foolish I had been to allow my mind to dare to dream. After awhile, I turned and walked slowly back through the cornfield, running my hands along the corn tassels, enjoying the texture of it and the soft brushing sound it created.

Halfway through the cornfield, I looked up to see my best friend Samuel walking towards me. I smiled broadly.

"What sound does it make?" Samuel asked in sign, pointing towards my hand.

I paused to consider.

"Soft but with a hint of coarseness like the coat of a horse," I signed.

"Do you hear a song in the sound of it?"

"Not today."

My response brought a frown onto Samuel's face. Not to hear a song was unlike me and he knew it. Samuel was the only one who knew about my music. The only one except for Elise, I corrected myself.

"Why? What are you allowing to take away your song?" he asked.

"Nothing important," I insisted.

"If it isn't important, then listen for the song."

Obediently I closed my eyes and tried to turn my mind away from the violinist, the girl with the golden hair, and even away from Samuel. As my hands brushed the tassels, I focused only on the feel, the sound, the smell, the taste of the wind, and the Maker of it all. Music began to play in my mind softly at first and then slightly stronger. With eyes still closed, I began to sign what I heard to Samuel.

"Brushes are softly creating a beat on a low-sounding drum the way your Daett's heartbeat felt against your cheek when he carried you in his arms. Violins begin to play sweetly like honey tastes in your mouth. First the flutes and secondly the clarinets blow feeling soft and giddy, the way fizz from root beer floats up into your nose."

Samuel laughed with delight.

"The brass instruments can't be left out but since this song is quiet, their sound is like a finger tapping you gently on the chest. Perfect harmony is achieved like a quilt; each piece unique and beautiful alone, but together it makes a masterpiece."

I opened my eyes.

"Bravo! Beautiful!" Samuel signed with enthusiasm.

"Thank you." I smiled and we began walking slowly towards home. "What are you doing out here?"

"Looking for you! Some of us are going for a ride to the lake. Would you like to come? There will be plenty of good food for a picnic and beautiful girls to look at and flirt with!"

"You are a rogue, Samuel. Thank you for the offer but thanks to you, I have a new song. I am going to go squirrel away in the woods and write it down."

"Your loss," Samuel said, smiling. "See you later."

Hours later while sitting up in a tree high above the earth, I felt like I was all alone in the world. My song was written but still I felt the urge to write words not notes. Pen in hand, I smiled as I wrote. It felt like a conversation.

Dear Elise,

Here is my latest song. I hope you enjoy it. My best friend, Samuel, inspired it today when he asked me what I heard around me. Samuel is deaf and before you, he was the only one who knew about my music. In describing the world around me and what it caused me to hear to him, this song began to play in my soul.

When I was five, I fell from the hayloft of our barn and broke my arm. The pain was excruciating like sharp, white, hot flames of fire piercing me. My mother tried to comfort me and I tried to remain stoic like I knew my father would be. You see, I didn't want to disappoint him by appearing to be weak. Therefore, I began to focus on the pain which perhaps seems contradictory but not for me. As I focused on the pain, I began to think about what the pain felt like, what it must look like, and what kind of sound it must make. A song began to form and as I composed it, I forgot I was in pain and the desire to cry left me. Later I heard my father telling a friend what brave a young man I had been.

"John barely shed a tear. He just laid there with his eyes closed like a brave little man. He must have been praying the entire time."

I could not tell him what I was doing while lying there or that God did get me through the pain but with a song. In fact, I haven't shared that story with anyone before now. Although my father would not understand, my music is the easiest way for me to pray to God. It feels like it connects me to Him like an unbroken bond. I am honored that you have chosen to be part of my conversation with God and I know that you understand, for I can hear the sound of your soul crying out to your Heavenly Father when you play your piano. Thank you for that gift.

Sincerely,
John

Satisfied, I climbed down the tree and began to make my way home through the woods. I hid my letter to Elise inside my shirt. After I completed my after-dinner chores tonight, I would slip away and place the song and the note for Elise to find them.

♫

I refolded the note thoughtfully. In a strange way, I felt connected to the boy and the man. No one else—not any teacher, maestro, or critic—had ever heard in my playing what this stranger had, and it made me feel naked before him. John knew me extraordinarily well and he was a stranger. What a sad fact it was that the person who knew me best was a stranger!

Unable to wait, I went directly to the piano and began to play John's new song. It was beautiful, peaceful, and it soothed my soul. Later as I lay in bed, the music continued to play in my mind, lulling me to sleep but not before a question entered my mind.

27

I wonder what John looks like?

The next morning was one that I had been dreading for days: the beginning of chemotherapy. Next to the word "cancer," chemotherapy is the other big C word that strikes dread the moment you hear it. When my doctor told me that the course of treatment for me would include chemotherapy, I felt numb. Cancer was terrifying, but I had come to terms with it or so I thought. *I am going to beat this. I am young and healthy. The surgeons would go in and remove it and I would be done with cancer and get on with my life.*

Then the oncologist explained that leukemia wasn't something that could be surgically removed and began using words like "chemotherapy" and "bone marrow" or "stem cell transplants." I felt like my world was crumbling away yet again. All that I could think about was the pitiful children in turbans on the St. Jude Children's Research Hospital commercials.

My God, on top of everything else, I am going to be a vomiting bald woman. Is there no end to what cancer would take from me?

Walking into a room filled with IV poles tethered to cancer patients in recliners huddled under blankets, I felt scared and oddly like it was the first day of school. As the nurse expertly accessed my port, I averted my eyes. Not watching tricked my mind into believing the needle didn't really hurt. As I turned my face, I found that I was looking directly into the kind, faded blue eyes of the lady sitting on my right. She smiled sympathetically.

"First time?" she asked.

"Yes."

"My first day, I was scared to death. I wasn't sure what to expect and how it would affect me. It isn't any fun but the girls here get me through it."

The nurse smiled at her fondly.

"We do what we can," said the nurse.

"I have come to look at chemo as a weapon in my arsenal to battle cancer. By the way, my name is Marge."

"It's nice to meet you, Marge. I am Elise."

The cool sensation of IV fluid entering my bloodstream followed by the taste of saline distracted me. I didn't know what I expected. Instant vomiting perhaps? The fact that something was entering my blood and not my mouth still struck me as very strange. After a few seconds had passed and nothing extraordinary happened, I opened my eyes. I hadn't even realized that I had closed them. Marge was knitting something soft, sparkly, red, and frilly, her bamboo needles flying so fast they were a blur.

"What are you making?" I asked, wanting to talk about anything but chemo and cancer.

"A ruffled scarf," she said, smiling.

"It's beautiful and intricate. You are very talented."

"Oh, honey, this scarf is so easy to make. It's just knit. The yarn makes it look much more complicated than it is. You, see the yarn is called self-ruffling. I simply knit into the top of the strand of yarn and without any more effort than that, it creates a beautiful ruffled scarf. Why, I can make one in a couple of hours, which is a good thing because every female in our family is wanting one for Christmas! I have a big family so it will take me from now until Christmas Eve to make one for everyone! I have to live long enough to make all the scarves! It gives me one more reason to fight. Do you knit?"

"No, but it does look interesting." And it really did. The rhythm and repetition of it reminded me of playing the piano in an odd way.

"I could show you if you want. We will be here for a while."

"Thanks, Marge. I will think about it. I would love to learn. My grandmother loved knitting. But I have to warn you, she tried to teach me how to knit one summer and it was a disaster. Nana loved knitting dishcloths. She said they were fast and fun to knit and something every-one could use all year long. Plus she said the pattern that she used was so simple she didn't have to think about it. She could knit a dishcloth while watching TV and it made her feel good to be productive while 'wasting time.' Anyway, she tried to teach me how to knit and somehow my wash-cloth landed up being a bowl."

Marge laughed along with me.

"I understand. I was seven when my mother started teaching me how to knit. She had a great amount of patience and I used up every single ounce of patience that she had," Marge said, chuckling. "It took us all winter, but Mother finally succeeded in teaching me how to knit. By the time I had finished my first project which was a scarf, I was hooked on knitting. I've always liked to challenge myself to learn new stitches and I love intricate patterns. However, I eventually became too cocky. I thought I was a great knitter and did not need to check my gauge."

"A what?" I asked.

"Gauge," Marge answered. "Before every pattern, it will tell you to 'check your gauge.' Gauge is the number of stitches and rows per inch of knitting. This is to ensure that your project will turn out to be the correct size. I had decided to knit myself a sweater. I looked at a lot of patterns before choosing one. I went to a specialty yarn shop and I bought really luxurious merino wool yarn, bamboo knitting needles, and hand painted buttons. I spent over $200. I started knitting happily, without first knitting a gauge swatch. I was shocked when I ran out of yarn but I figured that the amount of yarn in each of the skeins that I bought were less than than the amount of yarn in the skeins in the pattern. I went back to the yarn store and bought two more skeins of yarn. A week later I went back again and bought two more skeins, which means I spent $60 more for yarn, bringing my total very close to $300. I completed the sweater and I was thrilled with the results. It was absolutely beautiful and looked just like the picture on the pattern that I had bought and followed. I was excited to wear it for the first time. I put the sweater on and it was huge! I could have fit another me in the sweater and it would still have been loose on me! I had followed the pattern to the letter! I knitted exactly the amount of stitches in every row and the number of rows the pattern called for. So what on earth happened? Well, the lady at the yarn shop said that my knitting was very loose and hadn't I realized that when I knitted my gauge swatch so I could adjust the pattern?"

I was cracking up and Marge laughed right along with me.

"That is the story of Marge Learns the Importance of Gauge," she said wryly. "Every knitter is unique: some of us, like me, tend to knit too loosely which is why I knitted a sweater much larger than intended; and others, like you, tend to knit too tightly which is why your dishcloth became a bowl. But practice makes perfect and once you have knitted for a while, you figure out the correct amount of tension to have while knitting."

I suddenly felt very cold. I started shivering and couldn't seem to stop. The nurse was instantly there, covering me with a blanket and checking my temperature. It was comforting to have her hovering over me, nurturing me the way I had often wished my mother would.

Marge reached over and patted my arm sympathetically.

"It's the chemo, dear," she explained. "I'll stop my gabbing so that you can close your eyes and rest. It'll do you good to take a nap."

I protested but only halfheartedly. Between the blanket, the clinking sound of knitting needles, and the humming of the machines, I drifted off to sleep. My last thought was if I were going to have to go through cancer and chemo, I'd rather sleep through most of it.

Later at home, I was overwhelmed by nausea. I had thought I would be prepared for it. I couldn't have been more wrong. This was an all-consuming nausea. Walking into the kitchen for a glass of water to take my medicine with, my sense of smell was assaulted by the odor of the apples in the basket on the kitchen table. I ran to the bathroom vomiting; only I had nothing left so I dry-heaved until finally the episode passed. Too weak to make it out of the bathroom, I lay down on the tile floor, my head on the soft, pink rug. The coolness of the floor actually felt good. I had never felt so alone.

The music of one of John's songs came unbidden into my mind. As I played it over in my mind, I could visualize the notes on the page, the keys on the piano. By the time I was able to get up from the floor, I had an overwhelming desire to talk to John. Having no way of knowing how to get in touch with him, I sat down and once again wrote him a letter.

Dear John,

Today your music has helped me through a difficult time. Thank you so much. Music has always been a part of my life. When I was a child, I had a small red piano, a child's piano styled after a grand piano. I loved that little piano. Morning, noon, and night I played the piano or rather, I banged on the piano. My mother was driven to distraction and wanted me to stop. It was my father who encouraged her to let me be. Dad was always my biggest fan.

When I was three, the banging had given away to very rudimentary one-finger playing. By ear, I would pick out little tunes such as "Jesus Loves Me" and "Twinkle Twinkle Little Star." Mother was relieved it was no longer just banging. My father thought I had talent and signed me up for piano lessons, although Mother argued that I was too young. I was very excited the day my father took me to my first lesson. My teacher's name was Mrs. Peach. She was an elderly lady with gray hair piled high on her head in a bun. She was rather severe, and expected me to practice, practice, practice! I adored her and our hour-long sessions every Wednesday afternoon at four o'clock. The little red piano gave way to an upright Starr piano. It was a beautiful antique black piano made in Richmond, Indiana.

To my mother's distress and my father's pleasure, I practiced for hours every day. By the time I was ten, my skill level had surpassed that of Mrs. Peach. To her credit, she told my father she had nothing more to teach me and gave him the name and number of another piano teacher she thought would be an excellent instructor for me. Dr. Wooten was nothing like Mrs. Peach. He was a professor of music and loved music. Where Mrs. Peach was austere, he was flamboyant. Like Mrs. Peach, he demanded practice and perfection. He pushed me harder and faster than she ever had and I loved it. Soon the world of Beethoven, Bach, Liszt, Handel, and the great composers opened up to me, filling my world with beauty. It was as if the world became more beautiful, the colors more vibrant. This was the beginning of my journey into music, John.

Over the years, I have had many teachers, professors, and conductors. Eventually, music became my area of study then my career path, and finally my area of expertise. Along this journey, I had lost not my joy in music but that enthusiasm I had when I was banging on that little red piano. I had lost the awe of discovery that I felt the first time I played "Ode to Joy." Through your music, you have given me back that joy, the awe of music. So once again, John, I thank you. On that note, I have a question I would like to ask you. Would it be possible to meet face to face sometime?

Sincerely,
Elise

♫

My heart beat fast with excitement and with fear when I read her request. To talk to her face to face would be wonderful, but I was terrified of how she would react to me. I am not her equal in intellect. I am but a humble farmer who hears music in his head. Besides there was danger in meeting her, getting to know her. It was best to know one another only through music. Was it out of fear or simple avoidance? I do not know, but a week had passed before I had the courage to lay more music at her door and, that time, there was only sheet music in the package.

♫

A week slowly went by without any response from John. My request to meet him must have scared him away, but why I wondered. Still I couldn't break the habit of checking daily at my door until finally one day an envelope was there. I was disappointed and yet strangely relieved to receive only music from John. Although I would have loved to see John face to face, discuss music with him, play music with him and to put a face to the music, right now the two big Cs were successfully draining me of all but the will to vomit. I simply did not have the energy for anyone or anything. In fact, his music sat on the piano for nearly a week before I played it. Ironically enough, it was entitled "A Harvest Party." I couldn't have imagined anyone feeling less like a party but me. Still, Dr. Wooten would have chided me. Once I had told him that I didn't feel like playing the piano today. He had stared at me through his wire-rimmed glasses, his bushy eyebrows shooting up nearly to his hairline.

"How do you suppose your feelings factor into this situation, Miss Snow? All that matters right now is Bach. Put your emotions and your thoughts behind you and focus on the music and what Bach wants you to feel right now, in this moment, as you play his song. And play it you will, Miss Snow, and you will play it well."

And I had, not just that day but every day after that until the big C arrived on the scene. Surely, this would have merited a respite from Dr. Wooten? Somehow, I thought not. Okay then: if John wanted me in the mood for a harvest party, then to a harvest party my piano and I would go. It was golden sunshine, cool breezes, caramel corn, hot apple cider, pumpkins, and bales of hay all on five sheets of paper front and back. When I finished playing the piece I was hungry for the first time in weeks, but because I had been so sick, there wasn't much to eat in the house. The thought of venturing out into the chaos known as Wal-Mart overwhelmed me. Then I remembered passing an Organic Grocery store while returning home from the Cancer Center the other day when I had taken an alternate route due to road construction. My memory did not fail me and soon I found myself in a pleasant, clean store that felt vintage; it reminded me of Oleson's Mercantile from *Little House on the Prairie*.

"May I help you?" asked a cheerful, deep voice.

I turned and found myself facing a smiling, handsome young man. His smile was broad and so genuine that even his eyes seemed to smile. I could not help but smile back and after weeks of vomiting, it felt nice to use my mouth for something different for a change.

"I am just here to look for some groceries," I said. Good grief! How lame was that! As if anyone comes to a food store to buy anything but food.

"My name is Nathan Beckett. Welcome to my store," he said, extending a rough but warm hand.

"Hello, I am Elise Snow."

I had forgotten how good the touch of a man's hand could be. Even after the handshake was over, I could feel the warmth of his hand on mine. I tried to focus as he explained the simple layout of the store to me. I really needed to get my life back. The joy I felt from the most basic of human interactions was beyond pathetic and reminded me how lonely my life truly was.

I wandered the rows of the store carefully making my selections. Just because I felt hungry didn't mean I should jump back in with both forks, but I certainly wanted something besides toast, oatmeal, and broth. I was making my way to the front of the store to check out hoping that the fine-looking Nathan would be the one to wait on me when a young woman dressed in plain clothes with a cap on her head entered the store carrying a large basket covered with a brightly quilted cloth. Nathan saw her coming and that magic smile of his turned on full force.

"Rachel, it is good to see you! What delicious goodies have you brought me today?" he asked.

"Just some homemade breads and jellies," she said shyly. I noticed that she did not look Nathan in the eyes and her cheeks flushed a bright pink. "I have been busy with harvest and canning and all, so I haven't made as much as I would have liked."

"I am grateful for anything you bring. My customers love everything you make, Rachel."

"Thank you for letting me sell my baked goods here, Mr. Beckett. It is most kind of you."

"Nonsense! It is good for my business," said Nathan, smiling.

I waited patiently as Rachel handed the basket to Nathan.

"I will come back in a day or two?" she asked hesitantly.

"Sounds good," said Nathan. "I am sure to have money for you."

"Thank you," she said as she turned and left the store.

"If you like homemade bread and jams, Rachel's are delicious and free of any additives or preservatives," Nathan said to me as I sat my items on the counter. "You are welcome to take a look."

I lifted the quilted fabric off the basket and the smell of fresh bread wafted up to my nose. I anticipated a wave of nausea and I was pleased that the nausea did not come. The big, fluffy loaves of bread really did look wonderful. I gave in to temptation and bought a loaf of the bread and a jar of my favorite jam, blackberry. Instead of bags, Nathan carefully placed my selections in a cardboard box, deftly packing and fitting everything into the box.

"We reuse everything here," he explained. "Some people bring boxes or bags from home, while others choose to use what I provide. If you can use the box at home, you are welcome to keep it; otherwise, I encourage you to bring the box back next time you come back to my store."

"Very slick," I said, smiling at Nathan.

"I try. By the way, welcome to our community."

"Thank you."

On the way home, the smell of Rachel's bread permeated my car and my stomach growled in anticipation. Ahead, a horse-drawn buggy plodded along. After checking for oncoming traffic, I passed them. I glanced in the rearview mirror and saw Rachel sitting in the buggy; a young man, very handsome with golden hair, lean, tall, and with a strong posture sat next to her, hat on his head and reins in his hands. My mind began to imagine all the possible relationships between the two: brother, father, husband, and I wondered what her life was like and how it would feel to be surrounded by a family and community. Suddenly, I felt very alone.

CHAPTER FOUR

The golden days of August faded into September. With harvest upon us, I did not have time for music or Elise. At night she haunted my dreams, and songs filled my thoughts while I labored in the fields. Occasionally I heard snatches of her piano playing in the wind, but with Daett and my brothers in the field with me, I could not pause to listen or venture closer to her house. The sounds of harvest made my fingers itch for pen and paper, so I stored them in my mind for a later time.

One day, I was working in the part of the cornfield closer to the house. Music danced in my mind as my hands and body toiled. Interrupting my musing came the sound of screaming. I dropped everything and ran towards the sound. As I broke free of the cornfield, I saw my Daett had beaten me to the door of the house. I ran inside to see Rachel on her knees next to Mamm who was lying in a crumpled heap on the kitchen floor.

"Ruby?" cried out Daett. "What happened?"

Mamm did not respond. Her face remained still and white, her eyes closed.

"I don't know what happened, Daett," said Rachel, sobbing. "We were cooking and all of a sudden she just collapsed. She didn't say anything to me about feeling poorly."

"John," Daett said urgently. "Call for an ambulance, quickly."

I pushed my way through my brothers and sisters who had gathered anxiously in the kitchen and ran down the lane to an English neighbor's house across the road. I felt shaken to my core as I told the 911 operator our situation and our address. It seemed like an eternity before the wail of sirens could be heard in the distance. I had never felt so helpless in my life. All we could do was pray and ask God to be merciful to us. As they loaded Mamm into the back of the ambulance, Daett asked if he could ride with her to the hospital. He barely waited for their response before climbing in next to her. As the ambulance pulled away, I could see Daett's stricken face through the back window; tears were coursing down his face. It was the first time I had ever seen him cry.

I used to take showers but the chemo had me as weak as a kitten and it was easier to take a bath. I had gotten into the habit of bathing at night. I didn't have to rush like I would if I bathed in the mornings before going to my chemo treatments. The warm baths also relaxed me and helped sleep to come a little easier. Tonight's bath had started off uneventful. I had my iPad plugged into a speaker up on the vanity and I was relaxing amongst the bubbles and warm water while watching a show I was streaming. However, when I shampooed my hair, everything changed. I had lathered up the shampoo and washed my hair like normal. Then I leaned forward and began rinsing my hair in the water cascading out of the faucet. Without warning, my hair simply slid off my head. Every single hair rinsed off my scalp, leaving me horrified and speechless. For a few moments, all I could do was stare down at my blond hair swirling around in the water pouring down upon it. For a brief insane second, I actually considered picking it up and trying to stick it back on my head. *Like that would work!* I snorted. There was simply nothing to be done but to shut off the water, dry off, and to clean my hair out of the bathtub so it wouldn't stop up my drain.

I didn't cry until I cleaned the steam off the mirror and looked at my reflection. The woman looking back at me from the mirror was a stranger. To say she was bald was an understatement because she was completely devoid of hair; she didn't even have the benefit of eyebrows, and I swear that even my eyelashes were nearly gone. The woman in the mirror was pale and gaunt and she looked old, really old. If I had the strength left in me, I would have screamed in rage. I reminded myself that I had planned for this event; I had been warned about this possibility. However, none of my preparations made this any easier. Right before I started chemo, I had visited a hairdresser who cut off most of my long locks in order to create a custom wig for me out of my own hair. Reluctantly I took out the wig and tried it on. I had really hoped for the best but no matter what angle I looked at myself from, the effect was still the same: I looked like a bald woman in a wig trying to look like she still had hair. Somehow the absence of eyebrows and eyelashes made the wig look bizarre. Worse still, the stupid thing made my scalp itch like crazy. I pulled the wig off my head and threw it into the trash with disgust. *A scarf wound around my head or a hat would have to do*, I thought. Due to the stress of losing my hair, it took me awhile to fall asleep.

The following morning, the sound of sirens captured my attention, rescuing me from self-pity. I looked out the window just in time to see an ambulance whiz past my house. Sitting there wondering who was ill and what could have happened, I began to think about the very real possibility of my own mortality. If I collapsed or worse, died at home, there would be no one to call for help. How long would I lie before someone found me? It was a very disturbing thought. I had come to grips with the possibility of dying, but the thought of being a rotting corpse like seen on popular crime shows was not something I was willing to accept. Surely dignity in death would not be an unreasonable wish. However self-absorbed Mother might be, I would think she would still want to say goodbye to me and she couldn't do that if I became compost before she even knew that I was dead. What a perplexing and sad situation to be in: dying and worried if anyone would even find you.

Through the open window came the sound of horse hooves. I looked up to see a buggy going up the road and I thought about Rachel. I could check with Nathan to see if he could help me get in touch with her. Since

I had seen her in a buggy on my road, I felt it was highly likely that she lived close to me. Perhaps I could pay her to clean house for me several times a week. Living alone, my home didn't get very dirty but asking someone to be your cleaner sounded more legitimate and less creepy than asking them to be your corpse checker.

I did what every woman does when she feels lousy about her appearance: I went shopping. A few hats, scarves, and outfits later, I was feeling better about the world. As I walked down the street, I received what I interpreted as an admiring smile from a man. I would have batted my eyelashes at him had I had any, a minor detail hidden by brand-new sunglasses. Had I removed my hat, he would have been in for a shock. Upon entering the Cancer Center, the smell of sickness that permeated the building assaulted my senses. The smell of cancer is sharp, distinct, and unmistakable. My happiness gauge decreased substantially.

"Nice hat," said a smiling Marge. "Have you been shopping?"

"Yep," I admitted as I sank down into the chair next to her.

"Shopping is just what the doctor ordered," said the nurse, smiling as she prepped my port for access.

"May I get that order on my chart also?" asked Marge.

"I'll see what I can do," she replied.

"When I looked in the mirror, I found a bald woman looking back at me. I tried on my wig and found out to my surprise that I could in fact look much worse," I said to Marge as I turned my head to avoid watching the needle pierce my port. "I still looked like a bald woman but with a wig on my head. It was truly hideous!"

"Where is the wig now?" asked Marge.

"By now, I would imagine it is in the landfill."

Marge laughed so hard her knitting needles were bouncing up and down.

"Thanks," she said. "I needed a laugh today. If it helps you feel better, my wig is in a box, shoved in the back of my closet. I never even wore it outside of the house."

"Did you look like a bald woman in a wig too?" I asked in mock surprise.

"Worse," she replied, smiling. "I looked like a bald fifty-year-old with a twenty-year-old head of hair on my head."

"Uncle," I said, giggling, "you win the Who Looked Worse In Their Wig contest!"

I closed my eyes and leaned back into the chair. My shopping spree had drained me. I felt ridiculous that something so mundane could make me as tired as if I had put in a full day of work. The chill that seemed to always accompany my chemo treatments caused me to shiver.

"That reminds me," said Marge, "I brought something for you."

I opened my eyes. Marge was smiling at me and holding out a flowered gift bag.

"Oh, Marge, you didn't need to bring me a gift."

"I wanted you to have something to bring you comfort, something from me. Well, go on," she urged. "Open it."

I pulled out the tissue paper, reached into the bag, and pulled out a beautiful yellow afghan.

"It is beautiful and so soft and warm! Did you knit this?"

"Yes, I did. I am so glad that you like it."

"I love it! Marge, this is so special. It must have taken forever to make. You are so talented. Thank you so much. I don't know what to say," I said as the warmth of unexpected tears filled my eyes.

"You are very welcome," said Marge, smiling as she patted my hand.

I spread the blanket out over me, letting my fingers enjoy the luxuriousness of the yarn.

"Yellow is my favorite color. When I was five, we moved to a new apartment. I was sad to leave the only home I had ever known and my best friend and neighbor, Penny. In order to placate me, my parents let me pick out anything I wanted for my new room. I picked out yellow carpet, yellow curtains and bedspread; even my furniture was yellow. It was the brightest, cheeriest room I had ever seen and I loved it. This blanket would have fitted in my room perfectly. Right now it is just what I needed to warm me up and cheer me up. It's like sunshine in blanket form!"

"God has a way of knowing what we need and providing it before we even think to ask Him for it," said Marge. "By the way, there is something else in the bag."

"Oh, Marge, you shouldn't have!"

"Just shush and open your gift!"

Reaching into the bottom of the gift bag, I pulled out a tissue-wrapped bundle. After carefully unwrapping it, I found four of the prettiest knitted hats I had ever seen. All of the hats were very soft and beautiful slouch berets in different colors. One even had a hand-knitted flower on the side. No one had ever given me a gift of such thoughtfulness and care. I could not contain the tears anymore, so I simply wrapped myself up in my new blanket, buried my face in the softness of the hats and, for the first time since my diagnosis, I allowed myself to cry in front of someone else. Marge reached over and her hand found mine under the blanket. I looked over at her. She had tears rolling down her cheeks as well. Neither of us said a word; we didn't need to.

Mamm looked so frail lying in the stark white hospital bed connected to wires and machines that made continuous beeping, chirping, and humming. I felt hopeless and afraid. I could not imagine our home, our family without Mamm.

Rachel reached over and took my hand.

"It will be okay, John. You will see. God will give us a miracle."

"You don't know that for sure, Rachel. I am trying to believe, to have faith, but my heart is so full of fear."

"I understand. Truly I do, John. But we can't lose hope. We must cling to our beliefs and pray for Mamm. She needs our faith right now, not our fear."

"Jah, you are right. Ach, little sister, when did you become so wise?"

"You mean you are just now noticing I am a genius?" Rachel said, smiling at me.

"Don't get all big headed on me just because I gave you a compliment," I teased as I tugged on one of her Kapp strings playfully.

"Would you two be quiet so an old woman can get her rest?" a voice said querulously.

"Mamm!" exclaimed Rachel joyfully. "You are awake!"

"Jah, I'm awake but my head feels all woozy. What happened?"

"We don't know, Mamm," I said. "You collapsed in the kitchen while cooking lunch. We were all so worried. We didn't know what had happened to you."

"Where am I?" she asked and I could hear the hint of fear in her voice.

"You are in the hospital, Mamm," replied Rachel.

"Why do they have it so dark in here?" Mamm asked. "You can't see your hand in front of your face, much less be able to care for the sick. Goodness, I must've slept the day away! Light a lamp for me, John, or whatever kind of light they have in a hospital."

Rachel looked at me with fear and puzzlement in her eyes. I shook my head at her, warning her not to alarm Mamm.

"Jah, okay, Mamm," I said. "Just let me check with the doctor first to make sure it is okay."

Mamm nodded her head. Rachel reached out and held her hand.

I found Daett down the hall talking to the doctor. They both looked up at me when I approached.

"John, the good doctor here was just going over the results of the scans they did of your Mamm's head," said Daett.

"She is awake," I said.

"Well, that's good news," said the doctor.

"Jah, but…," I paused, not quite sure how to say the necessary words aloud.

"What is it, John?" prompted Daett.

43

"She wants to know why it is so dark in her room and asked me to light a lamp. I am worried that she may be blind, Daett."

Daett looked at the doctor with a mixture of fear and anguish.

"What does this mean?" he asked.

"Well, as I told your father, John, your mother has bleeding in her brain. I told him that we would not know what kind of injury this had caused and what the effects would be until she woke up. Now that she is awake, it seems as if it has affected her eyesight."

"Will this be permanent?" I asked.

"Only time will tell," he replied.

Daett stood there silently twisting his hat in his hands. I wish I had words to comfort him, to strengthen him. The words he wanted to ask but could not seem to bring himself to say out loud hung unasked in the air. As his eldest son, I decided to help him in the only way I could in this moment and ask the hard questions myself.

"Doctor, has the bleeding stopped?"

"At this time the bleeding seems to have ceased but again, we will know more in the hours and days ahead. We will take repeat images of her brain to see if the bleeding has truly stopped and if it is reabsorbing the blood."

"Is this something that could...," I paused, struggling to find the right words with which to ask the question that terrified me. "What I mean to ask is could this be fatal?"

Daett's head snapped up and he stared at the doctor, waiting for his response and dreading it all in the same moment.

"I am sorry to not be able to give you the definitive answers you need and want right now. This is something that could be fatal, but that depends on if the bleeding has stopped and the extent of the damage that has been done."

"So for now we just wait," I said.

"And pray, John," Daett said as he placed a hand on my shoulder. "We pray and believe in God for His will to be done."

We went back into Mamm's room. Daett walked over to the bed, bent down, and gently kissed her forehead. Being that our father was not overly affectionate, the moment was all the more poignant.

"Abram," she said, smiling and reaching up a hand to touch his beard. "Why is everyone behaving as if they can see in a dark room?"

"Ruby, the room is brightly lit," said Father softly as he gripped her hand. "It's your eyes that are dark."

"What?" Mamm said with a voice that suddenly sounded high and thin with fear. "What are you saying to me, Abram? Are you saying that I am blind?"

"For now I am saying you are blind," said Daett. "But the doctor says that this may only be temporary."

"What has happened to me to cause this?"

"You had some bleeding in your brain."

"Am I going to die?" asked Mamm as tears began to silently slide out of her beautiful, sightless eyes.

"Now, don't think like that, Ruby. Keep hope and keep faith. The doctor said that you waking up is a good sign and he is encouraged by that."

"But what if my sight does not come back, Abram? How will I cook, clean, sew, and be a good wife and mother to you and the children?"

"That is a bridge we will cross if and when we have to," Daett said. "But if we have to cross it, we will cross it together just like we have with every other storm we have braved together. You are not alone in this, Ruby. I am here. I will always be here for you."

The tears became a torrent and Daett took Mamm into his arms, holding her tightly and stroking her back and hair with his work-roughened hand. We had never seen our parents embrace and it felt like we were intruding upon a very private moment, so we slipped out quietly out of the room. I couldn't resist one last glance back into the room before shutting the door. The image of my parents embracing was indelibly imprinted upon my heart and mind and, as sad as the moment was, witnessing their love and devotion to one another was one of the most beautiful sights I had ever seen.

I sat out on the screened-in back porch seeking solace in the night. Marge's yellow blanket was wrapped around me like a warm hug, and a coordinating yellow hat was covering my bald head. One of my favorite night sounds is those from crickets and tonight they were out in abundance. With a cup of chai tea to sip on, the moment should have been near perfect but it wasn't. As a city girl, the darkness of the country seemed to stretch on for an eternity. I realized for the first time that one of the drawbacks of having only Amish neighbors was the lack of light and sound. However, the bonus of the lack of streetlights was an abundance of stars. The sky was vast and dark, with brilliantly bright stars dotting the velvet black expanse. The feeling that I was completely alone and very small was overwhelming. If only I had someone to talk to.

The thought of John came to me unbidden. I found myself wondering where this mystery music man was and what he was doing tonight. Is it possible to miss someone you do not know? To miss seeing a face you have not yet seen? It must be, because I missed John and I longed to talk to him. I reached for pen and paper and began to write my heart to this man I did not know, to talk to him in the only method of communication with him that I had. When I finished, I folded the pages and put them away. This letter was not one I could give to John or anyone for that matter, but it still felt cathartic to have had an outlet for my thoughts.

Stretched out on the chaise lounge, warm from tea and Marge's blanket and my thoughts calmed from writing, I drifted off to sleep.

The day had been long and hard. My body was tired but my soul was restless. With the rest of the house asleep, I took to the solace of the fields. An invisible cord seemed to pull me towards Elise. Why I felt the need to be close to this girl I did not know. I only knew that I needed to be, must be near her tonight. When I reached the edge of the field, I stopped suddenly hesitant. Her house glowed in a way mine did not but like mine it was silent, allowing me to hear the night sounds. The music of the night hummed in my ears: the crickets chirped the soprano, the wind swooned in the alto, owls were the confident tenors, and the bull frogs croaked out the bass line. I closed my eyes and for a moment I allowed myself to enjoy the music.

When I opened my eyes I was close to her home and, as I looked at the house more closely, I realized that she was on her back porch. At first I was nervous, afraid that she had seen me, but then I realized that if she had she would have said something or made some sort of move-ment. Emboldened, I walked quietly forward until I could see her better. She was lying on a chaise, completely swaddled in a yellow blanket and sleeping soundly. All I could see of her was her face peeking out from her cocoon, and I realized that this was the first time that I had seen her face up close. She was unbelievably lovely. I felt inexplicably drawn to her and protective of her. It wasn't safe for her to sleep out on the porch alone but it wasn't like I could walk up onto her porch and tell her to go inside. So I did the only thing I could think of: I lay down in the grass next to her porch and kept watch over her all through the night.

CHAPTER FIVE

I awoke refreshed to the sound of singing birds and the sun on my face. I allowed myself the luxury of lying there for a while feeling the soft blanket against my skin and the warmth of the sunlight. Eventually I got up and slowly started my day, feeling stronger than I had for many days. While sitting at my kitchen table reading the morning paper, I heard a knock at the door. I opened it to find a sweet-faced Amish girl standing there.

"May I help you?"

"Jah, my name is Rachel," she said with a smile. "Rachel Yoder. Nathan said you had asked about help around the house?"

"Yes," I replied, smiling. "Come on in. Would you like a cup of tea?"

"Thank you, that would be nice."

"The house is old and not real big, and there is only me," I said as we walked to the kitchen. "So it shouldn't be too hard of a job for you."

"You are all alone?" she asked, unable to hide the curiosity in her eyes.

"Yes," I answered. "I inherited the home from my grandparents. After many years on the road, it was time to rest. Of course you will have noticed my lack of hair."

I touched my head self-consciously.

"I did wonder," she admitted

"I have cancer and this was the only place that has ever been sort of

48

home to me. I used to come visit my grandparents here and I have many good memories. Anyway, I needed to be stationary for treatment so I moved here."

"Where did you live before?" she asked as she accepted the cup of tea I was handing her.

"I am a concert pianist—so everywhere and nowhere," I said as I sat back down at the table and gestured for her to do the same. "I have visited many interesting places and even though this has been forced upon me, I am enjoying living in a home instead of a hotel for a change."

After a moment's hesitation, she sat down across from me looking at me shyly. From the look in her eyes I could tell that she didn't understand the concept of a travelling life, but she was interested. Oddly enough I was finding it very easy to talk to her and since my only human contact lately had been at the cancer center, I was finding her company refreshing and comforting.

"I have never even left Indiana," she said, smiling shyly at me over-top her teacup.

"Well, maybe someday you will."

"I hope to visit my cousins in Pennsylvania next year for my cousin Rebecca's wedding. Daett says that if we go, he may take us to see Hershey park. They give you free chocolate there and have lots of rides!"

"That sounds like fun," I said, smiling.

She smiled back quickly and then looked down into her teacup as if it was uncomfortable for her to continue making eye contact with me.

"So back to the job: if it is something you are interested in, I would like for you to come three days a week for light housekeeping. Being sick, I'm just not able to keep up with cleaning the house myself. Perhaps you could come on Mondays, Wednesdays, and Fridays? I could pay you $100 each day, so $300 a week? Does that sound fair?"

"More than fair!" said Rachel with wide eyes. "Are you sure?"

"Yes, I'm sure. Could you come from 8:00 a.m. until 2:00 p.m.?"

"Jahh! That would be great!"

Two cups of tea later, I not only had a new housekeeper and someone to check to make sure I was still alive, I also had a new friend named Rachel.

♫

I watched from a distance as Mamm worked with her therapist. Her bravery and determination was inspiring to me. Footsteps came up beside me and stopped. I looked up to see Daett standing there, hat in hand, staring at Mamm.

"She seems to be doing well," I said. "The therapist seems to have some really good ideas to help her adapt."

"Jah," Daett said, then he sighed heavily. "I just wish she didn't have to go through this. I wish her sight would come back."

"Perhaps it still will."

"The doctor doesn't seem to think so. He says that it would've come back by now if it were going to."

"God is the one that made her eyes, Daett," I reminded him gently. "He can heal them if it be His will."

"Rachel has gone to see a lady about a job," Daett said, clearly wanting to change the subject. "Nathan Beckett told her about it."

"What kind of job?"

"It's a housekeeping job for our new neighbor."

At the mention of her, my heartbeat picked up pace. I hoped Daett didn't notice any change in my demeanor.

"Rachel would like that. She loves caring for a house."

"Just like her Mamm," Daett said softly. "Life changes. It takes us on unexpected journeys, down paths we would never go voluntarily but yet through it all, God is faithful. That is our constant and as long as we keep hold to that, John, we will make it through this also."

I knew Daett had spoken more for his benefit than for mine, but all the same his words comforted and encouraged me. I placed my hand gently on his shoulder very briefly, kissed Mamm's cheek, and then headed for home. There was work to be done.

As I approached her house, I couldn't help but slow the horses down a bit. I don't know what I hoped for—perhaps a glimpse of her? Once home, I first went to the barn to put the horses up for the night. As I brushed their coats, the familiar smells of the barn: the animals, the leather of the saddle and bridles, the hay brought back so many layers of memories and sounds that my mind swirled with them. Daett's words about God being our constant truth, the unmovable, unchangeable God mixed with the smells and memories and began to form notes in my mind. The notes on the staff began to align to tell the story of the changing seasons of life, but one note remained unchanged throughout the song. This note, a G, did not ever cease. Sometimes the G was played by the clarinet in an alto-sounding voice. Other times, the flute sang it out in a high soprano sound. Then the oboe played it deep and low before the saxophone snatched it up. Finally the violin crescendo ended with a high and clear G for the final sound. "Unchangeable G," I would call it. I could not wait to write this down. I scrambled up the barn loft and eased my sheet paper and pencils out of their hiding place and began to put to paper the sounds I had just heard in my mind. I lost all track of time; all track of where I was and I ceased to be cognizant of my surroundings.

"John?"

I was so startled I nearly fell out of the loft. Quickly I shoved my music back into the box and covered it over with hay. This temporary hiding place would have to do for now.

"John?"

"Jah," I said as I began to climb down the ladder. "I am coming."

"Why were you in the barn so long?" asked Rachel with concern in her eyes. "You have been home for nearly two hours. Are you worried about Mamm?"

"Jah," I said and although I was speaking the truth, I was still lying to my sister. "I was just needing some time alone to think and to pray. It was hard watching her in therapy today. It is as if she is a child and is learning how to do things all over again but in a different way."

"Poor brave Mamm," sighed Rachel as she tucked her hand into the crook of her arm and led me towards the house. "She will be fine. Of that I am sure and certain, but you must come inside and eat with us, John. Daett is still at the hospital with Mamm and the little ones need their big brother John to pray over the evening supper and read the Bible to them before bed if Daett isn't home by then. I know it's hard but the little ones need us. We have to be strong for them and we need to keep things the same as much as possible for them."

"You are a good sister and daughter, Rachel."

"Jah, the best," she teased with a grin. "I got a new job today, John, making $300 a week! All of that money just for cleaning house for one lady! Can you believe it?"

"$300 a week? She must be a really rich lady!"

"Jah, I think she is. She is a famous pianist and has travelled all around the world. She showed me a scrapbook with pictures in it from places like England, France, Italy, and big cities here in America like New York and Chicago! She is still young but she has already seen so much of the world. And here I am seventeen and I have never even been outside of Indiana!"

"It would be fascinating to see those places," I said as we entered the house.

"What places?" asked little Ruthie.

"Faraway places," said Rachel as she bent to kiss Ruthie on the forehead. "Come on! It's time to eat!"

"I don't want to see faraway places," announced Ruthie as she climbed up into her chair. "I want to always stay close to the farm and Mamm."

"You canna stay forever with Mamm," said Caleb who dearly loved teasing little Ruthie. "One day you will be married and have children just like Mamm. You will have to live wherever your man lives."

Ruthie's face puckered for a moment and I was afraid the waterworks were about to start. Then the sadness cleared from her face and a smile lit her eyes back up.

"Then I will marry a man who lives near Mamm."

Caleb's mouth opened and then closed when he caught sight of my stern look telling him to let it go. Soon we were all sitting at the table, all except for Mamm and Daett. It felt strange to look towards Daett's empty chair and then to realize all my sibling were looking at me expectantly the way we normally looked at Daett. I am the oldest child in the family and the oldest male, so I supposed it was natural that in the absence of Daett my siblings would look to me. I am twenty-two nearly twenty-three; after me another son was born who would have been twenty but unfortunately he died of SIDS when he was only four months old. I am rare in my community in that there is five years between me and my next living sibling because Mamm's next pregnancy ended in a miscarriage. Rachel, age seventeen is next, then Abigail fourteen, Elias thirteen, Caleb eleven, Matthew eight, and Ruthie five is the baby in our family and spoiled by all of us. I loved my family so much and as the oldest, right now, the weight of that responsibility was weighing heavily on me. As I looked at their faces, I prayed a silent prayer to God asking him to give me the wisdom and strength to be the big brother that they needed me to be especially now that Mamm was ill and Daett was preoccupied with caring for her.

"Let us give thanks to God for our food," I said.

After we bowed our heads and silently prayed, we began to eat. As I looked at the dear, familiar faces around the table, I began to wonder what it would be like to have a family of my own to love, to pray over, to share meals with. Without conscious effort, the image of Elise at her piano with her long flowing hair came into my mind. The two thoughts, equally desirable, were at complete odds with one another for I could only have one but not both. I shook my head as if to shake these thoughts that I ought not have out of my head. She was a stranger to me, a stranger who had a hold on my heart. How could I turn my back on my family?

But how could my heart deny the feelings that had taken seed in my heart for the girl with golden hair?

I looked at the plate of food in front of me and tried to will myself hungry enough to eat. The nausea was under control with medication but still my appetite was poor. I took a bite and looked around the kitchen. It is still very much my nana's kitchen. There had been many wonderful family meals here shared by my grandparents and me. Now I eat alone. My thoughts drifted as they so often do these days to John. *Does he have anyone to eat with? A family of his own perhaps?* I have many questions I wish I could ask him. *Why does this man enter my thoughts so often? His music draws me like a cord to him.* I pushed the plate away from me and went to the piano. I pulled out every piece of music that John had given me thus far and I began to play them. His music was pure, raw, unadulterated emotion. It was both cathartic and traumatic to play his songs. By the time I was done playing, I was emotionally spent. As I went around the living room, turning off lights and locking up for the night, I noticed a white envelope partially underneath the front door. I retrieved it and my heart sped up when I recognized the handwriting. It was John's. He had been here while I was playing his music! Why hadn't he knocked on my door? Was he afraid of scaring me? I sat down on the couch and opened his letter.

Dear Elise,

    I am sorry I don't have a song for you tonight but I promise I will soon. In fact, tonight a new song came to me. As soon as I have finished writing it down, I will bring it to you.

    Your playing is the most beautiful sound in the world. Your music is what I imagine heaven will sound like. To think that some-one as talented as you would play my simple songs is humbling.

Thank you for that gift. I cannot express into words what it means to me.

I would also like to meet you someday but for reasons that are difficult to explain, I cannot meet with you yet nor do I know if that can ever be possible. Please have patience with me a little while longer.

In God's Rich Love,
John

His note could not have come at a better time. It was almost as if he knew that I was lonely and in need of comfort. Strange to think that I did not have a face to go with his name but yet I had such a strong connection to him. If I were really honest with myself, I would admit that I was feeling attracted to him even though I had no knowledge of his age. How wonderful it would be to have someone in my life to care for me, someone to share this horrible journey with me and to support me! Yet how unfair it would be to ask someone new into my life during such a difficult season of my life and when my future was so uncertain. Sighing, I knew that I would never sleep so I decided to go for a walk.

The air was cool so I grabbed my grandmother's old sweater from the coat closet in the kitchen. The warmth of the familiar garment wrapped around me was comforting. There was still a hint of my grandmother's scent attached to it, making it almost seem as if I were wrapped in her arms. With a smile on my face, I began to walk down the country road.

I had gone quite a ways from my home without seeing a car or another person until I saw a man and a dog walking towards me. When we got closer to each other, I recognized him as Nathan Beckett from the store. I smiled and raised my hand in greeting. He responded, his eyes lighting up with recognition.

"Hi—Elise, right?" he asked as we stopped to talk.

"Yes," I replied. "How are you, Nathan?"

"Great! It is a wonderful evening and Chet and I are enjoying our walk especially now that we have run into you. You must live nearby?"

"Yes, I live just down the road."

"Me too. Well, down the road and down another lane," he said, smiling. "The only cars that come down my road are either coming to see me or lost. Do you mind if I walk with you?"

"No, but aren't you going the other way?"

"Well, I was, but you've just given me an excuse to turn around and head back towards home."

"Company would be nice," I admitted. "So did you grow up here?"

"Born and bred. Most of my family still lives here or near here, so holidays are huge and exhausting but lots of fun. What about you?"

"No, I am from New York and everywhere else my suitcase took me. My grandparents are from here and I used to come spend summers with them when I was younger. They were wonderful. When they passed away, I inherited their home. As you can tell," I said as I self-consciously touched my hat-covered baldhead. "I am ill and needed to be located in one place for the time being for treatment. I didn't want to be on display in New York for all my coworkers to see, so I came home to the only place that ever felt like home."

"So you traveled a lot?"

"I am a concert pianist. I have toured since I was sixteen so yes, I have traveled a lot. It is strange but nice to be in one place for longer than a day."

"Wow! That's impressive! I bet if I were more cultured I would have recognized your name," he said, smiling.

"Oh, I doubt it."

"If you don't mind me asking, is it cancer?'

So here it was: the big C question. One of the main reasons I hate making new acquaintances in my current circumstance. He sensed my discomfort.

"You don't have to answer that," he said.

"No, it's okay," I lied. "It is getting easier to talk about. In fact, I am proud of myself. I went through denial and now, I am having my second conversation of the day about the elephant in the room. I do have cancer; the type of cancer that I have is called leukemia."

"I am sorry."

"Me too," I said honestly as I fought back tears. "But changing subjects, please, what prompted a young man like you to open a store?"

"Not just any store—Beckett's Organic Grocery," he said, smiling. "I am that rare creature that is perfectly content to be a small-town resident. While many of my peers couldn't wait to leave for a big city adventure, I never wanted to live anywhere but home. My family has been farmers for generations and while I appreciate the produce, I've never been drawn to grow anything more than I can eat and share with friends. My brother was the one on the tractor with Dad and I was the one at the roadside stand with Mom. I started with a small produce stand at a local farmer's market, which I still do on Saturdays throughout the season, and progressed to my own store. I like to think of my store as a throwback to the old general store. Fortunately for me, I am close enough to Indianapolis to draw a faithful following from the weekend crowd who like the experience of shopping authentically organic. I'm a pretty boring guy compared to you, huh?"

"No," I said thoughtfully. "I'm envious of you. It must be wonderful to have that sense of belonging and to know what you want in life. Mine has been the life of a vagabond, and music has been my only home."

"Still you must have experienced so many wonderful places and people. Although I don't want to live anywhere else, I dream about traveling someday. What has been your favorite place?" he asked.

"Venice," I responded without hesitation. "It's not like any place else in the world and no matter how many times I visit the city, I always experience and see something new."

"Now there is a place that is on the top of my list," said Nathan. "I love to read, always have, and every book that I read that is set in Venice makes me want to go even more."

"This is me," I said as we neared my lane. I hesitated then I took a brave step. "Would you like to come in for a cup of coffee?"

"Thank you—I would love to."

For the second time that day, I found myself welcoming a stranger into my home. Perhaps my recluse days were behind me. My grandmother certainly would be pleased.

He sat down at the kitchen table and watched as I put the tea kettle on to boil, ground the beans, and placed the fresh grounds into the French press. I sat the brewing pot onto the table and then got two cups from the cupboard. As I sat down opposite of him, he smiled at me.

"It is nice to see a fellow coffee connoisseur at work," he said.

"Why am I not surprised that in this era of fast one-cup coffee makers, the organic grocer is a slow-brew man," I teased him.

"I see you are a Bible reader," he commented.

I turned to see him looking at the worn black leather Bible that had been my grandfather's.

"That was my grandfather's," I said. "He would sit at this table drinking coffee, reading his Bible, and talking to God every morning. The house is exactly like it was when my grandparents lived here. I haven't changed anything. Which is why Poppy's Bible is still on the kitchen table. It may seem crazy to you but it makes me feel closer to them, plus I don't have the energy to do a lot of decorating."

Nathan nodded thoughtfully. I could tell by the way he handled the Bible reverently that he was a believer.

"I can tell this was a well-loved Bible," he said, smiling.

"Are you a Christian?" I asked him.

"Yes," he said as his face lit up. "Are you?"

"I believe in God. My grandparents were the love of God personified. When I would stay with them, I went to church with them. I always loved it. The music was pretty, the people friendly, and peace and joy permeated the building," I responded evasively.

Nathan seemed to sense that I didn't want to talk about the state of my soul and didn't pursue the matter further much to my relief.

"What was the name of the church they attended?" he asked.

"Fellowship Chapel," I answered. "It was a beautiful white church with a steeple. It looked like it belonged in a picture in a magazine."

"That's where I go to church!" Nathan exclaimed. "It's a wonderful church. You are right: the people are still very friendly, and the peace of God is there. If you would like to go to church with me on Sunday, I would be happy to pick you up."

"Thank you," I said, smiling. "That's very kind of you. Right now I'm to avoid crowds because the chemotherapy makes me susceptible to catching illnesses. However, I really would like to go to Fellowship again. So perhaps once I have finished with my chemo, I'll take you up on your offer."

"Great," he said, smiling back at me.

We sat at the kitchen table for an hour talking and drinking our coffee. It felt natural and easy. For that hour, I didn't think about cancer. It was freeing. Later as I lay in bed, I realized that I also had not thought of John during my time with Nathan. I didn't know if I should be pleased about that or not. John had become a part of my daily life. In a very strange way, I felt as if I had cheated on John, a man whose face I had never seen, a man I knew almost nothing about. His music told me enough; it told me that we were soul mates.

I snorted in disgust as I rolled over and hit my pillow with my fist. Why even think about men and relationships when I had cancer coursing through my bone marrow trying to kill me? It wasn't fair to either of them or to me! But life is very often not fair.

So many nights lately, sleep has evaded me. I found myself once again in the hayloft finishing my latest composition. My music used to be only for myself and for God, but now it is also for Elise. I found myself concentrating on how the music would sound on the piano. She seemed to be filled with a deep sadness and I so wanted to make her smile. After the song was complete, I carefully folded the music and put it in an envelope I had brought out with me along with the note I had written to her earlier. I climbed down from the hayloft and set out across the field towards her house. The house was dark and quiet as I crept up on the porch like a thief and slid the envelope under the door. There was no reply for me and I felt slightly disappointed.

As I walked back through the field in the dark, the sound of talking and laughter came from the direction of the woods. It was an odd time of night for anyone to be out, so I quietly went closer to investigate. There was a couple locked in an embrace—an Amish couple. I smiled and started to turn to go away when the couple pulled apart and I saw their faces. My heart froze. It was Rachel, and the man was Amish to be sure and certain. He was a family friend, Daniel Lapp, and he was a married man and the father of three *kinner*. I hurried away from the house, my heart hammering inside my chest. The thought of Rachel, the sister up until a few moments ago I had thought was an innocent girl, in an illicit relationship filled me with a rage I didn't know I was capable of! How could she do this to Daniel's wife and children? How could she do this to Mamm and Daett? Such selfishness was beyond my comprehension. I did not trust myself to see either one of them right now, so I put as much distance between them and me as quickly as I could. Fortunately, I made it back to the house and into my room before Rachel made it home. It seemed as if an hour passed before I finally heard her creeping through the house. Part of me wanted to confront her, but it was not our way to behave in such a way. So I lay in bed stewing in anger, until finally sleep engulfed me in the early hours of dawn.

CHAPTER SIX

I managed to make it through breakfast without Rachel realizing that I was angry. She was too busy trying to feed our siblings to notice me or my mood. I ate quickly then headed out to work. I told Daett as he hitched the buggy to go into town to see Mamm that I would chop firewood.

"Good thinking, John," he said, smiling. "It never hurts to have plenty of firewood."

Truth be told I needed to work off some steam, and chopping wood is a great way to express anger in a productive manner. I headed into the woods alone with my ax, although my brother begged to come with me. The air was crisp and cool, perfect for hard work. I found a tree to my liking and began to steadily chop away at it. I found a steady rhythm and began to take pleasure in that. It would be a perfect beat for a sharp, angry staccato piece. Finally the tree fell and I chopped it into pieces, loaded the logs into the wagon, and headed towards home. I was tired and hungry. My fury was now at a low smolder. I entered the house to find the girls running around the kitchen, hurrying to put lunch on the table. Little Ruthie came flying past me with a bunch of mums clutched in her chubby little hand.

"Whoa, little one!" I said as I caught her up in my arms. "Now where did you get these beautiful flowers? They better not be from Mamm's flower garden!"

"They are from Mamm's flower garden, but it's okay because they are for Mamm. Rachel said I could pick some for the table for Mamm's welcome home lunch, and I also get to pick some for Mamm's bedside table."

"What's this?" I asked Rachel in surprise as I let my wiggling sister go.

"Jah, Daett called our neighbor this morning and asked them to let us know that he is bringing Mamm home today."

As if on cue, I heard the sound of hooves coming down the lane. I went outside followed by most of my siblings. I helped Daett get Mamm down from the buggy and into her wheelchair. Her face looked washed out and worn but she smiled just the same.

"It is good to be home," she said as I guided her into her chair at the table. "The food sure smells wonderful, Rachel. It will be nice to eat a good home-cooked meal after that awful hospital food."

I excused myself with the pretext of helping Daett unhitch the horses and putting away the buggy. I found him in the barn whistling while he worked.

"Come to help an old man, John?" he said, smiling.

"Jah, and to ask why they let Mamm out of the hospital so soon."

"Because I insisted that they let her come home that's why," he said in a voice that dared me to challenge him.

"But why, Daett? She was getting the care she needs there."

"Her place is here with her family, John. We can care for her better than any outsiders at a hospital. She is my wife and this was my decision."

"But Daett…," I began.

He whirled around, his eyes grey as an angry storm.

"The Englishers wanted her to go to a nursing home for rehabilitation! I refuse to put my wife in a place like that! They said it would only be for a few weeks but people go there to die, John. She is my wife and I need her with me. She can get better here surrounded by her family and her people, not with strangers. Your sisters will care for her better than any strangers ever could!"

He strode out of the barn as if to avoid any more discussion. The realization that my Daett had shown vulnerability to me for the first time in my life caused me to soften towards him. In many ways, he was right. Mamm needed her family just as surely as plants need sun and water. I just prayed to God He would make us sufficient for her needs.

♫

Walking with Nathan became a nightly event quite by accident. He just simply kept showing up each evening. He was pleasant company and easy to talk to, and he even seemed to sense when I needed to be quiet. The chemo treatments were beginning to really make me weak. If it were not the thought of Nathan walking the road alone, I would have been tempted to stay curled up on the couch binge-watching shows on Netflix. When I told Nathan this, he smiled.

"Good! You need to stay active and keep your strength up," he said.

"If not for you, Rachel, and my chemo friends, I would be a hermit. To be honest, the real reason I wanted to hire Rachel was so I wouldn't lay dead for days undetected. Pretty morbid, huh?"

"No, I understand. It would be undignified to be found that way and hard for your family and friends," he said as he gently took my hand in his. "I am your friend, Elise. Even if you don't want me, you are stuck with me! And as your friend, I promise that I will check on you daily to make sure you are alive."

Tears sprang to my eyes. Nathan was indeed my friend. In the darkest, most uncertain hour of my life, God had richly blessed me with friendship and music. Unable to speak, I simply smiled and nodded at him. We walked back to my home in silence, holding hands the entire way. It was comforting and natural. It is strange how these two new men in my life evoked such different responses. Nathan made me happy and I felt at home with him. Music and notes from John made my heart beat faster and filled my entire being with nervous anticipation.

63

In addition to her new job, having Mamm at home and requiring a lot of care, Rachel was always very busy and I had not been able to talk with her about Daniel Lapp. Daett was determined to make our home safe and functional for Mamm and his ingenuity amazed me. Due to Mamm's limited mobility, Daett had converted our family room into a downstairs bedroom for himself and Mamm. A great deal of his time also went towards caring for Mamm. Because of this, Daett actually entrusted me with tasks that he normally took care of himself. A few days after I had seen Rachel and Daniel, we were eating breakfast when Daett told me that Mamm had a doctor's appointment that day. He also informed me that he had made an appointment with the farrier to tend to our horse, Blackie, who had been limping. Our farrier was none other than Daniel Lapp, and our appointment was scheduled for the same time that Daett and Mamm would be at her doctor's appointment. To my surprise, Daett did not want to reschedule our appointment with Daniel but rather asked me if I would take Blackie to his appointment. I agreed with alacrity and hoped that I would have time alone with Daniel so that I could talk with him about what I had seen. At the mention of Daniel's name, I involuntarily looked at Rachel. Her face flushed red and a myriad of emotions raced across Rachel's face, but she quickly hid her feelings behind a mask of placidness.

Later that day, I was both relieved and disappointed to find that Daniel was not alone in his blacksmith's shop; his two oldest sons were assisting him. However, as I watched him expertly care for Blackie, I wondered how a man like Daniel could betray his wife, his family, my sister, and his God. I wasn't naive enough to see Rachel as an innocent in this situation, but I did hold this married, older man more responsible than my very young and inexperienced sister. As I left the smithy some time later, I saw Daniel's wife, Lydia. I watched as she carefully spread a clean tablecloth over the picnic table underneath the large oak tree next to her husband's shop. She began to take containers of food out of a large picnic basket. Her youngest son was assisting her. Lydia turned and caught me watching her and I felt my face grow warm with embarrassment at being caught staring like a child without manners.

"Oh, good afternoon, John," she said shyly. "How are you?"

"Good," I said as I tipped my hat politely at her. "And you?"

"I am doing well," she replied, smiling. "God is good."

As she spoke her hand unconsciously went to her belly, and I saw the unmistakable swell of her belly indicating that a new child was on its way. A surge of pure, undiluted anger coursed through me. Before, my anger had been due to the feeling of my sister being deceived and seduced by an older man, but now my anger was increased by the betrayal of this precious family by their husband and father. My mind could not comprehend how a man could say he loves his wife and children and yet seek a relationship with another woman? I felt sick to my stomach. The affair of my sister and Daniel would only result in pain and misery. While I didn't want my sister to be hurt, I knew in that moment that I would rather her heart be broken than for Daniel's children to have their hearts broken. They were innocent. My sister was not.

I arrived home just in time to take Rachel to work at Elise's. She normally walked the short distance to Elise's house but when I arrived home, she asked if I would mind to give her a lift since the horses were already hitched up to the buggy. During my drive home I had turned over in my mind all of the things I wanted to say to her, but I took one look at her face and knew that now was not the time. She looked utterly exhausted; she had dark circles under her eyes and her face was pale. As angry as I was at her, I didn't have the heart to fuss at her right now. She sat down on the bench in the buggy with a sigh.

"Ach, it feels so good to sit down," she said with a rueful smile.

"You have a lot on you with Mamm being back home," I said as I turned the horses towards Elise's.

"Jah," she agreed, sighing again. "It's not just picking up Mamm's load of the household chores. I could cope with that easily, but Mamm requires so much care and it's wearing me out, John. I wasn't sure if I would be able to get all that I needed to get done before going to Elise's today but thankfully Mamm had physical therapy and was gone for a while, giving me the chance to get caught up on my chores. Thank goodness Elise is flexible with my hours and letting me come during the times that is best for me and our family."

"I know you like having the extra money, but it may be too much for you to have a job and take care of Mamm while picking up her load of the household chores," I suggested.

"Jah, I have thought of that," replied Rachel. "I feel bad to leave Elise after such a short time of working for her. I really like her and she is really sick, John. I don't think she would be able to cope with a home on her own."

This caused my heart to plummet. I knew she was right. I had seen for myself at a distance that Elise was becoming very frail indeed. I hated that she had no family and no one to care for her when she needed it most.

"Perhaps Mamm will get better soon and be back to how she was before the stroke," I said hopefully.

"Perhaps," Rachel said but from the tone in her voice I knew that like myself, Rachel did not think that Mamm would ever be the same again. It just hurt too much to say that out loud.

As we turned into Elise's driveway, my heart began to thud in my chest. It was unreasonable for me to be nervous. It was highly likely that Elise would not even see or notice me and even if she did, she would not know that the man driving the buggy was the one bringing her presents of music. Still, the palms of my hands were sweating and my throat was dry. Rachel was down and walking towards the doorway as soon as the buggy stopped. My heart thudded even faster as I saw the front door began to open. Elise stepped out of the front porch and smiled in welcome to Rachel. She was wearing a pale yellow hat and smiling beautifully at Rachel. I nervously licked my dry lips. *What should I do? Should I nod my head or raise my hand in greeting? Would I be expected to speak to her?* Then I remembered: she knew my name. My heart froze. If Rachel introduced me, Elise would have to wonder if I was the John bringing her music! What if she said something in front of Rachel? I couldn't risk my parents finding out about my music right now, not with Mamm so sick. In the end, my anxiety was for naught. Elise welcomed Rachel inside, followed her into the house, and shut the door without even glancing in my direction. I should've been relieved but I wasn't. I was strangely disappointed and a little upset. She hadn't even looked at me. It was like she didn't even know I existed.

Cancer has given me perspective or rather it has put things into proper perspective. I used to be mad if the right kind of water wasn't in my dressing room or if the local coffee shop couldn't make my favorite brew. Expensive dinners in an exclusive restaurant with Donovan were the highlight of my life; now I am happy when I keep tap water down, and coffee has become a thing of the past. Just the smell of coffee makes me extremely nauseated, but occasionally tea will soothe my belly and warm my body. As for expensive dinners, I am fortunate if I can keep down half a can of protein drink. Oddly enough, life is sweeter. Before I was incredibly busy, stressed, and shallow; often the only parts of a city that I would see apart from the views from a plane or taxi were hotel rooms, rehearsal rooms, and concert halls with the occasional dinner with Donovan thrown in. Now I find joy in the simple things and every day that I wake up alive is cause for celebration. The favorite events of my week are: my talks with Marge, my walks with Nathan, the days that Rachel come to my house, and above all my notes and music from John. Today finds me basking in the joy of having someone in my home with me. I sat on my couch wrapped up in my yellow blanket from Marge and watched Rachel as she whisked around cleaning my house with an incredible amount of energy. I couldn't remember ever having that much energy but I know I once did. As I watched Rachel and listened to her talk and sing, I noticed that she seemed pale and in spite of her energy, she had dark circles around her eyes. She switched the vacuum cleaner off and began to wind up the cord.

"Rachel," I began hesitantly. "I hope I don't offend you, but you look tired to me. Are you okay?"

To my surprise, she looked up at me and burst into tears.

"Oh my dear," I exclaimed. "I'm so sorry. Please, come and sit down on the couch with me."

After a moment's hesitation, she did as I asked. I watched as she wrung her hands and struggled to get her emotions under control. I patiently waited and didn't pressure her but merely handed the box of tissues to her. She smiled at me gratefully.

"One of the bonuses of being sick," I said wryly. "I always have tissues now—in every room of the house!"

To my relief, this brought a slight smile to her face. Slowly the tears stopped.

"I'm sorry, Elise," said Rachel.

"Please don't worry about it," I reassured her. "I've traveled so much that making friends has been a rare event in my life. In the short time I have known you, I would like to think that we have started to become friends."

She smiled at me in relief and in a rare display of affection, she reached out and patted my hand.

"Thank you for being so kind to me when you are going through so much yourself. I do think of you as a friend. It has been hard on me these past few weeks," she admitted. "Mamm, that's my mother, had a stroke and was in the hospital. So all of her household chores and caring for the little ones naturally fell on me as the oldest daughter. I was doing fine. I've cooked and cleaned and cared for children my entire life. But this week, my Daett got upset because he felt like the hospital was wanting to put Mamm in a nursing home to die. We couldn't get him to understand that they only wanted Mamm to go for a short while for rehab. You see, our people always take care of our own elderly. It is very rare for someone in our community to go to a nursing home. Daett had a maiden aunt and she became very sick. I'm not really sure what was wrong with her; I don't think Daett even knows because he was a young boy at the time. Because his aunt did not have any children to take her in, it would have fallen upon someone in the family to take her in. She was so sick though, and it sounded like she needed the kind of care that only nurses can give and the hospital convinced her siblings that the best thing would be to put her into a nursing home. Daett remembers visiting her in the nursing home. He said it smelt so bad and many of the patients were crying out. His aunt was only there for a short while before dying and Daett is convinced that she died because she felt unwanted by her family and her heart broke. To Daett's mind, sending Mamm to a nursing home would be telling her that we don't want her and he is afraid she would die. I love my Mamm. She has been a wonderful Mamm. But caring for her is really hard. She cannot do anything for herself, Elise. She will only let me attend to her more personal hygiene because she is too embarrassed to let any of my younger sisters her with that. She is blind and she is paralyzed on one side. She can stand and pivot to sit in a chair if she has a lot of assistance. Because of that we moved their master bedroom down to the first floor, which means it was one more huge task that we had to get done quickly."

Rachel flushed and her gaze dropped.

"I love my Mamm and I don't mean to complain about caring for her. I am very grateful that Mamm is still with us, but caring for her day and night and having all of the extra work on top of it all is wearing me out."

"And you just got the job of cleaning my house adding to your load. I am sorry, Elise. I understand if you want to take a break from cleaning for me until your mother gets better," I said.

"Oh, Elise! I didn't mean to make you feel like I can't handle working here too. I'm sorry," said Rachel, her face flushing red. "I hope you haven't been displeased with my work."

"You didn't make me upset at all," I reassured her. "Like I said, I think we are becoming friends and friends share things that are bothering them with their friend. Lately everything has been about me and my health. It is nice to focus on someone else for a change. As far as your quality of work, you are incredible! My grandmother would be pleased and she was a stickler about keeping her house clean. She couldn't have done better herself. Selfishly, I would love to have you working for me forever! It's wonderful to have a clean home especially when you can't care for it yourself. But more than that, I really enjoy your company. However, as your friend, I don't want you to overwork yourself and I don't want you to feel obligated to me. You have a job with me for as long as you want but if you feel like it is getting to be too much for you, I will understand if you need and want to take a break from this job. Your mother should be your main focus right now, not cleaning up after me."

Rachel gave her a watery smile.

"That's awfully nice of you but for now I would like to continue working for you. Mamm is getting better and it wouldn't hurt to turn over some of my duties at home to my sisters. I'm not doing them any favors by trying to spare them extra work. After all, one day they will be married with a family of their own and I want them to be well prepared."

"As you wish," I agreed. "You know I am delighted to have you but if you ever need to take time off, I will completely understand."

"Thank you, Elise," she said, smiling. "You are kind. Well, I best be getting back to work."

With that, Rachel rose to her feet briskly and got back to work. Soothed by the sounds of someone else in the house with me, I presently dropped off to sleep. I awoke to her gentle tapping on my shoulder. I opened my eyes to see Rachel looking at me apologetically.

"I'm sorry to wake you up, Elise," she said. "I am getting ready to go home. I didn't want you to wake up to find me gone."

"Thank you," I said. "The house looks wonderful. Oh, before you leave, I want to pay you today."

I went to my grandmother's secretary to retrieve my checkbook, wrote Rachel a check with an additional bonus to our agreed amount. She took the check, looked at it, and gasped.

"Oh, Miss! I can't take this! It's too much," she protested.

"You have more than earned it," I said firmly. "Now, I won't take any arguments. You are worth every penny and then some."

I watched from the window as Rachel walked down my long driveway until I could see her no more. Then, with a sigh, I locked the front door and went to the kitchen. I couldn't find anything that I felt I could eat and keep down, so I decided to drink as much as I could of a can of protein drink and to call that dinner. Since I found it more palpable out of a glass instead of the can, I poured the thick liquid into a glass and took my 'dinner' to the back screened-in porch. This had become one of my favorite spots of the house, and the gently worn chaise lounge was my usual seat. I ran my hand along the arm of the chair admiring the aged fabric of still beautiful if somewhat faded cabbage roses. This had been my grandmother's favorite spot as well and she had spent a great deal of time here. I knew this because in addition to the floor lamp conducive to reading, there was a side table next to the chaise lounge that was so old it was now fashionable again thanks to the popularity of farmhouse decor. The table had two shelves and my grandmother had positioned it to where the shelves were accessible to whomever was sitting in the chaise lounge. While the top of the table had what my nana called "pretties" displayed on its surface as well as a pretty glass coaster with a crocheted coaster inside of it, the shelves held books including a Bible, Nana's magnifying glass, and a small glass jar that held pens, pencils, highlighters, knitting needles, and a crochet hook. On the other side of the chaise lounge was a small wastebasket and a beautiful quilted bag. When I first discovered the bag, I opened it up and found that it contained Nana's knitting project and accoutrements. The sight of the unfinished knitting on the needles brought tears to my eyes. I wish that I had taken the time to learn how to knit from Nana during one of my visits. If I had, I could finish the project for her. Nana had always been busy and even when she had finally sat down for the evening, she would pull out her knitting. I teased her that the only way she could justify sitting down was if she was doing something worthwhile like knitting. Suddenly, I remembered something that had happened the last time I had come home for a visit. I had come directly from England. I had jet lag and my sleep schedule was discombobulated. I had woken up very early; the dawn was just beginning to creep across the sky. The house was very quiet and I thought that Nana and Poppy were still sleeping, but then I smelt coffee in the air. It smelled too delicious to resist so I got up, wrapped up in my dressing gown, thrust my feet in my bunny slippers, and went downstairs in search of caffeine. When I arrived in the kitchen I saw Poppy at the kitchen table, a steaming cup of coffee next to the open Bible in front of him. Poppy was bent over the book, tracing the words with his finger, his lips moving as he quietly read aloud to himself. I had crossed over and kissed the top of his head.

"Good morning, Poppy," I said. "Is Nana still sleeping?"

"No, no," he answered without lifting his eyes up from his Bible. "She is on the back porch. Coffee is in the percolator."

I smiled as I poured the dark, rich brew into a blue willow china cup. My grandparents' coffee could rival the espresso of any coffeehouse in boldness. By the time we ate breakfast, the coffee had been percolating since dawn. I probably would hate it if anyone else had served it to me but over the years, my taste buds had adapted to the stuff and I actually missed it when I was away from home. The amount of cream and sugar that I added to it had always caused Poppy to tease me that I liked a 'little' coffee with my cream and sugar. Coffee cup in hand, I had went out to the back porch. Nana had been sitting in her chaise, her reading glasses perched on her nose and a well-worn Bible was in her lap. She had looked up at me and smiled sweetly. I had always known that my grandparents were deeply religious but until that morning, I never realized how deep their faith actually was and that reading their Bible and praying was part of their daily lives.

I took another drink of the protein drink and shuddered. I put the glass down and on impulse I picked up Nana's Bible. It opened up to John. I noticed that one verse was highlighted, underlined and circled! Curious, I read the verse which was the sixteenth verse in chapter three.

"For God so loved the world, that he gave his only begotten Son, that whosoever believeth in him, should not perish, but have everlasting life."

I noticed that there were words written in the margin; they were written in Nana's shaky script. My finger traced the words as if touching her writing brought me closer to Nana. Then I read the words she had written.

"Dear Lord, please save the soul of my precious Elise. Let her know that she is loved by you and that you love her so much, that you sent your Son to die for the remission of her sins. Thank you for your mercy and grace, and thank you for answering my prayer."

Tears began to pour down my cheeks. I had known my grandparents wanted me to be a Christian like them. They had taken me to church whenever I was with them and had talked to me about God, His love for me, and the plan of salvation. But until that moment, I had not realized how deeply they must've wanted it. To think of my precious Nana praying for me filled my heart with both love and sorrow. Then a thought struck me; I got up and went into the kitchen. Poppy's Bible was still on the kitchen table where he had left it. I had not been able to bring myself to move it. I opened up Poppy's Bible and found John 3:16. Poppy had also underlined the verse and he had written in the margin as well. Through my tears, I read his words:

"Amen! Precious Lord, thank you for your saving grace. I pray that Elise will come to know you as Her Saviour. In Christ's Name I pray."

Suddenly I felt like I couldn't breathe. I had to get out of the house. I grabbed Nana's sweater and practically ran out of the house, barely remembering to grab my cell phone and keys. Without even really seeing where I was heading, I blindly walked as fast as my weakened body would let me, as if trying to escape an unknown pursuer. It wasn't until I heard my name being called that I finally looked up and took stock of my surroundings. Nathan was stepping off a porch and walking towards me with concern on his face.

"Elise, is everything all right?" he asked as he reached my side.

"I'm fine," I lied. "I just needed to get out of the house for a bit. I was feeling cooped up."

"Are you sure?" he asked as his soft brown eyes scanned my face for reassurance.

"I promise," I said, smiling reassuringly. "I've been looking at some of my grandparents' belongings and it just brought home to me how much I miss them."

"I am sorry. It can't be easy to be surrounded by so many memories."

"Usually it is comforting, but today it just got to me. Too much alone time as of late, I guess," I shrugged.

"Speaking of that," Nathan said with a smile, "I have someone I want you to meet."

My curiosity aroused, I followed Nathan across his yard and up onto his front porch. He took me to a small basket that held a sleeping kitten that was curled up in a ball of grey fur.

"Oh, how sweet!" I exclaimed. "How old is it?"

"She is twelve weeks old," answered Nathan. "She is one of a litter of five. All of her siblings have been adopted, so now I just have her and her mom. I thought I would keep her to be company for her mom, but the oddest thing has happened."

"What's that?" I asked, my own troubles now forgotten.

"Now that the kitten is weaned and a competitor for food and my affection, her mother no longer wants her here!"

"Surely not! Are you sure her mother doesn't want her here with her?" I exclaimed, pushing aside the uncomfortable memory of my own neglectful mother.

"I am 100 percent positive," insisted Nathan. "Princess—that's her mom who was named so because she acts like a princess—hisses at her and rebuffs all of the kitten's attempts to play with her or to cuddle with her. What's more, she keeps carrying her outside!"

"What?" I exclaimed.

"I kept finding the kitten outside and I wondered how she was getting out. She is too small and doesn't have enough strength to push her way out through the cat door. Thankfully, she never ran away or got hurt; she would just sit on the porch waiting to be found. I would take her back inside, only to find her outside some time later. Then yesterday, I was sitting out here on the porch when I heard a sound at the door. I looked and saw Princess at the front door. I watched as she butted the cat door open with her head. She came outside carrying the kitten in her mouth by the scruff of her neck. She dropped the kitten down and then ran back into the house as fast as she could! The kitten looked up at me nonplussed like this was an ordinary, everyday occurrence! Obviously, Princess is trying to get her last remaining kitten to leave the nest!"

I collapsed into a chair laughing. Nathan sat down next to me smiling, enjoying my amusement. Finally, my laughter dried up and I wiped my eyes.

"So what are you going to do?" I asked him.

"Well, that's where you come in," he said as he looked at me.

"Me?" I asked, perplexed. "I don't know anything about cats. I wouldn't know how on earth you would go about getting Princess to accept the kitten."

"Oh, I've decided to accept defeat and to allow Princess to rule the roost uncontested. Even Chet, who is easily triple Princess' size and weight, is submissive to her and acknowledges her as his alpha! No, I thought that perhaps you would like to adopt the kitten. She is a very sweet kitty. She is smart and affectionate. She loves to play and makes me laugh with her antics. She would be a lot of company for you."

I stared at the little kitten. As I watched her, she stretched in her sleep and I noticed that her little paws were bright white, contrasting beautifully with her glossy grey fur. She yawned broadly, revealing small sharp white teeth and a pink moist tongue. Then she opened up her eyes and looked directly at me. Her eyes were big and a beautiful shade of green. She stood up and stepped out of the basket and stretched out in a downward facing dog position before coming to stand in front of me. We looked at one another as if we were assessing each other.

"I think she likes you," said Nathan.

"What's her name?" I asked.

"I haven't named her yet because I wasn't sure that I was going to keep her. If she went to a new home, I wanted them to be able to name her. I've just been calling her Kitten," confessed Nathan sheepishly.

"What do you think?" I asked the kitten. "Would you like to come home with me and adopt me as your human?"

In a move so fast it stunned me, the kitten leapt with a single bound up onto my lap. She looked up into my eyes and said a sweet, high-pitched "Meow" and thus completely melted my heart. She then began to sniff, look at, and paw my sweater. I had only buttoned my sweater halfway and, finding the opening of my sweater, the kitten crawled inside, snuggled up into my sweater, and began to knead her paws on my abdomen with closed eyes and purring loudly. I could feel the tiniest prick of her claws through my shirt and onto my skin, but it was not enough to hurt me or cause me to bleed. I looked up at Nathan in wonderment.

"What is she doing?" I asked.

"She is doing what is called *smurgling*. Kittens tend to do this when nursing from their mother in order to push the milk out from their mother. They create a memory from this and of course the memory is associated with happiness. Sometimes they will recreate that memory by kneading or smurgling whenever they feel comfortable. I would say that it clearly indicates that she likes you. Her mother hasn't let her do that on her since she was weaned. She must see you as her new mom," said Nathan with a smile.

Unexpected tears flooded my eyes. Hesitantly, I reached my hand out and began to stroke her fur. She was so soft and warm, and an empty spot in my heart that I hadn't even known that I had was filled. I wrapped my arms and hands in a protective gesture, holding her and supporting her just like I would an infant. I looked up at Nathan with shining eyes.

"I'll adopt her!"

"Great," he said with relief. "She has her basket, a carrying case, a few toys, a food and water bowl, some food, a litter box and litter—by the way, she is housebroken and has never had an accident. She has seen the vet and has had all of her inoculations, and she was spayed at eight weeks."

"Wow!" I said with astonishment. "I need to reimburse you. That all had to cost a lot!"

"Nonsense," said Nathan with a wave of his hand as he stood up. "I will gather everything up and take it to the car. How about letting me give you a ride, since you are going home with much more than you came out with?"

"I would be grateful for a ride home," I admitted.

"Good. Now sit there and rest with her while I get everything together, and then I will pull the car around to pick you two up. But first, I want to take a picture of you and kitten."

"Oh, Nathan, I probably look terrible," I protested.

"Nonsense," he said as he held up his phone. "Smile."

And so I found myself at home with the sweetest little kitten in the world. Nathan patiently taught me all I needed to know to care for her and then he left. Usually I would feel a loss when people left, but now I had this sweet fur ball. Despite being so small, she filled the house with life. We played and her antics made me laugh. I practiced several different names on her but she didn't seem to respond to them and wouldn't look up until I called her kitten.

"What am I going to call you?" I asked her as she ate. "I don't want to just call you kitten. That makes it seem like I don't love you enough to name you."

A memory popped into my brain randomly. It was my seventh birthday and I had asked for two years for an American Girl doll like some of my friends had. These dolls were beautiful and came with a book about their life and the historical events that occurred during their lifetime. However, Mother stated they were too expensive and that I already spent too much time playing with dolls and not enough time practicing the piano. I had opened all of my presents and of course there was no doll. Mother had gotten me clothes, most of which she said I could wear to recitals and auditions. I was playing with my friends when the doorbell rang. I thought nothing of it until I distinctly heard my father's voice.

"She's my daughter, Muriel" Father was saying angrily. "Today is my baby's birthday and I want to see her. Please don't keep her from me today of all days."

"She doesn't even want to see you," Mother was saying coldly as I hurtled myself down the hallway and into my father's arms.

Father wrapped his arms around me tightly and as the familiar smells of aftershave and cigar smoke enveloped me, I was truly happy for the first time in months. Even though I was so young, I realized that night that my father did love me and want to see me and that my own mother had been lying to me. My relationship with my Mother was never warm or close, so the only reason she would have for keeping me away from the parent I was close to was to hurt him. She didn't care that she was hurting me also.

"I have something for you," Father had said with a smile. He handed me a big box. I tore into it with a fast beating heart. When I saw that he had brought me not only an American Girl doll but the very doll that I wanted more than any other, Kit, I squealed with happiness. Looking back on that memory, I realized wryly that my father had understood my mother very well. He had also given me nearly every single accessory that the American Girl doll company sold for the Kit doll. Additionally, he gave me a large antique trunk that opened up and had little drawers, a place to hang up her clothes, a mirror, and ample room to hold not only Kit but all of her belongings. I loved it. Father had carried it into my room for me because it was very heavy and he watched with joy as I and my friends eagerly arranged the trunk like a little bedroom using the doll furniture Father had given me. Father had a pet name for me, I remembered with a smile. He had called me Kitten. I had wanted to call him Daddy but Mother had insisted that I call him Father as soon as I could say it. Before he left, Father had given me the key to the trunk's lock and then knelt down and looked me in the eyes earnestly.

"Kitten, I want you to take good care of Kit and all of her belongings. They were expensive. Okay?"

"I promise, Father," I said solemnly.

"I know, you will, Kitten," he said with a smile. "Now when you aren't playing with her, I want you to put Kit and all of Kit's belongings including her furniture and clothes into the trunk. Then I want you close the trunk and lock it. And I want you to always keep the key on you."

"I promise, Father," I said again.

"Now don't you forget," admonished Father. "If you aren't playing with her, never leave her home open and unlocked even if you are home. You wouldn't leave your home unlocked, right? So this will be a good way to remember to lock your own home someday."

I now realized why Father had done that. He hadn't wanted just to teach me to lock up my home. He hadn't wanted my mother to get rid of my doll, and that had been the only way he could think of to keep my doll safe for me. Mother had always hated my doll and that "big, old, dirty, ugly" trunk. I had loved them both. In fact I still had Kit and her trunk, and she had moved into this house with me. Kit and all of her accessories looked new because Mother allowed me very little playtime. I hoped someday to give her to a daughter of my own, and I planned on letting Kit get worn out with love and play.

Watching the kitten eat and thinking about Kit had triggered another memory.

I had attended the birthday party of a little girl whom I went to school with named Shelby. The fact that Mother had allowed me to go to her tenth birthday party was remarkable. Once I realized who the girl's parents were, I understood why Mother had given her permission. It was the first time that I had eaten real birthday cake. The only time Mother allowed cake in our home was when it was on our birthdays and Christmas. However, the cake was a recipe that Mother had obtained at her weekly diet class. I once asked her why she went to a diet class every week because she was skinny. She replied coolly that she went so she could stay skinny. The cake was made with a boxed cake mix and a can of diet soda. Mother did not put frosting on it, but she did allow me to put two squirts of whipped topping on it. I had always looked forward to those cakes but after taking one bite of Shelby's birthday cake, I realized just what I had been missing. Not only that, but her mother gave us two scoops of ice cream to go with our generous slices of cake. By the time the party was over, I was on a major sugar high! However, the surprises weren't over yet!

At the end of the birthday party, Shelby's mother gave every one of us a treat bag to take home with us. I was on cloud nine! Inside the bag was a stuffed marmalade cat, a tiara, a costume jewelry set, a three-pack set of fruit-flavored lip balm, a diary with a lock and key, and two full sized Kit-Kat bars which Shelby explained were her favorite candy bar. Everyone started telling which candy bar was their favorite. Then Shelby noticed I hadn't said which candy bar was my favorite and asked me. The truth was that I had never had a candy bar before but I was too embarrassed to tell my friends this, so I lied and said that Kit-Kats were my favorite candy bar as well. Fortunately for me, I found that I loved the Kit-Kat candy bar and as it was the only one I had eaten, it truly was my favorite. Knowing that my mother would confiscate and throw away the chocolate, I quickly hid them inside the inner lining of my jacket. My mother was known to search my room, my purse, my backpack, etc. and I quickly became adept at creating hiding places for things I did not want her to find. At the beginning of the winter I had slit open the lining of my jacket and, using super glue, I adhered strips of Velcro that were left over from a sewing project I had worked on with Nana that past summer, making an interior pouch inside my coat's inner lining. I was able to slip the Kit Kat bars into this hidden pouch.

When we got into the car, Mother immediately asked to see the gift bag. She looked through the bag with disdain on her face. I was sure she wanted to throw it all away but didn't because she was afraid that if Shelby found out, then so would her parents. I had to eat the Kit-Kats at school knowing that if I ate them at home, I would have to dispose of the wrappings in the trash and Mother would see them. *It had been worth it,* I thought, smiling. A thought occurred to me.

"That's it!" I suddenly exclaimed. "I will call you KitKat because you are an unexpected sweet treat!"

At the sound of her name, KitKat looked up at me from her food and meowed. Then she went back to eating. Wondering if this was just a fluke, I tried it again.

"KitKat," I said in a singsong voice.

KitKat looked up into my eyes, swished her tail, and again said, "Meow." Then she looked down at her food and up at me as if to say, *Can I please eat without interruption?*

"All right, KitKat it is," I said with a smile. "I'll let you eat in peace now."

As I watched her eat, I realized with some amazement that for the first time in days, I was hungry. I made myself a boiled egg, toast, and tea. I ate it all and did not experience any nausea. It was a delicious feeling to feel full and not to be sick.

That night she followed me up the stairs and watched me with interest as I put her sleeping basket next to my bed and sat a small dish of water next to her bed. I had noticed how much water she tended to drink and I didn't want her to have to go all the way to the kitchen for a drink during the middle of the night. Then she followed me into my bathroom, jumped up on the countertop and watched me with interest, cocking her head to one side as I went about my nightly routine. Occasionally she would meow at me as if talking to me; Nathan had told me she was talkative and he was right. When I was finished, I picked her up gingerly. She didn't protest at all but rather snuggled up against my chest and rubbed her head against me with a sigh. I carried her like a baby to the bedroom and it felt so good to be holding her in my arms. I tried to put her in her sleeping basket but she refused to put her little feet down and protested greatly when I tried to sit her down. She looked up at me with such mournful eyes that I felt guilty.

"Oh, all right, " I said. "You can sleep with me."

This time she made no objections when I laid her down on my bed. I got into bed and turned out the light. My hand went instinctively to where I had laid down the cat, only to find the spot empty. I hadn't even had time to look for her or to wonder where she was before there she was on my chest. She tucked her head up under my chin and began to smurgle on my chest. Her purring and the warmth of her little body was very comforting and before I knew it, I was asleep.

CHAPTER SEVEN

An odd sensation on my ear and a strange sound woke me up. My brain had tried to interpret these oddities by explaining them in a dream featuring a nurse at the cancer center attaching a leech to my ear to "suck the cancer out of me" while I introduced KitKat, who was slurping up water out of a dish, to Marge. I struggled to wake up and realized that KitKat was nursing my earlobe. She was making noisy, slurping sounds as she nursed and she purred loudly as she also smurgled on my neck. It was sweet but weird and I wasn't really sure how to handle it. I felt sorry for KitKat. She must still want mothering and the poor baby had essentially been rejected by her mother which was a feeling I understood all too well. I would be lying if I didn't admit that I liked her thinking of me as her mom. It was nice to be loved and needed, to care for someone instead of being cared for. So I lay there and let her nurse as long as she needed to. As I lay there I began to wonder for the first time that if I were to live, would I ever be able to have a child of my own? I had not even thought to ask if the treatments would render me incapable of having a child. My only concern had been to survive, but I now realized that I also wanted to thrive. I loved playing the piano and music was as much a part of me as my skin but as I took stock of my life, I knew that I had not been living my life to the fullest. My life had consisted of concerts, rehearsals, and getting from one event to the next. Oh yes, I had a boyfriend in the form of Donovan Shane but with a flash of insight, I knew that our relationship had been nothing like the type of love I wanted, the type of love I deserved. For the first time in a long time, I could think of Donovan Shane without pain or regret or longing. In fact, I was glad he had dumped me! Truly that had been the nicest thing that he had ever done for me!

KitKat was done nursing and I had a strong desire to talk to someone about all that I was thinking and feeling. I wanted to share with someone that this tiny little fur ball had come into my life and in just a few hours, I had fallen in love with a cat! Finally, I understood my animal-loving friends! Animals love unconditionally and give fully of themselves. Why couldn't humans do the same? With a pang of longing, I realized that I wished to share my news with John. I would love to sit with him on the back porch and tell him all about KitKat but since I couldn't, I decided to write to him instead.

Dear John,

Something rather wonderful and unexpected has happened to me. I now have the sweetest little kitten that you could ever see and her name is KitKat! She is absolutely lovely. KitKat is twelve weeks old, has soft grey fur, white paws, and big, beautiful light-green eyes. She is very playful and funny. And she is very smart. It may seem silly that I am so excited and happy about a cat, but I have been so lonely. Actually I have been lonely all of my life but now that I live most of my life by myself, I am realizing just how isolated and sad I have been. I am an only child. My mother was not very maternal. She is from Chicago and her family is very rich. Consequently, Mother was raised by a nanny. She never really talked about her nanny very much; all I know is that she was an older woman who was strict, stern, and not affectionate. Once I understood this, it gave me insight as to why my mother is the way that she is, but it doesn't make it any easier or less hurtful.

However, my Father was delightful and he loved me very much. He was very affectionate and gave me enough love for two parents. He actually grew up in this very house but back then my grandparents owned the farmland as well. My grandfather's family were German Jews who fled Germany before the Holocaust. Poppy—that's what I called my grandfather—told me that his parents were Messianic Jews, which means they had converted to Christianity and embraced Jesus as the Messiah. Poppy's father said that one night God came to him in a dream and told him to flee Germany and to tell all of his Jewish family, friends, and acquaintances to flee to America for their safety and they must do so by month's end. God also told Him that they were not to leave behind a trace of their lives and to shake Germany off the soles of their feet as they left.

His father went to the rabbi at the synagogue and told him as well; he begged him to tell his congregation to flee Germany. The rabbi scoffed at him and refused to take him seriously because he viewed him as a traitor to his faith. Why would God speak to a heretic and not a rabbi, he asked my great-grandfather. "Perhaps because God knows that I am listening for His voice and you are not." Both of my great-grandparents told all of the Jewish people they could find while packing up their lives, arranging to have their belongings shipped to America, transferring their funds to a bank in America, and saying goodbye to Germany and everyone they knew there. It was difficult on my great-grandmother. Apparently my great-grandfather was a wealthy banker in Germany and they led a prosperous lifestyle there. My great-grandmother was especially sad to leave behind her home which was by all accounts a grand home. However, she trusted in her husband and in God and although she grieved in secret, she did not challenge her husband about leaving. Poppy was eleven years old so he did still have memories of Germany. He said that as they left Germany, his mother asked her husband if he thought they would ever return to Germany. His father replied, "Das Deutschland, das wir lieben, ist nicht mehr. Wir werden sie nie wieder sehen" which means: "The Germany we love is no more. We will never see her again."

Poppy raised Father to be bilingual and likewise, Father raised me bilingual as well. When I toured Germany for the first time with the orchestra, I visited the town where Poppy came from. I took hundreds of pictures and hours of video for him. I did find several very elderly residents who remembered my great-grandparents but out of all the Jewish families that Poppy could remember and saw mentioned in his parents' archives, not a single person remained. Everyone that he could remember had fallen victim to the Holocaust. Very few actually heeded the warning and left. When I showed the pictures and videos to Poppy, he wept and wept. I felt that my heart would break with him. The silver lining is of course the fact that by emigrating to America, Poppy met my nana, fell madly in love with her, and had a son who in turn had me.

Poppy became a farmer and loved working the land. My grandfather had hoped that my father would follow his footsteps and one day take over the farm. However, my father didn't like farming and he became an attorney instead. He was my grandparents' only living child so when it became too hard for my grandparents to carry on farming, they sold the farmland and kept only the farmhouse and five acres. I believe they sold the farmland to the Amish.

Unfortunately, when I was five years old my parents divorced. While my father never admitted it to me, I believe that Mother is the one who wanted the divorce. In spite of everything, my father always loved my mother. He never remarried. Mother has been married four additional times. After two stepfathers had come and gone, I quit trying to get to know the guys. Mother used me to hurt my father. She fought to have full custody of me but thank God my father was given visitation rights. Still Mother did all she could to keep us apart. Father and I mostly spoke in German with one another and it nearly drove Mother crazy! She hated that she didn't know what our conversations were about so she couldn't control them. Although originally we conversed in German so I could become fluent in the language, it later became our language of choice in order to reduce Mother's interference in our conversations. Of course when we were sitting at the table eating a meal as a family etc., we conversed in English for Mother. But when it was just a conversation between us two, we spoke in German.

After the divorce, we wrote our letters in German so that we could be discreet and to prevent Mother from reading them. Father was truly a marvelous father. When I was thirteen years old, my father was killed in a boating accident in Lake Michigan. It was the fourth of July and there were a lot of boats full of people drinking and celebrating the holiday. A man who was driving a speedboat while drunk plowed into my father's boat while going at high speed. My father was killed along with two of his passengers. The man who caused the accident walked away from the crash with only minor injuries. The grief I felt over losing my father threatened to overwhelm me. Poppy and Nana were also devastated but together and with the help of God, we made it through. I miss my father and think of him every day.

As you've probably guessed from what I have already written about them, my paternal grandparents were wonderful. I spent every summer and most holidays here with them. Mother has always dropped me off whenever she wanted to go away with some man. Considering how many men she has dated and married, I spent a lot of time here with my grandparents. To me this farmhouse has always been home. Poppy was a big man, powerfully built with large hands that would engulf my own, yet he was extremely gentle and kind.

I loved going for walks with Poppy. He would hold my small hand in his big, work-roughened hands and off we would go on our 'adventures' as we called them. Through him, I learned the name of all the trees and plants in the area. Poppy was very intelligent and he could have gone to college and chosen a different profession but he loved being a farmer; he loved feeling the dirt with his bare hands and the satisfaction of producing a good harvest. He didn't talk very much but when he did, I listened. Often I would see him working or sitting with a far-off look in his eyes. When I would ask him what he was thinking about, he would just smile and say evasively, "Oh, just a pondering." He was introverted and shied away from crowds, but he loved people and would quietly do things for them. He never wanted any recognition for his good deeds. At his funeral, countless people came up to me and told me all of these wonderful stories about Poppy.

One of our neighbors told me that after her husband had passed away in 1962 of a massive heart attack, she was left to care for their home and five young sons alone. She said that same week, Poppy just showed up and mowed her lawn and even did the trimming. He did that every week during the warmer months for years and would never accept anything more than a glass of water from her. She said he wouldn't even take a cookie but instead would tell her to save all the cookies for her sweet children. When her boys got old enough, he taught them how to mow and trim the lawn; he taught them how to change the oil, change a flat tire, and countless other things around the house. Gradually, he didn't have to do as much because the boys were old enough to do the chores on their own. Then one by one the boys grew up, got married, and moved away to start a life of their own. Without a word, Poppy went back to tending to the grass and outdoor maintenance for her and continued to do that until the day he died.

Poppy died when I was eighteen. He had a massive stroke while sitting at the kitchen table reading his Bible. Nana left his Bible there; she couldn't bear to move it. Neither can I. In fact, I read out of Poppy's Bible yesterday while sitting at the kitchen table. Nana lived for four years without him. She never got over the heartbreak of losing him. Nana died of breast cancer three years ago. Now Poppy and Nana are with Father in Heaven and I must confess that I am jealous of them but one day, we will all be together again.

My house has a back porch that is screened in. There is a chaise lounge back there that I love to sit in. Apparently it was Nana's favorite spot as well because I found her knitting, books, reading glasses, and Bible next to it. I opened her Bible and it fell open to John. Nana had underlined, highlighted, and circled John 3:16. Next to it she had written a prayer for me. Then I looked up the same scripture in Poppy's Bible. He had also underlined John 3:16 and had written a prayer in the margin for me. It really touched my heart. They loved me so much and now that they are gone and my Father is gone, I feel bereft. It is a lonely feeling to realize that there is no one left to love you. Which is another reason why I am very thankful to have KitKat: now there is someone in the world who loves me and will miss me when I die.

Thank you for 'listening' to my rambling. This morning, I woke up wanting to talk to you and this is the only way I have to contact you.

With great affection,
Elise

I folded the letter and slid it into an envelope. A thought occurred to me and I wondered if I dared to act upon it. After some hesitation, I decided to chance it. With my wireless photo printer, I printed out a copy of a picture of me age seven beaming and holding Kit tightly to me and the picture Nathan had taken of me and KitKat. I tucked the pictures inside of the envelope with a wry smile. I was behaving like a teenager with a crush. Then I pulled out the letter to add a postscript.

P.S. I have included a couple of pictures for you. One is me with the doll named Kit that my father bought for me on my seventh birthday. The second one was taken by a friend of mine yesterday. It's the first picture of me and KitKat.

I folded the letter back up and placed the letter and the pictures inside of the envelope. Before I could change my mind, I took the letter out to the front porch and placed it under the doormat. Then I went back inside where I was greeted with a meow from KitKat.

Rachel wasn't the only one whose workload had increased. With Daett taking Mamm to therapy three times a week plus her many doctor appointments, the load of his work fell on me and my brothers, with me taking the brunt of it. In some ways, I was grateful for the work because it kept me busy. I worried about Mamm and Rachel but in spite of all of my worry for them, the majority of my time my mind was consumed with thoughts of Elise. Music has always been a part of me. I hear music good and bad everyday but Elise was causing me to hear notes, sounds, and combinations of notes that I had never heard before. She inspired me to create music unlike anything that I had composed before. I wanted to make beautiful music for her to play, to make her smile. It broke my heart to know that she was ill and alone. The only thing I could do for her was to bring her music. I waited until I was sure everyone was asleep before sneaking out of the house and to the barn again. I worked on the new piece of music for a while but my mind was restless. Eventually, I set it aside. I wished I could sit on her porch with her and talk with her. I looked through my sheets of music and picked out another song to take to her. Then I took out a blank sheet of paper and began to write. I set out to write a short note like always, but I found myself pouring out my thoughts to Elise.

Dear Elise,

I have brought for you a new song. This is a cheerful tune and I hope that it brings you some joy. Hearing you play my music has brought me great happiness and I wish to repay your kindness. I am thankful that God brought you into my life. The gift of your friendship has been an unexpected and wonderful blessing.

Is it possible to miss someone you don't know? I ask because I find myself missing you and thinking of you all the time. Although I suppose you aren't really a stranger to me: we have met through music. In many ways, music is more honest than a conversation. Words can be misleading and misunderstood, but music cannot lie. Music clearly conveys the breadth and depth of feelings and the truth of our experiences. In fact, I think you are the only one who truly knows me. Samuel knows about my music but he cannot hear it and thus he cannot hear the truth it contains. He also doesn't understand the consuming need inside me that drives me to compose music but when I heard you play for the first time, I knew that you understand because you feel it too. It's the same reason you practice for hours on end, at all hours of the day, no matter how bad you feel.

While I am grateful for our shared music and for your notes, I must confess I long for more. However, it would not be fair of me to ask that of you right now. There are circumstances and obligations to my family that keep me from being able to meet with you in *person. I pray that someday soon we can meet face to face. Please consider agreeing to meet me in person one day.*

Ever yours,
John

As I placed the note inside the envelope, I thought of all the things I wanted to say to Elise but could not. Oh, how I longed to hold her in my arms, to tell her that I was feeling emotions that I had never felt before, and to ask her to be my girl. Then reality came crashing into my mind and snatched away my lovely dream. How could I ever hope that a girl like her would ever love a boy like me? Even if the impossible happened, I could never leave my family behind now. They needed me too much. With a heavy heart, I walked towards Elise's home pondering if I should just turn around and never bother her again. But then I remembered how much joy she said my music had brought her and my steps became more sure. And how, I asked myself sadly, am I ever going to let her go?

When I arrived at Elise's house, it was shrouded in darkness and all was quiet. I paused for a moment and looked up at the upstairs windows wondering which ones were hers and I hoped that she was resting well. I took great care to step lightly, trying to make as little sound as possible. Weighted down by the rock she always used to keep the envelopes from being blown away, I found an envelope addressed to me. Joy flooded my heart. I removed the letter addressed to me and slid the one I had brought for Elise under her door. Then I rapidly made my way towards home; I could scarcely wait to read the letter. Halfway across her yard, I decided to go into the woods instead. For a reason that I couldn't really explain, I felt uneasy about going to the barn tonight. So instead, I headed deep into the woods.

Close to the spot where I had buried my music, I had built a tree stand. Daett was not a hunter but he had not objected to me and my brothers' hunting. My maternal grandfather had taught me how to hunt and had given me my first shotgun. In turn, I had instructed my two brothers who were old enough to hunt as well. I had built the tree stand for us to use in deer season; however, my brothers did not seem to be as enthusiastic about hunting as I was and had little patience for sitting up in the cold early hours of the morning waiting for deer to come. Secretly, I was glad that my brothers very rarely wanted to accompany me. While I was glad to provide much needed meat for my family, the act of killing the animal brought me no joy. For me the attraction of hunting was being high up in the tree, away from the rest of my large and noisy family and in the peace of the woods. The sounds of nature are magnified in the woods. The chirping of the birds seem to echo and bounce off the trees, the wind rustled the leaves of the trees, and the sounds of the forest animals all seemed to make a concert of nature that satisfied and calmed me. Being one in a family of nine, being alone is nearly impossible and thus I cherished my time in the woods and happily volunteered to be the hunter for the family. It was to my tree stand where my feet now propelled me.

I climbed up to the tree stand agilely and sat down with my back resting against the tree. Thankfully I had a small flashlight with me and was able to open the letter and read it. My breath caught in my throat as I pulled out the pictures she had enclosed. The first was a picture of a beautiful little girl with long blond hair pulled back by a headband. She clutched a doll tightly to her chest as if she were afraid that someone would take the doll away. She was laughing and crying at the same time. The second picture was of Elise and a cat. She was even more lovely up close than far off. Her beautiful hair was gone and the knitted hat she wore on her head brought out the blue of her eyes. She was holding a darling little gray kitten in her arms; her face was next to the little kitten's face and you could tell by the huge smile on her face that she was smitten with the cat. *Lucky cat*, I thought. Although she was absolutely lovely, I could tell that she was very ill. In addition to the baldness, she was so pale that her skin seemed almost translucent and dark smudges were under her eyes. Still, the pictures were wonderful. I was glad to have received them, to be able to see her face even when apart; but I knew that photographs were strictly forbidden. These were the first pictures I had ever owned. I would have to keep them well hidden. As I read the letter, I could almost imagine her voice speaking to me. I imagined that it was soft and sweet. I loved getting to know her and about her life. It made me sad to realize how alone she really was, and I wished desperately that I could be with her and to hold her in my arms. I had known she was sick, but seeing the evidence of her illness with my own eyes made my heart ache and caused me great fear. I prayed that the physicians caring for her would be able to cure her of her illness. With a sigh, I forced myself to my feet. After some thought, I put the pictures and letter back in the envelope and then tucked the envelope inside my shirt, underneath my undershirt and next to my heart. I snuck back into the house and was halfway across the living room, congratulating myself on not disturbing anyone, when I heard Daett's deep voice. My heart sunk.

"John," he said quietly. "Where have you been at this late hour?"

I turned and met his troubled gaze.

"I couldn't sleep so I went for a walk in the woods and I spent a little time up in the deer stand. It's a good place to think and pray."

Daett seemed to think this over for a few moments and then he nodded his agreement.

"I can imagine that it would be," Daett said. "Anything in particular keeping you awake?"

I shrugged my shoulders. It was hard to keep things from Daett and Mamm, but unburdening myself to Daett would only result in adding to the already heavy load on his own shoulders. I answered his question as truthfully as I could without upsetting him.

"I am worried about Mamm, and I worry that you are trying so hard to take care of her and us that you aren't taking care of yourself."

I paused and thought about my next words very carefully.

"There is also a situation that I have encountered that has me greatly troubled and I do not know what if anything I should do about it. I could use your advice, Daett," I said honestly.

I noticed that the tightness in Daett's face and shoulders loosened ever so slightly. He clapped a hand to my shoulder.

"Come let's go into the kitchen and sit down at the table. I will go get us a couple of root beers and then you can tell me what is troubling you."

A couple of minutes later, I was sitting across the kitchen table from Daett drinking root beer and eating oatmeal raisin cookies.

"A while back, I saw a married man from our community with an unmarried much younger girl from our community who is not his wife. They didn't see me. They were embracing and kissing. I didn't know what to do so I just snuck away without them seeing me. I thought about confronting the man and I went to his place of work but his boys were there. No matter what he has done, his boys are innocent and I didn't want them to hear anything hurtful about their dad. As I was leaving, his wife and youngest son came; she had brought him lunch. The worst part is she is pregnant, Daett, pregnant! How can a man betray his wife and children like that? How can he deceive and seduce a young innocent girl too naive to realize that what she is doing could have horrible and eternal consequences?"

"I don't know, John," Daett said, his face grim. "I've never had a moment's thought for another woman since the day I fell in love with your Mamm. My wife and my children are the treasures that God has blessed me with and He has placed me as their protector. Did you see the face of the young lady?"

I remained silent.

"John," Daett said in a voice that demanded I look up and into his eyes, "You forget that as my son, I know you very well. I can see on your face and in your eyes that you are deeply troubled by this. Yes, it is a horrible situation but something tells me this is also personal for you. If this involves one of your siblings, one of my children, you must tell me, John! As the head of this household, I have the right to know! You are not protecting this girl by keeping her secret. You said it yourself that in the end this will hurt not just the man's family but the girl and her family as well."

He was right. I knew he was right but if I told him, Rachel would never forgive me. The stress and strain of all that I had been carrying caught up with me and much to my embarrassment, my eyes filled with tears. I wiped them away angrily with the cuff of my shirt. I would not break down like a baby in front of Daett!

"John," Daett said with a softer voice. "I know you are probably trying to protect me because of Mamm being sick, but if it is about my family, you wouldn't be protecting me but hurting me. If you don't want one of your siblings to know that you are the one who said something because you are afraid they will be angry with you, well then rest assured that your name will not be mentioned."

I looked up into Daett's eyes trying to discern what I saw in the depths of the blue: pain, worry, fear but no anger. Would not I be the biggest hypocrite in the world if I betrayed Rachel while carrying around a secret of my own? However, my secret was an innocent one, I told myself, while Rachel's could destroy a family and ruin her chances of a good marriage, not to mention the eternal damnation of her soul. Suddenly all I wanted was to give this burden to Daett so he could carry it and I wouldn't have to. I looked at him and said with a hoarse whisper:

"It was Rachel. I saw Rachel in the arms of Daniel Lapp."

Breakfast the next morning was a subdued affair. Fortunately, Rachel was so busy cooking and caring for the little ones that she did not notice how grim-faced Daett was as he slowly and patiently assisted Mamm with her breakfast. Even the younger ones seemed quiet this morning as they sleepily shoveled food into their mouths. Only little Ruthie was cheerful and talkative.

"After breakfast, I need to attend to some errands," announced Daett. "And I need John to come with me. Elias, Caleb, and Matthew: you are to attend to the morning chores. John and I will be back shortly. Rachel, I want you, Abigail, and Ruthie to stay at home today with Mamm."

She looked up quickly, her eyes filling with dismay.

"But Daett, I am supposed to go to my job at the English lady's house today. She is relying on me," she said tremulously. I had never heard her challenge Daett before.

Daett fixed his eyes sternly on her. At first she met his gaze unflinchingly but within seconds she dropped her gaze, unable to withstand Daett's glare.

"Your Mamm needs you more, and your Mamm comes before the needs of an Englisher!" he thundered. "You will stay at home and attend to your Mamm."

"Yes, sir," Rachel said softly knowing that she was defeated.

It was with dread that I turned the buggy in the direction of the bishop's house. I was greatly regretting confiding in Daett about Rachel and Daniel Lapp for although I knew that what we were about to do was the right course of action, I dreaded the coming storm and I felt guilty to be exposing someone else's secret when I had several of my own. But I rationalized with myself that my secret was not causing anyone harm, whereas Daniel Lapp's could destroy his family and Rachel. I could live with my guilt but I would not have been able to live with myself if I had done nothing while Rachel's life was ruined and the Lapp family broken up. Our bishop was in his sixties but looked much younger. He took his role very seriously as well he should and while he was firm in his beliefs and his duty to his congregation, in my experience, he was also kind.

Bishop Troyer welcomed us into his home and we followed him into his living room. After we accepted ice tea from his wife, we sat in silence awkwardly. Daett waited until the bishop's wife had quietly withdrawn from the room before speaking.

"We have a grave problem," Daett said with a solemn face. "John came to me last night with a troubled heart. He had seen something that upset him a great deal. I confess that I am angry, upset and hurt, and I am at loss as to what I should do about it. I prayed about it and then I decided that the best course of action was to come see you, especially as it concerns not just our family but another family in the congregation."

Through this rather garbled discourse, Bishop Troyer sat quietly listening, occasionally nodding his head solemnly. I supposed that he often encountered people coming to him with trouble that they danced around before coming to the point. I snapped back to attention when I heard Daett saying my name again and Bishop Troyer's gaze focused on me.

"Since John was the one to see the...," Daett paused as his mind searched for the right word, "the sin being committed, I will let him tell you about it."

"The other night when I was out for a walk, I saw a courting Amish couple embracing and kissing. They didn't see me but rather their attention was focused only on each other. At first, I thought it was sweet and chose to sneak away without invading their privacy. However, as I turned to go away, they shifted their positions and I saw their faces," I started, taking a deep breath before continuing. "It was Daniel Lapp and my own sister, Rachel."

Bishop Troyer's face became as grim as mine and Daett's.

"Have you said anything to either Daniel or Rachel?" he asked me as he fixed his pointed gaze on me.

"No," I confessed. "I've thought about talking to Rachel but I just haven't been able to face it especially with Mamm being ill and Rachel having such a load on her. I did go to Daniel's shop with hopes of talking with him but two of his sons were there and then his wife, his pregnant wife, came by with his other son. They had brought his lunch to him. I'm sorry, Daett. I didn't want to trouble you and I carried this around for several days not knowing what to do."

"Well, you have done the right thing by confiding to your Daett and to me," Bishop Troyer said as he sighed heavily. "This is a serious matter and it is not something that I can overlook or ignore. I will have to gather some of the brethren and go to confront Daniel. When we are done talking with him, we will come to your home to speak with Rachel."

Daett agreed to this and then we left. I had thought that once I had unburdened myself, my heart would feel lighter. It did not. Instead I found that my heart was heavier feeling like a stone inside of my chest.

CHAPTER EIGHT

"**Y**ou are the only reason I am out of bed today," I said to KitKat who swished her tail in anticipation, her big, bright eyes watching my every move. "Are you hungry? Is that why you wouldn't let me sleep in?"

KitKat meowed back her response and of course I acquiesced to her majesty's every whim. We went down the steps, KitKat running ahead of me. She occasionally stopped and looked back, making sure I was still following her. We went to the kitchen and I picked up her food bowl. She chirruped in anticipation. As I spooned her food into her bowl, she rubbed my legs with her furry little body. I sat the food bowl down and KitKat bumped and rubbed my hand with her head in appreciation. As I sat at the kitchen table drinking a cup of tea, I watched her eat. It was amazing how much more my house felt like a home with this four-pound addition. She was a lot of company and 'talked' constantly. The weird thing was I was starting to understand her. One thing was for sure: she wasn't going to let me just lie down and die. Whenever I even thought about just lying around and wallowing in the depths of despair, she would come and meow and pester me until I got up and played with her.

A knock at the door brought me out of my thoughts and KitKat looked up towards the sound. Then she looked down at her food and back at the door. Curiosity won and she ran towards the door to see who

98

was there. Halfway across the living room, she stopped and looked back, meowing at me.

"I'm coming," I assured her.

When I reached the door, I saw that John had slipped an envelope for me under my front door. I picked it up and then I went to place it on the piano before I answered the door. I would read it later and play the music after Rachel left.

I opened the door expecting to see Rachel, but a young Amish woman I didn't know stood there. She was a little older than Rachel and pretty but not as pretty as Rachel.

"May I help you?" I asked.

"I am Leah. Rachel cannot come today and she didn't want to let you down so she sent me," she said shyly. "She asked me to give you this."

She handed me a folded note. Her eyes met mine briefly but she quickly looked away.

The note from Rachel was short and to the point:

I am sorry but I am unable to come today. My Mamm needs me. I have asked Leah to come in my place as I did not want to let you down. I will give Leah the money I would earn from today. Thank you for your understanding,

Rachel

What else could I do but let Leah in? For the next few hours she worked quickly and efficiently. Like Rachel, she seemed to have never-ending energy and although she didn't talk to me like Rachel did, she made a lot more noise. It felt like a cleaning cyclone had entered our normally peaceful home. We retreated to our favorite spot, the screened-in back porch. For whatever reason, KitKat loved the big rug on the porch. She would stretch out on it, showing me her belly, and would knead her paws on it while purring like crazy.

KitKat was such a sweet-natured kitten so I was surprised when she took an instant dislike to Leah. I had always thought that it was an invention of cartoon storytelling that cat's fur would stand on end but I found out it was not. I heard KitKat making a sound I had never heard her making before. I looked at her and noticed that in addition to the very low, growly grumbling sound coming from my tiny kitten, her hair was literally standing on end! She was staring into the house with a malevolent glare. When the vacuum cleaner roared to life, KitKat was freaked out! She shot into the house running faster than I ever knew a cat could go. I followed her to make sure she was okay and barely made it into the living room in time to see KitKat flying up the stairs. Leah was oblivious to the chaos she had created. I went into my bedroom and saw that my pillows were shaking and a small gray tail with a white tip was sticking out from underneath them. KitKat was burrowed underneath the pillows shaking like a leaf. I closed the bedroom door in order to muffle the noise and got onto the bed. I left her where she felt safe but began to gently pet her and I sang a German lullaby that Father used to sing to me. Slowly the shaking stopped and was replaced with purring. KitKat finally emerged from the pillows and climbed up on me and nuzzled up under my chin. Heaven. She began giving me a bath with her tongue.

"Thank you for the kisses," I said to her as I stroked her fur. "I love you so much. You are such a sweet baby, KitKat."

What a gift this little bundle of fur was to me! If the love I felt for her was even half of what a mother feels for a child, then I couldn't wait to have one. She gave me a purpose; a reason to live and not die. Then she found my ear again and latched on.

"And now it's just weird," I said to her. She didn't care. She just kept on sucking. I sure hoped the Amish girl didn't come inside my bedroom without knocking. If she did I would be the talk of the Amish! I could hear it now: 'Did you know that crazy lady down the road thinks her cat is a real baby? I saw it with my own eyes! She was letting her cat nurse her earlobe! Her earlobe! How nuts is that?' "Ah well, I love you anyway, you freaky little kitten. I guess I will keep you in spite of your ear fetish!"

The bishop had refused Daett's request to accompany the brethren to the Lapp household to confront Daniel. Although Daniel had committed a terrible sin, he was still a part of their congregation and a soul they wanted to save. I suspected that this was the primary reason for the denial. Our church teaches forgiveness, not revenge or retribution. And right now Daett's eyes were full of rage and hate. He was a father angry about an older man, a trusted man of our community who had taken advantage of his little girl. When I heard the bishop's edict, my opinion of him increased exponentially. While I shared Daett's feelings towards Daniel, I did not want Daett to do something that he would later regret.

I went about my chores with a feeling of dread in the pit of my stomach. I knew that Rachel was going to be upset and hurt and while I hated that for her, I knew that one day Rachel would realize that the ending of her affair with a married man had saved her life. Girls in our community have two goals: to be married and to become a mother. Unmarried women are very few and have a difficult existence. They do not have enough education to obtain a well-paying job. Mostly maiden women depend on family for their survival. They live with their parents until they pass away. Then they are typically shuffled around the family and community, going to whomever wants or rather needs them at the time. If a new child has been born or if there is sickness in the family, the maiden aunt will come and fulfill the need. For the length of time that her services are required and in exchange for her work, she is provided with a place to stay and food to eat. It is an arrangement that suits all involved.

I have an unmarried aunt, an older sister of Daett's, named Fannie. She is a short, pleasantly plump lady with wispy gray hair and a sweet, kind, and patient manner. While it is not the way of our people to have favorites, secretly Aunt Fannie is my favorite aunt. I always liked it when Aunt Fannie came to stay with us which was usually when Mamm had a new baby. Aunt Fannie made the most delicious gingerbread which I loved and even though she was there to work for us, she seemed to genuinely be happy to be with us and to care for us. Aunt Fannie and I had become especially close when she came to stay with us the summer little Ruthie was born. Each week, it was my job to drive Aunt Fannie into town so that she could acquire whatever food or resources that we needed. While we were not told the details of the circumstances, the pregnancy and birth had been very hard on Mamm and it was many weeks before she was able to resume her normal role in our household. To my delight, this meant that we had Aunt Fannie with us all summer and most of the fall. Aunt Fannie had a knack of making you feel comfortable in her presence. She would often sit quietly and listen while others poured their hearts out to her. I am still not sure quite how it happened but one beautiful fall afternoon after driving Aunt Fannie to and from town all summer, I found myself telling Aunt Fannie all about my music. Immediately I regretted my disclosure but my fears were groundless, and Aunt Fannie quickly set my mind at ease. She not only promised to keep my secret but she also did not condemn me and that was oddly gratifying. It was Aunt Fannie who caused me to first consider the possibility that my "sin" might actually not be a sin. Furthermore, she suggested that my music might be a gift, a blessing, and a calling. She had referenced the parable of the talents and told me that she thought my talent was God-given and meant to be used for the glory of God and not buried under years of tradition.

Shortly before the winter, she had been asked to come to Pennsylvania to care for an elderly lady who suffered with dementia. She was to live in the Grossdaadi house with the elderly lady who was *die Groossmammi* of the family. The lady required constant supervision and total care as if she were a child. She had not come back to Indiana and as far as I know, she is still living with and caring for the elderly lady in Pennsylvania. I miss her daily. One of the things I miss most about her is her smile. Although I had never heard anyone say it out loud, I know that Aunt Fannie was probably pitied by the women in her family and community. Yet in spite of all of that, Aunt Fannie was always happy. Being around her was a balm for the soul as she was truly a caring, giving and joyful lady.

How I would love to be riding in a buggy with Aunt Fannie again, I thought. What a relief it would be to talk over my troubles with her and to listen to her sage advice! Then I realized that although I might not be able to go for a buggy ride with Aunt Fannie right now, I can write to her! I resolved that tonight while writing Elise, I would also write Aunt Fannie a letter. I suddenly felt ashamed that I had only thought to write Aunt Fannie when I needed her advice. I resolved to do better about staying in touch with her. Sadly, I suspect that Aunt Fannie is used to being forgotten. Such is the fate of many unmarried, elderly ladies in our community.

I was at the piano playing quietly when Leah came to let me know that she was done and leaving. I don't know why but I instinctively covered John's music and notes. Leah had been polite to me and was a cleaning machine but not very personable. While Rachel was cheerful and friendly, Leah was quiet and frigidly reserved. She seemed to disapprove of me although I wasn't sure why other than the fact that I didn't dress like her. I guiltily hoped that Rachel would come back soon as I wasn't sure if KitKat and I could tolerate having the unfriendly Leah in our home three times a week. If that were the case, I may have to reconsider having someone come to my home at all. After the front door shut behind Leah, I heard KitKat's tiny, high-pitched squeaky meow. I turned to see KitKat's little face peering between two of the staircase spindles trying to see if the coast was clear.

"She is gone," I said with a smile.

KitKat chirped back at me and bounded down the stairs happily, her little bell jingling. The mood in our house was once again cheerful with the gloomy Leah gone. I wondered what John had thought about my pictures and worried that my baldness would scare him away. More than anything, I hoped that he would bring me a picture of him. How is it possible to desperately long to see the face of one you have never seen before? I know that when I look upon his face for the first time that I will know him. How could I not? I realized now that I was falling in love with a man I had never met with face to face and I couldn't stop myself even if I wanted to.

I was walking from the barn to the house when I saw the brethren coming. My chest constricted with pain in anticipation of the pain that was getting ready to strike my sister, my family. My guilt threatened to choke me. How dare I tell my sister's secret when I had one of my own? Then I reminded myself that my secret didn't run the risk of hurting anyone. While that might not be entirely true, it was inescapably clear that Rachel's relationship with Daniel Lapp had caused pain and damage to not only the Lapp family but also to our family and also to our extended families and the people of our community.

Daett invited the brethren in with a grim face. My brothers and sisters all looked nervous and concerned. They knew having all of the brethren come to our home was an ominous event. Daett told all of the children to go outside except for me and Rachel. I snuck a quick look at her and when I saw the stricken look on her face, regret smote my heart. I hoped that in time she would realize that I had done this for her as well, and that she deserved a man of good moral character and not the lying, cheating Daniel Lapp.

"Is your wife well enough to be here for this?" Bishop Troyer asked Daett as he looked at my very pale-faced mother who sat in her rocking chair by the fireplace, her sightless eyes shining brightly with unshed tears.

"As much as I wish that I could protect her from this, I cannot," Daett answered gravely. "She is my wife and Rachel's Mamm, so I did not think I could in good conscience keep this from her. She and I talked this morning."

Mamm's hand fluttered up to her face and she wiped away her silent tears with a white handkerchief embroidered with yellow flowers. Rachel's face was ashen and she sunk to the floor next to Mamm as if her legs could no longer hold her up. She reached up and grasped Mamm's left hand and opened her mouth as if to speak but no words came out. Mamm's hand gripped Rachel's hand so tightly that her knuckles were white. She was Mamm's first daughter and they had always been extremely close. What thoughts were racing through my sister's mind? Was she feeling regret? Wishing that she could take it all back? Or was she merely scared that her secret relationship had come to light but still determined to be with the man she thought she loved? Was Mamm feeling guilt? Wondering what she could have done differently in raising Rachel? The minor notes of sorrow and regret combined with the low sounds of guilt and the shrill sounds of fear. In my mind the notes began to arrange themselves upon the grand staff. I shook myself back to the present. Music is my refuge, my way of coping with and interpreting my feelings and my way to talk to God. But right now, I needed to be here no matter how uncomfortable it was.

"Rachel, it has come to our attention that you are in an adulterous relationship with Daniel Lapp," Bishop Troyer said with his stern gaze fixed on her. "You know that to have a romantic relationship with a married man is a sin and contrary to the Biblical teachings of our church. Daniel is a husband and a father with another child on the way. We have talked with Daniel and with his wife and he has confessed and repented of his sin."

At this, Rachel uttered a moan and then buried her face in her apron. Her shoulders began to shake with silent sobs but the faces of the brethren were not softened in the slightest. Mamm's hand reached out and fluttered around as she sought blindly to comfort Rachel. Daett's large, work-roughened hand grasped Mamm's hand, engulfing it and stopping her hand before it reached Rachel's head. He then gently but firmly disengaged her other hand from Rachel's grasp and held that hand as well. Her face turned up towards Daett's face, her sightless eyes trying to see in spite of the futility of her efforts. Mamm looked puzzled for a moment and then understanding and sorrow dawned across her face. Daett was silently telling her as the head of his household that right now there would be no comforting of Rachel but rather she must accept the consequences of her sin.

"We have instructed Daniel that in order to avoid shunning or excommunication, he must repent and confess his sin to the congregation of the church. Thankfully, Daniel has seen the error of his ways and confessed his sin. He has asked forgiveness from God, from us, and from his wife. He has agreed to repent and to confess his sin to the congregation."

At these words, Rachel looked up at him in horror. For some reason, this made me mad! What did she think would happen? She has been in the faith since birth and took her vow this past spring. She knew full well that a relationship with a married man would not end well and that it would eventually come to light. If it had not been me, someone would have eventually seen them together. She knows as well as I that the Bible states that those sins which are committed in secret will be shouted from the rooftops. I wondered if she had deluded herself into believing that one day Daniel would leave his family and his faith for her? If she had thought that, she was even more innocently ignorant than I thought.

"Do you have anything you wish to say to us or to your parents?" asked Bishop Troyer.

Rachel continued to look stricken and unable to speak. All she could manage was a negative shake of her head. Large fat tears silently coursed down her cheeks and she could not look anyone in the eye.

"Will you confess your sin and repent for your sin?" Bishop Troyer asked her sternly.

Rachel took a deep shuddering breath and forced herself to look up. She looked at me with a pleading look in her eyes which smote my heart. I wasn't sure what she was wanting from me until she reached out a trembling hand towards me and then I understood. I grasped her hand and helped her to stand up. Once she was standing, Rachel let go of my hand and faced the brethren bravely. In spite of the situation, I admired Rachel in that moment. The bishop and the brethren faced her with stern faces that could've been carved from stone. They were severely intimidating but Rachel faced them bravely.

"It is true that I am in love with Daniel and he with me," Rachel said in a clear voice. "I am sorry for the pain that this causes my parents and my family. I am sorry that this has deeply hurt his wife and children. It was not our intention to hurt anyone; we simply fell in love."

The bishop's face became thunderous at these audacious words and Daett's face went white with rage. Mamm began crying in great gulping sobs. Rachel turned and went to Mamm. She placed an arm around Mamm and it was then that I noticed that she was also crying.

"I am sorry, Mamm," she wept. "I am so sorry."

The fact that she so quickly became seemingly contrite and brokenhearted after her audacity probably saved her from being instantly shunned, for I noticed that Bishop Troyer's face became slightly less angry although I think that Daett's rage increased.

"The fact that you will apologize to your Mamm is good but you must truly be repentant. You must confess your sins, beg for forgiveness, and forsake your sin if you wish to remain in the church. Are you willing to do this?" asked Bishop Troyer. "If you will not repent and confess, we will have no choice but to shun you."

Rachel didn't answer right away. She hesitated and looked up at Mamm's face just as she had often done as a child when searching for an answer. Although Mamm couldn't see her, she seemed to sense Rachel's gaze. Mamm tugged her left hand which was still held tightly by Daett, trying to break free of his grasp. He released her hands and took a step back. Mamm reached out with trembling fingers that found Rachel's face and gently brushed away her tears.

Mamm only said one word. And one word was all it took.

"Please."

Rachel's face twisted in despair? Sorrow? I wasn't quite sure. She looked up at Bishop Troyer and at Daett.

"Daniel has denounced me?" she asked.

Her question seemed to displease them but I understood my little sister's motive. I didn't like it but I understood it. She would bear shunning and even excommunication in order to be with the man she loved but if his repentance meant that he would no longer have a relationship with her, then the cost was not worth it. My anger flashed hot and got the better of me.

"Would you rather he denounce his wife, his children including his unborn child, and his God for you? If he would do that, he would prove himself all the more to be a liar and a cheater! Why would you want a man like that? More importantly, how could you do that to his wife and children? I love you, Rachel, but right now I am ashamed of you!"

She recoiled at the force of my anger and blinked as if something unpleasant had blown into her eyes. We had always been close and this was the first time that I had not taken her side.

"Let's remain calm," instructed Bishop Troyer, although I couldn't help but think that he looked a trifle smug, as if I had said words that he had been longing to say himself but felt that he could not. "Although like your brother I find your question to be disturbing, I will answer it because I fear that if I do not that you will try to discover the answer yourself and in so doing, cause even more pain to the Lapp family. Yes, Daniel has confessed his sin, begged for forgiveness, and promised to abstain from sinning any further. He has also agreed to confess his sin to the congregation and to ask them for their forgiveness."

Rachel bowed her head as if in submission and for a moment, I hoped she was going to comply. Then with a tremulous voice she spoke and shattered my hope and our parents' hearts.

"I confess that I am guilty of being in love with a married man. I confess that Daniel and I are in a relationship. But I cannot promise to stay away from him. I have to see him and to talk with him," she said defiantly as she raised her head and looked Bishop Troyer in the eyes.

"You are not to talk to Daniel," thundered Bishop Troyer, his face flushed in anger. "You will leave them alone, Rachel. Leave him to his wife and children. They are hurting and trying to heal and move forward as a family. For their sake and for both your soul and Daniel's, I insist that you refrain from speaking to him and that you keep your distance from him and his family. I remind you that if you wish to remain in the church, you will confess your sins before the congregation, repent of your sins and in the words of Christ, go and sin no more! What will it be, Rachel? Will you confess your sins and stay away from Daniel?"

"I can't," she said, her eyes brimming with tears. "I love him!

Father let out a choked exclamation, his face suffused with anger. Mamm began to sob again in earnest and she buried her face in her apron as if it would hide her from the shame that Rachel was bringing upon our family.

"You love him?" Bishop Troyer spat out the words, his voice dripping with disgust. "Love is from God. Love is pure. Love is kind. What you feel towards Daniel is a sin and is not love but rather lust! You have played the part of a harlot and nearly destroyed a family and debased yourself in the eyes of God."

I looked at my sister. I didn't think I have ever seen anyone ever look so forlorn as she did in that moment. The defiance was still in her eyes, but as she looked at the faces of my parents, myself and the brethren, her shoulders sagged under the weight of their condemnation. While I agreed with most if not all of Bishop Troyer's words, it upset me to realize that he saw my sister in the role of seductress and placed all the blame squarely on her shoulders. That was not at all a fair assessment of the affair considering the facts that Daniel Lapp is much older than Rachel and as a married man, he knew exactly what he was doing whereas Rachel being innocent did not. However, this wasn't the time to squabble with the Bishop. Right now the focus was on stopping this adulterous relationship before it destroyed two families and multiple lives.

"Very well," said Bishop Troyer. "You leave us with no choice. From now until such time that you repent and forsake your sinful ways, you are shunned. You have broken your commitment to the Lord Jesus Christ and also to the congregation. We shun you to help you to see the error of your ways and to remind you that if you persist in sinning, you will be excommunicated from the church and worse still, you will one day stand in judgment before God and be cast into everlasting torment. We shun you for the good of our church, to help prevent the corruption of the church, and to put a fence around our congregation to protect them from the wiles of the devil. As of this moment, you are shunned, Rachel Yoder."

With that the brethren turned as if one body and put their back towards Rachel. Slowly and with pain in his eyes, Daett did the same. Mamm had tears coursing down her cheeks from her sightless eyes, but I realized that she could not see what was happening. I gently shifted her shoulders, turning her away from Rachel. Mamm realized what I was doing and complied. I was the last one to turn my back on my little sister. Her face was white and the pain and grief of the past few minutes had already seemed to age her face. Turning my back on my little sister was the hardest thing I have ever had to do.

I dreamed of John last night. I dreamed I was in my living room playing his beautiful music when he came up behind me. He placed his hands on my shoulders and stood so close to me that I could feel the warmth coming off his body. I felt so happy, so at peace. Little KitKat rubbed my ankles and tried to capture my foot as it pressed and released the damper pedal. John kissed the top of my head and he whispered in my ear, "I love you." I twirled around to put my arms around him and to tell him that I love him too but he was gone. I began searching for him and when I couldn't find him, I became frantic and tearful. When I woke up, I had tears on my cheeks. How can I be falling in love with a man that I don't even know? I have done it before, I reminded myself wryly. Although in my defence, I had thought that I knew Donovan Shane. I was wrong. I felt myself beginning to spiral down that familiar path of self-loathing and insecurity. *No!* I told myself. *You will not do this.* I went to my spot on my back porch and opened up my Bible and began to read. As I read the anxiety began to melt away, and peace flooded over my soul. The Words felt like they had been written just for me as I read:

"There is no fear in love; but perfect love casteth out fear: because fear hath torment. He that feareth is not made perfect in love."

1 JOHN 4:18

At that moment, KitKat jumped up on my lap and meowed at me loudly. I sat my Bible down and smiled at the little grey furball. She slowly blinked back at me, letting me know she loved me. I rubbed my hand down her silky head and back. Then I picked up her little paw and began to look at how perfectly her paw was formed. I looked and felt her little pink pads on the bottom of her paws, her little sharp claws that were retracted back and barely showing, and the way that her little toes splayed was absolutely adorable and utterly perfect.

"You were made perfect in love," I whispered to her, but I knew those words were just as much for me as they were for her. Just then, Nana's Bible caught my eye. I picked it up and, noticing a lace bookmark, I opened it up at that location. A scripture was highlighted and circled. Next to the scripture, Nana had written, "For Elise." With tears streaming down my face, I read the scripture verse Nana had marked for me:

For whosoever shall call upon the name of the Lord shall be saved.

ROMANS 10:13

The last time I had gone to Fellowship Chapel was after Poppy passed away, so it was just myself and Nana. The preacher had delivered a sermon about salvation and at the end of his sermon, he invited the lost to come to the altar to accept salvation. When no one came forward, he then asked everyone to bow their heads and close their eyes. He said that he was going to pray the sinner's prayer written by Rev. Billy Graham and that if there were anyone who wished to be saved, to pray the prayer with him. He said we could even pray it silently. Nana held my hand tightly during the prayer and said the words along with the preacher. My heart had felt heavy and as if it were being squeezed in a vise. I wanted to say the words but something held me back. I could tell Nana was disappointed that I hadn't said the prayer, but I wondered how she had known that I didn't say the prayer silently. In fact, curiosity got the better of me and I asked Nana.

"Well, dear," she said in a sad voice, "I knew the moment I opened my eyes and looked at your face. You see, when you get saved, you become a new creature in Christ. As the song says, you are filled with joy unspeakable and full of glory. In my lifetime, I have been privileged to see many people get saved and every one of them were grinning from ear to ear, their faces glowing. Your face didn't look like that."

Several days later, I had to say goodbye to Nana and head out on tour. It was the last time I would see her alive. When I reached my destination, I opened up my suitcase to find a note inside from Nana. She had written down the sinner's prayer for me on a Post-It Note. She had also written 'I love you" and because of that, I had folded it up and put it inside of the locket I wore that also contained pictures of Poppy and Nana. With trembling fingers, I opened up the locket and retrieved the piece of paper that I hadn't read in years. My heart felt heavy and tight just as it had years ago. I knew that the time had come to pray the sinner's prayer. With tears streaming down my face, I read the words aloud:

"Dear Lord Jesus, I know that I am a sinner, and I ask for Your forgiveness. I believe You died for my sins and rose from the dead. I turn from my sins and invite You to come into my heart and life. I want to trust and follow You as my Lord and Savior. In Your Name. Amen."

Instantly, the weight was lifted and peace flooded my soul. I was so happy and felt light and free. I wanted to share my joy with someone so I stroked KitKat's head and kissed the top of her head.

"KitKat," I whispered into her ear. "Mommy is saved! I asked Jesus into my heart!"

She meowed at me and licked my hand in response.

"You are so perfect, KitKat," I told her. "And now I have been made perfect through Christ."

I laughed. To think I had just described myself as perfect! I had spent so many years of my life trying to be good enough for my mother, for my instructors, for my directors, and then for Donovan. They had all looked at me and found something lacking, someone flawed. This led me to believe that I was deficient. But God looked at me and saw me as perfect because of the blood and love of Jesus Christ. For the first time in my life, I felt like I was good enough.

CHAPTER NINE

JOHN THE BELOVED

M y family was in great pain. Rachel was still with us. She still cooked and cleaned. She continued to assist Mamm. She was there but we behaved as if she did not exist. All of us—that is, except for Ruthie who at five is the youngest of our family and very attached to Rachel. Daett and Mamm did not correct her or stop her, but my younger siblings hissed and whispered at her. Eventually Ruthie succumbed to peer pressure. At supper, she looked at Rachel and then turned her head away so fast her little braids wrapped around her neck. She said loudly, "Rachel is bad and we can't talk to her." I heard Rachel's quick intake of breath and knew that Ruthie's words cut her deeply. I decided to take advantage of the moment and I was shameless in my efforts to save her soul.

"We are shunning Rachel because we love her," I explained to Ruthie. "The bishop placed Rachel under the Bann in hopes that it would help her to have a change of heart and to cease doing bad things. Do you understand?"

"Yes," she said as she nodded her head enthusiastically. "I promise I won't ever be bad like Rachel."

I kissed the top of her head and snuck a peek at Rachel who had her head bowed over her food and her eyes downcast as well. She had silent tears coursing down her cheeks. My heart couldn't take it. Without saying a word, I reached out and briefly touched her shoulder. Then I quickly left the house. I needed a break from the sorrowful atmosphere that consumed our home. The hard work of the day helped to release some of my frustration, but my mind continued to be in turmoil. At the end of the day, I set out for the woods with my rifle under the pretext of going hunting. I doubt I fooled anyone. Once I was up in the tree stand, I leaned back and lifted my head towards the sky. The sounds of the woods enveloped me. Unlike the sounds you hear in towns and cities which are abrasive to the ear and mind, the sounds of nature soothe the soul and calm the mind. I let the forest music work its magic. The warble of the songbird sang out a solo in a smooth soprano to the soft accompaniment of the alto notes of the leaves gently, slowly rustling in the breeze. A woodpecker rat-a-tat-tatted out the rhythm. The staccato bark of the coyotes joined in, and the chirping crickets did not want to be left out. A crackling of branches reached my ears, indicating that an animal was creeping through the trees and brush on a mission unknown to man. My fingers itched to grab paper and pen to put the notes on a staff before the notes vanished into the ether, but I forced myself to simply relax. My soul needed to hear the therapeutic music of the woods, not to capture it. Eventually, I felt myself began to relax. In the sanctuary of the tree where I no longer needed to be strong for my family, I finally allowed myself to let my emotions break and I began to weep.

A few weeks ago, I knew who I was and who my family was and where we belonged. Now at an age far too young, Mamm was disabled and blind. During the time of life where she should be attending singings, going on picnics, quilting a wedding blanket, and courting a young single man her own age, Rachel was having an affair with a married man and on the cusp of being excommunicated from the faith. And me? I was composing more music than ever before and ... I was falling in love with a woman that I barely knew. A woman who was forbidden to me. A month ago I was John Yoder, oldest son of Abram Yoder, nearly ready to kneel and take my vow. Now I had no clue what was next for me and my family. Dear God, please help me and guide me. Have mercy on me. Have mercy on my family. Dear God, I need you.

For me, prayer and music are one and the same. So I finally allowed myself to put pen to paper and prayed using music notes instead of words. The sounds of the woods became my cry out to God, and peace like a river poured over my soul. Peace. In the midst of my turmoil and sadness, God granted me peace that passed all understanding. Such wonderful peace!

During the night, I woke up feeling overwhelmed with soul-crushing sadness. I was unsure of where this feeling was coming from or why I was feeling this way. The weight on my chest made it difficult to breathe, much less sleep. I threw aside the covers, garnering a squeak of protest from KitKat. I murmured apologies to my cat who was already back to sleep and headed downstairs to what had become affectionately known to me as my prayer chair. The golden light from the lamp bathed the room in a comforting glow, creating an island of light in the vast darkness of the night. I reached for my Bible, held it close to my heart, and I began to pray. As I talked with God, clarity illuminated my mind and somehow, I knew that this sorrow was coming from John. He had brought me such comfort with his music and while I couldn't offer him the same type of comfort, I could pray for him and so I did.

In the early morning, a hot, rough tongue licked my face, waking me up. KitKat's little face was right in front of mine and she meowed with joy at the sight of my open eyes. She immediately jumped down and ran towards the kitchen. She looked at me a little confused before realizing that I must have fallen asleep in my prayer chair during the night. The sorrow was still present but not as strong. All I could do was to place John in God's hands and to pray for him but as I spooned KitKat's food into her bowl, a thought struck me. Praying wasn't all I could do: I could write to him. A few minutes later, I was sitting at my kitchen table with a steaming cup of tea in front of me along with paper and pen.

Dear John

Last night I woke up with my heart heavy and burdened for you. I was unable to sleep after that so I went downstairs to my back porch to my prayer chair. Yes, although it may sound silly, I have a comfy, worn chaise that has become my place to read my Bible and talk to God. I love being in that chair because when I am in the chair talking to God and reading His Word, I am at peace and happy. A few months ago, I would have laughed if someone suggested praying to me. I had a passing knowledge of God and what the Bible is, but I did not know Him personally. Now I can't imagine my life without Him... It may seem crazy that I have such a connection to you even though we have never met face to face, but I cannot deny that I do have and feel a deep connection to you. So much so that I know that right now your heart is breaking and I wish with all my heart that I could do something to help alleviate your sadness. You have shared your music with me and that has brought me an incredible amount of joy and comfort. While I can't give you anything as awesome as what you have given me, I do want you to know that my heart is hurting with yours and I am praying for you. You are not alone. I am with you in spirit and heart.

Love, Elise

Tears blurred my vision as I read the words Elise had written to me. I was not alone: Elise was with me. God was with me. I jumped down from the hay loft and headed towards the cornfield. I was going to her. I had to go before I had time to think this through because if I did, I knew that I would talk myself out of it. This was crazy. It didn't make sense and it went against every single thing I had been taught but it felt right: it was right. I had just made it to the edge of the cornfield when Daett's voice rang out.

"John."

His voice commanded my attention. My father would not be denied. I stopped walking but I did not turn around. With all my heart, I wanted to keep walking towards Elise.

"John," said Daett, this time louder and more firm. "I need you to come here."

Reluctantly, I turned around and walked away from Elise and towards my father. As I came close to Daett, I noticed that his face was more heavily lined than I remembered. His eyes were bloodshot and ringed with dark shadows, and his shoulders sagged under the weight of his stress. He looked old and worn out and that scared me. Daett had always seemed strong and invincible but the shame of Rachel's sin, the stress of Mamm's illness was taking its toll on Abram Yoder. My heart was smitten with sympathy and I knew that as much as I wanted to run to Elise and to hold her in my arms, I couldn't do that to Daett, to my family; not now and maybe not ever. But I couldn't bear to think of never just now. Never hurt too much; never was too final.

"Yes, Daett?" I asked as I came close to my father.

"I've been asked to come to the bishop's house to talk with him," Daett said with a heavy sigh. "He has asked me to come alone. Your Mamm is distressed. I didn't intend for her to hear about the bishop's summons but she did and her mind is consumed with worry of what will happen. Rachel is…in the house cooking but Mamm doesn't want her help right now. She upsets her too much. Abigail is looking after her but she won't be able to lift her into her chair or turn her, so can you help look after your Mamm until I get back?"

"Of course, Daett," I said without hesitation. "I will be glad to help Mamm."

Daett looked at me and almost smiled. "You are a good son, John. You are a great comfort to me and to your Mamm."

"I am glad," I replied.

I entered the house. Rachel's face was set in stone as she moved about the kitchen. I paused and wondered if I should say anything to her.

She was very close to Mamm and having Mamm reject her help had to hurt her deeply. However, she didn't glance in my direction but rather she just kept working with that closed look on her face that did not invite any conversation. I sighed and left the kitchen. I entered Daett and Mamm's bedroom and found both Mamm and Abigail crying. It was not going to be a good evening.

"What is wrong?" I asked.

"I can't get Mamm up," cried Abigail.

"I'm sorry I am such a burden," Mamm cried.

Once I finally had Mamm settled in her chair and both Mamm and Abigail soothed, I went into the kitchen to check on Rachel. She looked up as I entered the room and then quickly turned around and away from me. I realized that we had not had the chance to talk since she had been confronted by the bishop. She was very angry with me and must be feeling betrayed by me. She probably wanted me to leave the kitchen quickly but no one else was in the room with us, making it the perfect time to talk. Rachel has always been a pouter and I was well aware that she would probably give me the cold shoulder so severely that I would feel like I was the one under the Bann. Still, I had to try.

"Rachel…," I said and then paused. I hadn't expected a response but I waited just in case she chose to surprise me. Actually, I thought wryly, a one-sided conversation with Rachel might be easier than a conversation that included her sharply barbed tongue.

"I know that you are angry with me right now and that is okay," I continued. "I can take your anger but I could not stand to see you being taken advantage of by Daniel Lapp. You are my little sister and I have always and will always protect you. That is why I felt I had no choice but to protect you from having your life destroyed by Daniel Lapp. If the price I have to pay is you being angry with me for the rest of our lives, then I will consider the cost worth it because nothing is more important to me than you. Rachel, you are a beautiful, smart, and loving young lady. You deserve to be treated with respect. What God wants for you and what I want for you is for you to be loved by and one day married to a man that loves you with a pure love, untainted by sin. You deserve to be the one and only love of a good man, not a lying, cheating man."

Thinking I was done and not expecting a response from Rachel, I turned to walk away. Then a thought struck me and I stopped. I turned back around to once again face Rachel's ramrod straight back.

"The night I saw you with Daniel, I felt like I had been sucker-punched. I told no one for days what I had seen and that secret weighed heavily on me. I didn't know what to do but finally I had decided to confront Daniel. I went to his shop but his sons were working with him and I didn't feel like I could confront him in front of his sons. So I left but when I was in the parking lot getting ready to leave, I saw Daniel's wife arrive with their youngest child. As I watched, she and her son sat out a beautiful lunch complete with tablecloth on the picnic table. Her face was happy and the knowledge that her husband was cheating on her with my sister was like a knife to my heart. But then I saw the bulge of her abdomen and I saw her caress and cradle her abdomen with her hand and I realized that she was with child. That was when I knew that I could not keep quiet because the cost would be too great. Not only would me keeping silent allow your affair to continue, but my silence would destroy the family of three little boys and an unborn child would be born into a family that no longer existed. And one day my silence would condemn you to the same fate as Lydia Lapp."

At those words, Rachel whirled around, her eyes blazing.

"He wouldn't do that to me! He loves me!"

"More than he loves his wife, Lydia whom he married? More than he loves his children?" I asked. "Why do you think that you are so special that he wouldn't treat you with the same disregard as he has treated his wife? You have to know that he has a character flaw! It doesn't matter who he is with, he will cheat! If he will cheat with you, Rachel, then he has proven he will cheat on you!"

Rachel's face drained of color. Her mouth opened and then closed. She stepped back away from me, as if increased distance would protect her from the painful truth of my words. For a long moment we simply stared at one another, neither one of us saying a word. Then in a voice as cold as ice, Rachel spoke.

"Have you forgotten that because of you I am shunned? How dare you speak to me when the bishop has placed me under the Bann? You better keep your hypocritical words to yourself, *der bruder*, or you will find yourself in trouble. Since we no longer are looking out for each other, I would not have a problem in telling the bishop that you are disobeying his orders."

With that she turned away from me.

Feeling like she had gotten in the last word and gotten the better of John, Rachel whirled around and went back to kneading dough for bread. John looked at her back silently. Clearly, she hadn't accepted his words or comprehended what he had said. He had tried and that was all he could do. Sighing and with a heavy heart, John left the house. He went out the back door, putting his hat back on his head as he stepped outside.

Rachel continued to knead the dough roughly, tears blurring her vision and salting the dough as they dripped off her cheeks unhindered. She wouldn't have admitted to John but his words smote her heart and for the first time, doubt about Daniel Lapp began to creep into her heart. She hadn't known that Lydia was expecting a child. Daniel had told her that his marriage was over and although they continued to live in the same home, it was only for appearance's sake and for the sake of their children. Daniel had told her that he and Lydia hadn't lain together as husband and wife since she had gotten pregnant with his youngest son. He had known the words to say to ease her conscience. He had poured out his grief and loneliness to her, spinning a tale of an ill-used and neglected husband who had done all he could do to save his marriage without success. Now she wondered if anything he had told her was true. Had he even loved her or did he merely lust after her? Shame flushed her face, and her body felt hot and then cold. She had been a fool. Dear God, what a mess she had made. In that moment, Rachel felt completely and utterly hopeless and worthless. For the first time in her life, Rachel felt totally alone.

Feeling broken and bruised by all of the emotions of the day, I went to the barn to commiserate with the horses. I was feeding an apple to my favorite horse, Comet, when I heard someone enter the barn. I wasn't really in the mood to talk to anyone, so it was with reluctance that I turned around. Samuel was smiling at me and I nearly sagged with relief.

"Hi, Samuel!" I signed to him. "I am glad to see you."

"Hi, John," he signed back. "I wanted to come see you. I heard that Rachel is under the Bann and I thought that you might need a friend."

"Thank you. It has been very difficult for my family and I feel so guilty."

"Why?" asked Samuel with a perplexed look on his expressive face.

"I actually saw Daniel Lapp and Rachel kissing. I didn't say anything to them but I was upset. I went to his store to confront him but he had his sons with him so I left. As I was leaving, his wife came. She had brought him lunch. I saw that she was pregnant and that's what made me decide I had to say something about it. I confided in Daett and the next day he went to the bishop. When the brethren confronted Daniel, he confessed and begged for forgiveness. The bishop said he also repented. Rachel was more stubborn and she insisted that she loves Daniel."

"Wow!" signed Samuel. "I had no idea. Sorry, *der freind*."

"Thanks," I replied. "Rachel is hurt and angry. She feels betrayed by me. I tried explaining to her why I did it but she doesn't understand. You know how close we have always been. This is the first time that she has been this angry at me. I hope she will come to see that I did what I did out of love."

"She will come around," Samuel assured me. "She knows you love her and you are a safe person for her to unload her anger on. I bet that if you could see underneath all of her anger, you would find that the person she is angry with the most is herself."

"Maybe."

"No maybe—I know! Now come on, I want to show you something."

"Come where?" I asked

"Just come on," he urged, smiling. "I want to show you something, but we have to go for a ride."

After I told my family I was going for a ride with Samuel, we headed out. Riding with Samuel was always quiet as he couldn't sign while driving. Our route took us past Elise's eyes, and the longing to see her and be with her hit me so sharply that it nearly took my breath away. The evenings were getting cooler and the slight nip in the air was perfect. I closed my eyes and took a deep breath in. The country air was a mixture of hay, mowed grass, smoke from bonfires, and earth with a tinge of manure. The music made by the combination of the horses' snorts and whinnies, their hooves striking the pavement, the leather reins snapping, and the crickets' and frogs' singing soothed my raw nerves. By the time the buggy stopped, I was feeling much calmer and nearly happy. I opened my eyes and I was confused. We were parked in an empty field. I turned and looked at Samuel with a question in my eyes.

"Nice land, right?" he signed.

"Yes," I agreed. "It's a very nice land."

"I'm glad you approved—because I bought it today!"

"What? Wow! Samuel, that is great!"

"Thank you, thank you," said a smiling Samuel. "I am going to build a house and a barn. I have enough acreage for a small farm. Up by the road I'm going to build a small shop for my wife."

"That will be nice, Samuel" I agreed and then realization dawned. "Your wife?!"

"Well, she isn't my wife yet," said Samuel, laughing. "But Miriam has agreed to become my wife. She loves to bake and at home she works in a small Amish-owned bakery. It's been her wish to have her own bakery near the road of her home. That way when the kinner come, she will be close to the house. Maybe by then she could hire a young unmarried Amish girl to work it for her."

"Samuel," I signed. "I am very happy for you! I pray you have many happy years of marriage with Miriam."

"Thank you," said Samuel, smiling. "Your turn is coming! Who knows, maybe you and Leah will be next."

"Who knows?" I agreed but I felt like a hypocrite because I knew in my heart there was no way that I could marry Leah when I was falling in love with an English girl named Elise.

During the drive home, I again closed my eyes and listened to the music of an Indiana summer's night. The music calmed me. I felt the buggy turn onto our driveway and then the buggy stopped. Confused, I opened up my eyes to see why we had halted.

"Tell me," signed Samuel. "Tell me what you are hearing. I know that you are hearing music because I can see it on your face."

I nodded my head and then closed my eyes in concentration for a moment. Samuel was my best friend and I really wanted to convey to him the beauty that I was privileged to hear.

"The tempo is set by using a 2-inch frog guiro to mimic the sound of the crickets and a 4-inch guiro to mimic the sound of the frogs," I signed.

"A frog guiro?" asked Samuel.

"It's a Latin American percussion instrument. It is made out of wood, shaped like a frog, and has notches in its back. They come with a wooden stick. When you rake up the frog's back with the stick it makes a sound which, if using the 2-inch one, mimics the chirping of the cricket and if using the 4-inch one, mimics the sound of a frog. I've seen videos of people playing them on the internet at the library. This is the tempo of the song," I said as I reached out my hand and began to tap his chest so that he could feel the beat of the music.

"My die Groossmammi has always said that the sound of crickets herald that fall is near," signed Samuel with a smile.

"Mine too," I signed. "Using drum brushes, the drummers play the sound the wind makes as it blows through the trees. Several other percussionists beat out the clippety-clop of the horses' hooves on the road by striking wooden blocks with wooden mallets. A flute begins playing a song so soft and sweet like a lullaby. Then the other wind instruments join in, quietly at first and then stronger. The stringed instruments are added in and then the brass instruments join in shortly thereafter. The momentum of the song grows, the tempo increases, and the song becomes joyful, celebrating the beauty of a summer's night. Abruptly the song stops and a clarinet plays a solo that sounds curious in nature, suggesting that something unusual has been seen that requires more investigation."

"Perhaps he saw a firefly," suggested Samuel, his eyes alight with imagination.

"Yes, that's probably it," I agreed, secretly amused that Samuel felt the song was from a male point of view and since I was the composer, I suppose it was. "Then the firefly must fly away because the song changes back to the joyous mood with the entire orchestra playing, but it is slightly softer and slower than it was before."

"The der Bu is getting sleepy," signed Samuel.

"He is," I agreed. "The music slows and the brass instruments drop out of the song, then the stringed instruments and the wind instruments, until the flute is the only instrument left playing. The flute plays the same lullaby from the beginning as the brushes on drums mimic the wind, the wood blocks and mallets mimic the horse hooves and the 2- and 4-inch frog guiros mimic the crickets and the frogs. The flute grows softer until it is no longer audible and the percussion instruments begin growing softer until they too cease playing."

"The boy fell asleep on the way home and now the buggy has rode out of our sight," signed Samuel.

I nodded and smiled at Samuel. He started the buggy back up and soon I was home as well. I thanked him for the ride, for showing me his future home, and for being a friend when I needed one. Then I again congratulated him and he turned the buggy around and went home.

Chemo day, I thought gloomily as I trudged to the kitchen even though the thought of eating made my stomach churn. KitKat cheerfully ran past me and into the kitchen. I went to the refrigerator and retrieved the apple juice. As I closed the door and turned around, I caught sight of KitKat and chuckled. She was quietly standing by her food bowl, looking down at the nearly empty bowl as if it would magically fill with food. She wasn't complaining about the lack of food or in the delay of service; instead, she patiently waited for the food to come with total confidence that I would feed her. I wish I could feel the same when waiting on God to fulfill my needs. Before I did anything else, I filled KitKat's food bowl with her favorite food: tuna. I sipped the apple juice and watched her eat her food voraciously and wished my appetite could be half as good as hers. When she had finished eating, KitKat sauntered out onto the screened porch, found her favorite fluffy rug and a sunbeam, and settled herself down. She then proceeded to meticulously clean her body. It amazed me how thoroughly she cleaned herself and that in spite of cleaning herself with her own spit, she always smelled so good to me. Perhaps love isn't merely blind but also nose-blind, I thought wryly. Admittedly, I had some eccentricities; some I had never voiced aloud to anyone. One of my quirks is my oddity regarding smell and hands. It didn't matter to me how handsome, charming, and suave a man may be; if I didn't like his scent (his natural scent, not the one given to him by products) and if he didn't have hands that I found attractive, then I wasn't interested at all and nothing would change my mind. This had made things tricky for me at times. When a friend tried to set me up with a man they thought was perfect for me, they would have thought me nuts if I had told them, 'No thanks. I don't like how he smells. No, he doesn't stink; his scent just doesn't appeal to me!' or 'He is nice but his hands are just so unattractive to me!' Thus I would try to contrive a reasonable excuse and try to hide my quirkiness. John was a man I had never seen or smelt yet if I was honest with myself, I was falling in love with him. Love is wonderfully strange.

Nearly an hour later I was once again at the Cancer Center in order to receive my chemotherapy treatment. Getting ready and driving there has worn me out; because of this I was distracted, concentrating solely on trying not to pass out. It was some time after the nurse had accessed my port and started my infusion that I realized that the seat next to me was empty.

"Where is Marge today?" I asked the nurse when she came back to check on my progress.

She bit her lip and her eyes darted nervously about as if she were seeking out someone else to answer my question, and my heart sank.

"I'm afraid Marge is in the hospital," she finally said. "Her husband had called us this morning to let us know and he gave us permission to let any of the patients here know about her hospitalization if they asked."

"Do you know what her room number is?" I asked and I wrote down the number that she rattled off.

I tried not to worry and not to jump to conclusions. I told myself that there wasn't a reason to panic just because Marge was hospitalized. She could've simply been dehydrated or had a kidney infection or many other scenarios that didn't pose a threat to her life. Still my anxiety level increased, and I felt on the verge of panicking. Marge was my friend, my chemo buddy, and I don't think I had realized just how much she meant to me until that moment. She made my chemo treatments bearable with her friendship and stories.

As soon as my treatment was over, I left the outpatient center and went to the inpatient hospital building. I found Marge's room without any difficulty. The door to her room was open and when I looked inside, she appeared to be sleeping. A man sat on a chair pulled up next to the bed. He was holding her hand in both of his and his eyes were closed. Tears were quietly rolling down his cheeks and his lips moved in silent prayer. I stood awkwardly in the doorway, hesitant to intrude upon their time alone. Cancer teaches you how precious time is, to cherish every minute and to make the most of every moment. A hand touched my shoulder and startled me. I turned to see a young, pretty nurse standing there with a Dinamap machine.

"Excuse me, please," she said.

I quickly stepped to the side to give her room to enter. At the sound of the nurse and the machine entering the room, both Marge and the man opened their eyes and looked at the both of us. A slow smile spread across Marge's face and she reached out her free hand towards me.

"Oh, Elise," she said sweetly. "How lovely of you to come and see me! I'm sorry I had to bail on you today."

"I was so worried when I found out that you weren't at the infusion center because you are in the hospital," I said as I quickly closed the gap between us and took her hand in mine. Her hand was as cold as ice and I noticed with a start that her fingers and nail beds were dusky. "I missed you, so I had to come and see you."

"I am glad you did," Marge said, smiling. "I missed you too and I was so afraid I wouldn't get a chance to talk to you and say goodbye before I go."

"Go?" I asked. "Where are you going?"

"Home," she said with a sigh of contentment. "I finally get to go home."

"That is wonderful!" I cried with relief. "I am so glad you get to come home. It will be good to have you back with me on chemo days."

"Oh dear," Marge said, her eyes clouding over. "I am sorry. I didn't mean to mislead you."

"What do you mean?" I asked, my heart sinking. I was scared of what she was going to say and my first instinct was to run away in panic. But I owed it to Marge to be brave. She had been there for me, supported me. I would do the same for her.

With tears in her eyes, Marge spoke softly. "I am sorry to leave you, Elise. You are a sweet friend. But my body is done fighting. When I said I am going home, I meant my real home, my family home. While it breaks my heart to leave my sweet Roger," she said as she choked back a sob and turned to gaze in Roger's pain-filled eyes, "I am going home to heaven; I am going to get to see my Lord and Saviour! And as sad as I am to say goodbye to my Roger and our family and friends, I am so excited to get to see God! Now I know you don't want to hear that and it is okay for you to be sad. Cry all you want to for you, for the sadness you will feel when I pass from this world into the next, but don't cry for me,

Elise. Don't shed any tears for me for I will be with my beloved Jesus. Just think, Elise, I will be completely healed of cancer! I will never again be sick or experience pain! I will never grow old and I will live forever. I've never told you this, Elise, but I have a dear little baby boy who is waiting for me in heaven. And I can't wait to hold him, to see him happy and healthy. While I wait for Roger, I will spend my days praising God and getting to know my boy, Ben."

Tears were coursing down my cheeks and down Marge's as well but our tears were no longer tears of sadness but of joy. In that moment, I envied Marge. I couldn't imagine what heaven would be like and I wondered if its spectacular beauty could even be comprehended by the human eye and mind. I also envied Marge for knowing what it felt like to be loved so completely. I had never felt that type of love before, not even from my mother. As soon as that thought entered my mind, I knew that it wasn't true. I did know that kind of love because the love God had for me was an all-consuming, everlasting love.

"I love you, Marge," I said, smiling through my tears. "And I am going to miss you so much but I am so glad that you will soon be free of pain and be with your Ben and the Lord."

"Thank you," she said, smiling back at me. "Now sit down. Bring that chair over there next to my bed so I can tell you one last story."

I eagerly acquiesced to her demand and soon I was sitting next to her bed opposite from Roger. I held her right hand and Roger held her left hand. As she talked and slipped into storyteller mode, she got a faraway look in her eyes as she saw in her mind's eye her memories of her distant past made real again by the telling.

"It was Christmas Eve, 1978. I have always loved Christmas but that year, Christmas was extra special because I was carrying our first child and, as the Bible says in Luke, I was 'soon to be delivered.' In fact I was eight-and-a-half months pregnant. Christmas Eve was on Sunday that year and I was trying to get our breakfast on the table so we could eat and get to church on time. I was pouring Roger a cup of coffee when I suddenly felt a horrible stabbing pain in my abdomen."

Marge's eyes filled with tears and her voice faltered. She looked at Roger imploringly. He squeezed her hand and kissed her cheek.

"Let me tell this part of it, honey," he said and she nodded her head, unable to speak. Some wounds never heal in this life.

"I watched as coffee filled my cup but Marge didn't stop pouring the coffee. The coffee spilled over the cup, down the table, and onto the floor. I remember jumping up and wondering why the brown coffee was turning red. I looked at Marge and when I saw the look on her face, I knew that something was terribly wrong. She dropped the coffee carafe as her knees buckled. I caught her just as the carafe hit the floor and shattered into many pieces. The sound of the breaking glass caused me to look down and that is when I saw that a large amount of blood was pouring out of Marge like water. I carried her to the couch and laid her down. Then I ran to the phone and called 911. The house we lived in at the time was a bi-level and I was worried if the EMTs would be able to carry Marge on a stretcher down those steps. I was scared they would drop her and cause her and the baby even more harm. As it turned out, I worried in vain because the fire department came as well so there was plenty of strong men to carry her. They got Marge out of the house and into the ambulance safely. They let me ride with her and that felt like the longest ride of my life even though they were driving as fast as possible. Somehow, I knew that we wouldn't get to the hospital in time. I've never felt so helpless in all my life."

Roger's voice grew husky and I could tell that he was struggling to control his emotions. I waited patiently as he cleared his throat and looked deep into Marge's eyes. I could see that they were drawing strength from each other and I wondered what it felt like to have that type of love. It was beautiful to see that even after many years together, love still shone from their eyes when they looked at one another.

"As it turned out," Roger continued, "it didn't matter how fast they drove. Marge had complete placenta abruption. Her placenta abruptly and completely pulled away from her uterus and young Ben's oxygen supply was taken away. Later, her doctor told me that even if she had been in the hospital when it occurred, it would have been highly likely that Ben still wouldn't have survived. He also said that there would not have been any warning signs, and there was nothing that we did to cause it and nothing we could have done to prevent it. At the time it didn't help to hear those words but during the many sleepless nights that I had in the days to come, those words brought me comfort and eased my guilt a little. It was my job as dad to protect my son, and it was my job as husband to protect my wife. I felt like I had failed them both.

"When we got to the hospital, they immediately took Marge into the operating room to perform an emergency C-section. I felt so alone and helpless as I watched them wheel my wife and child away from me. Back then, fathers were not allowed in the delivery room. While I waited, two other men who were in the father's waiting room with me were congratulated and told that their children were born healthy. One had a daughter. The other man had a son. Both gave me cigars, one pink and one blue. For some reason I kept both of those cigars. I still have them. You would think that looking at those cigars would make me feel bitter or resentful but instead, looking at those cigars remind me that happy endings still occur. I was left alone in that room for what seemed like an eternity.

"As soon as the doctor came into the room, I knew the news wasn't good. He told me that my son—I had a son—was stillborn. He never took one breath outside of his mother's womb. His heart never beat outside of his mother's womb. His entire life, brief as it was, was spent inside of his mother's womb. At the time, that felt so unfair. But many years later, I realized that my son's entire life was spent sheltered, nestled inside of his mother. He was literally cradled in love all of his life. He never knew fear, pain, hunger, or grief. Ben never had his heart broken. Ben's life was pure love. Throughout Marge's entire pregnancy I talked to Ben, told him how much I loved him, sang to him and read him stories. Marge's voice and heartbeat filled his world and he could feel his mother's life every moment of his life. That brings me comfort. So when people say they are sorry that we never got to spend time with our son, they are wrong. We had nine months with our boy. For nine months he was completely and utterly loved and wanted.

"The doctor also told me that they had been unable to control Marge's bleeding and that in order to save her life, they had to perform a hysterectomy. In an instant, my dreams of being a father were taken away. They offered to let me see and hold Ben but Marge was still in recovery. I didn't feel like it would be fair for me to get more time with our son than Marge or to see him before his mother. So I asked if Marge and I could see and hold him together once she was ready. The doctor kindly agreed."

"When I woke up, I was in a great amount of pain," said Marge, taking over the thread of the story. "And I felt totally empty. I knew before anyone told me that my baby was dead. I could see it in the eyes of the nurses that were taking care of me. When I was well enough to leave recovery, they put me in a hospital room and Roger came to me and told me about Ben. He didn't tell me about the hysterectomy right away. He probably knew that I wouldn't be able to handle it yet and he was right. One knife-twisting pain at a time was all I could take. When I finally felt that I was ready, they brought Ben to us. They brought him in a bassinet just as they would've done if he were living. He was absolutely perfect. His color was dusky but other than that, he merely looked as if he were asleep. They had dressed him and wrapped him up in a blanket. I unwrapped him and looked at his sweet little hands and feet and counted his fingers and toes. The longer we had him with us the more that we loved him and felt like a family. Yes our baby was dead, but he was and always would be our baby boy. We named him Benjamin after my father and Roger after his daddy and we called him Ben. You may think it morbid but I asked them to take pictures of Ben and of us holding him. They did that for us and they also did his footprints and handprints for us. I also asked for the little knitted hat and sleeper they had put him in. I wanted something that had touched him. Roger went home and brought back the outfit we were going to bring him home in. Instead, that was the outfit that we buried him in. Those few keepsakes are all we have ever had of our son."

Marge paused and dabbed her eyes with a tissue. Then she took a deep breath and went on with her story.

"Ben's viewing was in the evening on Christmas Day and his funeral was the day after Christmas. I was still in the hospital and not allowed to leave. I have never felt so utterly alone as I did that day. I couldn't bear to think of my baby being buried in the cold ground, so we purchased a mausoleum. In order to get to the graveyard where Ben's mausoleum is located, you have to drive past the hospital where I was a patient. At our request, one of the funeral home's employees called the hospital and told my nurse that the funeral procession had just left the funeral home and would be driving past the hospital in just a few minutes. Fortunately, my room was located on the side of the hospital that faced the road. The nurse assisted me out of the bed and helped me over to the window. I asked her to leave me and she was reluctant to do so but I assured her I was fine and that I wanted to be alone. She finally agreed and went out of the room. At my request for total privacy, she shut the door behind her. As I looked out the window, I watched as the hearse carrying the body of my son drove past me. There was a small white house across the street from the hospital. Movement at the front door caught my eyes and I saw a man and woman come out of the house. The man was carrying a baby car seat that was covered over with a baby quilt that was a Christmas theme. They were smiling and looked so happy. The man put the car seat in the backseat. Then he stepped back and the lady stepped up and bent over the baby. I couldn't see what she was doing but I could imagine all sorts of things. Perhaps she was uncovering his face, putting a pacifier in his mouth, wiping away tear, or kissing his little face. And yes I realize that without any basis in fact, I have assumed the baby was a boy," Marge said, smiling wryly. "The lady stepped back and shut the car door. The man then helped her into the car before getting into the car himself. The car turned to the right and the little family drove off and out of sight. They went in the opposite direction as my son. They had no need of a graveyard for their child. I felt as if the grief would overwhelm me and my knees began to buckle. A breath of wind and the rustling sound of fabric came from behind me and just as I was starting to collapse, strong arms surrounded me from behind and held me up and a sweet, delightful fragrance engulfed me. Instantly, I felt peace that did truly pass all understanding and while my grief was not erased, I was comforted. I was not alone. That was undisputable. My hands rested on the arms wrapped around me and the fabric I felt was softer than any cloth I have ever felt before. I looked down to see what it looked like but while I could feel and touch the arms, I couldn't see them. You might think that I would have been frightened but I wasn't. The presence that I felt was so pure that it was almost unbearable to me in my frail, flawed humanity. But I trusted Him; I knew Who He was. I closed my eyes and allowed my body to relax. I didn't even try to stand; instead, I let Him hold me and I let His strength be the strength that I needed.

"The days and the weeks ahead were very hard. Roger and I wept over the loss of our son and the loss of the children we would now never be able to have. Yet the Comforter never once left me or Roger, and although I have never again been able to touch those strong arms or feel the soft fabric, His presence has never left me nor forsaken me. And His strength has always been sufficient."

For a while none of us spoke and all three of us cried for the baby boy who was stillborn. I couldn't imagine how much it had hurt and still hurt. It was clear that Roger and Marge still felt the loss of their child just as keenly as if he had died today. The loss of a child is a pain that can only be healed by one thing—reunion with the lost child.

"When I die," Marge continued, "I have asked that the mortician remove Ben from his coffin and to place him in my arms. Ben and I will be buried together. So now you know, Elise, why I am looking forward to dying. As much as I hate to leave Roger, I am equally as eager to be reunited with my son, not in death; although we will be dead to this life, in heaven we will be alive. Heaven is the place where I will finally see my son alive and hold his warm, breathing body in my arms."

A look of wonderment flooded her face and her eyes widened. She let go of my hand and turned to Roger, grasping both of his hands in hers.

"Roger," she exclaimed, "I just realized something. You said that Ben's entire life was spent inside of me but that's not really true! Yes, he did spend his entire earthly life inside of me but although his body is dead, he isn't really dead! He is alive with Jesus! Don't you see, Roger? What you said was even more true than you knew! Ben was born in heaven! He has never known pain or sickness or sin or hate! He has spent his entire life in perfect happiness! And soon I will be with him!"

Roger drew Marge into his arms and close to his chest. They both wept and laughed at the same time. And I watched in wonder. Here they were at the end of Marge's life and they were rejoicing. Finally I understood what Paul had meant when he wrote in 1 Corinthians 15:55, "O death, where is thy sting? O grave where is thy victory?" The death of those who believe in Christ isn't a defeat. It is a victory.

CHAPTER TEN

D awn was just creeping over the horizon when I made my way back across the cornfield. I had slipped an envelope containing a letter for Elise and a piece of music for her to play under her door. When I made it back home, I went straight to the barn and to work. When I finally entered the house, breakfast was on the table and everyone was in their usual seats except for me and Rachel. Because Rachel was shunned, she was no longer allowed to sit at the table with the family. Instead, a small table had been set up in the corner of the kitchen for her use. Her table and chair was placed such that her back was to her family and her face was towards the blank wall. I hated her separation from the family. While I understood that the purpose of the shunning was a form of tough love and that it was meant to force her to see the error of her ways in hopes that she would cease her sinful behavior and reaffirm her commitment to the church and to God, it felt that the shunning was pushing her further away from us. Even without Rachel contributing to the conversation, breakfast was a lively affair in our home. Sometimes I wished for peace and quiet but today I was grateful for the cheerful chatter generated by my siblings. In spite of Mamm's stroke and blindness and Rachel's shunning, some aspects of our lives had not changed and that gave me comfort.

While the family talked around me, my mind began to wander and as it so commonly occurred did nowadays, my thoughts strayed to Elise.

I knew she was beautiful, but I wondered what she looked like up close. I wondered what her voice sounded like, what color her eyes were, and what it would feel like to hold her in my arms. I missed her. I had never been in the same room with her but still I missed her constantly and longed to be with her. Every day it was becoming more difficult to stay away from her. I wanted to run through the field to her house, to meet her face-to-face and to hold her in my arms. She was so close yet so very far away. I envied Rachel for spending time with her. But while I wanted to spend time with her, my biggest fear was that my secret would be exposed. When I heard that Leah was covering for Rachel the day Daett refused to allow Rachel to work, I was terrified she would see one of the letters I had written to Elise or my name on the music on Elise's piano. Thankfully, I don't think that Leah saw any evidence that betrayed the fact that I had a relationship with an Englisher. I felt certain that if she had, she would have promptly gone to the Bishop out of anger and jealousy. Hopefully, Leah would not have to cover for Rachel again.

After breakfast, I hitched the horses to our buggy and rode to town to the bus station in order to pick up Aunt Fannie. Having her help and cheerful presence in our home would be a balm in Gilead. I arrived just a few minutes before the bus. When I saw her cheerful face, my heart felt lighter than it had in days.

"Aunt Fannie!" I called out to her.

She turned towards my voice, saw me and smiled even broader than before. She hurried towards me. Aunt Fannie is short, petite and plump; she walked on the tips of her toes and made quick, bouncy steps. One summer, I teased her and told her that if she had not been born Amish, she would've been a ballerina. She had laughed, patted her belly and protested saying, "Me, a ballerina? Not me! I like my food too much! Can you imagine one of those men trying to lift me up?" At that, we had all laughed.

In a few quick strides, I met up with Aunt Fannie and enveloped her in a bear hug.

"Aunt Fannie," I exclaimed as I bent to kiss her check. "It is so *gut* to see you! We are delighted to have you with us. I am afraid that we are in a mess, Aunt Fannie."

"John," she beamed up at me, "it is wonderful to see you, my dear nephew. Don't worry about a thing. I specialize in cleaning up messes."

I helped Aunt Fannie up into the buggy and then I put her bags inside. I planned on taking the long way home at a leisurely pace so I could have Aunt Fannie all to myself for as long as possible. We had barely pulled out of the parking lot before Aunt Fannie turned and looked at me solemnly.

"All right, John," she said, "tell me everything that is going on and I do mean everything! I can tell by your face, your tense shoulders, and the look in your eyes that you are under a great deal of strain. I made and brought you some of my famous molasses cookies."

"Those are my favorite cookies!" I exclaimed, my mouth already drooling.

"I know," she said, smiling. "Let's stop by the park so you can eat all of the cookies you want before your brothers and sisters get their hands on them. And while you eat, you can tell me everything that is troubling you."

"On one condition," I said. "We have to stop by the Quick-Mart first and buy some ice cold milk because I cannot possibly eat molasses cookies without ice cold milk."

"Agreed! I thought it was a given that we would be stopping for milk."

A few minutes later we were sitting on a quilt that Aunt Fannie had spread out on the grass underneath a shady maple tree. Aunt Fannie opened up the container of cookies and the delicious scent of molasses and spice wafted up, causing my mouth to water. I ate two cookies so fast I think I forgot to breathe.

"Your cookies are just as good as I remember," I said as I reached for a couple more cookies.

"I'm glad you like them," said Aunt Fannie, smiling. "Now talk to me, John."

Soothed by the calmness of Aunt Fannie, the delicious cookies, and the beauty of the park, I began to talk to her. I told her about Rachel's job. I told her about Mamm's stroke and how it had affected our family. I told her about seeing Rachel with Daniel Lapp and all that happened because of it. Then I fell silent and grabbed another cookie. I quickly stuffed it in my mouth as Aunt Fannie looked at me shrewdly. I averted my eyes and grabbed another cookie.

"John, that's not quite everything. You've told me about everything and everyone but you. There is no need to keep anything from me. You know that I love you and you can tell me anything," she said.

Suddenly my mouth was really dry and I couldn't swallow the cookie that I had practically shoved into my mouth whole. Aunt Fannie handed me the milk. Once I had recovered, she arched her eyebrow at me and I made the decision to trust her. I told her everything. I told her that I had been composing music again and about my beautiful new neighbor who played the piano and had played my songs. I even told her that Elise and I were writing and I kept bringing her my music to play. As I talked, I kept my face averted from Aunt Fannie's probing eyes and instead I stared at the duck pond. When I was done, I still couldn't look at her. I felt like I had stripped myself naked in front of her.

"John, look at me, please," asked Aunt Fannie in a tender voice.

I looked into her eyes expecting to see judgment, condemnation, sadness, and anger but instead I saw love.

"I understand what you are going through," said Aunt Fannie. "More than you could know. It's hard when you have been given a gift from God that you believe in your heart could be used to praise Him and to declare His glory. I am sure that your parents have never told you my story because that is the way of our people. Once a sin has been confessed and forgiven, it is never to be spoken of again. That can be wonderful and it can also be hurtful. I have been and will continue to be silent about my past. I have made my choice and I am comfortable with it. But right now in this moment, I am going to tell you why I understand your struggle and then I will never speak of it again unless I feel led of God to tell it like I feel led to tell you.

"When I started school, it was like a whole new world had been opened up to me. It was incredible and at the same time, it was scary. I don't know if you know this, but I went to public school through the third grade. Then our district started a school and from the fourth to the eighth grade, I went to an Amish school. I loved the public school and I cried in secret when I found out that I would no longer be going there. I loved public school because of the new world I got to glimpse and be a part of during school hours. On the first day of kindergarten, I was shocked and surprised when I learned that the school's bathroom wasn't outside. The teacher had to show me how to flush the toilet and how to turn the bathroom light on and off," Aunt Fannie said, smiling wryly at the memory.

"The lights were especially fascinating to me. I couldn't believe how bright they were and how much light they generated. The fact that I could have light by flipping a switch was fascinating and much simpler than lighting a kerosene lamp. Another thing I loved was snack time with store-bought goodies that I had never tasted before. My teacher, Mrs. Farris, was a great educator and she was very kind and patient with me. I'm sure it wasn't easy having me in her class, but she never once acted exasperated with me. She was a great storyteller and when she would read to us, she made the story come alive. I loved the stories in the books, but the illustrations in the books totally captivated me.

"One day she let me borrow one of her storybooks to take home to show my Mamm, brothers and sisters. I was excited and happy to share it with my family. Much to my surprise, when Daett saw the book, he became very angry. He said the only books that I should be reading were my school books and the book I brought home was only the vain imaginings of an Englisher. If the book hadn't belonged to the school, I think he would have burned it. Instead he confiscated it. When I asked him about it the following morning and told him that I needed to take the book back, he told me not to worry about it that he would take care of the situation. I can't tell you how embarrassed I was when my Daett walked with me to school, marched into my classroom, and handed the book back to my teacher. He was very stern and unfriendly. He told her that her job was to teach me how to read, write, and reckon not to fill my mind with useless stories. Later I apologized to my teacher. She told me I had nothing to apologize for; she was so kind. She asked me if I needed to not participate in story time. I begged her to please allow me to listen to the stories and I begged her not to tell my Daett about storytime. I felt so guilty in my heart for I knew that I was rebelling against my Daett, but I also felt that my deceit was justified. That was the first time I made the conscious decision to rebel against my Daett. It was the first time I chose to sin."

"Aunt Fannie, that wasn't...," I started to say before Aunt Fannie cut me off.

"I know what you are going to say, John," she said with a wave of her hand as if to dismiss my opinion on the matter. "And I even understand why you don't think it was a sin. Perhaps my Daett's views on fiction books is erroneous and his belief may not be supported by scripture; however, the Bible is very clear that children are to obey their parents and the Bible also makes it plain that rebellion is a sin. Looking back over my life, I see that first lie by omission and that first decision to rebel against my Daett started me down a path that would eventually bring me great heartbreak. Anyway, let's get back to my story.

"I liked my class, being in school, and learning. However, from the first time I had art class, I was in love with drawing. It was like a seed inside of my heart and soul that I didn't even know was there had finally been watered and exposed to the sun, blossomed, and became an amazingly beautiful flower."

"I know that feeling," I whispered.

"Over the next few years, art class was my sanctuary, my 'happy place.' I learned how to sketch and paint. My art teacher, Mrs. Toomey, told me that I was talented and encouraged me to practice outside of class. Instinctively I knew that if I asked my Daett for permission to draw or for art supplies, the answer would be no and all I would receive would be punishment courtesy of my Daett's wrath. Now I don't want you to get the wrong idea about my Daett. He was a good father and he loved me and I him. Daett knew that as our father and Mamm's husband, he was to be the spiritual leader of our family. He took that responsibility very seriously. While I didn't necessarily share all of his beliefs, I knew in my heart that he made the choices he did to protect my soul. I saw books as a window into a world that I would never see. Daett saw books as a door that would lead me into the world and away from God. At that point of my life, I felt that if drawing was taken away from me, I would die. Overly dramatic I know, but that is how I felt. Eventually, Mrs. Toomey guessed that I wasn't allowed to draw at home. When she asked me about it, I told her a partial truth. I told her that I lived on a farm and I had so many chores to do when I was home that I didn't have time to draw. I also explained that we didn't have or believe in electricity and at night, our home was lit by kerosene lamps and that was not enough light to draw by. Mrs. Toomey accepted my reasoning but I had an inkling that she also knew that my Daett wouldn't allow me to draw. When I told Mrs. Toomey that I wouldn't be coming back for fourth grade, I cried. On my final day of art class, Mrs. Toomey asked me to stay behind after class. She gave me a present. When she handed it to me, I was flabbergasted! I had never received such a gift. It was wrapped with beautiful wrapping paper and it had a huge bow on top. As awesome as the package was, what was inside was even more wonderful. She gave me a case full of art supplies: charcoal, colored pencils, a small set of watercolor paint, a couple of brushes, a large sketch pad, a small sketch pad, and paper. She also gave me instructional books on drawing and painting. I was so overcome with emotions that it was hard for me to get the words thank you out, but she knew how grateful I was: she could see it on my face and in my eyes. It was the most thoughtful and marvelous gift I had ever received. I went back to my classroom on cloud nine. Halfway through our afternoon, I realized that Daett would never allow me to keep my art supplies. Without a doubt, I knew that he would throw it all on the fire. I couldn't help it; I burst into tears. My third grade teacher, Miss Johnson, finally got me calmed down enough that I could tell her what was wrong.

"Miss Johnson had beautiful red hair and very fair skin with a smattering of light freckles across her nose and cheeks. When she was upset, she would develop hives on her neck. We knew that when she started getting blotchy, we had better settle down and behave! As she listened to me, Miss Johnson's neck got blotchy and her eyes narrowed. However, I quickly realized that she wasn't mad at me; she was mad at the situation. She told me not to worry about it that she would come up with a plan by tomorrow which was the last day of school. She had me leave the supplies at school that night and she locked it up in her cupboard. The end of the next day when the bell rang, I stayed behind. Once all of the other students were gone, she unlocked the cupboard and brought out a beautiful wooden lap desk."

"'I remembered the time that you brought a letter from your cousin in Pennsylvania and how you told us that writing letters was the main way that your family stays in touch with family and friends. You told us that you loved it when your family was cuddled up close to the fire on cold winter nights and before your family devotions, your family would take turns reading aloud to the family, letters that they had received. I thought that was marvelous. I inherited this writing desk from my grandmother. My grandfather, who was a very gifted furniture maker, made it for her. It has been in my attic just collecting dust and it would make me very happy for it to belong to someone who will use it.'

"I loved the desk at first sight. I had never seen anything like it. I protested and told her I couldn't take something that had belonged to her grandmother. But she insisted. Then she showed me the secret compartment that her grandfather had made into the bottom of the desk. It was totally undetectable and it would be very difficult to figure out how to open it up unless someone showed you how to do so. All of my art supplies fit into the hidden compartment perfectly. Miss Johnson had even bought me beautiful stationary and pack of pens and placed them in the nonhidden compartment. I was nervous taking it home because I was not sure what my parents would think. At first my parents were unsure if I should keep such a nice gift. My Daett went to Miss Johnson's house and she assured him that she really wanted me to have it. She told him that it was just sitting in her attic rotting away because she didn't write letters anymore. Then when she heard that I wrote letters to family and friends, she thought I would be able to use the writing desk. She told him that her grandfather had made the desk and she hated to see it going unused and decaying in her attic when she knew I would actually use it. And because I was leaving the school and had been such a great student, she wanted to give me a gift to remember her by. Her words convinced Daett to let me keep the lap desk. You see, Daett was a big believer in hand crafting items and he thought everything should be useful. Seeing how well-crafted the desk was and thinking of it rotting away and not being used made Daett decide he would let me accept Miss Johnson's gift."

Aunt Fannie paused to drink some milk and took a bite from her cookie.

"I was so scared of getting caught that I didn't draw anything for a month. When the itching in my fingers to draw something got so strong that I couldn't hardly sleep at night, I couldn't withstand it. So I waited until it was very late at night and I was sure everyone was asleep. Being the oldest girl, I had begged for and gotten my own room. It was very small; not more than a closet really, but it was a private place just for me like your room is for you. I had a straight-backed wooden chair in my room. Since my door didn't have a lock on it, I wedged the chair under the handle just in case anyone decided to pay me a late night visit. By the light of the moon and a kerosene lamp I sketched a picture, a portrait of my favorite dairy cow on the farm, Daisy. Since the light was dim, I stuck with charcoal as my medium. The picture wasn't perfect but drawing it was extremely satisfying. It's hard to explain but drawing made me feel like I was totally alive and like I had finally found myself."

"I understand," I said. "Writing music makes me feel the same way."

"I know you do, sweetie," said Aunt Fannie as she squeezed my hand. "The drawing in secret went on for years. Eventually I was bold enough to even sneak in some drawing in the daylight.

"When I was sixteen, I developed a crush on a boy and I did something that for an Amish girl went against my beliefs. I drew a picture of him. Then I did something really foolish. Instead of keeping the picture hidden with the others, I started keeping the picture with me at night. I would talk to him, kiss the picture, and then sleep with it under my pillow. One morning, I had trouble waking up and I was running late for work. At that time, I worked at an Amish bakery. I left without remembering to hide the picture. Mamm decided to wash all of the bed linens that day and she found my picture and showed it to Daett. He became so angry that he didn't even let me finish out my work day. When he walked into the bakery and I saw his face looking like thunder, my heart sank. I knew I was in serious trouble—I just didn't know why until we got home. He sat in stony silence the entire ride home. It was awful, John. The bishop came to the house. I had to convince them that I had drawn the picture from memory and that the boy knew nothing about the portrait. I had to apologize before the entire congregation. The boy had been talking to me and although we were not dating, I thought that we were on the verge of that happening. But when he found out about the picture, he was furious with me. Because I confessed and repented, I wasn't shunned but it felt like it. Girls that had once been close to me became distant; I wasn't invited to many social events and when I went to the singings, no young men asked to take me home. The days turned into months and then years.

"Eventually some of the people became more friendly and while I don't feel like an outcast anymore, I don't feel completely accepted either. Once I realized that I was going to be an old maid, I became very sad and angry; I shut down for a while. Like all Amish girls, I had dreamed of being a wife and a mother. I had sewn and quilted and collected marvelous items for my hope chest that my Daett had made for me. It was hard for me to realize that my dreams weren't going to happen and to let go of that dream. The day the boy of the infamous portrait got married was a horrible day for me. My heart still hoped and longed for him and I did not think I would be able to bear seeing him at church as a happily married man with a wife and kinner. This heartbreak took me down a dark path and I made choices and mistakes that put the final nails in my coffin. But that is a story for another day. Because of a praying Mamm, I eventually found my way back home and God healed my broken heart."

"What about your drawing?" I asked

"At first my drawing was a way to celebrate the mighty works of God and the awesomeness of His creation. My talent was God-given and I used it to praise Him and to think upon Him. But eventually I began using it for the wrong reasons and when I realized what I had done in drawing the picture of the one I was in love with, knowing how he believed, I was horrified with myself. I didn't draw again for years. In fact, I have only drawn once since I was sixteen years old."

"What did you draw and why?" I asked, very much intrigued.

"I drew a picture of you," she said with a smile.

"Of me?" I asked in surprise.

"Yes," she said, smiling. "I drew you. It was when you were in that horrible buggy accident when you were eighteen. You were in a coma and the doctor said that you would probably never wake up and that most likely you would die. You were my first nephew and we have always been very close. You are the closest thing that I will ever have to a child. I remember staring down at your beautiful face thinking that I could not bear it if you died. I was overwhelmed with the need to capture your face on paper so that I would always be able to see your face even if you were in heaven. I drew a picture of you, John. I captured you, your personality, the light in your eyes, and your beautiful smile. It is the best thing I have ever drawn. For some reason, I felt like I needed to bring the picture to you. It isn't large; I wanted to be able to put it between the pages of my Bible."

Aunt Fannie stood up and walked over to the buggy. She flipped open her suitcase and got her Bible which was lying on top. She took out a piece of thick paper, walked over to me, and handed it to me. I looked down and gasped. It was like looking into a mirror! She wasn't exaggerating when she said she had captured me.

"Aunt Fannie, you are amazingly talented!" I exclaimed.

She turned pink and smiled at the compliment.

"I am glad you like it," she said. "Something tells me you know exactly what to do with the portrait."

"I do," I agreed.

"Good," she said, smiling.

"Now let's pack up and head to the house," she said. "They are probably wondering what on earth happened to us."

Within minutes we were back in the buggy and headed towards home. I had my picture hidden inside my shirt. I was so glad Aunt Fannie was home with us.

"John," said Aunt Fannie as we neared home, "remember the parable of the talents? When God gives us a talent, He expects us to use it for His glory and according to His will. And when you do, He will increase your talent. I believe that God has given you this talent. My life story is different from yours. Learn from my mistakes so you won't make the same ones, but don't let fear of making mistakes keep you from taking a leap of faith."

"I won't," I promised as I turned the buggy into our driveway. "I promise."

Aunt Fannie was right: I did know what to do with the picture. It was the only portrait of me that existed and I knew that a very special young lady would love to have this picture of me. When we arrived home, the family was happy and excited to see Aunt Fannie. After supper was over, the dishes washed and put away, and the chores done for the day, we all gathered in the living room for prayer and devotions. Afterwards, Aunt Fannie asked Daett if it would be all right if she gave out the gifts that she had brought for us. Daett looked surprised but assented. Aunt Fannie had a gift for everyone. Aunt Fannie gave Daett new sturdy work gloves that she had sown herself. They were much better than gloves from the store. Rachel and Abigail each received a dozen handkerchiefs that had been beautifully embroidered. Elias received a book all about birds commonly seen in Indiana which is perfect as he loves watching birds. He had even saved up his money and bought himself a pair of binoculars this year. Caleb and Matthew each got a ball and Ruthie received a doll that had been knitted by Aunt Fannie—even its clothes were knitted! She loved it. Mamm received a beautiful, warm, and soft shawl that Aunt Fannie had knitted for her. Mamm smiled, really smiled for the first time since her stroke. Then Aunt Fannie turned to me.

"John, I'm afraid that I didn't make anything for you or buy you anything new. However, I do have something that I have treasured for many years that I want to give to you," she said with a smile.

She handed me a brown cardboard box that was tied up with twine. I used my pocket knife to cut through the twine and then I opened the box. Inside was a beautiful wooden lap desk. I was overwhelmed. I didn't know quite what to say. As I looked up at her, I felt tears welling up in my eyes.

"Do you like it?" she asked.

"I love it," I answered her. "Thank you so much, Aunt Fannie. I will treasure it always."

I stood up and enveloped her in a hug. Afterwards, she smiled up at me and patted me on the cheek.

"Inside is paper, envelope, pens, and stamps," she said. "Now you have no excuse not to write me once I leave. In fact, none of you have an excuse because I expect John to share the writing supplies with the family."

That night after everyone was asleep, I slipped over to Elise's house with the letter that I had written that evening. I had enclosed the portrait that Aunt Fannie had drawn of me and another piece of music. The music that I was taking her was written by me after I woke up from the buggy accident and had come through months of physical therapy successfully. The music was about God's grace, the miracle of healing, and the peace that children of God have in the midst of a storm. The music began dark, sad, and suspenseful, signifying my accident. This was followed by a haunting melody that was initially discordant but eventually resolved, depicting my time in the coma and the voices that eventually began to pierce the fog. Then with harmonic jubilation, the song ended in triumphant praise. This morning I had woken up before dawn and instantly felt like I needed to pray for Elise so I had. The burden and the need to pray for her had stayed with me the entire day. I hoped that this letter, music, and picture helped bring her some comfort.

CHAPTER ELEVEN

Saying goodbye to Marge was extremely hard because I knew in my heart that this would be the last time I would see her in this life. As I walked out the door of her hospital room, I turned around for one last look. Roger and Marge were holding hands and looking into each other's eyes; their love almost radiated off them.

"I want that kind of love," I whispered to myself. Almost immediately, my thoughts went to John. After Donavan I didn't think true love existed for me but since John had started writing me and bringing me his music, I had begun to think that maybe I was wrong. Perhaps true love would find me after all.

The next morning, the ringing of my cell phone woke me up. Before I even answered the phone, I knew Marge was gone. Roger's voice was broken and thick with tears. He told me that Marge had passed away during the night. She had asked him to sleep next to her one last time so he had crawled into her hospital bed and held her in his arms all night long. They had talked and told each other how much they loved each other and promised one another that they would be together forever in heaven. Then they had fallen asleep. Roger woke up when the nurse entered the room around dawn to take Marge's vital signs. There were none because Marge had died during the night while sleeping in Roger's arms.

My heart was broken over the loss of my friend but I also rejoiced that she was now completely healed of cancer and no longer in pain.

Marge was now in Heaven with her God whom she loved with her whole heart and she was holding her son in her arms. Once I had cried all my tears, fear and depression began to set in. Marge was treated at the same Cancer Center as I was. What if I were to die next? John and I had just found one another and I was just beginning to fall in love, really in love for the first time. I wasn't ready to die.

The day was long and dark and the only bright spot was KitKat. She seemed to sense that I was unhappy and she made it her mission to cheer me up. She played and chortled and scampered. As sad as I was over Marge's death, it was impossible not to smile at KitKat's antics.

That evening, I realized that I hadn't checked my front porch for mail from John. Sure enough, I found a package waiting for me. I opened it up and pulled out a letter, sheet music, and a drawing of a handsome young man. His eyes seemed to pierce my heart and soul and I had a hard time looking away from his face. I knew this had to be a portrait of John. I was puzzled why he sent me a drawing instead of a photograph, but I was so pleased to put a face to the man that my heart was falling in love with. Convinced his letter might explain things to me, I hastily unfolded the pages and eagerly began to read.

Dear Elise,

I hope that you are well. Today I have felt the need to pray for you and if I am being honest, I have wished that I could be with you. I know we have not met face-to-face and don't know a lot about one another. However, I feel like we know each other very well. Something within my soul connects with yours and I cannot deny that I have feelings for you. Please understand that I am not telling you this because I want you to reciprocate those feelings or to pressure you in any way and I certainly do not want to come across as a stalker. I am telling you this because without first explaining my feelings, what I have to say next would sound weird.

Elise, all day today, I have felt an overwhelming need to hold you in my arms and to comfort you. I have felt the need to pray for you and to ask God to give you strength. I don't know what may be going on in your life but I want you to know that I am always here for you. Please never forget that.

Love,
John

P. S. This is a picture of me, drawn by Aunt Fannie when I was eighteen. I hope you like it.

As I read John's words, tears began to stream down my cheeks. While my heart was broken over the death of Marge, the knowledge that John cared for me just as I cared for him helped ease the pain and brought me joy. For the first time since I was diagnosed with cancer, I felt hope. The need to see John's face, to look into his eyes, and to be held within his arms was suddenly so strong that it nearly took my breath away. As I wrote John a note, tears dripped unimpeded off my cheeks, down onto the paper, and mingled with the ink.

I awoke before dawn with a feeling of anticipation much like I had felt as a child on Christmas morning. Quickly I scanned my memory to see what was causing me to feel this way but I couldn't think of a reason. Well, that wasn't entirely true: there was always the chance that Elise had responded to my letter. Just thinking about Elise made me smile. It was crazy but now that I had acknowledged my feelings for Elise, they were growing rapidly. I got out of bed and dressed quickly. My plan was to go to Elise's house to see if she had left a letter for me. I longed to hear from her, to have a connection with her. Within minutes, I was running through the field towards her house, towards her. With trembling hands, I lifted up the mat and with joy, I retrieved the note that was there. After replacing the mat, I took the letter and retreated to my tree stand.

Up amongst the leaves, I looked about me as if seeing my surroundings for the first time today. There was a hint of a chill in the air and I noticed that a few of the leaves were starting to change. It would soon be mid-September and it would officially be fall. Come October we would harvest the field corn and plant winter wheat. Without the camouflage provided by the cornstalks, I would no longer be able to watch Elise play the piano through her window. Even worse, she would have to close her windows to keep out the cold, and I would no longer be able to hear her beautiful piano playing. This caused my heart to constrict within me and I wasn't sure I would be able to bear the loss of seeing and hearing Elise. I opened up the note and began to read.

Dear John,

Words cannot express just how much your last note meant to me. What I have to tell you is very hard. Along with KitKat, you and your music are the best aspects of my life. This time last year, I was living the type of life that people are envious of: I was a concert pianist who traveled the world staying in luxurious hotels, eating at high-end restaurants, and playing in the most sought-after venues. I was also young and healthy at twenty-four years old. After months of ignoring the fatigue, loss of appetite, night sweats, and weight loss, I collapsed and found myself in a London hospital extremely ill. This was a shock for me because I had always been healthy and had never been hospitalized before. After so many diagnostic tests that I had begun to feel like a pincushion, I finally received the diagnosis of acute myeloid leukemia. I was utterly devastated. At the time, I had a boyfriend but he didn't handle my diagnosis very well. He very quickly decided that he didn't want a girlfriend with cancer. We parted ways and within days of our breakup, he was with another girl. My nomadic lifestyle has afforded me many acquaintances but none are friends or at least close friends. This house was the only real home

I had ever known. Since I needed to be stationary for treatment, I decided to come home. I go to a Cancer Center which has provided me with excellent care. While sitting in a recliner getting my chemo treatment, I met and made friends with a delightful lady named Marge. She has been an extraordinarily good friend to me and a tremendous support. Unfortunately, Marge passed away last evening and my heart is broken. So you see, knowing that you were thinking of me and praying for me yesterday means so much to me. I am not sure what the future holds for me or how long that future will be, but none of us are promised a set amount of time. However, one thing I do know for sure: I hope that you are a part of my future.

Love,
Elise

I slowly folded the letter and stared blankly into the woods. I felt like I had been sucker-punched. Fear threatened to overwhelm me. It was one thing to know that she had cancer, it was another thing altogether to hear directly from her that death was a possible outcome. My emotions towards Elise weren't something that I could define yet, but I knew that the thought of losing her terrified me.

The day passed by quickly. After supper, Daett asked me if I would help Mamm get to bed if she became too tired before he got back. Naturally I agreed but I wondered where Daett was going. It was not normal for him to leave the house in the evening. He must've seen the question in my eyes because he answered the question before I even asked it.

"The bishop asked me to come to his house this evening," Daett said with a heavy sigh.

Daett had scarcely been gone thirty minutes before Mamm asked if I could help her to bed. While Mamm was able to walk short distances with help, steps were more than she could do. Therefore shortly after Daett brought her home from the hospital, we converted what had been our family room into a bedroom for Daett and Mamm. As I helped

Mamm to bed, I noticed that she felt lighter and this caused me to look at her a little more closely. She looked pale, wane, and quite small. A frisson of fear and worry crept into my heart. I pulled the quilts up around her and tucked her in just as she had tucked me into bed when I was a child. Mamm smiled up at me sweetly.

"Thank you, John," she said softly. "I'm sorry but I am just very tired. I think I will go on to sleep."

"Of course, Mamm. You rest, and don't worry about a thing."

After I kissed her forehead, I eased out of her room and shut the door. I looked in the living room onto a domestic scene. My siblings were all engrossed in various activities while Aunt Fannie and Rachel tended to the mending. All day long my mind had been consumed with thoughts of Elise. By the time our work was done for the day, I knew one thing for sure: I couldn't let Elise die without first getting the chance to actually talk to her and to look into her eyes. Not wanting to wait a moment longer, I told Rachel that I was going out for a bit. She barely even acknowledged me and I knew that I would not be missed.

Because I was unsure exactly when Daett would be coming home and not wanting to chance him seeing me on Elise's front porch, I decided to be discreet and to go through the woods and around to her back door. As the lights of her house came into view through the trees, a wave of anxiety swept over me and I was tempted to turn back. Many questions and what-ifs went through my mind, but the fear of never knowing was greater. I stepped out onto her lawn and slowly walked toward her back porch. I was nearly to the back steps when I realized that she was sitting in a chair on the screened-in porch. I paused thinking that she surely must see me but when she didn't speak or move, I walked on. As I stepped up onto the steps, I could see that she was sleeping, wrapped up in a blanket with a kitten on her lap. I didn't want to scare her, so I knocked on the door lightly at first and then slightly louder. The kitten woke up first, gave me a cursory glance, yawned, and then dismissed me as she started licking her paw. I knocked again and this time, Elise opened her eyes and looked directly into my eyes. My heart stopped. My first instinct was to run and she must have somehow sensed that.

"Please stay. Don't run," she said.

So I stayed. I felt as vulnerable as if I were standing before her naked, my heart hammering wildly within my chest and my mind racing with a multitude of thoughts, and then there was no more time to wonder for she was there in front of me framed by the light from within. She was enchantingly beautiful, the most breathtaking girl that I had ever seen. I tried to speak but no words came out. I reached up and took off my hat because this moment felt sacred. I didn't know what to do or say, so I simply stood there with my hat in my hands looking mutely into her beautiful blue eyes. Without saying a word, she reached out her hand and I took it. Just the feel of her hand in mine made my body tingle, and my heart rate sped up. Still holding my hand, she drew me inside the house and shut the door.

The Phenergan I had taken for nausea had caused me to fall asleep in my favorite spot on the screened porch. KitKat had jumped up onto my lap and her purring and smurgling had added to my sleepiness. My dreams were of John as they so often were these days. In my slumber, we were together and all was wonderful. A sound began niggling at my conscious but I resisted waking up from my lovely dream. I didn't want to wake up yet again to the knowledge that it had all been a figment of my mind. *Please be here*, I thought. Then I heard the sound of his footsteps on my back steps. My mouth went dry and my heart began to race. John was here. I would finally get to see his face, hear his voice, and look into his eyes. I slowly opened up my eyes and looked into his. How I knew I don't know, but I knew that the man standing there was my John. I saw panic flair within his eyes and his body tense as if he were getting ready to turn and run away. I didn't think I would be able to bear it if he were to run away from me, so I spoke.

"Please stay. Don't run," I pleaded. Instantly the panic faded away and the tension ebbed away. He stayed. Slowly I stood up, lifting KitKat from my lap, incurring a protesting meow from her as I laid her down on the chaise. I walked to the screen door and without breaking eye contact, I unlocked and opened the door. He stood before me, the most beautiful man that I had ever seen. His hair was golden honey, his skin was kissed by the sun, and his eyes were a beautiful green with gold flecks in them. I had been scared that it would be awkward being face-to-face for the first time, but it was the most natural thing in the world. Looking into his eyes caused all of my anxiety and doubts to simply melt away. A slow smile spread across his face and my goodness, does that man have a spectacular smile! I reached out my hand to him. He took it and the warmth of his touch shot electricity through my hand and up my arm. I drew him onto the porch, and then I led him through the back door. John removed his hat then he stepped across the threshold and into the kitchen. He stopped and looked down at his shoes and then back up at me with a quizzical look in his eyes.

"Don't worry about your shoes," I said. "This is an old farmhouse with well-worn floors. You can't harm them."

John followed me into the living room. I sat down on the couch and after a brief hesitation, John sat down next to me. He then put his hat on the coffee table, before settling back into the couch and turning slightly towards me so that he could look at me. He smelled good and he was so good-looking that he nearly took my breath away. Suddenly I didn't know what to say. I had so many things I wanted to say to him and even more questions that I wanted to ask him but just now, I couldn't say anything at all. We sat there in silence just drinking in the sight of each other, yet it wasn't an uncomfortable silence.

Without warning, KitKat chirped loudly and leaped up onto John's lap. John laughed and stroked KitKat's fur with his big, work-roughened hand, making me instantly jealous of my cat. The little stinkpot began purring and smurgling on John's lap. Then she turned around three times before curling up onto his lap and going to sleep.

157

"John, this is my kitten, KitKat," I said with a wry smile. "Clearly you have captivated her heart without any effort at all."

"I hope she isn't the only one smitten with me," he said with a smile. I could feel my face flaming red hot, and my embarrassment made him smile even more broadly. He reached his hand out and softly stroked my cheek. "You are beautiful and I am totally smitten with you."

"Thank you," I whispered while thinking how gorgeous his deep voice was. "You are, too. Handsome I mean."

"I'm glad you approve," he said. "I was worried that I would be a disappointment to you."

"How on earth could you be disappointing to me?" I asked in confusion and then as I saw him subconsciously tug on his shirt. For the first time, I really looked at his clothes. I noticed that his pants were denim without crease or cuff; he wore a pair of suspenders but no belt; his shirt was blue and long-sleeved although he had folded up the cuffs; he wore black socks and shoes; and his hat was a wide-brimmed straw hat. His hair was longer than I had expected and it was cut in a bowl cut. Finally it clicked and I understood.

"You are Amish!" I exclaimed.

"Yes," John admitted. "I am actually Rachel's brother."

"Why the secrecy?" I asked. "Why leave me your music and notes on my porch instead of coming over and introducing yourself? Especially after Rachel began working for me."

"It's hard to explain but I will try," John said, smiling wryly. "Amish do business and are acquainted with English—that's what we call people who are not Amish—but we do not forge close relationships with the English. Forgive me for speaking so honestly, Elise, but from the first moment I saw you, I was captivated by you. I was scared of what would happen if I met you face-to-face and I knew that my Daett and the bishop would not approve.

"The bishop is the head of our church district and enforces the Ordnung, or the rules of the church. This may not make sense to you but by giving you my music, I am entrusting you with my most precious secret. You see, Amish do not play musical instruments because it is viewed as a means of self-expression, which can cause feelings of pride and superiority. Our church songs come from a High German songbook called the *Ausbund* which has no musical notes. Instead the tunes are passed down from generation to generation.

"To compose music as I do is also forbidden for the same reason of the fear that self-expression which they teach leads to sinful pride. If anyone in my church or family knew that I composed music, I would be in a great deal of trouble. This has been my struggle for as long as I can remember. Elise, I have always heard music in my mind inspired by the world around me, the emotions that I feel, and the things that I see, touch, taste, hear, and feel. My ability to hear the music truly feels as if it is a gift to me by God. Placing the notes of the song onto the measure is my way of thanking God and praising Him for the music. In times of distress, the music is my prayer to God when words simply aren't adequate. However, my Daett, my father, the bishop, and the people wouldn't see my music as praise or prayer but as sinful pride. I would probably be shunned."

"Shunned!" I gasped. "I didn't know that still occurred!"

"Oh yes, it's still practised," said John grimly. "I know it's hard for outsiders to understand, but shunning is done out of love and concern for the person's soul. It's supposed to make them face their sin and the consequences of their sin in the hopes that this will cause them to forsake their sin. Anyway, I had just made the decision to forsake my music and to take the vow when I heard the most beautiful music that I had ever heard. I followed the sound to the edge of our cornfield. There I saw you through your living room window playing your piano. That awakened within me the desire to hear my own music played."

"You mean you had never heard your music played before?" I asked in shock.

"No," he said, smiling wryly. "Until you, my music lived only inside of my head."

"It's amazing that you can compose music without hearing it! How can you know what notes sound good together and what instruments create the sound you want?"

"I'm not sure," he shrugged. "I've just always been able to compose the music inside of my mind. I can hear a sound and know where it fits on a scale. For years, I would secretly go to the library in town. I studied every book I could find about music and in the audio-visual lab, the world of music opened up to me as I listened to recordings of the music to Bach, Beethoven, Mozart, and Purcell. As I listen to the music inside of my head, the notes begin to arrange themselves on the staff; it's like they simply fall into place. Although my church tells me that my music is a sin, I've always thought of it as a gift from God. My Daett reads the Bible to us every night and then he prays out loud. His prayers are pure poetry. His love and devotion for God and his family rings out clearly in every prayer. For me, knowing the right words to pray is difficult but when I hear the music and put it on paper, I am praying in a language understood by God. My music is the way I pray and a song of praise to Him."

"John, that is beautiful!" I exclaimed. "Your talent is astonishing to me. I have played a lot of music throughout my career and your compositions rival the compositions of composers who went to college and studied music composition. I have so many questions to ask you but they can wait. However, I really must ask you: when you referenced Purcell, did you mean Henry Purcell the English composer?"

"From the 1600s?" he asked with a smile.

"That's the one!" I exclaimed. "I'm just surprised that a self-taught composer knows about Henry Purcell. Most people who are informally trained focus on the composers that everyone knows like Beethoven and Mozart. I'm impressed."

"Like I said, I consumed literally everything that I could lay my hands on about music. I soaked it up like a sponge. I still have so much I would like to learn and need to learn. However, I am thankful for the library. It was for me a blessing from God. I think because I had to be self-taught that God gave me the ability to comprehend and understand composition as well as I do. I'm not naive: I'm sure you can look at my music and see a hundred things or more that I've done incorrectly."

"Honestly, no. The errors are very minor and minimal. Clearly your talent is a gift from God! How can anyone think that something from God is a sin?" I asked.

"That is the question I have struggled with my whole life, Elise," he said as he reached out and grasped my hand. As soon as our skins touched, I felt a tingle and warmth that spread from my hand, up my arm, and into my heart. A memory came to me.

A few years ago, I had toured a glass factory in Murano. I had watched as the master craftsman created beautiful glass from silica, soda, lime, and potassium melted together in a special furnace. When the warmth from John's touch reached my broken heart, it melted those pieces and fused them together so perfectly that all traces it had ever been broken was gone.

She had known who I was from the moment our eyes met. That knowledge caused my heart to soar. Being with her felt so wonderful and natural; it was as if half of my soul had been missing and now that I had found her, I had the piece of me that had been missing. I couldn't bring myself to think about what this meant for my future. Right now, I just wanted to bask in the joy of meeting Elise and the marvelous journey we had embarked upon of getting to know everything about each other. It was a miracle but she hadn't been repulsed by me or by the fact that I was Amish. I had convinced myself that she wouldn't want me, a plain farm boy. She was a beautiful, world-renowned concert pianist; she would want a sophisticated man of the world. But when I looked into her eyes and she into mine, all of those fears had vanished. She was mine and I was hers. Where God would take us I didn't know, but I trusted that His will would be done in our lives.

We talked for hours but the time flew by so fast. We told each other absolutely everything that we could think of, making up for a lifetime apart. She told me of her childhood: about being a child prodigy; how her Mother had expected her to practise an incredible number of hours a day and to forgo having a normal childhood; how her mother was cold and distant; her father warm and loving; and how the divorce of her parents had broken her heart and limited the time she was able to see her father. Elise had described for me her life as a concert pianist who had traveled the world and how her only glimpse of what a relationship with a man should be had been a hollow misrepresentation of what true love really is. Her life sounded as foreign and strange to me as my life as an Amish boy and man was to her. We marveled how two people from such different backgrounds as we had could not only find common ground but felt as if we were two halves of a whole. There was no fear in stating how we both felt: we were in love. After talking for a few hours, I realized that Elise was looking tired. Without even thinking about it, I opened up my arms and just as organically, she laid her head on my chest and snuggled up to me as I wrapped my arms around her. Holding her in my arms filled a hole in my heart that I hadn't even been aware was there. She belonged in my arms and I never wanted to let her go.

In the late hours of the night, we had fallen asleep while talking. The sound of a cat meowing in my ear woke me up. I was momentarily confused by my surroundings and by the irate, little furball staring at me. Then I realized that Elise was in my arms and I knew where I was; I was with my beloved. KitKat must've noticed that my attention had wandered away from her and to the beautiful girl in my arms because she meowed angrily and loudly. Elise opened her eyes and smiled up at me lovingly.

"Hello," she said softly.

"Hello," I answered. "Is KitKat always this happy?"

"Only when she is hangry," she said giggling as she sat up, leaving my arms feeling bereft and lonely.

"I'm not familiar with that word," I mused.

"Hangry is an amalgamation of the words 'hungry' and 'angry' and it is a perfect description of KitKat whenever her little belly feels empty. The cat is serious about her food!"

"I can relate to that," I said as I followed Elise into the kitchen. I watched as she moved gracefully around the room tending to the needs of her kitten. She was lovely in every aspect and in every way. She turned around and saw me looking at her. She smiled and walked towards me.

"Oh, John!" she said in a teasing tone. "Why are you looking at me like that?"

"Like what?"

"Like you could just eat me up!"

I caught her in my arms and pulled her to me, breathing in the scent of her deeply.

"Because I really, really want to kiss you," I said in a husky voice.

Her eyes blazed with a look that I decided must be passion and she stood on her tiptoes as she placed her arms around my neck.

"Well then," she said in a whisper, "I guess I might as well confess something to you."

"Hmm?"

"I really, really want to kiss you too."

I didn't need any more encouragement. I bent my face down to hers and kissed her lips. Her mouth tasted sweet as honey and her kisses were as intoxicating as wine. I kissed her lips and then her eyelids, her cheeks, and then her lips again.

"Elise, I love you."

"I love you too, John," she responded without hesitation and my heart soared.

She loved me! I held her close and thanked God for blessing me with the love of an amazing woman. My heart was full to overflowing and I couldn't imagine a more perfect moment. I could've held her forever and I never wanted to let go. Suddenly I felt the impact of something landing on my shoulder. I turned my head and met the staring eyes of KitKat who meowed into my face loudly. Elise began laughing and her laughter was contagious.

"I guess she thought she was being ignored and that you should be paying just as much attention to her as you are to me," Elise was finally able to say.

"I've always heard that when you fall in love with a girl you have to remember that her family is part of the package, but no one ever mentioned cats," I said teasingly as I plucked the little furball off my shoulder. I held her like a baby and scratched her little white belly. Her eyes practically rolled back in her head and she began to purr loudly.

"You have just made a friend for life," said Elise with a smile.

"I hope so," I said as I looked into her eyes. "I hope I have her and you in my life forever."

"Are you sure?" she teased. "Forever is an awfully long time."

"I have never been so sure of anything in my life," I said. "You?"

"Positive," she answered but then her eyes darkened and a shadow passed over her face.

"What's wrong?" I asked.

"I'm just not sure how long my life will be," she replied hoarsely.

"Hey, I just found you," I said as I quickly closed the gap between us, causing KitKat to squeak in protest of being between us. She jumped down, allowing me to hold Elise close. "I am not going to let you go."

"It's not exactly up to you," she challenged in a muffled voice.

"God just brought us together. He wouldn't do that only to take you away from me."

"Do you really believe that?"

'Yes," I said emphatically. "I do believe that, Elise. God's timing is always perfect. He knows that you need me to help you fight and beat cancer and He knows that I need you because without you I am nothing but with you, I finally understand who I am and why He made me the way He did. He made me for you, Elise. I've always believed that the music He gave me was for His ears only and that only He would ever get to hear my music out loud. But that wasn't true. He gave me the ability to hear the music that no one else can so that I could capture the notes and put them on paper in order for you to bring them to life on the piano.

Without you, there is no music and without me there are no scores but together, we make a beautiful symphony of love that will forever be a song of glory to the Lord."

"I love you, John. But I would understand if you wouldn't want to be with a bald woman with cancer," she said with downcast eyes.

"Hey," I said. "You are perfect just as you are. I love you, Elise. I will always love you."

"I love you too, John," she replied.

After that, neither of us spoke again for a long time.

CHAPTER TWELVE

It was 3:00 a.m. when John reluctantly left my house and headed out into the darkness of the night towards his home. Having him finally in my presence in person and not on paper, it was hard to watch him walk away, especially when I didn't know precisely how long it would be before we were together again. I wouldn't be able to call or text him as he did not have a mobile phone and I couldn't just walk up to his parents' house and ask to see him. This was new territory for us both, but I was confident that together we would chart our way through the unknown. My complete and utter desire to be with him shocked me. When I had been involved with Donovan, I had liked him and I had even thought I loved him. But I had never felt this craving to be with him or experienced the feeling of completeness with him like I felt when I am with John. This then was true love, I mused. Cue the singing birds, I smiled wryly. I locked the house up and headed upstairs, holding a very sleepy-looking KitKat in my arms.

"What do you think?" I asked the yawning kitten. "Would you like having John as your father?"

"Meow," she answered.

"I am so glad," I said, smiling at her. "I think he will make you a wonderful father."

With all of the excitement and the empty feeling I had without John, I thought it would take forever for me to fall asleep. I was wrong. My head had scarcely hit the pillow before I was sound asleep. My dreams were lovely and full of John and his kisses. When I woke up, I stretched and smiled at the remembrance of how wonderful it had felt to have his lips on mine. I couldn't wait to see him again but until then, I would have my memories of last night to keep me company. As if on cue, KitKat meowed loudly.

"And you," I agreed. "I have you to keep me company as well."

After forcing myself to drink some protein drink for breakfast, I went upstairs to inspect my wardrobe for an outfit suitable for Marge's funeral. It was shocking and scary to see how thin I had actually become. With the baldness, gauntness, and black clothes, I looked exactly like what I am: a cancer patient. As I stood there hating my appearance and how I looked, I remembered Marge and that I was trying to find a dress to wear to her funeral. Just thinking about Marge brought a smile to my face. She had brought such joy to my life in the midst of my illness. That's when I realized that the best way to honor Marge's memory was not to dress in black.

Later that day, I walked up to my friend's casket to tell her farewell. Roger turned and when he saw me, he smiled through his tears. His trembling hand reached up and touched the soft yellow hat on my head.

"I'd recognize that hat anywhere," he said. "It looks beautiful on you. Marge is looking down on us and I know she is happy to see you enjoying your hat. Thank you for wearing it and thank you for wearing a yellow dress. You are a ray of much needed sunshine today, and Marge would love that."

Marge's funeral was a celebration of a life well lived. She had touched many lives including mine. I looked around me at the crowd that had filled the chapel to overflowing and I noticed that like me, many were wearing hats, scarves, and shawls made by Marge. I wondered how much different this scene would be if the funeral was for me. While I was sure my death would be mentioned in newspapers and maybe even on a TV news show or two, the amount of people who would truly mourn my death was very small indeed. For that, I had no one to blame but myself.

I had lived my life for music and for music alone. I had spent hours cultivating and honing my piano skills and very little time nurturing relationships. Music is a powerful force and can do much good but I had hidden behind it instead of using it to spread joy. Sitting in my friend's funeral service, I vowed that going forward I was going to change.

With Marge gone, someone had to pick up the knitting needles and to carry on her legacy. Before doubt could set in, I stopped by a yarn shop on my way home from the funeral and made a new friend out of the shop owner, Joanne, who was no doubt excited for one of her biggest sales of the year. My first project was to be a very simple dishcloth knitted entirely in the knit stitch. The pattern was recommended by the lady at the shop and she had also directed me to the cotton yarn I would need. Within an hour, I had signed up for several knitting classes, a knitting group, and I bought: a book of patterns for knitted washcloths; two sets of knitting needles in the indicated size in case I should lose one; a bag full of yarn; a bag to carry around my knitting project; and every accoutrement for knitting that Joanne said I needed. Then I headed home. I had a lot of knitting to do and now that I craved to be with John every minute of the day, I was glad that I had a new hobby to keep my mind and hands occupied. That's when I decided that once I learned how to knit, I would learn how to knit scarves. I also determined that the first scarf I knitted would be for John and I determined that as I knitted, I would pray for him and pour my love for him into every stitch.

The day passed by as if I were in a dream. While my body was busy working on the farm, my heart and mind were consumed with thoughts of Elise. I couldn't believe how blessed I was to have a girl like her love a boy like me. It was hard not to tell my family that I was in love and I was sure that everyone could see the fact plastered on my face. The fact that no one seemed to notice and no one said anything to me was astonishing to me. However, I was grateful that I had time to process what this meant for my future and a chance to pray and think through the decision that I had to make. I was completely taken off guard that the only person who saw something had changed with me was the person who was blind. I had lifted Mamm out of the chair into her bed and was turning to walk out of the room when she stopped me.

"John," Mamm said as her hand reached out blindly for me.

I turned and walked back to her, capturing her hand in mine.

"Yes, Mamm. Is there something else you need?"

"Can you just sit for a bit and talk to me?"

"Of course," I said as I pulled a straight-back chair close to the side of her bed and sat down.

"Since before you were born I have prayed for you. It has always been my desire that you would love God with all your heart, that you would serve Him to the best of your ability, that God would provide you with a wonderful wife, and that you would be happy. I have always felt that there was a part of you that you kept hidden from us and I wish that you didn't feel the need to keep secrets from me and Daett."

These words caused me to shift uncomfortably but before I could speak, Mamm put a hand on me, stilling me and silencing me.

"John, I feel a change in you and today I feel like you are happy. Have you found a special young lady?" Mamm asked gently.

"Yes, Mamm," I smiled. "I have."

"I am pleased, John." Mamm smiled. "That is an answered prayer. I love you, my baby boy. If you love her, then I know that I will too."

It had been years since Mamm had called me her baby boy and hearing her say it brought tears to my eyes. I stood up and kissed her gently on the check.

"I love you too, Mamm," I said.

I tucked the quilt in around her shoulders like she had used to do for me when tucking me into bed when I was a child. Looking down at her, I could see the toll that her illness had taken on her in the lines on her face and this smote my heart with sadness. I placed my hand upon her head for a moment and whispered a prayer. Mamm smiled sweetly, her eyes closed.

"I am tired," she said. "I think I will go to sleep quickly tonight."

I bent down and kissed Mamm's cheek. Then I automatically bent down my head so that Mamm could smell the top of my head like she always did.

"You have the best smelling head in the world," Mamm said with a smile. "Good night, John. I love you. I will see you in the morning."

"Rest well, Mamm," I said as I turned to leave the room. "I love you too. I will see you in the morning."

When Daett came to bed an hour later and bent down to kiss her cheek, he found that it was cold. Mamm was now forever asleep. It had been both the happiest and the saddest day of my life, and a day that had changed my life forever.

While my sisters and Aunt Fannie washed and dressed Mamm's body, Daett asked if I could go to an English neighbor's house to call the funeral home and to call and leave a message for Mamm's oldest sister, Lydia, with her English neighbors who have been kind enough to allow Lydia to use their phone occasionally and have offered to take messages for her. I didn't even think about it: I just automatically headed towards Elise's house. She answered the door quickly, took one look at my face, and opened up her arms. All of the emotions that I had been holding in broke free and I went into Elise's arms sobbing like a child. We some-how made it to the couch where Elise held me as I cried. She stroked my hair and intermittently kissed the top of my head much the way that my mother used to do when I was a small child. Gradually I gained control of my emotions and I sat up mopping my face with my handkerchief. Then I looked at her beautiful face and attempted a smile.

"I'm sorry," I said as I cupped her face in my hands and kissed her gently on the lips. "Thank you for letting me cry on your shoulder, literally."

"There is no need to apologize," she said softly. "I am glad that you came to me. What's wrong, John?"

"Mamm died," I said, my voice breaking. "My Mamm is dead."

"Oh, John," Elise said with tears welling up in her own eyes. "I am so, so sorry. Is there anything that I can do?"

"Yes, actually. We don't have a telephone and I need to call the funeral home and I need to call and leave a message for Aunt Lydia in Pennsylvania. I will pay you back for the long distance call."

"Of course; my house phone is in the kitchen but there is no need for you to pay me back. I won't accept any money."

I followed her into the kitchen. While I telephoned the funeral home and Aunt Lydia's English neighbors, Elise sat next to me quietly. Just having her there with me brought me comfort. I wished I could have her by my side when I went back home, but I knew that was impossible. When I had finished the last call, I took Elise into my arms and kissed her, gently at first and then gradually deeper and more intensely. I poured all of my love and heartache into that kiss and it was difficult for me to end it. I rested my forehead against hers and we looked into each other's eyes.

"I could kiss you without stopping for forever and still I would want for more," I said, smiling wryly.

"Mmmm," was all Elise managed.

"Mamm somehow knew about you. No one else picked up the fact that I was walking on air! In spite of her blindness, Mamm saw more than any of them. She asked me if I had met someone special. She could sense it somehow. Mamm told me she was happy for me and that even before I was born, she prayed for me to be happy and for God to bless me with love. God answered her prayers with you, Elise. I am so blessed to have you. I know it isn't fair but I need to ask you to be patient with me because for the next few days it will be nearly impossible for me to get away. Please know I wish so much that I could tell everyone in the world that the most beautiful and amazing girl in the world is my love but right now is not the right time."

"I understand completely. Right now, you focus on you and your family. I will be here for you whenever you are able to come back to me. I love you, John. I am not going anywhere."

I thought that my heart would break as I watched John's horse and buggy driving away from me. If I loved him this much, felt this close to him and longed to be with him this much after being a couple for one day, I could only imagine what the future held for me. My desire to support him during this time threatened to overwhelm me but I knew that for now, I had to support him from a distance. The feeling of soft fur rubbing up against the bare skin of my calf captured my attention and caused me to smile. I looked down to see KitKat twining herself around my leg.

"Hello, KitKat," I said. "Thank you for the lovings. Momma sure did need them right now."

She looked up at me and meowed a response. Her sweet little face and eyes truly looked concerned. She melted my heart. I bent down and picked her up and kissed her forehead as she purred her appreciation.

"I love you, baby," I said to her. She looked back at me and gave me several slow blinks. I had read online that when a cat blinks at you slowly, it is their way of saying I love you. Still carrying KitKat, I went upstairs to get ready for bed but I doubted that I would be able to sleep a wink. Several hours later I was lying in bed, staring up at the ceiling and listening to KitKat's sonorous breathing in my ear. For some reason, KitKat's favorite place to sleep was with her little face buried against my neck up near my ear with one paw up in my ear and scalp and the other paw on my cheek. Her back paws rested on my shoulder. Occasionally she would smurgle and her little claws would dig into my skin a little, causing me to wince. However, the pain was worth the exchange of having KitKat's warm, little furry body snuggled up against me.

As I lay there, my mind kept busy. My thoughts were largely consumed of John and rosy dreams of love, marriage, and family brought me happiness and hope. Then the dark seeds of doubt took hold and I began to worry. I didn't know much about the Amish and I wondered if John would even be allowed to date me or marry me. I remembered that he had said that they did still practice shunning and I wondered if John would be shunned if he chose to be with me. Could I live with myself if I caused him to be separated from his family? The one thing that I knew about the Amish is that they had large families and I knew that because of my chemotherapy, there was a chance I would be barren. Would John want to marry me if I couldn't provide him with children? Then the absurdity of worrying about these things when my relationship with John was only one day old hit me. With a snort that caused KitKat to protest in her sleep, I shelved my worries for another day and finally fell asleep.

The next day passed quietly for me. Being a Saturday, I didn't have to go for chemotherapy and was able to just rest at home. I basked in the joy of knowing John and loving him. The memory of his kisses and how it felt to be in his arms made me hot and dizzy. Then I would remember that his Mamm was dead and I would feel guilty for being happy. KitKat and I spent much of the day on the back porch. I knitted while she chased bugs and sunbeams and napped. It had only been two days ago that John had walked up onto my porch and into my heart. I wondered how John was holding up. The ache to be with him was so sharp it fairly took my breath away. To distract my heart and mind, I watched YouTube videos and learned how to cast on, do a knit stitch, and how to bind off. Then I listened to an audiobook as I knitted a very simple knit-only pattern. At some point in the afternoon, it began to rain. The sound of the raindrops hitting the tin roof was hypnotic as was the rhythmic clicking of my knitting needles. Before I knew it, my eyes were getting heavy and I dropped off to sleep.

In my dream I looked around me curiously. I was standing in the middle of the road with cornfields on either side of me. The corn was tall and golden, and the sound of the wind swishing through the stalks seemed to be the only sound in the world. I looked behind me and then in front of me. There were no indicators as to where I was or where I was meant to be going. I decided to go forward because in my experience, no good ever came from going backwards. It was a beautiful sunny day with just the perfect amount of warmth to the air. As I walked, I enjoyed feeling the wind blowing through my hair. That thought caused me to stop dead in my tracks. I reached up with my hand and touched the top of my head and felt hair! Lots and lots of hair! *How had it grown back so fast?* I wondered. Then with a shrug, I walked on. Presently, a driveway appeared on my left and down the long lane, a large white farmhouse stood proudly. A lady in a long blue dress with a white apron and white cap stood on the front porch. She waved at me smilingly and beckoned for me to join her. I walked down the road noticing a big barn, a buggy, a garden, and a washing line filled with clothes that all seemed to be shades of blue blowing in the wind. When I reached the porch, the lady smiled at me warmly.

"Hello," she said. "You are Elise, aren't you?"

"Yes," I said, surprised that she knew my name. "I am Elise."

"I am Ruby. Would you come join me on the porch? It's the perfect day to sit out on the rocking chair drinking lemonade."

I climbed the steps and sat down in a beautiful rocking chair. Ruby sat down in a rocking chair next to me. Between us was a table and on the table was a tray that held a pitcher of lemonade, two glasses, a plate of cookies, and napkins. I wondered if Ruby had somehow known that I was coming, but how could that be since I myself hadn't known? I gratefully accepted the offered lemonade, realizing that I was suddenly very thirsty. The lemonade was delicious and I almost drank the entire glassful in one drink. Ruby laughed and refilled my glass. Her laugh was lovely, high and tinkled like wind chimes.

"My son John always drinks his first glass of lemonade down in one gulp like that," she said as she handed me a napkin with two cookies on it.

"John is your son? My John?" I asked in surprise.

"Yes—well, he was mine first," she reproved gently. "John is my firstborn son and he is a good man. When I learned that he loves you, I wanted so much to meet you. I was very grateful that this meeting was arranged for us."

I found this curious. I wondered who arranged our meeting but she continued to talk and the ginger cookies smelt divine. I bit into the cookie. Heaven.

"I know that you know this," she continued. "But I wanted to let you know that John is a very special young man. He has a gift that God has given to him that is also a test of his faith and commitment to God. He will need you, Elise, to pray for him, guide him, and most of all to support him. Many times in the days ahead, John will feel like he is all alone and he will need you to remind him that he is never alone. John will have a choice to make. I can't tell him which road he should choose and you won't be able to tell him either. That choice will be up to him and God. One path will be hard but will bring him great joy.

"Sometimes God places a calling on our lives that is challenging and questioned by those around us. Some people may never truly believe that he is called to this by God. The other path would be an easy choice and would be approved by many but while it is safe, it will not be fulfilling. If he choices this path, he will never reach the potential that God has given him the talent to reach. I am sad that I will not be able to be with John during this next phase of his life, but I am very thankful that God has blessed him with you."

"Thank you. That means a lot to me. You raised a wonderful son."

"You are kind, my dear," Ruby said, smiling, and she reached out her hand for mine. I placed my hand in hers and she squeezed it gently. "Now this will be our only chance to have a chat. I want to hear all about you."

It was surprisingly easy to talk to Ruby and we talked for what seemed to be an entire afternoon. We laughed, cried, drank all of the lemonade, and ate all of the cookies. When they were gone Ruby smiled, but her smile was tinged with a hint of sadness. I knew.

"I have to go now, don't I?" I asked regretfully.

"Yes, my dear, I am afraid that you do," she said as she stood up. She opened up her arms for a hug and I eagerly gave her one. In a short span of time, I had come to like and love her.

"I will miss you," I said as tears began to flow.

"I know and I will miss you," Ruby said as she wiped my tears away with her apron. "But we will meet again and that time, there will be no goodbyes."

"I like the sound of that," I said as I attempted to smile and failed. "John is going to miss you so much."

"Ach, I know. I will miss him as well but someday we will be together again," she assured me.

As I headed down the driveway, I turned back to wave goodbye. She was wiping her face with her apron but she released her apron with one hand and raised it to wave goodbye back to me. When I reached the road, I turned back for one more look and felt a stab of sadness when she wasn't there. I looked to the left and to the right. Whereas before I had felt that I must go forward, I now knew that I had to go back. Thus I turned right and headed back the way I had come. Eventually, I began to realize that my home was just ahead and to my right and my pace picked up. The wind now had a chill to it and I could no longer feel it blowing through my hair. I reached up and with disappointment, my hand felt my bald head. Just as I reached my driveway, a voice began to call at me and it felt as if my name had hooks that grabbed hold of me and strings that began to pull me towards someone that I could not see. I opened my eyes and found that John was there looking down at me with concern on his face.

"Hi," I said with a smile. "It's quite nice to wake up to your handsome face. I could get used to that. In fact, this is starting to be habit for you, isn't it?"

"Sorry," he said ruefully. "I just couldn't stand it. I wanted to see you and to say good night. The house is so full of our family and friends that I knew I would be able to sneak away. I may not get so lucky in the days ahead so I thought I would take advantage of it while it lasted. You were really deeply asleep though! It was quite hard to wake you up!"

"I was having a dream," I said slowly. "At least I think it was a dream. It was very, very real, John. I can still taste the lemonade and ginger cookies and hear her musical laugh."

"What are you talking about?" he asked.

"Let's go inside and I will tell you all about it. It has gotten cold out here while I slept."

"And dark," John said with a hint of reproof in his voice as we walked into the house. "And your back porch door was unlocked. It isn't very safe for you to be asleep out here in the dark with your door unlocked. Actually, I have a confession to make."

"A confession? This sounds ominous. Are you hungry?"

"Goodness no! I have been fed by every female in sight today! I think that women believe that food will cure grief!"

At this I chuckled as we sat down on the couch. I grabbed a blanket and spread it over both of us. John reached out his hands and placed my hands in his. I looked down at our intertwined hands: his engulfed mine and that made me feel sheltered and cherished. Work and the outdoor elements had roughened his skin. I loved the feel of him and it astonished me how much effect the simple act of hand holding had on me. I loved everything about this man including his beautiful hands.

"What is your confession?" I asked him.

"One night I came to your house to drop off an envelope and I came the back way. When I approached your house, I saw that the light was on in your screen porch. Then when I came closer, I could see that you were sound asleep on the chair. Now I would simply wake you up and take you inside but back then you didn't even know who I was and I would've scared you to death. I couldn't just walk away leaving you unprotected. So I decided to stay outside your porch and watch over you."

"All night long?" I asked in amazement.

"Yes," he said, smiling. "I stayed there until you woke up in the early hours of the morning and went inside. Then I snuck home."

"John...," was all I managed to say as my eyes filled with tears. The love and devotion that he gave to me even before we were together overwhelmed me. Since I couldn't figure out what words to say, I chose actions to say it for me. I leaned forward and kissed him.

"Now tell me about your dream," prompted John afterwards.

As I told him about my dream, John listened intently, a look of wonder slowly spreading across his face as he listened to me.

"I have no idea how it could be but Elise, you have dreamed about my Mamm and things that you couldn't have known. The words spoken to you by Mamm sound just like her. Whenever she entertained visitors, Mamm always offered refreshments. If the weather permitted it, she loved sitting outside on the porch with her visitors and she would serve them lemonade and cookies, ginger cookies to be specific. There is no way that you could have known that," John said with a tone of wonder. "Plus I don't think I ever told you that Mamm's name is Ruby."

"No, you hadn't told me her name but she did. What do you think it means?" I asked.

"The only explanation I can think of is that somehow God arranged for you and Mamm to meet and visit each other. It sounds impossible, I know, but with God all things are possible."

"I believe that," I said with a smile as I caressed John's face with my hand. "Because our love is a miracle."

His kiss, deep and passionate, demonstrated his agreement with me. Then I stopped thinking and simply basked in his love.

CHAPTER THIRTEEN

The next morning we removed all of the furniture and decorations, including those hanging on the walls, out of the living room. Then Aunt Fannie and my sisters scrubbed the room clean. Once they were finished with the cleaning, we put chairs all around the room up against the wall so that people would have a place to sit. After lunch, I drove the buggy and took my older sisters to T. Hess-A. Lonians Funeral Home and waited while they tended to Mamm. Because we had family that lived away and we had planned on having Mamm at the house for three days prior to her funeral, we had chosen to embalm Mamm. Fortunately the mortician, Mr. Thaddeus Hess, was one trusted by our people and therefore frequently used by our community. He understood our wishes and customs. This meant that no makeup was applied to Mamm's face and Mr. Hess allowed my sisters to be the ones to dress Mamm, fix her hair, and apply her cap. Another reason that our people used Mr. Hess was because he had an arrangement with the Stoltz family who owned a buggy shop where they built, repaired, and sold Amish buggies.

The Stoltz family had built a custom buggy which would hold a coffin and had a business agreement with Mr. Hess to transport deceased Amish in the manner which was fitting and in keeping with their beliefs. Once my sisters were finished, we waited in our buggy for Mamm's coffin to be loaded and then we followed her on her final journey home. When we got home, Daett and my brothers were waiting for her. I joined them and together we carried Mamm inside her house. Mr. Hess had placed the unadorned wooden catafalque in the center of the living room as requested on top of the round Amish knot rug that Mamm had made.

We gently lowered Mamm's coffin down onto the waiting surface and then stepped back. The plain wooden coffin was unadorned and would remain so as was our custom. A ray of sunshine danced on the surface of the coffin and illuminated the dark but vibrant colors of the rug and highlighted the grain of the unvarnished wooden flooring.

"Would you like to see her?" Mr. Hess asked, his voice cutting through the quiet of the room.

Daett swallowed hard and blinked his eyes rapidly as if trying to hold back tears. After a moment's hesitation, he nodded yes, answering the question. Mr. Hess went to work and with deft, well-practised movements, he opened and lowered the lid of the coffin. He then moved back from us a discreet distance, as if to give us space and privacy. His movements were remarkably quick and silent, and his demeanor was respectful and professional. We waited for Daett, allowing him the chance to see Mamm first. He made a strangled sound that startled and surprised me. Daett was not one to show his emotions; in fact, this was the second time I have ever seen him cry. Hoarse, rasping sobs shook Daett's body and his hands gripped Mamm's coffin for support. Without taking his eyes off Mamm, Daett spoke only one word to us.

"Come."

Without hesitation, we joined Daett at Mamm's coffin. Death isn't pretty and although I had seen death often enough on the farm, I wasn't prepared for how much it hurt to see Mamm dead. Her skin was blanched nearly white, and she had dark blue discoloration around her bloodless lips. The tips of her fingers were blue and she had purple mottling on her hands. She looked as if she were made up of wax and mentally, I corrected that thought. *No, she isn't made out of wax but rather out of clay. 'For dust we art and to dust we shall return,'* echoed in the recesses of my mind. I knew that it was important for me to say goodbye to Mamm and seeing her dead body was part of that process, but that didn't make seeing her dead any easier. My siblings were all crying along with Daett. I wanted to cry; crying may ease the burning ache in my eyes and the curious lump at the back of my throat. But the tears simply wouldn't come.

"Is that Mamm in the box?" I heard little Ruthie's voice ask.

I looked down to see her standing next to me. Her little face upturned as she waited for my response.

"Yes, Ruthie," I said gently. "It's Mamm."

"I want to see Mamm," she said as she held her arms up, wanting to be picked up so she could see into the coffin.

I looked at Daett for his wishes. After a couple of seconds, he slowly nodded his head. I didn't really want Ruthie to see Mamm like this but Daett was her father, so I picked her up so she could see Mamm. She looked at Mamm and her little body shuddered. She buried her face into my chest and she began to cry.

"That's not Mamm," she wailed.

Aunt Fannie came and took Ruthie in her arms. Ruthie went to her readily and clung to Aunt Fannie. She held Ruthie close as she made soothing noises. In a way, I envied Ruthie's ability to cry; I hadn't shed a tear since crying on Elise's shoulder the night Mamm died.

The next few days passed in a numbing haze. So many people came to pay their respects to Daett and our family and to say goodbye to Mamm that whenever anyone came near me, I automatically stuck out my hand to shake theirs and said thank you. I appreciated the amount of support that we had from our extended family and community, but having to hear hundreds of "I'm sorry for your loss" and having countless women crying on my shoulder and hugging me as if their hug could replace the absence of my Mamm's arms was incredibly exhausting. I didn't even feel like I had time to grieve the loss of my Mamm. Perhaps I would be able to grieve after the funeral. But for now, there were too many people to greet and the work of preparing Mamm's grave.

During this time, Leah was frequently at our home. I knew that she was there to help and support Rachel, but she continued to look at me with a glint in her eyes that made me uneasy. She would frequently bring me food or something to drink and she would try to start a conversation with me. I tried to be nice to her but at the same time I felt guilty. The last thing I wanted to do was to make her think I was interested in her when in fact I was in love with Elise. However, I didn't know how to let Leah know that I was spoken for without saying who that lady was, and she would definitely want to know the name of my love.

It is our custom to dig the graves of our dead by hand. It was back-breaking work but I welcomed it gladly. Grave digging got me out of the house and away from all of the people including Leah, and it was an outlet for the strong emotions that I was experiencing over Mamm's death.

The sky on the day of Mamm's funeral was brilliantly blue and cloudless. My grief was so strong that I felt betrayed by the beauty of the day; surely, the world should be weeping with me. For three days we had dug Mamm's grave by hand and her burial site was now ready for her. We carried Mamm's coffin to the funeral buggy and loaded her inside. We stepped back but Daett stayed close to her with his hand resting on the wood.

"Would you like to ride with her?" Mr. Hess asked Daett.

Daett nodded his assent without saying a word. Then he climbed into the back of the funeral buggy and sat down next to Mamm. As our buggy followed behind Mr. Hess's, I could see Daett. He was sitting with his head bowed, and his hands were resting on Mamm's coffin. The funeral was held in the bishop's barn as it was the largest one in our community. When we arrived at the bishop's farm, we carried Mamm's coffin into the barn and placed it in the middle of the room. Then Mr. Hess opened the coffin for the service. Throughout the two sermons and the singing, Daett stared at Mamm's face. For the first time in my life, I realized that my parents were in love. I had always known that they loved each other but since they are my parents and not very demonstrative, I had never thought about them as being sweethearts.

Now as I looked at Daett, I could see that his heart was broken and his song of despair began to build itself inside of my mind. The sound of

his heart shattering like glass was mimicked by the nonharmonic over-
tones of the triangle, and the mournful sound of the cello sang out the
bass notes of the cry of a brokenhearted man. A sweet, high and sorrowful voice sang out from the violin intermingling with the deep voice of
the cello, the lady and the man forever bound together by love and promise now saying goodbye as death ripped them apart. The mocking tones
of the grim one came lilting out of the tenor sax. Just like the friends and
family who now surrounded us and joined us in mourning Mamm, the
rest of the orchestra joined in the song macabre. When it seemed as if
grief would consume us all especially Mamm and Daett, the clear, tenor
voice of the trumpet rang out triumphantly declaring that He Who had
left His throne above to be born as a mortal babe, lived a blameless life,
died as a sacrificial Lamb, opened the gates of death with His cross and
took back the keys, thus defeating death, hell, and the grave. Then He
arose from the dead, ascended to take His place on the throne next to His
Father, and is alive forevermore! Now through Him, we can be saved
from sin and live eternally with Him. Because of Him, Mamm and Daett
would one day be reunited, we would all be reunited and never again
would we die or have to say goodbye.

The song of triumph grew louder and stronger until the song of sorrow
was completely eclipsed and silenced. This was farewell not goodbye,
because we sorrow not as those without hope or with dead hope, for ours
is a living hope because of the resurrection of Jesus from the dead. Just
as the love of God is eternal, Mamm and Daett's love which came from
God is also everlasting and in the end they win.

Once the funeral was over, we embarked on one last journey with
Mamm. This time we took her to the cemetery where her body would be
laid to rest. To outsiders we may have appeared to not be grieving as we
quietly stood around Mamm's grave, because it isn't our way to display
our emotions. However, to those who knew us, our sorrow was etched in
the lines and pallor of our faces and droop of our shoulders.

Throughout the long day, I had longed for Elise's comforting presence. Once we were all gathered around Mamm's grave, the bishop

prayed a final prayer. Mamm's coffin was lowered into the ground by ropes and then one by one every member of our family threw handfuls of sod down onto Mamm's grave. This one last symbolic gesture seemed to drive home the finality of Mamm's life. This was the last contact that I would have with Mamm and I found it to be a bitter and harsh substitute for our usual hug and her kiss on the top of my head. Usually the pall-bearers were members of the extended family or friends of the deceased but myself, Daett, and my brothers had decided that we didn't want any-one but ourselves carrying Mamm. This meant that burying Mamm was our job. As we picked up our shovels, Daett turned and addressed our friends and family in a voiced cracked by grief.

"Whenever my sons and I would head out of the house to go to work, my beloved wife would always give us a hug and then she would kiss and smell the tops of our heads. She would always tell each son and indeed every child that their head was 'the best smelling head ever'! I asked her about it once. She told me that one day when she was still a girl at home, her Daett and brothers headed out to attend to the day's work. Her young-est brother was named John and he was very attached to her and she to him. When he was born, her Mamm was sick for a great many weeks thereafter and the care for the babe had fallen to her. Consequently, they formed a very close bond. Every time he went out, she would hug him and kiss the top of his head and tell him that he had 'the best smelling head ever.' But the day came that John thought that he was a big boy now and he was teased by his older brothers about being the baby. So John told her 'no more kissing, hugging, and smelling me like a baby. I am a man!' She didn't like it but she knew he was growing up and she agreed to stop babying him and treating him like a baby. She said she didn't really know why but that day, she wanted so much to hug, kiss, and smell his head before he left out for work but she remembered her promise to him, so she pushed down those feelings and went about doing her own chores. That morning was foggy. John rode in the buggy with his Daett to go into town for supplies that they needed. A car traveling way too fast and unfamiliar with our country roads and the fact that Amish horses and buggies are frequently traveling these roads drove through a four-lane stop sign without slowing down at all. The car hit the horses and buggy. Her father was injured but survived and didn't have any lasting damage. But John was instantly killed. When she saw his body in the coffin, she kissed the top of his head and smelled his hair one last time. Death, however, had taken away the scent of the brother she loved and replaced it with the scent of decay. She told me that if she could've gone back in time, she would've listened to her heart and hugged, kissed, and smelled her brother that morning.

"Regret costs us much and permanently scars our hearts and souls. Because of the loss of her beloved brother gone without a farewell kiss, she never let any of us leave the house without a hug, kiss, and smell of the head. And in honor of her beloved brother, we named our firstborn son, John. The Bible tells us that John was beloved by Jesus. John," Daett said as he looked into my eyes, "you are beloved by your Mamm and by me. All of my children are beloved to me and to your Mamm. Now I would much rather be getting a hug and kiss from my beloved wife but instead, I've asked the bishop if we can sing her favorite hymn as my boys and I do this one last thing for our wife and Mamm."

The shovels went into the earth with a scrape as rocks and pebbles grated against the metal and the dirt thumped onto the top of Mamm's wooden coffin. Daett looked at me and nodded his head, indicating that he wanted me to begin the song. Because of my natural musical talent, it had always been easy for me to learn the melodies over the years. Consequently, whenever my family sang at home, I was considered to be the song leader or "*vorsinger*." Unconsciously we established a rhythm with our shoveling to which we began to sing "Das Loblied," or "Hymn of Praise." We do not sing in harmony but rather in unison. While my musical side craved to layer in the harmonic voices, the fact that we sing in one voice perfectly suited these people who lived in unity of belief, thought, values, and way of life. In a world filled with people who long to be unique and noticed, the Amish disdain the promoting of one's self. Instead we strive to be a member of a family and a part of a community, not an individual. While we do wish to be set apart and different from the world, we all adhere to the Ordnung which dictates every single aspect of our lives, thus we are identifiable by our faith and beliefs not by our individuality. We are truly a people living, working, praying and singing in unison for the glory of God.

Finally Mamm's grave was completely filled and covered with earth. We had done all that we could for Mamm. Now she was in God's hands. As we turned to get into our buggy and go home without Mamm, I caught sight of a figure standing at the edge of the graveyard. My heart leaped within me as I recognized Elise. She briefly raised her hand and then lowered it. We were all utterly exhausted; thus my family was intent on getting into the buggy and going home and failed to notice Elise. For this I was grateful. Just knowing that she had been there filled my heart with joy in spite of the situation. I could imagine Mamm up in heaven looking down upon us; she probably had nudged the nearest angel and said, 'See that beautiful girl there? She is my son's beloved.' In spite of it all, I felt a frisson of happiness break through the gloom of grief.

The days following the news of the death of John's Mamm were extremely difficult for me. I longed to be with him, to comfort him and hold him. There were moments of temporary madness when I nearly got in my car and drove to his house, but then I realized that this would add to John's stress and I would talk myself out of acting rashly. Still I craved him: the feel of his lips on mine, his arms holding me, and the lovely, masculine smell of him. I thought about him constantly and was nearly mad with longing for him. This was love and I knew now that what I had experienced with Donovan Shane while intense had not been love.

Nathan had provided me with information regarding the funeral arrangements. He was planning on attending the funeral and offered to take me with him. As much as I wanted to be there for John, I was afraid that it would make things even more difficult for him. After all, it would seem strange if the lady that his sister cleaned for came to the funeral. On the day of the funeral, I found myself watching the clock. Nathan had told me that Amish funerals typically lasted two hours. KitKat chased after me as I paced through the house. By noon, we were both worn out. I lay down on the couch and KitKat climbed on top of my chest, lay down, and fell asleep. Her purring soothed me and I followed her into dreamland. When I woke up, I looked at the clock and was surprised to see that two hours had passed. KitKat woke up as well and licked my face thoroughly. Then she jumped down, stretched, then walked into the kitchen and up to her food bowl. She stood there without meowing but just patiently waited for food. I smiled and honored her faith in me by filling her food bowl with her favorite cat food. I sat down at the kitchen table and watched her eat. I thought about John and how much I wished that I could be there to support him. I looked at the clock for the millionth time that day and realized that soon the graveside service would be taking place. Suddenly I had an idea. I went upstairs, washed my face, and picked out a hat to wear. Then I went downstairs and told KitKat that I would be back soon. I drove to the country lane adjacent to the cemetery and parked my car alongside the road. Thankfully the land next to the Amish cemetery was a small wooded area. The trees provided me with much needed shade and coverage. From beneath the branches of a massive oak tree, I watched in fascination as the dark procession of black buggies traveled down the road and turned into the cemetery parking lot. The men hitched their horses to the posts while the women assisted their children out of the buggies. I watched as John and the other pallbearers carried the plain wooden coffin containing his Mamm to her grave. I couldn't hear what was being said nor could I see the expressions on their faces, but the body posturing revealed the fact that the family members were suffering under the weight of grief. When I saw that John was filling in his Mamm's grave along with the help of his Daett and other male family members that I assumed were his brothers, I began to weep. Oh, to be with him and to comfort him!

Finally they were finished and people began to leave. John and his family were the last to go. Right before he got into the buggy, John turned and looked directly at me. My heart leaped within me and I raised my hand in greeting. John responded in kind and then hastily got into the buggy. No one seemed to notice and for that I was grateful. The one that I was there for had noticed me, had known I was here for him, and that was all that mattered to me.

Our house had never been so full of people. Everywhere I went there were so many family and friends that it was impossible to navigate through the house without tripping over someone once or twice. I am by nature an introvert so having a full house was difficult for me. Since we had family from Pennsylvania staying with us in addition to Aunt Frannie, our house was bursting at the seams. Daett had even given up his bed to Mamm's sister, Aunt Lydia, and her husband, Levi, while he slept on the couch. Since the weather was warm and I relished having some privacy, I had moved out to the barn where I was sleeping in the barn loft in a sleeping bag on top of the hay, giving my room up for guests. It was really quite comfortable. I had an oil lamp, my Bible, my pictures of Elise, and paper and pencils. It was a sanctuary for me in the midst of tumultuous times. While I wanted to go and see Elise, there were so many eyes watching and Daett wasn't sleeping well. At any given time of the night I knew that he could be awake pacing through the house and peering out the windows. In any case, I was exhausted and between that and my sad mood, I wouldn't be good company for Elise. Additionally, I wanted to put the song that I had written inside my mind during Mamm's funeral, "A Song of Grief and Triumph," on paper before I forget the notes. For an hour, my concentration was absolute as I completed this task. Once I was done, I was utterly spent and more than ready for sleep. I hid the song away in my hiding spot along with my paper, pens, and picture of Elise just in case anyone surprised me in the morning. Then I climbed into my sleeping bag and extinguished the lamp. In spite of my sorrowful heart, I was asleep within seconds. I'm not sure how long I had slept when a sound woke me up. I lay there in the dark listening and then I heard the sounds of someone moving about in the barn below me.

"Who's there?" I demanded as I lit my lamp, sat up, and held up the lamp to illuminate the barn below me. Daett nearly jumped out of his skin—he was so startled.

"John!" he exclaimed once he saw my face. "You gave me a *fashrekka*! I had forgotten you were sleeping out here!"

"Sorry, Daett." I grimaced. "If it's any consolation, you scared me too! I thought you were a horse thief."

Daett sighed and pushed his hat back on his head. He looked so weary and sad. His grief over the past few days had aged him. His weariness and sorrow saddened me and stirred my compassion.

"Would you like to talk about it, Daett?" I asked.

"I'm fine," Daett said unconvincingly. "I'm just having trouble sleeping. Your uncle Levi snores the loudest and most strange-sounding snores that I have ever heard. His snores sound like the squeals of a drowning pig!"

"That sounds awful," I said, chuckling. "Well, I have an extra sleeping bag up here if you would like to sleep up here with me. If you spread it out on top of the hay, it's actually a rather soft and comfortable bed. I brought it out in case I needed extra cover but it's been plenty warm and I haven't needed it."

Daett hesitated only momentarily. Then he sighed and nodded.

"I'll give it a try," he said.

A few minutes later the barn was once again plunged into darkness, but this time sleep didn't come as quickly or as easily. We were both quiet and lost in our own thoughts. My thoughts were of Elise and I wondered briefly if Daett's thoughts were of Mamm. This question was answered a few minutes later when Daett spoke, breaking the silence.

"Did I ever tell you how I met and fell in love with your Mamm?" Daett asked me.

"No," I answered, somewhat surprised. "I never really thought about it. I guess I assumed that you met each other at church. But now that I think about it, you grew up here in Indiana while Mamm grew up in Pennsylvania. So how did you meet?"

"I was nineteen years old. It may seem hard for you to believe but I was a shy young man and it was really hard for me to speak to young ladies. When I liked a young lady, it would take me a long time to work up the courage to speak to her. By the time I would get up the nerve to do so, another young man would already beat me to the punch. It was very frustrating," Daett said, chuckling. "I despaired of ever finding a wife. It was the end of May, I can't remember the exact date now, but no doubt your Mamm would've been able to tell you when disaster struck.

"A massive storm system bore down on Pennsylvania. Two huge category 4 tornadoes tore through an area heavily populated by an Amish community. Many families lost their homes and barns as well as their belongings and livestock. The devastation was terrible. Ten people including three children lost their lives. It is our way to care for our people and typically when a family suffers a loss like this, the Amish church group that the family belongs to will rally around them and meet their needs. However, in this situation, nearly every family in the group was affected and in need of help themselves. Amish bishops and preachers all across America got together groups made up of men who volunteered to take their tools and supplies and to travel to Pennsylvania to help their fellow Amish in need. I volunteered to go.

"I stayed for two weeks and I helped build so many barns and houses that I lost count. It was one of the most exhausting experiences of my life but it was also one of the most rewarding. You will find out, John, when you sacrifice and act selfless to meet the needs of others, that is often when God will reward you by meeting your needs and sometimes even your wants.

"On my sixth day in Pennsylvania, I was on yet another devastated Amish farm. This particular family had lost the house, their barn, most of their livestock, and their Mamm and her infant daughter. In spite of all of that horrific loss, the family was so gracious to us and thanked us multiple times. It was a hot day and at noon we had taken a break for lunch which was provided to us by local Amish ladies. I was sitting under the shade of a tree drinking some water and visiting with another young Amish man who was also there helping. He told me that his family had been mercifully spared: no one in his family had been killed or injured, and they had very little damage to their house or barn. I looked up and saw the most beautiful girl I had ever seen walking towards us carrying a pitcher of lemonade. She was smiling at us and her smile was as bright as the sun. My thoughts must've shown on my face because the young man, Amos, looked at me and asked me:

"'What has struck you dumb all of a sudden? Are you suffering from heat stroke?'

"'The most beautiful young lady in the world is walking towards us,' I stammered out. 'Do you know her?'

"Amos turned to look and see who was coming towards us. When he saw her he burst out laughing, much to my indignation and chagrin.

"'Know her?!' he exclaimed. 'Of course, I know her! That's not the most beautiful girl in the world! That's my sister, Ruby.'

"When Ruby reached us, Amos was still laughing. She ignored this as if it were a normal occurrence. I was to learn that laughing is something that Amos does a lot. But at the time, his laughter made me nervous because I was afraid that Ruby would ask why he was laughing. To my relief she didn't. She merely asked if we wanted more lemonade. I agreed to this readily and held out my glass for her to refill. I hoped that this would distract her from the jocularity of her brother. Fortunately for me her attention was captured by her task but unfortunately for me, her brother's attention remained squarely on the subject matter of my opinion about her beauty.

"'Ruby,' said Amos as he stopped laughing at me so he could speak, 'you will never believe what my new friend, Abram Yoder, just said to me.'

"My face flushed red with embarrassment and I wished that the ground would open up and swallow me. Then I thought about getting up and running away but instead I stayed frozen in place, staring at the ground like it was the most fascinating thing I had ever seen.

"'What was that?' asked Ruby in her beautiful voice.

"'He said that you are the most beautiful girl in the world!' Amos roared as he collapsed in laughter yet again. 'I told him you aren't beautiful! You are my sister!'

"To this day I still don't know how I got the courage but instead of continuing to act like a frightened little mouse, I squared my shoulders, lifted up my eyes, and looked directly into her gorgeous green eyes.

"'I stand by my statement,' I said as I continued to look into her eyes. 'You are the most beautiful girl in the world.'

"Ruby's gaze held my own and everything else seemed as if it faded away.

"'Thank you,' she said softly. 'You are too kind. What did my brother say your name is?'

"'Abram,' I answered her. 'My name is Abram Yoder.'

"'Nice to meet you, Abram Yoder. My name is Ruby Lapp.'

"By this time Amos's laughter had faded away and he had picked up on the fact that there was most definitely sparks flying between me and his sister. He slung an arm around my shoulder and spoke to me in a loud whisper.

"'You know, I have an idea for you, my friend,' he said with a gleam in his eyes. 'Tonight there is a singing in the Fisher's barn. I am planning on taking my girlfriend who really is the most beautiful girl in the world and I am not very happy about having to give my sister a ride as well. So since I would like to be alone with my girlfriend, you would be the best friend in the world if you would give Ruby a ride to and from the singing! What do you say?'

"'I would love to give you a ride, Ruby,' I said. 'Would you do me the honor of allowing me to escort you to and from the singing?'

"'I would love to,' she said with a smile.

"Relief and joy flooded my heart. I couldn't believe that she had agreed to accompany me. That night I followed the directions that Amos had given me and drove a buggy I had borrowed to their house. Ruby was outside sitting on the front porch swing. When she saw me coming, she leapt up off the swing and porch and nearly ran towards me. Her excitement for my arrival made me think of the passage of the Bible where Abraham's servant has brought home a girl named Rebekah as a bride for Abraham's son, Isaac. As they were arriving, Isaac looked up and saw the camels coming. Then Rebekah looked up and when she saw Isaac, she got down from her camel and went to him."

Daett paused for a moment as we both think about a young Rebekah running to meet a bridegroom that she has never met yet somehow she instinctively knows that he is her betrothed. It was a beautiful story and I knew that there was a song residing in that passage of Scripture waiting for me to write it. *One day*, I promised myself and God, *when you let me know the time is right, I will put the notes of Isaac and Rebekah's song onto the waiting stanzas*.

"When I saw Ruby's eagerness to greet me, it brought that passage of Scripture to me. I knew then that she was the lady for me. She was my beloved, John. I loved your Mamm and she loved me. She truly lived up to her name and epitomized Proverbs 31:100. Ruby was a virtuous woman and her price was far above rubies. She was priceless and irreplaceable. My heart is broken, John, and I don't think I will ever recover from her loss."

Daett's voice broke and he began to cry. I didn't know what to do. He had always been so strong. Throughout my life, he had been my protector and comforter. Now our roles were reversed. As always, music is what God provides to me for every emotion and situation that I face and tonight was no exception. To my mind came "Ausbund Hymn 100." This hymn was written by fourteen different Amish men while held prisoner in the Passau prison in 1537. These men were persecuted and imprisoned for five years during which time some of them died. Yet they held fast to their faith and their belief in God. Instead of wallowing in despair about their situation, they praised God and wrote this hymn as a song to worship God while in the bowel of a prison. Consequently this hymn is one

193

of my favorites and one that I turn to in times of difficulty as it reminds me to praise God always. In the dark barn that was filled with the sound of my Daett's grief, I began to sing "Ausband Hymn 100." By the time that I had reached verse 8, Daett had begun singing through his tears along with me:

> *Awake, you Christians all.*
> *And grasp it courageously*
> *With a sound rich in joy,*
> *Reach for this crown*
> *Which God has promised to us.*
> *Through His Holy Spirit*
> *He wants to show us His help,*
> *That we may praise Him*
> *In affliction most of all.*

By the time we had finished all fourteen verses, both of our voices which had started out weak and cracked were strong and true and our hearts were comforted. Mamm had told me one time: "Whenever you feel overwhelmed or sad and like God has forsaken you, begin to praise God either with scripture or in song. The Bible tells us that God inhabits the praises of His people. So when we praise Him, He inhabits our praise and we are assured that He is with us and our sorrow will be lifted." In the now quiet dark, I smiled. Mamm had been right.

CHAPTER FOURTEEN

S leep was eluding me. I couldn't stop thinking about John. I wondered how John was and if he was able to sleep. It had been days since I had seen him and I longed to feel his strong arms around me and his lips on mine. I wanted to breathe in his clean masculine earthy scent and to hear his beautiful deep voice. At 4:00 a.m., I gave up trying and went downstairs with KitKat following close on my heels chirping the whole way. I went into the kitchen and gave an ecstatic KitKat a snack. Then I decided to make myself some tea. A few minutes later I was on the couch with a steaming mug in one hand and a remote in the other. I quickly realized that there was nothing on TV except for repetitive news and infomercials. Sighing, I turned off the TV and looked at KitKat who was now meticulously grooming herself.

"So what do you want to do?" I asked KitKat. She paused from licking between her claws to meow at me and then went back to licking. "Well, that's all well and good for you but I don't bathe by licking myself with my tongue."

Although watching KitKat cleaning herself was entertaining, in five minutes she was done and sound asleep in the corner of the couch, leaving me bored yet again. I was cozy under the blanket and KitKat was on top of my feet, keeping me both captive and warm. With limited entertainment options in my current position, I looked around for something to occupy my time. Luckily for me, I hadn't changed anything in the house since my grandparents' time and I do mean anything. Which meant that there was a magazine basket next to my side of the couch. I lifted it up onto my lap, expecting to dislodge a bunch of dust but found none. Rachel really was a world-class cleaner. The magazine basket was veritable treasure trove of vintage publications. Some of the issues were twenty years old. Looking at the magazines made me smile. I hadn't thought about it for a long time but in the evenings, Poppy had loved reading *National Geographic*, the *Saturday Evening Post*, *Reader's Digest*, and *Guidepost*. As a child I had loved pouring over these magazines, especially the *National Geographic*. Once again I found enjoyment in reading the articles and looking at the pictures until nearly dawn, when I finally fell asleep and dreamed of exotic lands and unusual customs.

I woke up to a very insistent KitKat who was standing on my chest and meowing very loudly at me. When she saw me open my eyes, she jumped off my chest and walked towards the kitchen. She paused and looked back to see if I was following her, and when she realized that I was not, she began meowing at me again.

"All right! All right!" I said as I threw the blanket off and got up. "You shouldn't be hungry. I filled your bowel at four this morning."

After feeding my insistent kitty, I went and got a shower and dressed. I was just finishing my second cup of coffee and starting to feel more human when I heard a knock on my door. I went to answer it with my heart pounding. I was hoping that John would be standing there. Instead, it was Rachel.

"Hello," she said shyly. "I've come to clean for you. I'm sorry I haven't been here in a week. Have you been okay?"

"Come in," I said, smiling. "I missed you but I have been fine. I am sorry about your Mamm."

"Dank," she said as she came inside. "And Dank for the fruit basket that you sent to us. It was much appreciated."

Within minutes Rachel was in full force cleaning mode, and KitKat had run up the stairs to hide from the vacuum cleaner underneath the bed. I had to leave Rachel alone as I was scheduled to begin the consolidation phase of my treatment with chemo that afternoon. She voiced her under-standing and assured me she would be fine. KitKat refused to come out from under the bed to tell me goodbye.

Chemo without Marge was more difficult. Her chair had been filled by a very elderly man who was nearly deaf and slept and snored loudly the entire time. Consequently I had begun wearing earbuds and listening to either music or audiobooks during my treatments and while I found that I enjoyed the feeling of solitude and of being surrounded in story or music, I deeply missed my friend Marge. I had forgotten how tired and rotten chemo made me. I had difficulty staying awake while driving home, and I had barely made it into the house when the nausea hit me hard. I stumbled into the downstairs bathroom and was violently sick in the toilet. A warm fuzzy body rubbed up against my legs, purring loudly, and I realized that sweet little KitKat was trying to comfort me. I smiled weakly at her but before I could speak, I had to vomit yet again. I vom-ited until I no longer had anything left in me and I was simply retching and dry-heaving. I collapsed onto the floor and laid my head down on the cold tile floor. I was utterly exhausted and spent. Within seconds I was asleep.

I heard John's voice and I thought I was dreaming. But then I felt his strong arms around me and I felt him pick me up.

"*Oh der Schatz*," I heard him say but I was too weak to say any-thing back.

He carried me upstairs and laid me down in my bed. I felt a cool washcloth washing my face and warm blankets covering me. Bliss. I heard whispered voices and wondered who else was here but I was sim-ply too tired to care. John was here with me and KitKat was purring by my side. All was well.

Most of our family left the day after Mamm's funeral and life had gotten back to normal as was possible without Mamm. At Daett's request,

Aunt Fannie stayed on, much to my relief. Rachel went to work at Elise's and I envied her so much. At dinner we were all pretty quiet, even the little Ruthie. Rachel was back at the table with us.

The Sunday before Mamm's death, Rachel had made a confession before the church and begged everyone's forgiveness. I suppose the bishop had felt bad for our family and since Rachel had abided by everything requested of her including confessing, repenting of her sin, and promising to forsake sin, he had lifted the Bann on her sooner than expected. Since little Ruthie really needed Rachel right now, I was very thankful for this. Aunt Fannie was good with her too, but Rachel and Ruthie had been close all of Ruthie's life. However, I was most grateful that Rachel had been reconciled to the church and our family before Mamm's death. I wasn't sure if Rachel would have been able to bear it if Mamm had died while Rachel was still shunned. That evening, I had assisted Rachel in getting Mamm into bed. We had kissed Mamm good night and turned to leave when Mamm called out Rachel's name. We both stopped and looked at Mamm.

"Rachel," Mamm said. "I wanted to tell you how happy I am that you have repented and that you are no longer shunned. Having to turn my back on my child was the hardest thing I have ever done. I want you to know that I have never once stopped loving you and I have always been thankful that God blessed me with you as my daughter, my firstborn daughter. I know what you have been through was painful and it breaks my heart that you have felt such hurt. You may not understand or believe me but although I know your feelings were real and strong, what you had with Daniel Lapp was not love. Since before you were born, before any of my children were born, I prayed to God that my children would serve Him and love Him; that they would always be in His will and that He would provide my children with mates that would love them, treat them well, and serve God with them. God has always answered my prayers. Granted the answers were not always what I expected or wanted, but God knows best and I trust Him. That is why I know that God has a good man for you, Rachel. A man who will love you purely and truly the way that

Abram loves me. I know your heart is broken right now but one day a good man will love you so well that your heart will heal completely with barely a trace left that it was ever once not whole."

"Oh, Mamm," Rachel said as she laid her head down on Mamm's breast like she did as a babe. "I love you, Mamm. I'm so sorry that I caused you and Daett such pain and shame. Please forgive me."

"Of course I forgive you, *dochder*," Mamm said as tears ran down her cheeks and into Rachel's hair.

"I forgive you as well, *dochder*," Daett's said as he strode past me. He knelt down next to Rachel and wrapped his arms around Rachel and Mamm both.

It was a moment in time that felt sacred. The sights, sounds, word, emotions, and tears would forever be with me, indelibly imprinted upon my mind. God's grace and forgiveness were clearly demonstrated to me that night as I watched my parents forgive my sister and reconciled themselves with her, bringing her back into the family fold without impunity.

This evening, Rachel was the first one to speak and her voice and words jarred me out of reminiscence and back to the present.

"I went back to work today," she said. "I feel sorry for that English lady."

"Why?" I asked, unable to stop myself.

"She had to start back on her chemo treatments today. The last time she was taking those, she was so sick and vomited all the time. Even the smell of water would make her sick. She's already a little thing—she doesn't have any extra weight to lose."

"That's so sad," commented Aunt Fannie. "Does she have any family to help her?"

"No," answered Rachel sadly. "She is an only child and her Daett and grandparents are dead. Her Mamm is still living but she isn't close to her. From the little she has said about her Mamm, I don't think she has a good Mamm like I did."

"Your Mamm was one of the best," said Aunt Fannie. "Perhaps I can do something to encourage your English lady."

"You are so thoughtful, Aunt Fannie," Rachel said. "You are always doing and caring for others."

"That she is," Daett said. He had been so quiet lately that when he spoke we all looked up at him in surprise. "Fannie has always put others first and been a nurturer even as a little girl. She is a couple of years older than me and was always looking out for me. But when I started school, Fannie took me under her wing and became my fierce protector. In fact, her devotion to her little brother got her in a whole mess of trouble once!"

"Aunt Fannie got in trouble?" asked Ruthie, her eyes wide and round.

"She sure did," said Daett, chuckling.

"Now Abram, you don't need to tell everything you know," said Aunt Fannie, looking quite flustered.

"Remember der Bu, Fannie?" asked Daett teasingly.

"Of course, I do," Aunt Fannie said. Her face was beet red and she was fanning herself with a placemat.

"Tell us about it, Daett," asked Rachel and the rest of us chimed in as we begged him to tell us about Fannie and der Bu.

"Well, der Bu was ornery as he could be. For some reason, he took a dislike to me and was determined to make my life difficult."

"He was jealous of you, that's what it was," interjected Aunt Fannie.

"Jah that's probably true," agreed Daett. "Every day he did something to torment me: he put a frog in my desk, getting me in trouble with die Tietschern; he knocked my lunch out of my hands; he would throw the ball deliberately hitting me in the face and would insist it was an accident; he sat behind me and he would sharpen his pencils to a fine point and then he would jab me with it; and he called me names. It got so bad that I didn't want to go to school anymore."

"What a horrible child!" exclaimed Rachel indignantly and the rest of us chimed in, agreeing with her and declaring our outrage that anyone would dare to treat our Daett that way when he was a little Bu.

"Of course my Mamm and Daett wouldn't let me skip school. During family prayers, Daett read to us from the Bible about forgiveness and then he would look me in the eyes and tell me that I was to be like Jesus and to forgive der Bu and turn the other cheek," Daett paused and chuck-led. "As it turns out, he should've been looking Fannie in the eyes. It was a beautiful spring day and die Tietschern let us eat lunch outside that day. It had rained the night before and die Tietschern instructed us to stay away from and out of mud puddles. I was sitting with some of my friends eating my lunch. Our Mamm was a wonderfully gut baker and she loved making all kinds of yummy things. She would always wrap up a piece of whatever yummy dessert she had made and put it in our lunch pails. And because our Daett was a dairy farmer and Mamm thought that you had to drink milk when eating dessert, we always had an extra thermos full of milk in addition to a thermos of water. I was a growing boy and the dessert and milk helped to keep my hunger at bay until Nachtesse.

"That day, Mamm had packed me three soft molasses cookies which as you know is my favorite dessert. I was happily eating and talking with my friends when der Bu grabbed my cookies and my milk thermos and took off. He sat back down where he had been eating and proceeded to eat my cookies. Now he was a lot older and bigger than me so I was afraid to confront him. I was naturally upset over losing my milk and cookies but my main worry was how to get the thermos back because I knew that I would be in trouble with Mamm if I didn't. Once I was finished eating what I had left of my lunch, I went to Fannie to ask my older and wiser die Schweschder what I should do. When I told her what der Bu had done, Fannie became angrier than I had ever seen her. She got up and marched over to where der Bu was sitting and said to him loudly:

"'Are you a Sau or are you a Bu?' she demanded.

"He looked up at her with a look of utter ignorance on his face.

"'What?' he asked.

"'I asked you if you are a Sau or are you a Bu?' she said loudly.

"'I'm a boy, of course,' he said snidely.

"'No. I don't believe you are a Bu,' she replied. 'You are obviously a Sau because only a Sau would steal food and milk from an innocent little boy. Since you are a Sau, you need to sit where die Sau sit and not where der Bu sit.'

"She twisted his arm behind him painfully, causing him to howl. She forced him up on his feet and marched him to a mud puddle. Then she pushed him hard, causing him to fall face first into the mud puddle! She went to the table, picked up my thermos and the one remaining cookie, as well as the rest of der Bu's sandwich. Der Bu had rolled over but was still sitting in the mud puddle. Fannie threw his sandwich down into the mud next to him and looked at him coldly.

"'There,' she said severely. 'Since you want to behave like die Sau, you can eat like a Sau.'

"With that, Fannie turned her back on der Bu and walked to me. She gave me back the remaining cookie and my thermos of milk. She was my hero!" Daett finished his tale and smiled fondly across the table at die Schweschder.

We were all laughing so hard tears were streaming from our eyes. It felt so gut to laugh, so wonderfully gut. Mamm would be happy to see that we were able to laugh even though we were heartbroken over her death.

"Wow, Aunt Fannie!" I said. "Remind me to never get you angry at me!"

"Did you get in trouble?" asked Rachel.

"Of course!" exclaimed Aunt Fannie. "Die Tietschern spanked me with the paddle, Mamm spanked me with a switch, and Daett spanked me with a leather strap. My backside was sore for a week or more! Ach I tell you that Sunday was pure torture for me! The service went on for four hours that day and whenever I would squirm trying to get a little relief, Mamm would pinch me severely! That was her way to correct us quietly in church. By the time church was over, not only did I have a sore backside, my left upper arm was also sore and covered with small bruises from the pinches! As if all of that wasn't bad enough, I also had to stand up in front of the school and apologize to der Bu and to die Tietschern and the rest of the students for my behavior. The bishop came and talked to me and prayed for the Lord to remove my 'vile temper.'

He told me that an Amish man wouldn't want to marry a woman with a temper. Hmmm, maybe that's why I never got hitched!"

This caused us to laugh again. Once our laughter quieted, she spoke again.

But you know, I felt like the biggest heichle because even though I apologized, I did not feel remorseful at all! I still don't! That was the end of der Bu picking on you too, wasn't it der Bruder?"

"It was indeed," agreed Daett.

"I saw him at church Sunday," said Aunt Fannie. "He is very fat, his nose looks like a pink snout, his big ears stick out, and his head is bald! I think he really is a Sau!"

Throughout the rest of the evening, I couldn't stop worrying about Elise. I wanted to go check on her but I wasn't sure I would be able to sneak away without being seen. However, Daett went to bed early and shut his door firmly. Before long the house was silent, with everyone happily back in our own rooms and beds including Aunt Fannie who was happily ensconced in what had been Mamm and Daett's room before they had moved downstairs.

I waited until it had been quiet for an hour before slipping out of the house and through the field to Elise's. Her house was quiet but I could see a few lights on. I knocked on the door but she didn't answer. I debated on what I should do. Perhaps I should just go back home, but I couldn't shake the concern that I had for her. I felt the key she had given to me that was in my pocket. Her trust in me warmed my heart but when she had told me why she wanted me to have the key, it nearly broke my heart. Although the cancer had eventually made her too weak to clean the house, at first the real reason she had hired a house cleaner was because she was afraid that she would die alone and not be found for a while.

"What does it say of me as a person that I could die and no one would miss me?" she had asked me.

"I would miss you," I had said.

Still she had persisted and wanted me to take the key. She was sick and what if she couldn't answer the door and KitKat needed food? I had finally agreed to take the key and I must admit that it made me feel good because I felt that she was under my protection now. Now that I was here, I couldn't shake the feeling that something was wrong, I made the decision to use the key and let myself into her house. I called out for her but she didn't answer me; however, KitKat came bounding to me, meowing insistently and after rubbing herself on my legs, she began to walk away. She stopped and turned to look at me and meowed loudly before she began walking again.

"Are you wanting me to follow you?" I asked her.

She meowed in response and I found myself following her. She led me into the bathroom where Elise was lying on the floor. I rushed to her side and called out her name. She was so pale and quiet but thank God she was still alive. Her eyes opened very briefly and then she closed them again as if it was just too difficult to wake up. I picked her up. Dear God, how had I not realized how frail and thin she had become? She weighed next to nothing. I easily carried her up the stairs and to her room. I managed to get her into her bed and covered her up with her blankets. Then I went to her bathroom and got a washcloth, dampened it with warm water, and rubbed one corner of the cloth on the soap. I went back to her and washed the dried vomit around her mouth with the soap corner of the cloth, and then I rinsed the soap off with one of the other corners of the cloth. She stayed asleep through it all. KitKat had snuggled up next to Elise and was purring loudly.

"You are a good girl, KitKat," I said to her as I patted her head. She licked my hand in response as if to say thank you.

I pulled the straight-backed chair in the corner up close to Elise's bed and sat down beside her. I was holding her hand and praying silently when I heard a floorboard creaking. KitKat's head shot up, her ears straight up and alert.

"What are you doing?" a voice hissed.

I looked up; I was shocked to see Rachel standing in the door of Elise's bedroom staring at me with a mixture of surprise and anger on her face. I stood up but was momentarily unable to speak—I was so shocked to see my sister standing there.

"I asked you a question," Rachel hissed as she took a step into the room and looked at Rachel's sleeping figure. "What are you doing?"

"Rachel, I can explain," I began.

"Well, you better!" she snapped.

I crossed the room quickly and quietly. I left the room and motioned for Rachel to follow me. She looked at Elise again who had thankfully remained asleep and then reluctantly followed me down the stairs and into the living room.

"I didn't want to wake Elise up," I explained unnecessarily.

Rachel just stared at me, her eyes hard.

"We are in love, Rachel," I said. "Elise and I are in love. I am here because I was worried about her. I found her lying on the floor in the bathroom with dried vomit on her face. I carried her upstairs to her bed and washed her face and tucked her in. She seems okay, just exhausted. I was just watching over her to make sure she is okay and I was praying for her."

"How did you get in?" she hissed.

"What?"

"You said that when you arrived you found Elise on the floor of the bathroom. If that is true, then how did you get in her house?" she elaborated further through gritted teeth.

"I have a key," I explained.

Rachel stared at me dumbfounded.

"You have a key?"

"Yes; you know that Elise is sick. She gave me a key in case of events like what has happened tonight," I explained.

"And is that the only reason you have a key to an English lady's house?" Rachel asked with a hard edge to her voice.

"What do you mean?" I asked cautiously.

"You seem awfully comfortable in her house and in her bedroom," Rachel said through gritted teeth. "You run to Daett and the bishop to tattle about me and Daniel while you are secretly having an illicit relationship with this Englishwoman? You *heichle!*"

I stepped back from her, startled by her venom. I knew that my family would be unhappy about my relationship with Elise because she is not Amish, but I had not anticipated Rachel's anger towards me or that she would compare my pure and loving relationship with Elise with her illicit love affair with Daniel Lapp. Her words hurt and they made me angry.

"Rachel," I said, struggling to keep my voice calm. "I can see why you would think that my secret relationship with Elise makes me a hypocrite. However, it is not the same as your situation at all. You were having an affair with a married man; a man who has a wife and children. And his wife? *Sie* is an *ekschpeckte!* Your affair with Daniel was adulterous! It was sinful. My relationship with Elise is pure. We are not having sex. Our love is true and from God. We are not committing a sin. There is no comparison between your sinful adultery and my love for Elise!"

Rachel slapped me across the face, hard. My hand went to my cheek. I was shocked. Rachel had never been violent towards me before, not even when we were children.

"How dare you!" she exclaimed. "If your relationship with Elise is pure, then why are you keeping it secret? Is not what you are doing against the Ordnung?"

"Yes, it is against the Ordnung," I sighed. "I have kept it a secret because it started very innocently. Then as our relationship progressed, Mamm had a stroke and then passed away and everything happened with you. There was just so much going on with our family that I didn't want to add to the stress and pain, but I am planning on telling Daett and the family once things have settled down a bit. Rachel, there is something about me that you don't know because I have never been able to tell you. Please sit down and listen to me for a moment. Please?"

She hesitated for a moment and then to my relief, she nodded and sat down on the sofa. She crossed her arms and wrapped them around herself as if to create a protective cocoon where she would be safe. I sat down next to her and I bared my soul to my sister. KitKat came down the steps and looked at us quizzically. Then she walked over to the sofa and, after staring at me just for a second, she jumped up onto my lap. The warmth of her instantly calmed my nerves a little. I began to pet her and scratch her head as I talked to Rachel.

"Listen and tell me what you hear," I told her.

She looked at me startled. Whatever she had been expecting me to say, this was not it.

"Please," I prompted her. "Humor me. Close your eyes and tell me what you hear."

After a few seconds, she closed her eyes. I did the same. We sat in silence for several minutes before speaking.

"Now what?" Rachel asked, looking bored.

"What did you hear?" I asked her.

"Nothing," she said, shrugging.

"Nothing at all?" I pursued.

"Well, just the ticking of the clock and KitKat purring," she said with a smile as she looked at the now sleeping furbaby on my lap.

"Let me tell you what I hear," I said. "I hear the sound of a beautiful and calming lullaby. A stick and a soft mallet striking two woodblocks mimics the tick tock of the clock. The traditional Australian Aboriginal instrument, the didgeridoo at a frequency of 20 to 30 vibrations per second reproduces the purring of the cat. Then the piano begins to play a beautiful melody. The cello and violin join in and then the woodwind begin to play softly. As the song progresses and builds, the brass instruments join the chorus singing the happy song that says, 'This is home where I am safe and loved.' Sleepiness comes born on the wind of the flute as the brass fades out. Then the cello and violin soften and then cease. Lastly the piano becomes more and more quiet until its voice is also silent in slumber. At last all of the instruments are still and all that remains is the soft tick-tocking of the stick and soft mallet softly striking two wood blocks mimicking the continuation of time and the didgeridoo softly purrs like the sleeping cat."

We sat listening to the clock and cat for a few minutes, neither one of us speaking. Rachel looked at me, her expression bemused.

"That is what I hear; it's what I have always heard. The world to me is music waiting to be written down on paper and then released back out into the world that created it. I honestly had no idea that I was unique and that where I heard music, others simply heard sound until one day when I talked to Daett about it. He told me that was foolishness and that I was to stop indulging these childish fancies. But he didn't understand that the music was a part of me. At first I listened to Daett and I really did try not to hear it. However, no matter how I tried not to, the music was there! How can I live in this beautiful world that God has created and not hear the symphonies that it creates? For years I learned all that I could about music, instruments, and composition."

"But how?" asked Rachel.

"I would often go to the library. I would listen to music there and I would borrow books and learn all that I could. I taught myself how to compose music and to put it down onto paper. Then I began to put the songs I heard around me down on paper while up in my deer stand or in the barn loft at night. And I hid my music from everyone, Rachel." I sighed. "I don't know how to explain it to you but when I compose a song, it feels like I am praying to and praising God. I know that this gift of music was given to me by God. And if my music is from Him and for Him, then how can it be sin? I have struggled with this issue for years. I had come to the conclusion that no matter what I felt and believed, I would not be able to be Amish if I continued to write music. So I determined to stop. I was going to get rid of all of my music and I was going kneel and take the vow.

"Then one day while I was in the cornfield working, I heard the most beautiful music. I followed it and I saw Elise through the open window and heard her playing her piano. It awakened the desire within me to hear my own music played aloud. I wrote a note to Elise asking her to play my music and I placed it in an envelope along with one of my compositions. I placed it under Elise's door. Then as I hid in the cornfield, I listened to her playing my song. It was beautiful; she was beautiful. I listened and I cried. I knew I could never be the same. That moment in time had changed me forever. We corresponded for a while. We wrote notes to one another and I continued to bring her music to play. Through music and notes, we began to fall in love. Eventually we decided to meet one another face to face. I was so scared. What would she think of me? Would she find me attractive? Would she be dismayed that I was Amish? I had so many fears but the love I felt and the desire to be with her overcame them all. One look into her eyes was all it took. As soon as our eyes met, I knew that she loved me just as much as I love her and that we were made by God for one another."

"And I love John with all my heart and soul," said Elise.

Rachel and I both looked up to see a very pale Elise standing there.

"You shouldn't be out of bed, der Liewer," I said as I jumped up and hastened to her side.

"I'm fine," Elise said. "Just a little weak."

"Come and sit down with us on the couch," I urged her.

"I will sit down," she said, smiling. "But at the piano."

Elise sat down on the piano bench and smiled at Rachel.

"I want to play one of John's songs for you," she said. "When I moved here, I was broken. My heart had been broken because the man that I thought I loved didn't want a sick girlfriend. I was diagnosed with cancer and scared that I might not live. I was alone without anyone to support me and quite frankly I was very depressed. Then John started writing me notes and bringing me the most beautiful music to play. He shone a light into my dark distressed world and made life worth living again. I didn't know anything about him. I didn't know his full name or what he looked like. I didn't know his background or anything about his life. But through his music and our correspondence, I began to fall in love with him. For the first time in my life, I am truly happy. I now know what true love really is. I can't imagine my life without John. This song is the very first song that John brought to me. It's entitled 'Spring Morning.'"

Elise began to play. It was the first time that a member of my family had heard my music and I found that I was quite nervous. I couldn't watch her to see her reaction. Instead, I closed my eyes and simply enjoyed Elise's superb playing. As the music filled the room and wrapped me in its beauty, all of my fear, stress, and worry vanished. I was transported to the day that God gave me the song and I once again rejoiced and praised the Lord. Everything and everyone else melted away and in my heart, mind, and soul, I began to talk to Him. Suddenly everything became clear and all doubt was gone.

I praise You, I said to Him within my soul. *I love you and with my life I vow that I and my family will live a life of praise to You in everything we do. Your will is my will. I commit myself to you. As for me and my house, we will serve you, Lord.*

When I opened my eyes, I saw that Elise's face was shining as if illuminated from within. I then looked at Rachel. Tears were coursing down her cheeks and she had a look of awe on her face and wonder in her eyes. She looked at me as if she were seeing me for the very first time. Truly something wonderful had happened.

"John, Elise—that was glorious!" she exclaimed.

"It is wonderful, isn't it?" said a smiling Elise as she dabbed her eyes with a tissue. "John has a gift, a talent that comes from God."

"Yes, he does," agreed Rachel as she turned and looked at me. "John, I can't believe that you have composed glorious songs like this one my whole life and I never knew. I am just in awe. I understand the consequences if you choose to pursue a career in music, but I agree with Elise. God has given you this talent, John. Music like that can only come from Him. Remember the parable Jesus told about the talents? You can't bury this talent, John. God gave it to you and you must share it with the world. And you are right: the love that you two share is beautiful and the kind of love that most people pray to God for. It's the type of love I thought I had with Daniel but now I can see it was just a cheap, tawdry imitation of the real thing."

With that, Rachel buried her face in her hands and began to sob. Elise got up and moved swiftly to her side and wrapped her arms around her. Rachel allowed it and laid her head on Elise's shoulder and continued to cry. My heart broke for my sister. I sat down on the other side of Elise and I wrapped my arms around both my sister and Elise.

"Rachel, *die Schweschder*, you are beloved to me. You are a beautiful, sweet, hardworking young lady. You deserve to be loved and treasured, and one day much sooner than you think, God is going to send you a der Mann who will love you as truly as I love Elise," I said.

"Thank you," she said in a muffled voice.

In spite of it all, in that moment, I was certain that my sister was in God's hands and I need not worry about her anymore. God makes all things work together for our good.

Once I had convinced John and Rachel that I was okay and had kept down a glass of water and four saltine crackers to prove it, they went home. I watched until they were out of sight. Every time John left, it felt like he took a piece of me with him. How was it that a man that I didn't even know existed a few weeks ago was now the most important person in my life? As if sensing that I was feeling lonely, KitKat rubbed up against my legs and meowed. I looked down at her and smiled.

"I also can't live without you," I said as I bent down and picked her up. She nuzzled up to me, purring as I patted her and scratched her head. I buried my face in her fur and kissed her. "How can you smell so good when you clean yourself with your spit?"

KitKat meowed at me and blinked. I really think she understands everything that I say. Still carrying KitKat, I went over to the couch and sat down. I placed her on my lap and covered us with a blanket. She looked up at me and then at the blanket. She then thoroughly sniffed the blanket before burrowing herself in it. She began smurgling and purring loudly. I smiled. The blanket was a new one that I had ordered with KitKat (and myself) in mind. It was very soft and fluffy. It made me happy that she was enjoying it just as I had anticipated. When I first adopted KitKat, I had to read everything I could find on kittens. I wanted to be able to care for her properly. I had read that a cat's purring is both inhalation and exhalation with a consistent pattern and frequency between 25 and 150 hertz. Various investigations have shown that sound frequencies in this range can improve bone density and promote healing. As I felt the vibrations from KitKat's purring, I wondered if the fact that the frequencies of cat's purring helped to heal the bones and muscles of cat's meant that it may also provide help for some humans. One thing was for sure: holding a purring kitten on my lap sure did ease my loneliness and make me happy. I yawned and looked down at KitKat and smiled.

"You also make me sleepy," I said to KitKat who made absolutely no reply as she was now sound asleep. Within a few short minutes, I was asleep too.

When I woke up the following morning, I was surprised to find that KitKat was still lying on me sound asleep. She looked so peaceful that I hated to make her move. So I lay there gently stroking her soft grey fur and looking about me. Sometimes we become so accustomed to a place that we stop seeing it properly. For the first time in a long time, I really looked at the room. Evidence of my grandmother was everywhere: from the curtains that she had sown to the lace doilies she had tatted and the hand-knotted rugs she had made on the wooden floor. There was also evidence of my grandfather in this room: he had made the wooden rocking chair for my grandmother when she was expecting my father; the crown molding and trim around the windows had been built and put up by him; the fireplace mantle and the built-in bookshelves that surrounded the fireplace had also been built and installed by him. My grandparents had never been wealthy but they had the talent to make a house beautiful for little money and with a lot of skill. This personal touch was what made this house a home and why I had not been able to part with the home when they passed away. For the first time since I had been diagnosed with cancer, I allowed myself to daydream about the future.

Suppose I married John. He would probably not object to living here, especially since his family lived next door. I dreamily envisioned a child sitting on the rug playing with blocks and with KitKat. I imagined playing board games in front of the fire as a family while drinking hot chocolate. My imagination rang with the laughter of children yet to be born as they ran down the stairs and out into the yard to play. My hand unconsciously moved to my flat stomach and I wondered what it felt like to have a baby growing inside of me.

Then an insidious dark thought slid into my mind and caused all of my rosy dreams to come crashing down. I remembered my oncologist talking to me about chemotherapy before I started taking it; she had said that most chemotherapy drugs can damage a woman's eggs, affecting her fertility. I tried to remind myself that she had also said that the type of chemo being used had a low risk of damaging eggs and that my youth meant I had more eggs which increased my chance of keeping some fertility. I thought about the little that I knew about the Amish, including the fact that they all seemed to have very large families. The fear was there no matter how I tried to dislodge it: would John want to marry me knowing that I may not be able to bear him a child?

KitKat stirred, stretched, and blinked her eyes up at me. A look of concern crossed her face and she came up to my face and began to lick away the tears as they slid down my face. A barren woman, that's what I was; a broken, barren woman.

♫

We walked in silence for a few minutes. I had much that I wanted to say but I waited, letting Rachel take the lead. We were almost halfway home before she finally spoke.

"Why didn't you tell me about Elise?" she asked. "Did you think you couldn't trust me because you saw me with Daniel?"

"No," I said emphatically. "Your relationship with Daniel had nothing to do with it."

"Then why didn't you tell me about Elise?" she persisted and as she spoke, she suddenly stopped walking, turned sideways, and stared at me with her eyes wide.

"What?" I asked. "Why are you staring at me like that?"

"I have always thought we were close. I've thought of you as my friend as well as my brother. Up until Daniel, I had confided in you about everything and I thought you did the same to me. But obviously I was wrong! You kept your music a secret all of your life. So really the question isn't why didn't you tell me about Elise but why have you lied to me by omission my entire life? Clearly you have never trusted me. You have never felt about me the same way I have felt about you."

I turned to face Rachel and put my hands on her shoulders. I could see the hurt in her face and the pain in her eyes. My heart ached at the thought that I had caused that look. She looked up at me, unshed tears gleaming in her eyes.

"Rachel, I am sorry. I never meant to hurt you. I have never distrusted you and I have always thought of you as one of my best friends as well as my sister. When I told Daett about my music, it was a disaster. That experience caused me to be ashamed of my music and I didn't want to get you in trouble as well. It was my personal cross to bear. Regarding my relationship with Elise, it is extremely new and it caught me by surprise. When I started writing her notes and taking her some of my music to play, I never expected to fall in love with her."

"But you did," she said softly.

"Yes, I did," I admitted with a wry smile. "Love took me by surprise."

"What are you going to do?" she asked and I could see the worry in her eyes.

"I don't know how I am going to handle it," I said slowly. "I always thought that one day I would marry a good Amish girl, have lots of children, and be a farmer like Daett."

"Well, you can still get married, have lots of children, and be a farmer," said a smiling Rachel and then she gasped, smiled, and clapped her hands together. "Oh, John, Elise could become Amish. I know it would be hard, but if she loves you she could do it!"

"No," I said, shaking my head regretfully. "Elise is a highly-skilled, highly-trained classical pianist. She has been playing the piano since she was three years old. Music is a part of her, just as it is a part of me. There is no way that the two of us could give up music."

"Not even if it is a sin?"

"That's just it, Rachel. I don't believe it is a sin. In fact, I feel like God gave me the talent I have. When I write my music and hear it played, it feels and sounds like I am talking to God with my music."

"That sounds wonderful," she said softly. "Your talent is from God. I may not understand it but I do believe that your music comes from God. I'm sorry for questioning you. I am just being selfish. I don't want to lose my der Bruder."

"You are not going to lose me," I assured her.

She smiled at me but her eyes did not look convinced.

"But you are going to leave the Amish?" she asked.

"Yes," I said, finally admitting this truth to myself as well as to her. "I will leave the Amish."

The enormity of this realization seemed to take the air out of my lungs. I had to sit down quickly before I passed out. Fortunately, there was a downed tree close to me and I sat down on the log and buried my face in my hands. I felt Rachel sitting down next to me. She put her arm around me trying to comfort me.

"Are you okay?" she asked me.

"Yes," I said as I looked up at her. "It's just that is the first time I have admitted to myself that I am leaving the Amish."

"Because you love Elise," Rachel said matter-of-factly.

"No," I said and she looked up at me with surprise. "I mean yes I do love Elise, but that isn't the only reason why I am leaving the Amish. I am leaving the Amish because God gave me this gift and I feel that I have to use that gift. For so long I believed that my music was sinful but now I know that denying my gift and not using my gift would be sin."

Rachel looked at me with eyes filled with tears and understanding.

"I am proud of you, John," she said, smiling at me. "I really am. And if I am being completely honest, I am also a little bit jealous of you."

"Jealous?" I scoffed. "Why on earth would you be jealous of me?"

"Seriously? First of all, the kind of love that you have with Elise is amazing. It's the type of love that most of us dream of having. Plus it helps that she isn't married to anyone else," Rachel said with a grimace. "But more than that, I am jealous of the walk that you have with God and because you have found your purpose. Right now, I feel like all I have done is cause pain. I don't have any purpose to my life. Most of the girls my age can't wait to get married and have a bunch of kinner."

Her voice trailed off and I looked at her sharply.

"And you don't want that?"

"I do—it's not that," she said, biting her lower lip.

"What is it?" I asked. "You are biting your bottom lip. You always do when something is bothering you."

"You know me all too well, der Bruder." She smiled wryly. "The truth is that I want a husband and children more than anything. To be a wife and mother has been my hope and dream since I was a little girl and Mamm made me my first doll. But I am scared, John. I am really scared. Can you imagine that? Being scared of the thing you want the most? I guess that's why I was in a relationship with a married man. It wasn't likely that he would want to marry me and ... and I made sure that our relationship never got physical enough for me to be at risk of pregnancy. Honestly, if you hadn't told Daett about us, our relationship would have ended soon anyway. Daniel was becoming increasingly frustrated with me and pressuring me to have, you know."

Her voice trailed off in embarrassment. My heart sunk and I looked at my sister, really looked at her. When had my kid sister become a woman? How had I not seen the load she had been under? Thinking of that jerk Daniel pressuring her for sex made my blood boil and I was so proud of her for not giving into his manipulation.

"I am sorry, Rachel," I said softly.

"It's okay," she said as she brushed away a tear.

It wasn't but I let it drop for now, determined instead to get at the heart of this matter.

"You said you were afraid," I prompted. "What are you afraid of?"

"Do you remember when Leah's Mamm and her *bobbel* died in childbirth?" she asked.

"Yes. That was the saddest funeral I've ever been to," I replied as the image of the young mother holding her infant son lying in a pine coffin came unbidden to my mind. I had been terrified that the same fate would happen to Mamm every time she had been expecting a baby.

"I was there," Rachel said, her voice cracking.

"What?!"

"I was there, John," she said as tears began to flow down her cheeks. "I had spent the night with Leah. Her Mamm went into labor around midnight. Leah and I helped as much as we could, bringing the midwife towels and boiling water. Everyone was excited and happy that the *bobbel* was coming. Her Mamm was so brave and she hardly cried out at all. I told Leah that her Mamm was much quieter than my Mamm was when she had her *bobblin*. Leah said proudly that her Mamm was born to birth *bobblin* and always popped them out like it was nothing. She said her Mamm's *bobblin* were always born fast too. But dawn came and still no *bobbel*. About an hour after dawn, we heard the most awful screaming I'd ever heard. Leah and I ran into the room. I'll never forget what I saw, John. There was so much blood. The midwife looked scared and she had to use the forceps to deliver the *bobbel*. Leah's Daett screamed for the oldest son, Jacob, to run to the phone box and to call for an ambulance. As awful as the screaming was, when Leah's Mamm went quiet, the silence was even worse. The *bobbel* was born but he never made a sound. Leah and her Daett were on each side of her Mamm begging her to wake up but she never did. When the ambulance came, the paramedics worked on both of them but it was too late; both Mamm and *bobbel* were dead. That's why I am scared to have a family of my own. What if I die like Leah's Mamm did? Or worse, what if my bobbel died but I lived? I'm not sure I would be able to handle that big of a loss."

I pulled the now sobbing Rachel into my arms. I tried to comfort her. Silently I began to pray, asking God to comfort Rachel and to give me the wisdom to know what to say to her.

"I'm sorry you've carried this fear for so long all by yourself," I said. "Fear is an insidious and evil thief that robs us of our peace of mind, our joy, our hopes and dreams. What you saw that night would've frightened anyone, Rachel. I understand why it has made you afraid of having children of your own."

"Thank you, John," she said as she pulled away from me and wiped her eyes. "Thank you for listening to me and for letting me cry on your shoulder."

"That's what big brothers are for," I said as we resumed walking to the house. "And big brothers are also for giving advice."

"Oh? Do you have any sage advice for me, der Bruder?"

"Just this: don't let fear direct the course of your life."

"That's awfully gut advice." Rachel smiled at me.

CHAPTER FIFTEEN

O ur days passed in the bliss that only new love could bring. Harvest time was busy for John and his family, so we snatched time together whenever we could. Because of his Mamm's death and his family's need of his help during the harvest, when he could, John would come to me for a brief very early morning visit. I would brew him coffee and we would share a cup together. As we sat at the kitchen table, John would read the Bible aloud to me. Then we would pray together. We asked God for guidance and wisdom on how to navigate the days ahead and we thanked Him for bringing us together and the love we shared. Before John left we would share some kisses, and those kisses gave me the strength to make it through the difficult treatments for my leukemia. I had known kissing could be pleasant but while kissing John, I came to understand firsthand the meaning of the Song of Solomon because his mouth was most definitely sweet. And I enjoyed kissing my beloved very much. If he could, John would visit me late in the evenings. We talked and shared stories of our lives, our hopes and dreams. We made tentative plans for our future together and we played with KitKat who demanded her fair share of our attention. She had become very enamored of John and would scarcely leave his side when he was with us. Before he left he made sure that all the doors in the house were locked, including the one behind him as he left. I had been on my own for a decade and had thought for years that if I were to ever have a boyfriend, I would chaff of any behaviors or actions that seemed possessive or protective. However, now that I had the love of a good man, I found that I didn't mind at all. In fact, I rather enjoyed it. I was blissfully happy and because of that, I was reluctant to bring up any subjects that could cause any friction between us. However, I knew that one day soon we would have to discuss the difficult things in order for our relationship to progress.

In addition to having John in my life, I felt like I had gained a sister in Rachel. She and I were becoming quite close. In fact, she would even come to see me on days when she was not scheduled to clean my house. It was the first time that I had forged a close friendship with another girl and I absolutely loved it. John was my love, my confidant, and my best friend. He was my first best friend in fact, but Rachel was also becoming a dear friend. I was able to discuss with Rachel things that I couldn't really discuss with John: some because it would've been inappropriate and others because he simply wouldn't be interested or understand. To my utter delight, I found out that Rachel was an excellent and accomplished knitter. She told me that her aunt Fannie had taught her to knit and that had inspired her mother, who hadn't knitted since her marriage, to begin knitting again. Rachel very graciously agreed to teach me how to knit. I had finally completed the washcloth that I had begun with the help of online videos but I was not sure what to do with the loose ends of the yarn left dangling. Rachel taught me how to weave in the ends.

The more I knitted, the more I loved it. I loved the feel of the yarn in my hands and how the bamboo needles glided in and out of the yarn smoothly. Knitting was soothing to me and helped when I felt anxious or worried about the future. I had gone back to the yarn shop to purchase more yarn. Occasionally there would be a free pattern displayed near a corresponding type of yarn and I found them fascinating. While daydreaming about all the different projects I would like to achieve, I came across yarn that was soft, bulky, and lovely. A free pattern for a prayer shawl was hanging next to the yarn. Above the pattern was a small sign that stated, "Fellowship Chapel invites you to take part in our Prayer Shawl Ministry. We are seeking knitters and crocheters who would be willing to knit or crochet prayer shawls for donation. The donated prayer shawls will then be given to patients in our local nursing homes as well as patients currently receiving treatment for cancer at the Cancer Center. If interested, please take the free pattern which is a design that can be worn by both men and women. We ask that as you knit, you pray for the person who will receive and wear it. Once you have shawl(s) ready for donation, please contact the church using the phone number and contact information printed on the back of the pattern." Instantly I knew this was something I wanted to do. I took one of the patterns and then I had a thought.

"Ma'am, would it be okay if I took more than one of the prayer shawl patterns?" I asked the lady behind the counter.

"Of course," she said, smiling. "Take all you want."

I retrieved four of the patterns: one for Rachel, one for her aunt Fannie, and two for me since I had the tendency to mislay things. Then after consulting the pattern for how many skeins of yarn I needed, I had to decide what colors I wanted to buy. After ten minutes I was at an impasse; thus, I made the only rational choice available to me: I purchased skeins of every color. I also bought: another tote, this one for the prayer shawl knitting project; multiple sets of the size of knitting needles required (again in case I lost a needle), multiple tapestry needles since I had lost all but one of the needles I had previously purchased; tips for my knitting needles because KitKat kept stealing and playing with my other ones; a measuring tape, a pair of scissors, and a magnetic pattern board. Once again, I left the yarn store happy as a lark and carrying multiple shopping bags that were completely full. I couldn't wait to show Rachel what I had purchased.

As soon as she came into my house the following day, I told her she had to come see what I had bought. I took her upstairs to the attic to Nana's sewing room. This third-level attic space was one of my favorite places in the house. It had been my nana's happy place as well; however, until yesterday, I had avoided the space because it had felt like the room was in stasis and simply waiting for Nana to reenter and to resume sewing. The staircase was behind a door and the steps went straight up. At the top of the steps was a small landing with a window. Other than a nice big full bathroom, the space was one big room with three large alcoves, dormers with window seats, and a built-in wardrobe and drawers.

One area of the attic room was a bedroom with nice thick curtains that you could pull closed, thus separating the bedroom area from the rest of the space. The curtains had always made me think of Ebenezer Scrooge and had afforded me many hours of imaginative play as a child. The bedroom was outfitted with an antique bedroom set which included: a white wrought iron bed covered with a patchwork quilt sown by Nana; a vanity table with a large, round, attached mirror, drawers, and a seat; and a dresser. The area also had a large round, braided rug and a fireplace. One of my favorite aspects of the bedroom area was the two reading wall sconces on the wall behind the head of the bed. These were perfect for reading in the bed. Another alcove had been my nana's sewing space; I had left it just as it had been when she was alive.

Across from the sewing area was an alcove set up as a sitting area. KitKat had followed us up the steps chirping the whole way. Next to the bed was a window with a window seat with a tufted cushion. Since the room hadn't been in use, I had covered her sewing machine and the furniture with a drop cloth and told Rachel she didn't need to clean it. However, when I had arrived home with the yarn, I had decided to make use of Nana's attic once again. KitKat had been so excited to find more stairs to run up and down and another area to explore. I had spent the evening happily organizing my yarn and I was so tired afterwards that I decided to sleep in the bed in the attic. This morning, I had dusted and cleaned the attic so it would be nice when Rachel came to see it. When we reached the top of the stairs and Rachel saw the room, she gasped.

'Oh my!" she said excitedly. "What a *wunderbaar* room!

"Yes, it is, isn't it?" I agreed. "I used to love coming up here as a child. In fact, once I was older, I would sleep in this room for the summer. I loved sleeping here especially when it rained. I loved lying in bed listening to the sound of the rain on the tin roof. This space was primarily used by my nana as her sewing room. She loved to sew and her handiwork is in every room of this house."

Rachel walked into the sewing area; she ran her fingers across Nana's sewing machine and along the stacks of fabric on the shelves. Her eyes shone and she looked like a kid in a candy store who has been told that he or she can have whatever they want!

"Do you sew?" she asked me.

"Yes," I responded. "I'm not the greatest seamstress in the world but I enjoy sewing. Whenever I would come for a visit, Nana would have a project for me to complete with her help. She would tell me that I had a talent for sewing but that I needed more practice. Traveling the world playing the piano wasn't conducive to a sewing hobby."

"Perhaps now that you're settled down here, you will be able to sew more. I love to sew," she said shyly. "My favorite things to make are quilts. I could teach you if you would want me to. We could start with a simple pattern."

"I would love that!" I exclaimed. "But only if you will let me pay you for your time."

Rachel demurred but I persisted.

"If I were to sign up for classes at a hobby shop or fabric store, I would pay for the lessons. Your time is just as valuable as theirs if not more especially now that you have so much on your shoulders with Mamm gone."

After a brief hesitation, she smiled and nodded.

"Jah, okay."

"Speaking of hobby stores, I went to the yarn store again today. Have you been there? It's an awesome shop!"

"Jah! It is a wonderfully gut store," she enthused. "Two of the families in our church supplies them with yarn. The men raise sheep and once a year the sheep are shorn. Then the mamm and older girls take the wool and make it into yarn. They even hand-dye the wool. Another family raises alpacas and makes yarn from their fleece as well. It's such soft yarn."

"Is the name of the family Stoltz?" I asked.

"Yes!" Rachel looked at me surprised. "How did you know?"

"Because I bought a lot of yarn today at the yarn shop with the name 'Stoltz Family Farm Homespun Yarn.' I smiled. "That's actually what I wanted to show you."

I opened up a cabinet and pulled out one of the bins that I had put the yarn in. I handed Rachel one of the skeins of yarn.

"I bought eight skeins of yarn in every color. Nana had these empty bins that fit on these shelves perfectly. Each one of the bins contains a different color," I said excitedly.

"You bought forty-eight skeins of yarn?" asked Rachel incredulously.

"Yes," I said, chuckling. "I know it sounds crazy, but I think this will be a creative outlet for me and it's also for a good cause. During my chemo treatments, I met a wonderful lady named Marge. We became friends. Marge was a knitter and when I lost my hair, she gave me a beautiful hat knitted yellow which is my favorite color. She also knitted me a yellow blanket which was incredibly thoughtful because I often feel very cold during chemo. Sadly, Marge passed away. When I went to her funeral, I saw many people there wearing knitted items that she had made them. I had been thinking about honoring Marge by carrying on her knitting ministry. I have started teaching myself how to knit. Yesterday I went to the yarn shop where they had a flyer for a Prayer Shawl Ministry. A local church called Fellowship Chapel is wanting knitters and crocheters to knit or crochet prayer shawls which will then be given to patients in nursing homes and patients at the Cancer Center. I decided I would like to be part of that ministry and thus I bought forty-eight skeins of yarn!"

"That sounds like a wonderful thing to do," Rachel said, smiling. "But do men wear shawls?"

"They call it a shawl but it isn't the triangle shape that I think of when I think of a shawl. The pattern isn't feminine or masculine and it can be either wrapped around a patient's shoulders or be used as a lap blanket. See, this is the pattern," I said as I handed her the flyer.

Rachel took the flyer and read it with a smile.

"This is an easy pattern and such a thoughtful idea for those who are sick." She smiled. "I love to knit and I would be happy to donate as well."

"You know," I smiled at her broadly, "I was hoping that you were going to say that. When I was at the yarn store, I got carried away. I remembered that you had told me that you knitted and Aunt Fannie knitted. I was hoping that you two would want to help me. I brought home two extra patterns and two extra knitting needles just in case."

"You know me very well," said Rachel, laughing. "You knew I would look at this lovely yarn, hear the worthy cause and say, 'Let me help.' I am sure Aunt Fannie will be glad to help also. Do you want us to pay you for the yarn?"

"Absolutely not! You have the most kind and giving heart of anyone that I have ever met," I told her seriously. "And you love God. When I read on the flyer that they want you to pray for the person that will use the blanket, my mind thought of you. Rachel, you are exactly the type of young lady who would sit knitting and praying for someone you have never met."

Rachel's smile faltered and then faded.

"I'm not as good of a person as you think," she said softly. "In fact, I'm terrible."

Rachel's head was bent but I could see tears dropping down onto the skein of yarn she was holding in her hands. My heart broke for her.

"What is wrong, Rachel?" I asked as I put an arm around her.

"I'm so ashamed," she sobbed. "I know it sounds silly, after all I confessed my sin in front of the whole church, but somehow I am more embarrassed to tell you. It's prideful but I must admit I worry that if I tell you it will change how you view me."

"Rachel, I am your friend and I am a flawed human being. I promise not to judge you nor will anything you tell me change the admiration or affection that I have for you. I hope that you know you can trust me. Please, come and sit next to me on the couch and talk with me."

Rachel nodded her assent and then accompanied me to the couch. KitKat had found a sunbeam shining onto the braided rug and had fallen asleep while basking in the sun. I sat silent waiting for Rachel to speak. I didn't want to pressure her.

"It all began as an innocent flirtation," she began. "Of course, I was lying to myself because how on earth could a flirtation between a married man and a woman not his wife be innocent? Sin is insidious that way; it can start out so small and then before you know it, you find yourself on a path you had never foreseen. For me that path was a relationship with a married man named Daniel Lapp. It started when his wife, Lydia, had fallen ill and was placed in the hospital. The Lapps needed help; in particular, the Lapp children needed cared for. Of course the Lapps have plenty of family and thus they had lots of help. However, it was flu season and it hit our community especially hard, including the family members who were helping to care for the Lapp household. Those of us who were not sick or not caring for sick family members of our own were very few indeed. I was one of the few and it was felt that I could be spared more easily than any of the others. I settled into the routine of going to the Lapp home early every morning and coming home every evening. Either Daett or John would take me there and Daniel would bring me home at night. I prepared three meals for them daily, cleaned their home, and cared for the children. Daniel complimented me on the meals and bragged on how well the house and children were cared for. At first I was merely flattered and thought he was being appreciative of my help. However, before long, I began to realize he was flirting with me.

"He is a handsome older man. It was nice to be appreciated by a man and not by one of the young boys my age. It made me feel like a grown woman. In the beginning, Daniel and his children took me home in the evenings. Then, his grandmother got better and she came to stay with Daniel and the children. She has severe arthritis and while she is able to walk short distances and to stand for a minute or two, she isn't strong enough to care for young children or take care of a house. However, when the children were settled for the night, it was fine to leave them in her care for a short while. That's when Daniel began taking me home alone. We talked and he made me laugh. We became friends.

"I noticed that he was taking me the long way home and that he kept his horse at a slow pace. It happened so slowly that I didn't understand what was happening until it was too late because by that time, I had fallen in love with him. We started parking the buggy in a secluded area and spending time alone. Then his wife got better and came home. She was still weak but the womenfolk in her family were over the flu and they didn't need my help anymore. However, my relationship with Daniel didn't end. We would sneak and meet each other whenever we could. At first it was so exciting. I was in love with being in love. Then he began pressuring me to take our relationship further. I told him nee! Instead of accepting my answer and respecting my decision, he became more aggressive. I became scared but I didn't stop our relationship because I was in love with him. One night a few weeks ago, John saw me and Daniel kissing. He was extremely upset and eventually he confided in Daett and together they told the bishop."

She paused and wiped her eyes with her handkerchief. I got up and went over to the mini fridge that I had bought and installed in the sewing alcove. I fetched a bottle of water for myself and Rachel. She accepted it with a grateful smile and drank down half the bottle in one huge, long gulp.

"Thank you," she said. "I needed that.

"Once the bishop found out about our affair, he first confronted Daniel who confessed everything, declared his remorse, and begged forgiveness. I wasn't as remorseful as Daniel or as smart, and therefore I was shunned."

"Oh, Rachel," I said, my eyes welling with tears. "I am sorry. That must've been difficult."

"Yes, it was," she said. "But it was just as hard if not harder on my family. The shunning served its purpose because it helped me to see the error of my ways and showed me what I had to lose if I persisted in my sin. Time away from Daniel and words John spoke to me put perspective on our relationship. I was finally able to see it for what it was: a cheap and tawdry affair that had never been about love. I prayed to God for forgiveness and confessed my sin publicly. Thankfully, God did forgive me and before Mamm passed away, I was able to reconcile with Mamm and Daett. They both forgave me and were so good to me. I also confessed my sin and apologized to my church and bishop. And I promised to refrain from the sin."

I looked at Rachel closely. She was chewing her bottom lip and she was twisting the handkerchief in her hands. Clearly something was still bothering her.

"Do you worry that some still hold your sin against you?" I asked her softly.

"What?" She looked up at me in surprise and then shook her head. "No, our people are not like that. Once a sin is forgiven it is forgotten, otherwise it isn't truly forgiven. The problem is that I cannot seem to forgive myself."

"Rachel, I'm not trying to minimize how you feel but you are a young, innocent girl and I can't help but think that Daniel Lapp manipulated you and the circumstance; I feel like he took advantage of you and your sweet, compassionate, and caring nature. What I am trying to say is that I feel like you are being too harsh on yourself."

"How?" she asked incredulously. "I committed a sin in having an affair with Daniel."

"Yes, you did," I agreed. "I'm not saying that you are innocent; your adultery with Daniel was a sin. But Daniel is an older man, a married man, and as I stated before, he manipulated you. Now I'm not saying that absolves you of your sin but I truly do not believe that you would have had an affair with Daniel or even thought of him in that way if he had not taken advantage of your innocence and your kind and caring heart."

"That is true," she said slowly. "I had never looked at him and thought of him as being attractive until he began paying me a lot of attention and pouring out his problems to me. But like you said, he tempted me but it's still my fault, my sin that I yielded to the sin."

"Rachel, do you believe the Bible to be the Word of God?" I asked her in a flash of spiritual intuition.

"Of course," Rachel said in a shocked voice.

"Since moving into this house, I have been reading my grandparents' Bibles quite a lot," I explained. "Over and over, I read in the Bible of the merciful grace and forgiveness of God. My grandparents had both written prayers in their Bibles for my salvation. Through the reading of the Word of God, I realized that I was a sinner in need of salvation and I asked God to forgive me of my sins and to be my Lord and Savior."

"Elise, that is wonderful!"

"Thank you. The more I pray and the more I read the Bible, the more I love my God. When I first got saved, I began to look back on my life and some of the sins that I had committed began to haunt me and brought me much guilt. Then one night, I was reading Hebrews 10 which tells us how Jesus gave His life for our sins. Verse 12 tells us that Christ offered for all time a single sacrifice for our sins. Nevermore is it necessary for us to offer up a sacrifice to God for our sins because Jesus Christ paid our sin debt in full by willingly giving up His life as a sacrifice. His job complete, he ascended to Heaven and took his rightful place next to His Father. Then I read verse 17 and Rachel, when I read it and believed it, that burden of guilt was lifted and I have refused to pick it up anymore because in verse 17 Christ gives us an assurance stating: 'And their sins and iniquities will I remember no more.' I realized that God no longer remembers my sin and if He doesn't hold my past sins—which were for-given and blotted out by the blood of Christ—then why should I punish myself for things that God Himself has chosen to forget?"

"The sea of forgetfulness," Rachel said as she suddenly looked like she was lit up from within.

"Excuse me?"

"The sea of forgetfulness," she repeated. "There is a song that we sing, not in church but at home and at singings. I don't know the name of it but the words of the chorus are: 'They're underneath the blood, on the cross of Calvary, as far removed as darkness is from dawn; in the sea of God's forgetfulness, that's good enough for me, Praise God my sins are gone.'

"That's beautiful!" I exclaimed. "The composer captured the meaning of Hebrews 10:17 perfectly. It may seem foolish but I suggest that whenever memories cause you to feel guilt and shame, start singing that song to remind yourself that your sins are forgiven and forgotten."

"I don't think that is foolish at all," smiled Rachel. "I think it is a wunderbaar idea!"

"Good. By the way, I think you sing beautifully."

"Thank you, but John is by far the best singer in our family and in the church district too!"

"Well, it seems I still have a lot to learn about John." I smiled.

"As his sister, I can tell you all the things that he wouldn't want you to know," she said with a mischievous smile.

"Hmmm, I'm going to take you up on that offer. But first, come and pick out the colors of yarn you would like to knit with."

Long after she was gone, I stayed in the attic room. After avoiding the room and pretending it wasn't even there, I now didn't want to leave. Everywhere I looked brought back so many wonderful memories. Nana tried to teach me to sew and while I could sew a little, I never really applied myself to it as I would much rather spend my free time reading. Mother had thought that reading was a waste of my time which could be better spent by practicing the piano. Consequently when I was with her, I could only read for a few short minutes. I became quite good at being sneaky. I would hide a paperback novel underneath my clothes and then in the few minutes I got to spend alone time in the bathroom, I would read a few paragraphs. When I was at the farm with my grandparents, reading was not only allowed but encouraged. In the attic there was a built-in bookcase that was filled two rows deep with books and more books stuffed along the tops of the books. To me it was heaven. Although I did have favorite authors and books which changed as I grew, I didn't care if the book was fiction or nonfiction. If it was a book, I read it. One summer I was helping Nana clean up the attic and in one of the knee walls, I pulled out first one big heavy box and then a second one. I had asked Nana what was in the boxes that made them so heavy. She had smiled and said, 'Open up and see.' So I did and I found a veritable treasure trove of old *National Geographic* magazines, a few old editions of *Readers' Digest*, and even a few *Readers' Digest* condensed books. I was overjoyed! I had reluctantly pushed them aside for later and was ready to help Nana as promised but when I looked over, she was already standing up and closing the door of the knee wall. I had protested and insisted I would help her and read later. Nana had smiled at me and told me that the only reason she had wanted me to help her clean out the knee wall was because she and Poppy had thought these two boxes might still be in the knee wall. She hadn't told me what we were looking for because she didn't want to get my hopes up in case the boxes weren't there. But how did she and Poppy know that I wanted something new to read? She had smiled and said:

"By my count you've read the book *Harriet the Spy* twice this week! So naturally we concluded that you had read every book you brought with you as well as all the books we have in the house."

"You are right, Nana," I said. "I have read every book in the house and all the books I brought with me. But you are wrong about one thing."

"Oh?" she queried with a cocked eyebrow. "And just what am I wrong about?"

Harriet the Spy, I said matter-of-factly as I picked up an especially enticing *National Geographic* that must be about cannibals if I was interpreting the picture on the cover correctly.

"What about it?"

"It's my favorite book and I often read it simply because I want to visit with Harriet, Sport, and Ole Golly. So just because I am reading *Harriet the Spy*, it doesn't mean that I am out of new reading material. I sometimes pick her overtop new books."

"I see," Nana said with a hint of a smile twitching at her lips. "Is that all I am wrong about?"

"No; I haven't read *Harriet the Spy* twice this week. I've read it three times this week, although in your defence I was reading the book when I came so I suppose it's more like two-and-a-half times. Guess how many times I've read *Harriet the Spy*? I challenged her.

"Hmmm, let me think," she paused as she tapped her chin with her forefinger. "Ten times?"

"Nope." I grinned at her madly just like *Harriet the Spy*. "I've read the book *Harriet the Spy* twenty-three times!"

"Wow!" was all Nana had to say.

Feeling rather smug, I opened up the *National Geographic Magazine* and made myself comfy on the window seat and began to read.

CHAPTER SIXTEEN

Harvest kept me so busy that I almost didn't have time to worry about the future. Many of my friends had enlisted in the eighteen-week instruction period required before they would take the vow and join the church. I had seen the looks and whispers and if Daett hadn't been so shielded from the world by his cocoon of grief, he would have been asking why I wasn't taking the instruction classes. In November I would be turning twenty-three and I knew the bishop would shortly thereafter be visiting me and asking me why I had not yet joined the church and would pressure me for a decision. At that point, I would have no choice but to announce my decision to not join the Amish church to Daett. I didn't want it to be something that was forced by the bishop and I felt that I owed it to Daett to tell him my choice first. Then I realized that there was one person who deserved to know even before Daett and that was Elise. I couldn't believe that I hadn't thought of it before. When I was with her, I was so completely happy and consumed with being with her that it hadn't dawned on me that she didn't know that I wanted to plan a life with her outside of the Amish community. I decided to remedy this soon. As much as I dreaded upsetting Daett with the news that I would not be staying in the Amish church and that I am in love with an Englisher, I couldn't wait for our relationship to be out in the open. It would be nice to just walk to her house and tell everyone where I was going instead of trying to be sneaky and deceitful. That afternoon, Aunt Fannie asked if I would take her to town for some supplies that she needed. We turned onto the road but I kept the horse at a slow pace.

"There is a white farmhouse coming up on our right," I told her.

She shot me a quizzical look but said nothing. As we passed by Elise's house, it took all my resolve not to turn the buggy into Elise's driveway. I knew that Aunt Fannie and Elise would like one another but I couldn't just take Aunt Fannie to Elise's house and say, 'This is the woman I love.'

"Well?"

Aunt Fannie's voice jarred me out of my reverie. I glanced over at her to find that she was looking at me sharply as if her sight could pierce my brain so that she could peer inside and find out what she wanted to know.

"Well what?" I asked, buying myself a few more seconds at least.

"You know very well what I am asking about! What is the significance of the white farmhouse? There has to be a reason you wanted me to look at the house." At those last words, understanding began to dawn in her eyes.

"Wait a minute. This wouldn't happen to be where the beautiful piano-playing neighbor lives, would it?" she said.

"As a matter of fact, yes." I blushed. "It is indeed where Elise lives."

"Ah... Elise." She smiled. "I think I'm beginning to understand. Since we last were able to talk privately, your relationship with Elise has progressed."

She said this rather smugly as a statement of fact and not as a question. I again glanced at her and noticed that she was looking rather satisfied with herself.

"Aunt Fannie, you look like the cat who got the cream," I teased.

"Oh no, you don't," she scolded me. "I'm not going to let you change the focus to me. Spill the beans, John. Tell Aunt Fannie all about it and don't leave anything out at all!"

I told Aunt Fannie all about my relationship with Elise and answered all of her questions. By the end of my telling her of our story, Aunt Fannie was misty-eyed and dabbing her eyes with a handkerchief but smiling.

"Why are you smiling and crying?" I asked her. "Is it because you are happy I have found love but you are sad that I will be leaving the Amish?"

"Oh, John, you are such a man," she said, laughing. "Haven't you ever heard of happy tears? Ach well, never mind. I am very happy for you, John, and for Elise. I won't lie to you; it does make my heart a little sad that you will not be continuing in the faith of our fathers. Thankfully you hadn't taken the vow so you won't be placed under the Bann and your family and friends will still be able to maintain a relationship with you. But I know that you are not naive and you are well accustomed to our ways and beliefs. Even though you are a Christian and family, it will be expected that our relationship with you to not be as close as it is now."

"I know and I understand," I said as a cold hard knot settled in the pit of my stomach. "I would never want to put my family and friends in a difficult position, so I will be careful and keep my distance as much as I can."

"I know you will, John. But I want you to know this in your heart and mind and never forget it: my love for you my dear nephew will never change, never cease, and never be diminished. I will always be here for your whenever you may need me no matter what."

My heart was deeply touched and I tried very hard to remain stoic.

"Thank you," I said gruffly. "*Ich liebe dich.*"

"I love you too, John."

Shortly thereafter, we arrived in town. While Aunt Fannie did her shopping, I went in search of a telephone booth. Because so many people have cell phones, the need for telephone booths was greatly diminished and thus they were hard to find. Fortunately, I was able to find one and called Elise's cell phone.

"Hello," her beautiful voice sang out to me through the telephone receiver, making me weak in the knees.

"Hello, Elise. It is John."

"What a pleasant surprise!" she exclaimed joyfully.

"How are you feeling today?"

"Not too bad; just a little weak and slightly nauseated," she replied.

I knew Elise well enough by now to know that she wasn't one to complain and in an effort not to worry me, she always downplayed the severity of how ill she actually was. Knowing this, I knew that she was probably feeling exceedingly ill.

"Well, in that case I will let you rest."

"Nonsense," she said stoutly. "Talking with you makes me feel better. Besides, this is the first time that you've called me. Now tell me what you called about."

"Aunt Fannie asked me to bring her to town and on the way here, I told her about you and me. She is happy for us. As we went passed your house coming to town, I wanted to turn into your driveway and bring Aunt Fannie to meet you."

"I would love to meet her!" she exclaimed. "Oh, John, you must bring her by my house on your way home!"

"Are you sure it wouldn't be too much for you?" I asked.

"Absolutely not! In fact, it would be good for me. Please, John?" she pleaded.

So of course I said yes.

I hung up the phone and looked around the living room with a critical eye. Thank God for Rachel. She was an amazing housekeeper and because of her, I wasn't panicking that John's aunt Fannie was coming to my home for the first time. Even though I wasn't worried about how my house looked, I was still nervous. When John talked about her, his whole face lit up. She was very important to him and because of that, I really desired her approval of me. Then a thought struck me. John had mentioned that his church still practiced shunning. If he left the church to be with me and to compose music, would his church shun him? And if they did, would that mean his family would no longer be in his life? I sat down hard on the couch as the magnitude of the situation seemed to suddenly land on my shoulder. Would I be able to live with myself if I was the reason John was permanently separated from his family?

KitKat came up to me and rubbed up against my leg and purred at me. She was such a sweetheart. She always seemed to know when I was having a rough time of it. I smiled and reached down to pick her up. She gave a cute little high-pitched squeak that caused me to laugh.

"What on earth was that noise about?" I asked her. "I thought you were a cat and not a mouse!"

For the next few minutes, I played with KitKat. Feeling better, I decided to bake a batch of cookies. In the kitchen, I opened up Nana's recipe box and began looking through the cookie recipes, trying to decide which one I had the required ingredients and the time to make. When I saw the recipe card for maple-raisin oatmeal cookies, I automatically pulled it out. The card was yellowed with age and grease stains from buttery fingers bore testament to the fact that these delicious cookies had been made often and much loved. I quickly gathered what I needed and began making them. The smell of the ingredients and the making of the dough brought back so many wonderful memories of being in this kitchen and using the same bowl, utensils, and ingredients to make these cookies with Nana. I remember begging for a taste of the brown sugar and for Nana to allow me to eat a little bit of the raw cookie dough. By the time I heard the horses' hooves and the buggy wheels on the driveway, I had just taken the cookies out of the oven, off the cookie sheet pan, and placed them onto the cooling rack. The coffee was brewing in the French press. All was ready. I took off the apron and hung it on the hook and went to open the door.

John stood there smiling and next to him was a beaming Amish lady with twinkling eyes and a huge smile. I liked her instantly. Within a very few minutes, all of my anxiety was completely gone. We went into the kitchen and sat at the kitchen table. While we ate the cookies and drank coffee—both garnered much praise—Aunt Fannie regaled me with stories of a little boy named John. Aunt Fannie was a natural-born storyteller. I laughed so much that tears were coursing down my face. Hearing the story of John's childhood made me love him even more.

"Now I know I've been talking your leg off, but do you mind if I just tell you one more story?" Aunt Fannie asked.

"No more stories about me," grumbled John, although I could tell from his twinkling eyes he was enjoying this as much as me.

"Oh yes, please!" I cried out.

"This is one of my favorite John stories," she said and John groaned. "Yes, John, it's that story.

"When John was eleven years old, his parents were gone for the day, his Daett was participating in a barn raising, and his Mamm was at a quilting bee. Rachel was away having spent the night with a friend. I was on my way here from Pennsylvania but until I arrived, John was left in charge of the little ones and he was confident that he could do it. At that time, Elias was only fourteen months old and not yet potty-trained, but John said that he would be able to care for him and in truth he had changed many dirty diapers. An Englisher that we use as a taxi picked me up at the bus station and brought me to my *brudder's* house. When we pulled up to the house, John was outside in the front lawn with Elias who was totally naked! John was spraying Elias off with the garden hose while Elias was running around and shrieking with laughter! Thankfully it was a very hot summer day so little Elias didn't mind being sprayed with cold well water. I got out of the Englisher's car, strode over to John and Elias, and asked him what on earth was going on? And John said, "Es Bobbel had diarrhea all over him! He played in it too and he had *der schtuhlgang* from his hair to his toes! I'm trying to get him clean!"

By the time she finished the story, Aunt Fannie was laughing so hard she couldn't hardly breath and tears were running down her face. John and I were laughing along with her.

"Now if you recall, Aunt Fannie, my plan was a pretty good one! By the time you arrived, he was only 50 percent covered with *der schtuhlgang*!"

"Jah, when I looked at the amount of poop in his hair and between his toes, I agreed that your plan was the best one we had. I joined in if you remember. I grabbed the soap and towels and washcloths. I started scrubbing and you kept on spraying," she said as she wiped the tears of laughter from her eyes.

"I was never so happy in my life to see you," John said, chuckling. "I didn't want to admit it but I was totally in over my head."

"Jah you were," Aunt Fannie said. "You were over your head in *der schtuhlgang*!"

At that we all began laughing all over again! I had such a wonderful time visiting with Aunt Fannie and John that I did not want the visit to end. However, it did. Because of his aunt's presence, John shyly gave me a quick kiss goodbye before leaving. Watching him leave, I suddenly had an image of a naked baby boy covered with poop or *der schtuhlgang* as they called it and a young John trying desperately to clean the boy up with a water hose and I started laughing all over again. Life with John was going to be an adventure.

A little before 9:00 a.m., I began walking into Bishop Troyer's barn with the other menfolk. Being an unmarried and unbaptized male, I was one of the last to walk in. As we took our seats on the backless wooden pews, I looked across to the womenfolk who were already sitting on their side. Little Ruthie saw me and began smiling and waving at me. Rachel noticed and shushed her quickly. It was a beautiful fall Sunday morning, reminding me why autumn is my favorite season. The sun illuminated the world in warm, golden hues. The orange, red, and yellow leaves and the already browning grass seemed to glow in the sunlight. I looked about me taking it all in as if it was the first time I had seen the congregation worshipping the Lord. It's a sad testament of our humanity that we often take our surroundings for granted and although we see what is around us, we don't always observe. Today, I felt the strong need to not just see but to observe.

The Amish typically do not own cameras and thus we do not document the people and the events of our lives in picture form. We rely on our memories and stories. Once we were all in place, the *vorsinger* began singing the first hymn. After a few notes, the congregation joined in. All of our voices, male and female, young and old, sang in unity, lifting up our voices in praise to our God. Shortly thereafter, the preachers filed out to go and discuss privately who would be preaching today's sermons. The second hymn we sang was Loblied which literally means praise song.

As we sang, I looked over and saw Leah. Our eyes met and her face flushed pink. She smiled at me slightly and I acknowledged her with a slight nod of my head. The service was four hours long and by then, I was very hungry. I was enjoying the food and fellowship immensely. Samuel tapped my shoulder to get my attention.

"What are you thinking about so intensely?" he asked me in sign language.

"Nothing," I replied in sign. "I was just really hungry and I am enjoying the food."

"I know you better than that," Samuel signed to me with a frown.

"I never could fool you." I smiled wryly.

"No," he agreed. "Now spill it."

"I will but not here. Later, okay?"

"Okay."

Samuel's eyes widened a little and he nudged me. When I looked at him, he inclined his head slightly. I turned and looked to see what he had seen. Leah was walking towards me with a big smile on her face and a plate in her hand. I groaned inwardly. I needed to find a way to let her down easy. Leah reached me and kept on walking. I turned and looked at Samuel who shrugged his shoulders and looked just as confused as me. Then we both turned and watched as she approached Isaiah Miller. He beamed up to her and accepted the plate happily. I sighed in relief.

"Looks like you've missed your chance with the fair Leah," signed Samuel. "I suppose that when she saw you hadn't signed up for the classes and wasn't going to join the church yet, she decided she didn't want to wait for you any longer. I'm sorry if you were wanting to go with her but I am happy for Isaiah Miller. He has liked her since we were Gezewwel in school."

"I am very happy for them," I said in sign. "Leah is a very nice and pretty girl but she is not the girl for me."

"Meaning that another girl has already captured your heart?" Samuel asked.

"Maybe." I smiled.

"Who?" he asked.

"Later," I said.

"You keep saying that and I am going to hold you to it! Don't think I'm going to let you wiggle out of telling me everything!"

"I promise that I will tell you everything," I signed. "As a matter of fact, I am looking forward to it."

At that, Samuel beamed at me. I looked down at Leah and Isaiah and sighed heavily. Samuel's eyes narrowed.

"What?" he asked.

"I really want a piece of pie and now that Leah is Isaiah's girl, I guess I will have to get up and go get my pie all by myself."

"You are *faul*," said Samuel, laughing.

"Yes I am," I smiled.

We had just gotten home and Daett and I were unhitching the horse and buggy in the barn when Elias came running in.

"Daett, that big ole heifer is trying go over the fence again and messed it up real bad," he said. "She didn't get out but if she keeps working at it, she will. And some of the other cows are looking like they might join in and help her."

"Ach, that stupid old cow," grumbled Daett. "You would think that she would be content getting to eat the corn stover. Elias, finish unhitching the horse and put her away. Give her some food and water and a good brushing down as well. John, you come with me."

After we grabbed the tools and supplies that we needed, Daett and I headed out for the damaged fence. Sure enough, the cow nearly had the fence down. She probably would've already made her escape if the other cows had helped her, but fortunately for us the others had decided they would rather continue grazing the corn stover. We shooed her away with some difficulty but eventually she gave a snort of disgust and joined the others in eating the bounty of the leftover harvest. Daett and I worked along in companionable silence. I tried to get my nerve up to talk to Daett about me being in love with Elise, wanting to compose music and my decision to not join the Amish church but every time I opened my mouth to begin, I found that the words just wouldn't come out.

We were nearly finished repairing the fence when Elise began playing the piano. The song came dancing out of the open window, bringing tears to my eyes which I blinked rapidly away. She was playing one of my compositions. I averted my face from Daett and continued to work as if the music wasn't having an effect on me.

"That's lovely," Daett said.

"What?" I asked him in astonishment. Daett had stopped working and was looking at Elise's house with a strange expression on his face that I couldn't quite define.

"The music," Daett explained. "It's beautiful. It is perfectly suited to today. I don't know why, but the song makes me think of autumn and harvest."

"That's wonderful," the words were out before I could stop them.

Daett looked at me with a confused look on his face.

"Why is it wonderful?" he asked.

God had just given me the opportunity to talk honestly and openly with my Daett. I prayed silently for the right words to say, took a deep breath, and began talking to Daett.

"It's wonderful that the music makes you think of autumn and harvest because that is what the composer intended. In fact, the name of the composition is 'Bountiful Harvest,'" I said, looking directly into Daett's eyes.

"How do you know that, John?"

"Because ... I am ... the composer," I said.

Daett's eyes looked confused so I further clarified.

"What I am trying to tell you…, Daett…, is that … I am the one who composed this song."

"You made that song?" Daett asked in a hoarse voice.

"Yes, Daett."

He turned and looked at Elise's house and then again at me. I could see the questions in his eyes and the wheels in his head turning.

"How does the Englisher know your song?" he asked.

"Her name is Elise and it's a bit of a long story," I said gently. "Would you like to go over to her house and sit down on the porch and I can tell you all about it?"

Daett looked uneasy at this suggestion. Having farmed all of his life, his interaction with Englishers was limited and therefore he is uncomfortable around them.

"Elise can stay inside if you would prefer and you and I can talk alone," I said. "After we are done talking, if you want to meet her afterwards then I will get her and introduce you but if you don't want to, that will be fine also. What do you say? She makes a really good cup of coffee."

At those words, Daett's eyes lit up. He loved coffee and I was hoping that would be enough to sway his decision. It was. Daett nodded his assent.

'Gut." I smiled at him.

We walked the short distance to Elise's house. When I knocked on the door, she stopped playing the piano and came to the door. She opened the door and her face and eyes lit up with joy, causing my heart to beat fast.

"John!" she exclaimed in delight, stretching out her hands towards me. "What a wonderful surprise! It's absolutely marvelous to see you."

"It is wonderfully good to see you, Elise," I said as I captured her hands in mine. I brought her beautiful hands up to my lips and kissed them. "My Daett and I were mending the fence when we heard your lovely piano playing."

Her eyes flitted behind me, noticing Daett for the first time. She let go of my hands and tried to pull them away. I knew she was doing that for my sake because of Daett being there, but I did not relinquish my hold on her hands, letting her know that I no longer wanted to keep us a secret.

"Daett liked the song and your piano playing," I told her conversationally. "He said that the song made him think of fall and I told him that was good because that was exactly what I was striving for and the name of the song is 'Bountiful Harvest.' As you can imagine, Daett has quite a lot of questions about that and I need to talk to Daett and to tell him everything. However, if it is okay with you, I wanted to know if you would permit us to sit on your back porch for our talk. It's too long of a story to stand up for the duration and at home there are many distractions and little ears listening."

"Absolutely," she said with a smile. "Hello, Mr. Yoder. I've heard many wonderful things about you. It is so nice to meet you. Come on in and I will take you through to the porch. Would you like something to drink?"

"Thank you," Daett said in English for her benefit. "It is nice to meet you as well."

"Well, if it wouldn't be too much trouble, I did tell Daett that you make the most delicious coffee in the world," I said as I stepped into the house. Daett looked down at his shoes and then up at me and Elise hesitantly.

"Don't worry about your shoes, Mr. Yoder," Elise said, smiling. "These old wooden floors can stand up to anything and they clean up easily."

Daett looked relieved that he wouldn't have to remove his shoes and he stepped inside. KitKat ran around our legs, meowing her cute little chirping meow as she excitedly followed us through the house and out to the back porch. Daett and I sat down and Elise went back into the house, closing the door behind her for our privacy. KitKat stayed with us, having immediately jumped up into my lap as soon as I had sat down as though my lap were created solely for her sitting purposes. Daett noticed this, his lips twitching in amusement.

"Es Ketzli seems to be taken with you," Daett said with a smile. "So does es Meedel."

"Yes," I agreed with a smile as I felt my face blushing. "I like the kitten and the girl as well."

We sat in silence for a few minutes. I stroked KitKat's fur and scratched her head while she purred her appreciation. It felt odd to be sitting in Elise's back porch with my Daett. I had this conversation in my head countless times over the years but now that the occasion had come to tell Daett my secrets, I was having trouble finding the words to say.

Daett broke the silence first.

"John, I want you to know that you can tell me whatever it is on your mind," he said. "I've been waiting for months for you to come to me."

"You have?" I asked in astonishment.

"Of course, John. I am your Vadder. I've known for a long time that you had something troubling you. When you came home that night and told me that you had seen Rachel with Daniel, I was upset and distracted. I know that did upset you but I also knew that was not the only thing weighing on your mind. I hope you know, John, that there isn't anything you need to keep from me."

"Daett, do you remember when I was a little boy and I told you about the music?"

"The music?" Daett asked, his brows creased in concentration.

"Jah; remember how I told you that the world around me made music?"

Daett thought for a moment more and then understanding dawned on his face.

"You mean the time when you was very young and you asked me … wasn't the music that the wind blowing through the leaves and cornstalks make and the sounds of the birds make … beautiful?" he asked.

"Jah," I said as I nodded my head in assent. "Once I understood that it was forbidden to compose music, I tried really hard to shut the music out but I couldn't, Daett. The music is a part of me and it cannot be turned off or ignored. I went to the library whenever I could and through books, recordings, the internet and videos that I watched at the library, I slowly taught myself all that I could about music theory and music composition. I also listened to all the recordings I could find of music instruments so that I could know what they sounded like. I taught myself about tempo and what all the different notes mean. I taught myself how to draw the treble staff and bass staff and how to arrange the notes on the staffs. I knew that composing music would be seen as sin, so I went to great lengths to hide it from you and Mamm and everyone. Daett, I am sorry for that. I am sorry that I went against what you and Mamm taught me and that I lied to you."

"It's okay," Daett said huskily. "I forgive you."

"Thank you, Daett," I responded. "But I do have more to the story so you may want to hold off on forgiving me until you hear everything.

"Speaking of hearing, it's ironic but the only person who knew about my music was the one person who would never be able to hear it. But Samuel has always asked me to describe what music I hear and seems to enjoy it a lot when I sign the music to him. Having to do that has really helped me grow as a composer because it challenged me to think about not just what I wanted the music to sound like but what I wanted the music to convey. It's hard to explain and I don't expect you to understand, but when I compose a piece of music, it often feels like I am praying to God. Sometimes it is a song of gratitude like the song you heard earlier which is a song thanking God for a bountiful harvest and celebrating the beauty of fall and God's creation. Other times it feels like I am crying out to Him but my favorite times are when the music I write is a song of praise to the Lord."

As I said those words, I saw a look of surprise on Daett's face. Just then, the back door opened up and Elise came out of the house carrying a tray. She set it down on the table between us. We thanked her and she smiled at us. She told me to wait four minutes before pushing down the plunger and then she went back inside, shutting the door behind her. I resumed my tale.

"I had just decided that I was going to put aside composing music and pray to God every day until the music went away. And I was going to join the Amish church. Then one day I was working in the cornfield when I heard the most beautiful music I had ever heard. I walked to the music and when I reached the edge of the cornfield, I could see Elise playing the piano through the open window. She was breathtakingly beautiful. Hearing the piano music awakened a desire in me to hear my own music played out loud. That night I snuck over here and I left an envelope for her on her front porch that contained a note asking her to play the music and one of my musical compositions. The next day I was so worried that I wouldn't be in the cornfield and able to hear the music when she played it but by the grace of God I was. Thankfully I was, and hearing her play my music was glorious. I had naively told myself that once I heard one of my songs out loud, that would satisfy my desire. Instead it was a spark that ignited a fire within me. Elise and I began writing notes back and forth and I kept bringing her music to play. I began composing more music than ever before and the quality of the compositions was better also. Elise and I had never seen or talked to each other face to face but through our letters, I got to know her and I began falling in love with her. She fell in love with me too, Daett. Then she asked to meet in person. I was nervous, afraid that she would reject me once she knew that I am Amish. She is smart, beautiful, talented, and sophisticated. She has traveled all around the world playing the piano and I am just a farm boy who has an eighth grade education and the furthest I've traveled is Lancaster, Pennsylvania. I felt completely unequal to her."

"Now, John," Daett said sharply. "You are selling yourself short! You are a fine young man! You are tall and strong, and good-looking like your Daett! You are a *wunderbaar* farmer and hardworking. In addition to all of that, you are a very talented composer!"

I couldn't help but smile. Imagine, Daett coming to my defence like that. It was out of character for him but I quite enjoyed it.

"Thanks, Daett," I said as I pushed down the plunger on the coffee press. I poured out a cup of coffee for Daett and then myself. Elise had also placed a plate of her maple-raisin oatmeal cookies on the tray. "Try one of the cookies. They are delicious."

Daett reached out, took one of the cookies, and took a bite. After a few chews, his eyes brightened and he smiled at me. He finished the cookie and reached for another one.

"This cookie is delicious," Daett said as he raised the cup up to his mouth to take a drink of coffee. "So is the coffee. Your Elise can bake and make a good cup of coffee. Carry on with your story."

My Elise. Those two simple words caused the warmth and happiness of hope to bloom inside my heart. He hadn't yet heard the rest of our story and he was acknowledging us as a couple.

"Now where was I?" I wondered.

"Elise wanted to meet you face-to-face and you were nervous about it," Daett said as he reached for his third cookie much to my amusement.

"Right," I said. "I was nervous to meet her but there was nothing else that I wanted more in the world. When she opened the door and we looked into one another's eyes, all of the anxiety, fear, and doubt melted away. In an instant I knew that I loved her and she loved me; and I also knew that she was the one God had created just for me. We were able to talk freely just as if we had known one another for years. She makes me very happy, Daett."

I finally had the courage to look up from my coffee cup and to look into Daett's eyes. To my surprise, Daett's eyes looked misty. He took his handkerchief out of his pocket and wiped his tears away.

"John, your love story with Elise reminds me of when your mother and I first met and fell in love. I am glad that you have found love. Now, I won't pretend to understand about the music because that isn't something I understand but having heard the music and how you have described it leads me to believe that God did indeed give you the talent for music. You do understand that if you want to become a music composer and to marry an English lady, you will not be able to be a member of the Amish church?"

"Yes sir," I said as I swallowed hard. "I do understand. It was a difficult decision to make. I don't want you to think otherwise. I have agonized over this decision and prayed about it fervently. I am sorry, Daett."

"I'm glad to know you have given it a lot of thought and prayer," replied Daett. "I must admit that it will be hard for me. I've always prayed that my children would grow up to serve the Lord and to be good Amish men and women. My heart will grieve over you leaving the Amish, I can't deny that. But John you are my son and *Ich liebe dich*. Nothing will ever change that."

"Daett," I said in a choked voice, "you are a wonderful *Vadder and Ich liebe dich*."

"Well now," Daett said as he cleared his throat. "Why don't you get your girl so I can meet her and get to know her properly."

I went inside with KitKat close behind me. We found Elise in the kitchen pacing and chewing her fingernails. KitKat started meowing and running back and forth like it was a game. When Elise saw me, she stopped pacing and looked at me with eyes full of questions.

"How did it go?" she asked.

I strode over to her, gathered her into my arms, and kissed her thoroughly. By the time our kiss was over, her knees had gone weak and I was practically holding her up.

"It went well," I said with a smile. "In fact, he wants for you to come outside so he can meet you properly and get to know you."

We went out on the back porch. When Daett saw us, he stood up to greet us.

"Daett, I would like for you to meet Elise Snow," I said. "Elise, this is my Daett, Abram Yoder."

"It is nice to meet you," Daett said as he smiled and extended his hand to shake Elise's hand.

"It's very nice to meet you too," said Elise, smiling, and she reached out her hand to Daett.

I looked down at their two hands which were so very different, their contrasts made all the more distinct by the intertwining of their two hands. Daett's big hand engulfed Elise's more petite hand. His large hand was tanned, rough, and calloused from years of working hard outdoors while Elise's slender hand was soft, smooth, and unblemished. Even their hands were a testament to how different they were from one another. Yet two very important things brought them together: their love for me and their love for God. Elise sat down next to me. We held hands while we talked with Daett. It was uncomfortable at first but soon Daett and Elise were talking and laughing with ease. By the time Daett and I were ready to go home, he and Elise were firm friends. I hugged her goodbye and kissed her cheek.

"*Ich liebe dich*," I whispered into her ear.

"I love you too," she whispered back.

"Welcome to the family," Daett said as he turned and walked down the front porch steps.

My face flamed red and Elise's eyes danced with mirth and happiness.

"Thank you, Mr. Yoder," she replied.

Daett stopped walking and turned around to look at Elise. He still held his hat in his hand and there was something vulnerable about him. I wondered what it was.

"Call me Daett," he said in a gruff voice and noticed his hand was trembling slightly as he placed his hat upon his head.

"All right," said Elise, smiling. "Thank you, Daett. I enjoyed meeting you and look forward to seeing you again soon."

Daett's back straightened and his shoulders squared. All uncertainty left his face and he smiled the first true smile I had seen on his face since Mamm's death. He nodded at her and then headed for home. I took advantage of his turned back and quickly kissed Elise on the lips before I ran to catch up with Daett. I was so happy that it felt like I was walking on air.

CHAPTER SEVENTEEN

A unt Fannie and Rachel had made my favorite meal of chicken and dumplings, mashed potatoes, peas and corn. When I thanked them for the second time as I filled my plate with seconds, Rachel flushed with embarrassment.

"Goodness, John," she said. "It's just plain country cooking. Mending that fence must've made you work up a powerful appetite!"

"Just wait until he finds out what we are having for dessert," said a smiling Aunt Fannie.

"What's for dessert?" I immediately asked.

"Blackberry cobbler! And I made it all by myself!" Rachel said triumphantly. "Well, Aunt Fannie did give me some help."

"All I did was give you some advice," said Aunt Fannie. "You made the dessert alone. And mighty good it will be too!"

"I wish I had known that before I got so much food on my plate the second time around," I groaned. "I hope I have enough room for a big helping of blackberry cobbler."

"You're a big strapping boy," said Aunt Fannie, smiling. "You have a big enough appetite to finish your dinner and to eat a good-sized helping of blackberry cobbler and fresh churned vanilla ice cream."

"Fresh churned vanilla ice cream? Oh my!" I groaned again. "I'm going to have to pray extra long before bed tonight."

251

"Why do you have to pray extra long tonight?" asked Elias, looking confused.

"Because I am going to have to pray and ask God to forgive me of gluttony!"

"What's glootney?" asked Ruthie, stumbling over the word.

"Gluttony is simple to explain," said Daett with a mischievous smile on his face. "Gluttony is eating two heaped platefuls of chicken and dumplings, mashed potatoes, peas and corn, followed by a bowl full of blackberry cobbler and vanilla ice cream!"

Everyone, myself included, laughed and laughed. It wasn't so much that Daett's joke was that funny although it was cute. Rather, it was a relief to see Daett smiling again and sharing a laugh, as a family did more to help in the healing of our family's broken heart than anything else. Mamm would be very happy.

After everyone had been given a serving of blackberry cobbler and vanilla ice cream, I looked at Daett and he nodded his head slightly. On the walk home, we had agreed that I should tell the family of my decision. However, first he wanted to tell them news that concerned our whole family.

"I know that Mamm's death has been hard on all of us. I'm thankful for such gut children and for how hard you all work. All my daughters are gut at keeping house and cooking but you are all still es gezewwel and we still need some help. Thankfully, my dear sister Fannie came to help us. I am so grateful, Fannie. You have always been a gut schweschder to me. Your entire life, you have had a servant's heart. Since you became old enough, you've gone whenever and wherever you were needed and you have never said a word of complaint. But now you are getting older."

At this, Aunt Fannie started to protest.

"Now I'm not saying you are old, Fannie, just older. You can still work harder and faster than Rachel but it is true that we are both getting older. I think it's time for you to enter into a new stage of life."

"What do you mean, Abram?" she asked.

"Fannie, I want you to have stability and security. I want you to live with me, with us, permanently. Now I will be honest with you, Fannie. I do also need you. As my girls get older, they will get married and leave home and I will need your help even more. My boys will also grow up and start families of their own and one day all of es gezewwel will be gone and I will have an empty nest. It's selfish, Fannie, I admit that. I would like to have your companionship in my old age. You took care of me as a bobbel and it's only right that I...," Daett paused for a moment before proceeding, "let you take care of me when I'm an der Grobaart."

At this we all started laughing again. When the laughter finally settled down, Daett continued talking.

"Seriously though, Fannie, I would like for you to make your home with me and my family permanently. If I pass away before you, I expect one of my der soh will provide a home for you."

At this, we assured Daett and Aunt Fannie that we would love having her live with us.

"What do you say?" Daett asked Aunt Fannie.

"Of course," Aunt Fannie said with tears in her eyes. "I would love to make my home with my family permanently. I can't thank you enough. I have worried and prayed about my future. This is the greatest gift that anyone could ever give me."

"You are a gift to us, Fannie, and to me most of all," Daett said, his voice thick with emotion.

"I do have one stipulation," said Aunt Fannie.

"What is it?" Daett asked.

"If in the future you find someone else that you wish to marry, don't you let worry over me keep you from marrying again. I wouldn't be able to live with myself if I thought I kept you from being happy," she said.

"I appreciate your concern," Daett said. "However, I will never love again, Fannie. Nor will I ever marry again. Ruby was the love of my life and always will be. That will never change. Which is another reason why I want you to make your permanent home with me. I would starve to death if I had to cook for myself. And you make delicious blackberry cobbler."

"All right," Aunt Fannie said amidst the giggles. "I will make my home with the Yoder family. But if things ever change in the future...."

"They won't," interrupted Daett. "But if they do, I promise I will discuss it with you. However, my heart and mind will not change."

Looking into Daett's eyes, I knew he was right and now I understood how he felt. Mamm was his one true love just as Elise was mine. I let everyone finish their blackberry cobbler and vanilla ice cream before I told the family my news.

"I have something I need to tell everyone," I said.

Everyone turned and looked at me. I looked at each and every face. I loved my brothers and sisters so much. Inwardly I prayed that we would always stay close, but I knew that it was likely that we would grow apart as life took us in different directions and we became busy with work and families of our own. Still, my family would always be dear to my heart and I would do all that I could to ensure we were as close as we could be.

"First, I want you to know that everything I am getting ready to tell you, I have already told Daett. I've had a secret pretty much all of my life," I said. "It's hard to explain but I will try. I have always heard music in my mind. I know that makes it sound like I'm crazy but I'm not. When I hear the wind blowing the trees, the horses' hooves on the road, the sound of Elias chopping wood, and Daett sharpening a knife, I start thinking about what music notes fit the pitch, what tempo is correct, and what musical instruments could sing this song. Musical notes began to fill the stanzas on the pages I see inside of my brain. For me, the songs that I compose are a love song to God. Some of the songs He gives me are songs of praise, others are songs of petition, and others are songs of thankfulness. When I realized that this was unique to me and that it was seen as sin by the Amish church, I tried really hard to make the music stop but it wouldn't go away. This is why I haven't joined the church yet. I have wanted to and up until recently I was continuing to try to suppress the music and the desire to compose music. Then I met a girl.

"She is the most beautiful, wonderful girl in the world and she is a very talented, world-renowned pianist. Having heard her play the piano when I was working in the cornfield made me want to hear my music played out loud. So I took her some of my sheet music and wrote her a note. I left it for her to find on her front porch. She played my music and that made me want to hear her play even more of my songs. I continued to leave her notes and sheet music to play. She wrote me back and left notes for me. She didn't know I was Amish.

At first, we just knew each other's first names; hers is Elise. Over time we began to fall in love. Eventually, I also learned that Elise has a type of cancer called leukemia. Right before Mamm died, Elise and I decided to meet in person. I was really nervous. I mean, what if she didn't think I was handsome or what if she didn't like me because I am Amish? But when our eyes met for the first time, all of the fear, anxiety, and doubt vanished. I knew that she was the one for me and thankfully, she knew that I was the one for her. The more that we get to know one another, the more we fell in love. I can't imagine living without her. In fact, I am going to ask her to marry me."

"Does this mean you aren't going to join the Amish church?" asked Elias.

"Yes, that is correct. I will not be joining the Amish church but not just because of Elise. I truly believe that God has given me the talent to compose music. As much as I love Elise, I love God more. If I abandon the music, I would be abandoning God because music is the way I talk to God, and it is the way I tell others about God. I may not be joining the Amish church but I will continue to go to church. And I will always be your big brother. I love all of you and that will never change no matter what."

Thirty minutes later, I was tired but relieved. It felt really good not to have secrets from my family. My siblings had grilled me. They had asked me all the questions I was expecting and some that I didn't see coming. The one that had smitten my heart came from little Ruthie.

"Does this mean we can't talk to John anymore until he stops being bad?" she asked.

"No *der Schatz*," Daett said. "John hasn't been baptized in the Amish church, thus he won't be punished for breaking the Ordnung. Do you understand?"

"No," Ruthie said as she shook her head side to side.

"Very well. I will try to explain it to you in a better way," Daett said patiently. "Let's say that you are my child and as my child I have given you a list of all of my rules. If one of those rules are that you can't go outside to play until you finish your chores and instead of obeying me, you sneak outside to play without first doing your chores, would you get in trouble with me?"

"Yes," said Ruthie.

"Yes, you would because you broke Daett's rule and you had been told what the rule was and chose to ignore it anyway," Daett explained. "Now let's pretend that you are not my daughter and you do not have my list of rules. Let us also pretend that you are visiting my house and I come into the kitchen and I find you eating cookies. This makes me upset and I punish you because you were eating cookies right before dinner and one of my rules is no eating snacks before dinner and ruining your appetite. Is it right for you to be punished for a rule you didn't know about? Would that be fair?"

"No!" Ruthie said emphatically "That would be mean, Daett!"

"Exactly," Daett said, smiling at her. "When someone is not Amish, they cannot be punished for rules that apply only to the members of our church. Even though John was raised in the Amish church, he hasn't been through the classes we have to take before being baptized. Rachel has been baptized in the Amish church. She knows the rules. Does that make sense now?"

"Yes!" Ruthie smiled. "Have I been bapteased, Daett?"

"No, Ruthie. You haven't been baptized yet. You have to be a young lady before you can be baptized," Daett answered.

"Oh gut!" sighed Ruthie. "I was awffuy scared I was going to haff to sit all by myself and nobody could talk to me unless they had to and I wouldn't like that at all."

"Why on earth would you think you would be shunned?" asked Rachel, looking amused and curious at the same time.

Ruthie squirmed in her seat and turned red in the face. She didn't answer but just shrugged her shoulders. She looked at Daett and then back down.

"Ruthie, answer the question," Daett said gently. "Just this once, I promise that you will not be punished."

Instantly she lifted her head up and smiled, looking greatly relieved.

"I was afraid I would be punished because I snuck and ate some cookies before supper! But not too many! They are awffuy gut cookies but I only ate three or four," she said the last part doubtfully. "Or maybe six. But I still ate all my dinner and all my ice cream and cobbler!"

"What?" Rachel asked in astonishment. "You ate all of that?"

Aunt Fannie scooted her chair back and went to the cookie jar. She quickly counted the amount of cookies left and then turned around to look at us.

"Has anyone else eaten any cookies this afternoon?" she asked.

After we all said we had not, Aunt Fannie walked back to the table, sat down next to Ruthie, and looked at her earnestly.

"How do you feel?" she asked Ruthie. "Do you feel okay?"

"Yep!" Ruthie said emphatically.

"Well, I am glad!" Aunt Fannie exclaimed. "I am shocked but glad!"

"How many cookies did she actually eat?" Daett asked.

"Seven!"

For a moment we all sat in astonishment, staring at my little sister who apparently was a bottomless pit. Then we all started laughing. Looking around the table at my family all laughing and enjoying being together, I felt profound gratitude. I just knew that Mamm was looking down from Heaven laughing with us and utterly delighted that we were all doing well. We would never stop missing her and I know there will be many days ahead during which we will miss her intensely and cry. But God's grace is new every morning and the joy that He gives us would be our strength.

As soon as dinner was over, I told my family that I had a few visits that I needed to make and I wouldn't be home until late.

First, I went to visit Samuel. When I knocked on their door, Samuel's Mamm answered the door and welcomed me inside. After a brief conversation with Samuel's parents, I asked if we could talk privately. Samuel motioned for me to follow him and we went upstairs to his room.

"What is it?" he asked me in sign language.

"I have some news," I signed. "I have fallen in love with a beautiful girl and the best part is she loves me too."

Samuel smiled a huge grin. He signed, 'Wow!" and high-fived me.

"Tell me everything," he demanded.

So I did. I told him about hearing Elise playing the piano from the cornfield and that this had made me desire to hear my own music played out loud. That this desire was so strong it physically hurt, prompting me to write a complete stranger a note asking her to play my music transcribed on the sheet music I left for her. A look passed across Samuel's face that I had trouble defining but I knew that it was something bothering him.

"What is it?" I asked, pausing my story.

"Nothing—it's okay," he signed, feigning false bravado.

"Samuel, I know you better than that. Please tell me."

"Okay," he sighed. "I understand your pain."

"My pain?" I asked.

"Yes. You said that you wanted to hear your music played aloud so much that it physically hurt and I understand that," he signed. "I would love to hear my Miriam's voice saying she loves me just once. I would love to hear what music sounds like too. In church I watch as people sing and I wonder what it sounds like. The only time I get to hear music is when you sign it to me."

"Samuel, I don't know what to say to that. If what I said offended you, I'm sorry."

"No need to be sorry," he signed. "I wasn't offended. I just wanted you to know I understand your desire to hear your music played aloud. Go on with your story."

"Elise played my song. It was so beautiful I wept. Instead of taking away the desire to hear my music played, it made it stronger. Elise and I kept writing notes back and forth and I kept leaving my compositions for her to play. Gradually through the music and the notes, we fell in love. Eventually, we met face-to-face and it was wonderful.'

"You love her," signed Samuel. It was a statement not a question.

"Yes I do," I replied. "I love her and she loves me. I'm going to marry her."

"I'm happy for you. Does this mean you are leaving the Amish church?"

"Yes, I am."

Samuel nodded and for a while, we didn't say anything at all. Then Samuel tapped me on my shoulder to get my attention.

"John, you will always be my best friend," he signed.

"You will always be mine too," I replied.

Next I went to Bishop Troyer's house. As I brought the horse to a stop, he stepped out onto his porch. I jumped down, secured the horse, and walked over to him.

"Gut'n owed," I said as I stretched out my right hand towards him.

"Gut'n owed," he responded as he grasped my right hand in his and shook it.

"May I talk to you for a little while, Bishop Troyer?" I asked, trying to choke down my nervousness.

"Jah, come sit down over here," he said while gesturing towards a couple of wooden rocking chairs.

"Danki," I said as we sat down. "Bishop Troyer, I want to start by thanking you for being a gut bishop, for your prayers, your kindness, and Biblical teaching and preaching. I have looked up to you and you have been a gut example of Christ's love to me."

"I appreciate that, John," he said.

"Bishop, I wanted you to hear this from me and not second hand. I am not going to be joining the Amish church."

"Jah, I figured you would not be this time since you hadn't joined the classes," he responded. "I know that losing your Mamm was hard on you so I decided not to pressure you about it. But you know, John, that you must make that choice soon."

"I have, Bishop Troyer. I'm not going to be joining the Amish church at all," I said as gently as I could and it hurt my heart to see the look of pain that passed across his face. "Bishop, I want you to know that my choice is not a reflection on my family, our church, or you. It was a very hard choice to make and I prayed about it earnestly."

As I explained to Bishop Troyer, just as I had to my family not long before, why I was leaving the Amish, I saw the various emotions flit across his face: pain at the loss of a young man from out of his congregation; confusion as he tried to understand my reasons; relief at my declaration of my love for God and my desire to serve Him; resignation at the knowledge that he would not be able to change my mind; and respect for being man enough to come and tell him about my choice. When I was back in the buggy getting ready to leave, Bishop Troyer put out his hand to stop me.

"Before you go, John, I won't lie: it is hard for me to lose one from my flock. I will pray that one day you will come back to the fold. However, I want to tell you that although you will not be joining my church, our love for you will not end. My wife and I will continue to pray for you. I hope to meet your bride one day and I know my wife would like that as well. John, if you ever need me, I will be right here." He reached out his hand and I took it.

"Thank you, Bishop Troyer," I said, my eyes unexpectedly filled with tears. "Thank you for everything."

Then I urged the horse forward and headed for home. It was dark as I got close to home. I could see the lights shining in the windows beckoning me and showing me the way to go. Even the horse seemed to sense the fact that we were nearly home because his steps quickened independent of my urgings. As we pulled into the driveway and up to the house, the front door opened and a figure stood framed by the light coming from inside the house. I jumped down from the buggy and hitched the horse to the porch rail. I strode up the steps and gathered Elise in my arms. I was home.

CHAPTER EIGHTEEN

The morning sun streamed in from the bedroom window, waking me up. I moved a little, stretching and trying to wake up fully. KitKat, who was sleeping with her head on my shoulder, protested this disturbance of her sleep. Memories from last night surfaced in my still sleep-befuddled mind and just for a moment I wondered if it had all been a dream. John's declaration of his intention to spend his life with me and his determination to compose music even though that meant he would be leaving the Amish church filled me with awe and disbelief that I could be worthy of such love and sacrifice.

"He chose me," I said to KitKat, whose only response was to yawn and stretch her whole body out long and lean.

I began daydreaming about the future. I dreamed that by our wedding, my hair would have grown back even if only a little and I prayed that I would be in remission by then so we wouldn't have cancer looming over our heads. I wondered what type of wedding John would want. Considering that he had been raised Amish, I hoped that he would be happy with a small intimate ceremony. In my backyard there was a big, beautiful maple tree. I had always loved this tree. I had spent many happy hours of my childhood in, on, or under that tree. The summer that I was seven years old, Poppy made me a wonderful swing. I had watched in fascination as he had made it from start to finish. He had cut a section of wood off a 2x10 and drilled two holes in it at each end. Then he had sanded it until it was smooth and painted several coats of varnish on it. Poppy had threaded a large, thick, and sturdy rope through the holes in the wood before securing the ends of the rope on a large branch in the maple tree. It had been a wonderful swing and I had spent many happy hours swinging and staring up into the leaves on the tree and the sky peeking through. Often while I was swinging or sitting on a branch of the tree after climbing up it like a monkey, I would daydream about getting married and falling in love. Now that I was in love with John and he loved me back, the reality was even better than all of my daydreams put together. As I went about my morning routine, my thoughts were consumed with rosy dreams of my wedding and a life with John. I was drinking my second cup of coffee when realization dawned on me, stopping all of my daydreams immediately. I looked at KitKat who had already eaten her breakfast and was busy grooming herself.

"KitKat!" I exclaimed. "I just realized that John hasn't asked me to marry him yet. Surely he will, though, right? I wonder how long he will want to court me before he will propose?"

These thoughts caused me to realize how much I wanted to marry John and spend my life with him. Moreover, I didn't want to wait. Cancer had taught me that life is precious and as none of us are promised tomorrow, we should live everyday like it was our last. Ah well, I had a doctor's appointment in an hour. Time to stop daydreaming and to get ready.

Daett had talked with the bishop and I was to be allowed to stay home with the understanding that this would be a temporary arrangement and I would not try to influence any of my siblings to leave the Amish and that I would not expose them to the things of this world. Bishop Troyer had also graciously given his permission for me to continue helping Daett on the farm when needed even after I moved out. I was excited about the future and I had absolutely no doubts about my choice. Yet at the same time, I was nervous. Our community was all I had ever known and it was scary to think of a future without the security of the Amish community. I wanted to marry Elise as soon as possible but I doubted that I was worthy of her. I had little education and no worldly goods to bring into the marriage. And I would need to find a way to support a wife and family. I was sitting out on the front porch when Daett came out to join me, bringing me a cup of coffee.

"You are up early," Daett said as he handed me the cup of coffee.

"Never went to bed actually," I said wryly.

"Why not?" he asked. "Are you worried?"

"Jah," I admitted. "I've been trying to come up with a plan for the future. I love Elise and I want to marry her and have a family with her. The thing is I have only ever known farming and I don't know how I am going to support a wife and family."

"Ah, I see," Daett said. "A wife and family is a lot of responsibility but you are a hard-working young man. You are up to the task."

"Thanks, Daett," I said.

We sat there for a while in companionable silence drinking coffee and looking out at the fields. I had also loved living here. I hoped that Elise would want to continue living in her house. My life was almost completely changing; it would be nice if I would be able to live next door to my family and to continue to be surrounded by the fields and land that I loved so much.

"John, I've been needing to talk to you about something," Daett said, interrupting my thoughts. "It's about your Mamm."

"Mamm?" I asked as I turned to look at him.

"Yes," Daett replied. "Mamm and I made wills a couple of years ago. John, I'm not going to lie to you. I have always wanted for you, for all my children, to grow up to love God, serve God, and to be good Amish men and women. That was our desire and our aim in raising our children. We strove to teach you and your brothers and sisters about the Lord and the Ordnung. However, when you told me about the music, it confirmed something that your Mamm and I had already thought: that you were a special, talented boy and that you were different. We always loved you,

John, and we are so very proud of you. We thought perhaps that you would grow up to be der Vorsinger."

Daett paused for a moment and took a drink of his coffee before continuing.

"Still we both had a niggling doubt, your Mamm more so than me. Sometimes late at night when we couldn't sleep, your Mamm would talk about it with me. She would tell me that she worried that when you grew up you would choose a path outside of the Amish church and she was concerned about that. She wasn't worried for the reasons you might think. She wasn't worried about your soul. No, she would reassure me about that. She told me that you had a deep love for God and she knew that if you ever left the Amish church, it would be because you knew this to be God's will for your life. She worried that at first you would struggle to provide for yourself financially. We heard horror stories about youth who had left the Amish and once out in the world that was so new and strange for them, they didn't know what to do in order to survive. We heard that some of the ex-Amish became drug dealers or prostitutes and those who didn't resort to illegal means of employment struggled to survive because they only had an eighth grade education.

"When your Mamm's Daett passed away six years ago, your Mamm inherited some money. She asked me if she could keep some of it for her own to put back and save. We were doing well and we didn't need the money, so I told her that she could save it all. She opened up a savings account at the bank. Over the years when she made a little bit of money, she would put it in that account but she never used any of it. She would occasionally ask me if I wanted or needed any of it and she always kept me apprised of the amount she had in the bank. When we made our will, your Mamm asked me if it was okay if she left half of the money to me and half of the money to you and if I passed away before her, then all of the money would go to you. Again, I insisted that I didn't need the money; God has always supplied our needs and wants. We compromised: she left me enough to cover her funeral expenses and then the rest would go to you. So you see, John, you don't need to worry so much. Now the money isn't so much that you will never need to work, but it is enough money to take care of you and Elise until you find work."

"Daett, I don't know what to say," I said as tears pricked the back of my eyes.

"There's no need to say anything," Daett said with a smile. "Taking care of our children is what parents do; that's what your Mamm is still doing for you. One day, you will be a Daett and you will understand."

"That's one thing that I don't worry about," I confessed to Daett. "I don't worry about being a gut Daett or knowing what to do because all I will have to do is to follow the example you have set for me."

Later that morning, Rachel needed to go to town for some supplies. I offered to drive her. As we turned onto the road out of our driveway, I spoke to her.

"Rachel, I offered to drive you because I was wanting to have a chance to talk to you privately."

"What about? Is something wrong?" she asked with a hint of apprehension in her voice.

"No, nothing is wrong," I reassured her. "I was hoping to get your advice as a weibsmensch."

"Really?" she asked with an arched eyebrow. "What about?"

"Well, you know that I am in love with Elise," I began.

"No!" she gasped in mock shock. "I had no idea!"

"Very funny." I smiled at her. "Because I love her, I want to marry her and spend the rest of my life with her."

"She loves you too, John," reassured Rachel. "I'm sure she will say yes when you propose."

"That's exactly what I was hoping you could help me with," I said. "I have no knowledge about the engagement process of Englishers."

"Oh, John, that is so romantic!" Rachel exclaimed, clasping her hands together. "I would be honored to help you come up with the perfect proposal! The first thing you need to do is buy an engagement ring. Englishers always propose with a ring, and when English girls get engaged, they like to announce it to the world by showing off the ring.

Then you need to plan to ask her at the perfect place in a romantic and perfect way."

"Well, I just thought I would just ask her to marry me," I said, starting to feel really nervous. "I'm not perfect, Rachel. I'm not sure if I would be able to pull off a big showy proposal."

"That's all right," Rachel assured me. "You don't have to be perfect. You are right, though, you aren't a showy type of a person; neither is Elise. The proposal could be simple but it needs to be meaningful to her. Propose in a way that would fit who you both are together. Let me think for a moment......"

Her voice trailed off as she stared off into the distance. I could practically see the wheels turning in her mind. I was starting to get bored when she snapped her fingers and looked at me triumphantly.

"I've got it! It's perfect, it's simple, and it fits you two like a glove! Now, first things first, do you have any money for a ring?"

I thought about Daett's revelation to me this morning. I had tried to turn it down but he refused. I told Daett that I had been saving money for a number of years now in hopes of one day marrying and I had $12,000 saved. Daett had been so pleased with me but he still refused to allow me to decline the money and give it to him. When he told me that the amount of money I had inherited was $125,000, I was extremely shocked. Again I begged Daett to take all of the money and when he said no, I begged him to take some of the money. He was absolutely adamant about it as this was his and Mamm's wishes. I was humbled, honored, and relieved. We wouldn't starve or become homeless. Because of Mamm, I would be able to ask Elise to marry me and I would be able to provide for her. Daett did ask me to keep the inheritance a secret from my siblings as they wouldn't be inheriting money from Mamm. Still this meant that I could use some of my own money to buy a ring for Elise with a clear conscience.

"Yes," I told Rachel. "I have been saving money for a long time and I should be able to provide her with a nice ring."

"That's wonderfully gut!" Rachel beamed. "We need to find out her ring size."

"Rings have sizes?"

"Of course they do, silly," scoffed Rachel. "Look at your fingers and think of Elise's fingers. A ring that fits on her finger wouldn't fit on yours."

"That's true," I said, seeing the sense of it. "But now the size of your fingers look the same as Elise's fingers. You could try the ring on for me and if it fits you, it should fit Elise."

"Very clever," marveled Rachel. "I would love to get to try on rings for Elise!"

"Gut," I said with satisfaction. "After you're done with your shopping, could we go to the jewelry store?"

"Of course," Rachel said, looking as excited as a kid going to a candy shop.

"Then if the ring doesn't fit her," I said thoughtfully, "I will take it back and get the right size."

"Why don't you go on to the jewelry store and start looking at the rings while I go do my shopping? I know what you're like," said Rachel. "It will take you forever to make a decision about which ring to buy."

"You are probably right," I said wryly. "I will stop by the bank first to take out some money for the ring. So tell me all about this perfect yet simple proposal idea that you thought of."

I lit the candles in the room and looked about me one last time. I wanted tonight to be perfect as I had something of great importance to tell John. Thanks to Rachel's ministrations, my house always looked immaculate.

"The candles are lit, the gas logs are also lit," I said, taking inventory. "The coffee is ready and in the insulated pot to keep it warm, and the cookies are ready. Did I miss anything, KitKat?"

She meowed up at me, her tale flipped about, and her big, beautiful, green eyes shone with curiosity and happiness. She had been by my side during the dark times, giving me comfort. It was fitting that she should be here with me to celebrate this happiest of days.

"Yes, we are ready," I told KitKat. "All we need now is John."

At hearing John's name, KitKat's ears went straight up and she ran to the door meowing. I chuckled at her. She was as in love with John as I was. KitKat was not to be disappointed for within seconds, I heard the sound of horse hooves and wagon wheels in the driveway. I went to the front door, stooped down to pick KitKat up, and then opened up the front door. I watched John as he jumped down from the buggy, secured the horse, and then took the stairs two at a time. I opened the door for him and he came in and gathered both me and KitKat in his arms. KitKat let out a squeak of protest and we let her jump down. Then he pulled me closer to him, pressing my body to his so close that not even a piece of paper could have separated us. I breathed in the scent of him. I love his smell. I love everything about him. He is my beloved and I am his. Finally the embrace ended and I stepped back.

"Come in," I told him.

He stepped inside and looked around the room, taking in all of the details. He looked at me and arched his left eyebrow. A smile danced on his lips.

"Should I go?" he asked me in a teasing voice. "It looks like you are expecting company."

"No," I replied. "Not company."

"No?"

"Nope. I am expecting John my beloved."

"Ah, so you are expecting company!"

"No," I shook my head. "I'm not expecting company because John, you are not company nor a visitor. You are my heart and you are my home."

His eyes flamed with intensity of love and passion. He again gathered me into his arms and kissed me so completely that my knees gave way. He held me up with his strong arms. His love would never let me fall and come to harm. When the kiss ended, we were both breathing rapidly and our lips were red and swollen.

"Come," I said as I took John by the hand and led him over to the couch. "I have something wonderful and exciting that I want to tell you."

"What is it, Elise?" he asked me as he tenderly brought my hand up to his lips for a kiss.

"I had an appointment with my oncologist today...." I paused.

"Yes?" he prompted.

"She said that my leukemia is in remission! I don't have to take any more chemotherapy! John, I don't want to celebrate too soon, but I think that God has answered our prayers!" I exclaimed with joy. Tears flowed down my cheeks but they were tears of happiness. Then I noticed that John was also crying with relief and joy shining in his eyes. He pulled me into an embrace and together we cried and laughed. The ugly, dark, and heavy clouds of cancer and death had finally rescinded and were no longer hanging over our heads. When we were finally composed enough, John took some folded papers out from his jacket and handed them to me.

"This is a new song that I am working on," he said and I noticed that his hands were trembling slightly. Perhaps because of the news of my remission?

"I think the song is perfect for this wonderful moment," he continued. "Would you play it for me and give me your opinion?"

"Of course," I said as I got up and went to the piano. John followed me and stood patiently next to me as I smoothed the sheets of music and put them on the music desk. I noticed that the title was missing but I surmised that he hadn't decided on one yet. I looked at the notes, positioned my fingers, and began to play. The song was beautiful and sounded at first pleading as if the music was asking a question. Amidst the Grace notes were two distinctly separate yet complimentary melodies: one in the bass clef and the other in the treble clef. It was an absolutely lovely and brilliant composition of a musical conversation.

"Hmmm," John said thoughtfully as I continued to play the piano, "it doesn't quite have the right ring to it, does it? Perhaps I can remedy that."

I started to tell him that I thought the song was actually perfect just as it was when I noticed that John was getting down on one knee. I abruptly stopped playing the piano and twirled around to see John down on one knee, holding out an open ring box towards me. I was speechless.

"The name of the song is 'The Proposal,'" John said with a smile. "I haven't completed the end of the song yet because it depends on your answer."

"My answer?" I asked in a quivery voice.

"Yes," he said. "Which coincidentally is the answer that I hope you will give me when I ask you this question: Elise, will you marry me?"

"Yes! Yes, I will marry you, John!" I said and then we kissed, embraced, and laughed.

John took my left hand and slid the ring onto the third finger. I brought my hand up for a closer look and I gasped.

"John, this is a gorgeous ring! Oh, my beloved, I love it very much but I worry that you have spent too much. I don't have to have such a fabulous ring. I'm sure we could take it back and exchange it for a cheaper ring. All I need is you," I assured him. "I don't have to have a big gorgeous ring to have proof of your love or to convince me to marry you."

"Take it back?" John looked at me aghast. "Absolutely not! Unless you don't like it. Do you not like it? Or does it not fit?"

"Like it? I love it! I adore it! John, it's the most beautiful ring I have ever seen. And it fits perfectly! Thank you! Thank you for the ring but most of all thank you for loving me and for wanting to marry me! I love you so much, John Yoder. I love you with an everlasting love."

"I love you, Elise," he said tenderly as he gently slid me off the piano bench and onto his lap. "I adore you and I cannot wait to become your husband and for you to become my wife."

After that, we didn't speak for a long while but rather we allowed our kisses, caresses, and embraces to say it all for us. Unlike other men I had dated in the past, John did not attempt to take advantage of me and he took no liberties. Because of this not in spite of it, I was all the more assured of the purity and truth of John's love for me.

CHAPTER NINETEEN

It was the last Sunday I would be attending the Amish church, because I would be marrying Elise on the coming Saturday. Bishop Troyer had been very gracious to me in allowing me to continue to attend church and he had also granted me a very special request. At the moment it was the reason I was extremely nervous, which was why my right leg couldn't stop shaking. Daett cast me a look and then directed his look at my leg. With difficulty I stilled my leg, although I could do nothing about the internal tremulous feeling. Finally it was time. Bishop Troyer had looked at me and nodded his head.

I stood up and walked to the center of the room in between the men's section and the women's section. I looked at these faces that I had known all of my life. For a moment, I felt sheer panic. How could I do this? How could I leave everyone and all that I had known? Surely, God was asking too much of me. I closed my eyes and whispered a silent prayer. I felt an imperceptible shift in the atmosphere and a whisper of wind at my neck. God was with me. I opened my eyes and began to speak.

"I want to thank Bishop Troyer for allowing me to speak to you today and for being a good bishop to me. I have held a secret for nearly as many years as I have been alive and for that I am sorry. When I was little I didn't realize that I was different; I thought that everyone heard the things that I heard. You see for me, the wind blowing through the trees or the horses' hooves on the ground and all of the other things that we hear throughout our days sound like music. I don't just mean that they sound like music to my ears, but I truly hear the music inspired by the sounds I hear. Even though I knew it was wrong, I researched and learned all that I could about music. I taught myself how to write the music down on staff paper. I kept this hidden. In August I had decided that I would put away music and take the vow and join the Amish church. Then one day when I was working in the cornfield, I heard the most beautiful music coming from the house on the other side of the cornfield. I walked to the edge of the field and I could see a beautiful young woman inside of the house playing a piano.

"Her music awoke within me the desire to hear my own music played out loud. I wrote a note to her and snuck over to her house that night. I left at her door an envelope containing some of my music and a note from me. She played my music and she wrote me back. Eventually I realized that I was falling in love with her. At the same time, I began composing more music than ever before. It comes as naturally to me as breathing. I don't expect any of you to understand but when I compose music, it feels like I am praising God and also like I am praying to Him. If I was to deny the music, it would be to deny God. Because I believe that God has given me this talent for music and because I am marrying Elise, an Englisher, I have made the decision not to take the vow and I will be leaving the Amish church."

I heard some sharp intakes of breath and some muttering. I looked around at their faces and saw shock, sadness, anger, disbelief, and many other emotions reflected there but the one that caused my heart the most pain was the faces who looked hurt.

"I want to say to you that this was a really hard decision. Even now, I am terrified because I am leaving the only church and the only way of life I've ever known. I also want you to know that my decision is not in any way a negative reflection on my Daett, my Mamm, Bishop Troyer, or any of my family or church family. Bishop Troyer has been a very gut bishop to me. He has counseled me and told me the truth even when it hurt. Although I know he wishes I would stay in the Amish church and he has been open with me about that, he has been kind to me. I have stayed in his home as a child and I have heard Bishop Troyer in prayer for his church. He loves God and he loves all of us. There is no one that I respect more than Bishop Troyer.

"My Daett is a wonderful Vadder. He has lived the Ordnung before his family, brought us to church, read us the Bible daily, and led us in prayer daily. I am telling you this because I don't want there to be any speculation as to why I have left and I don't want it to reflect badly on my Daett or Bishop Troyer or any of our gut preachers. I want you to all know that my door will always be open to any of you and I will help any of you if ever the need be and if it is okay with the bishop and the preachers. Thank you."

I sat down and gripped my hands tightly together as they were trembling uncontrollably and my knees were knocking together. There were no more secrets. I felt free. Now I was ready to start a new life with Elise.

Many people wished me well, many told me honestly that they felt I was making the wrong choice and they would pray for me. I understood and appreciated their honesty.

The rest of the week was incredibly busy and before I knew it, the week was gone. I had worried that I would have trouble sleeping the night before the wedding because of my excitement. However, I was so tired that when I went to bed, I fell asleep almost immediately.

"John," a voice said, breaking through my sleep. "John, it's time to wake up."

"Go away," I groaned. I had been sleeping so well and it was deliciously warm under the covers. "It's too early to get up."

"Today is your wedding day, John," Daett said.

At these words, I opened my eyes and sat up. Daett was standing beside my bed, smiling at me. The sun was streaming in my bedroom windows, causing me to squint my eyes against the brightness of the sunlight. *My wedding day*, I repeated the words inside of my mind. It was amazing to me that the talented, sophisticated, and gorgeous Elise was marrying me.

"I'm so excited to be marrying Elise," I said to Daett as I got up out of bed.

"I'm happy for you, Son," Daett said. "Elise is a good young lady. Now get dressed. We have chores to do."

I smiled as he headed out of my room and downstairs. Even on my wedding day, Daett was still telling me to do chores and that made me happy because it made me feel like some things will remain the same even though my life would forever be altered after today. As I got dressed, I looked around the small room. Years ago, the room had been Mamm's sewing room. As our family grew, the room I shared with my brothers became increasingly short on space. I had gone to Pennsylvania for a few weeks the summer I turned thirteen. I went to stay with Mamm's parents and to help her Daett with work he needed help with at his farm. When I came back home, Mamm was so happy to see me and she acted as excited as a child on Christmas morning. She and Daett had me follow them upstairs and then into this room. At first I was confused: I wondered where Mamm's sewing stuff was, why she had turned it into a guest room, and why Mamm and Daett were so excited to show me the guest room.

"Do you like it?" Mamm asked me.

"Jah, it's a very nice guest room, Mamm, but where did you put your sewing machine and fabric?"

"Well, we have a nice family room and a lovely living room. They are both large rooms and we don't really need both rooms. We spend more time in the living room, so we did some rearranging and gave away a few pieces of furniture to a family in need. Then Daett moved my sewing things down into the family room and made me a very nice sewing area. The best part is there's a nice fireplace in there that will keep me warm in the winter and there is still a couch and a couple chairs including an armchair that your Daett likes. That means in the evenings when I sew, he can sit in there with me," Mamm answered me. "But John, you have misunderstood. This isn't a new guest room," she said. She turned to Daett. "Abram, why don't you explain it to him?"

276

"John, you have proven yourself to be a very responsible, hardworking, and gut young man. Mamm and I have noticed that since we have more growing sons than daughters, the boys' bedroom is too crowded. We felt that since you are the oldest and you work hard, it would be only right to make this room into a small bedroom for you."

"This room is just for me?" I asked incredulously as I looked around the room and this time I really observed things: I had a twin bed that I wouldn't have to share with anyone, and on the bed was the blue-and-white blanket that my Mamm had made for me; a dresser to put my clothes and belongings in; a braided rug that Mamm had made; and a bedside table on top of which was an oil lamp and a horse that my Daett had whittled for me. He had given it to me on my fifth Christmas and I had treasured it ever since.

"Yes, it is all for you," Daett had assured me.

The memory made me smile and it also caused me to realize for the first time that as happy as I was to be marrying Elise and embarking on a new life with her, I would miss my Amish life. I would miss our home, my family and friends, and I would miss the peaceful, honest simplicity of the Amish way of life. All of my belongings except what I had needed for today had already been packed up and taken to Elise's house—our house, I corrected myself. Daett was to take my suitcase for our honeymoon and a crate with the rest of my things over to Elise's home when he dropped Rachel off to help Elise get dressed for the wedding. As the next oldest son, Elias was going to be moving into my room and he was very excited about it. Looking around my room had made me realize there were a couple of things that I would love to take with me and I made up my mind to ask Daett if he would be okay with it.

When I went into the kitchen, all of my siblings and Daett and Aunt Fannie were already there. Amidst cries of 'Congratulations!' and 'Happy wedding day!' I sat down at the kitchen table. Daett prayed over the food and then we began filling up our plates. Once it settled down a little and became more quiet since everyone had their mouths full of food, I spoke up.

"Daett, I was wondering if I could ask you about a couple of things in my room," I said.

"What about it?" Daett asked me.

"I'm a little embarrassed to ask you about it, Daett," I admitted. "I don't want to seem greedy or selfish."

"Don't worry," Daett said. "Just ask."

"Well, I guess I'm feeling a little homesick already but as I was getting dressed this morning, I looked about my room and realized that there were a few items in my room that I would like to take with me to Elise's. It would help make her house feel more like my house too, I guess," I said, my face flushing red from being so honest about my feelings in front of my family. "Now Daett if you don't want me taking some of the items or none of them, I will completely understand and I won't be hurt one bit. But what I would like to take with me, if it's okay with you, is the blue-and-white quilt Mamm made for me."

"Well of course, John," Daett answered. "Mamm made that quilt especially for you."

"Jah, I know that, but since Mamm is gone, I thought you might want to keep it here."

"That's considerate of you, John, but your Mamm would want you to keep it," Daett said.

"The other two things have been in my room since you and Mamm turned that room into my room but they aren't necessarily mine. But if you could spare them, I would also like to take the braided rug that Mamm made and the kerosene oil lamp on the bedside table."

"Well, now, Elias, I would suppose it would be up to you," Daett said thoughtfully. "After all, the room will be yours, so it depends on whether or not you feel like you would need them. If Elias doesn't need them, then you are more than welcome to take them with you but if he needs them, then I would ask that you leave them."

"That sounds fair," I said. "What do you think, Elias?"

"I don't need them, John," Elias said stoutly. "I think you should take them with you to remind you of home."

"That's awfully gut of you, Elias," I said. "Danki."

"You're welcome," Elias said. "Besides, I was planning on taking my own lamp to my room. And I have a quilt Mamm made for me also."

Cries of "Me too!" echoed around the table. Daett was sitting at the head of the table placidly listening to the chatter as he ate his breakfast, a look of contentment on his face. I looked around the table at all of the faces so dear to me. I was looking forward to being married to and living with Elise, but I admitted to myself that I would miss mealtimes with my family.

The day went by fast and although the chores were the same ones that I had performed day in and day out, a sense that the day was far from ordinary hung about me.

At last the time came to get ready for my wedding.

My wedding!

Just thinking of that made me giddy with happiness. I went into town and went to the barbershop. It was the first time that I had ever had my hair professionally cut. I looked in the mirror afterwards. This one small change was startling. I hoped that Elise would like it. I returned back home where I bathed, shaved, and got dressed for my wedding. My suit was the first store-bought suit that I had ever owned. It felt strange yet freeing. Someone knocked on my bedroom door and I went to answer it. Rachel stood there and when she saw me, her mouth dropped open.

"John! You look so handsome and fancy!" she exclaimed. "Elise is going to fall in love with you all over again!"

"Thank you," I said, smiling.

"I came to tell you that I am ready to go to Elise's house to help her get dressed. Do you have your things ready to drop off at her house?"

"Yes. If you think you can carry the crate, I'll get the suitcase as it's the heavier of the two."

We got everything loaded up into the buggy and then Daett took Rachel to Elise's house. When he came back, we rounded everyone up and got in the buggy and headed to the church. As we rode past the familiar countryside and towards town, I felt unbelievably happy. Today I'm marrying the one whom my soul loves.

The seventeenth of December proved to be a gloriously beautiful and sunny day. I jumped out of bed as excited as a child on Christmas morning. I ran over to the window and looked outside. A light fresh dusting of snow caused everything to look clean and white. It was the type of snow that decorated the trees beautifully.

"It's a perfect day," I whispered to KitKat who promptly ignored me and buried her head in the blankets, unwilling to get up just yet.

I didn't have much of an appetite due to excitement, but I did manage to eat a piece of toast and drank two cups of coffee. After breakfast, I took the sheets off the bed and put them in the laundry basket. Then I made the bed with the luxurious new sheets that I had bought. I had washed them and they smelled delightful, and they were just as soft as I had hoped. I packed my bags and sat my toiletry back in the bathroom. All I would need to do was to grab the items I needed and I would be ready to leave for our honeymoon. Full of nervous energy, I went through the entire house, picking up and straightening up anything out of place. There wasn't much to do since Rachel does such a good job cleaning for me. Afterwards I was tired so I lay down on the couch. KitKat jumped up on me and lay down on my belly. Her purring lulled me to sleep and I took a refreshing nap. When I woke up, I ate an apple and then I took a long hot bath. I was very happy that my hair was growing back and I actually had enough hair to shampoo. Granted it was a very small amount of hair but it was hair all the same and I was thrilled with it. I put on my new silk undergarments that I had bought especially for my wedding. Since neither my mother nor maid of honor had arrived and I couldn't put on my wedding dress without help, I put on a soft, warm and fuzzy white bathrobe. The house telephone rang and I went downstairs to the kitchen in order to answer the phone as this was where the only phone was located. Being attached to the wall and not cordless, it was quite the antique but it served its purpose.

"Hello?" I said.

Hello, Elise," my mother's cool and impersonal voice answered me. "Happy wedding day!"

"Thank you," I said. "Where are you? I thought you would be here by now? Did you find a nice hotel in town? You know you would've been welcome to stay with me."

"Actually, I wasn't just calling you to wish you a happy wedding day but to let you know that I am not able to come. I watched the news and saw that it is so miserably cold in Indiana and you have lots of snow," Mother said in her cool voice. "You know that I just cannot take the cold weather at all any more. I am sorry, darling."

Although I thought I had steeled myself for the disappointment that I had known would come, sadness and loss poured over me like a bucket of cold water dousing the fire of my joy. Before I could stop myself, the words just came tumbling out.

"I should've known that you wouldn't bother coming to the wedding of your only child just like you didn't come to your only child's side when she was fighting cancer and death."

Her sharp intake of breath was deliberate and calculated and aimed to make me feel guilty. It was unsuccessful in its endeavor. Still, she was my mother and as such she deserved to be treated with respect. I prayed a silent prayer for strength and for God to hold my tongue.

"I am sorry, Mother," I said. "I shouldn't have spoken to you like that."

"No," she said coldly. "You should not have."

"I am just very disappointed that you aren't here to share this wonderful day with me," I said, barely able to keep the tears at bay.

"Yes, well, it couldn't be helped," Mother said stiffly. "You have no idea how much pain my arthritis causes me or how difficult it can be for me to travel. Besides that, the cold hurts me so much! It seems to me that if you truly wanted your mother at your wedding, you would have held your wedding here in California. Then I could've helped you plan an elegant wedding which would've been more in keeping with your status instead of this little country wedding you've planned too quickly."

I couldn't listen to any more of this. Today was the day I'm marrying my beloved and I did not want it stained with anything that could take away any of our happiness at all.

"Mother," I said kindly but firmly. "I'm sorry but I have to go. Today is my wedding day and I have much to do. I love you and I will talk to you soon."

I could hear her voice talking but I went ahead and hung the phone up. After staring at it for a moment, I unplugged the phone from the wall. Then I reached into my pocket, pulled out my cell phone, and turned it off just as it began to ring again and showed Mother's name and photo on the front. I was getting ready to head back upstairs when a knock on the door stopped me. I went to the door and looked out of the peephole before throwing open the door with a cry of gladness.

"Rachel!" I exclaimed. "I'm so glad to see you! You look lovely!"

"Thank you," she said, smiling at me. "I know it's not the type of dress you are used to bridesmaids wearing. Are you sure I look okay?"

She nervously smoothed down her snowy white apron that she wore overtop of her pale blue dress. Her thick, glossy brown hair was fixed on top of her head in a neat bun which was underneath her cap.

"You are absolutely gorgeous," I assured her. "Are you ready to help me get my wedding dress on?"

"Yes," she replied as she followed me upstairs and to my bedroom. I noticed that she was looking about her. At first I wasn't sure what she was looking for and then it dawned on me. I had told her that my mother was supposed to be coming for the wedding and naturally, Rachel assumed that she was here somewhere.

"My mother called right before you arrived," I said, trying to keep my voice even and neutral. "She called to let me know that she wasn't able to come for the wedding."

"Ach ke," Rachel exclaimed. "I am sorry, Elise. It must be hard to not have your Mamm here with you on your wedding day."

"It's okay," I said as I forced a smile. I don't think that Rachel was deceived for a moment but she didn't force the issue and for that I was grateful.

I took off the robe; then I pulled on my white pantyhose. I slid the garter with the blue ribbon up to just above my right knee.

"It's my something blue," I said to Rachel who was watching me with amusement. "My dress is my something new. My something old is my grandmother's locket. Oh, I better put that on before I forget it."

I crossed over to the vanity table and picked up the locket lying there. I slipped it over my head and felt the coolness of the metal against the bare skin of my chest.

"What is borrowed?" Rachel asked.

"Hmm?" I asked, being a bit distracted.

"What is your something borrowed?" she expounded.

"Oh no!" I sank down on the bed still holding the garment bag. "My mother was supposed to bring a pair of her earrings that I have always liked and I was going to borrow those to wear. I will have to pick out another pair of earrings. I have plenty so that shouldn't be a problem, but I guess I will have to forgo the something borrowed."

"Actually, I have something that you are welcome to borrow," Rachel said shyly. "It's not as grand as the locket or earrings but I brought one of Mamm's handkerchiefs for you to use today. I thought you might need one in case you tear up during the wedding."

Rachel reached into her pocket and brought out a white linen handkerchief and handed it to me. It was soft with age and a bouquet of yellow and blue flowers were embroidered in one corner. As I examined it even closer, I noticed that the bouquet was tied together with a blue ribbon. On the blue ribbon the initials R. L. were embroidered in white. Tears welled up in my eyes and I looked up into Rachel's waiting eyes.

"It's perfect," I said. "I would love to carry it today. Are you sure?"

"Yes," she said emphatically. "It would make Mamm very happy that you are going to carry it. And I want you to know, when I say borrow, I mean for you to borrow it permanently."

"I couldn't keep it. You or one of your sisters will want it," I protested.

"Nonsense," she said briskly. "I insist! Besides, Mamm had a dozen or more handkerchiefs that she made and embroidered so there are still plenty for me and my sisters to choose from. In fact, I am carrying one myself today."

"All right." I smiled at her. "Thank you, Rachel."

I opened up the garment bag and took out my wedding dress. Joy flooded over me. Today was the day that I got to put on the most beautiful dress that I had ever owned. It was the day that I would get to marry my best friend and the love of my life. I was the luckiest girl in the world.

"What a lovely dress," Rachel said in an awestruck voice.

I had forgotten that she hadn't seen it before. John and I had not wanted a long engagement and decided to be married quickly. It had taken those few weeks in which I had to plan the wedding for the seamstress at the wedding dress shop to perform the necessary alterations. Which meant that Rachel had not seen my dress before today.

"Do you like it?" I asked her.

"I love it," she exclaimed. "I've never seen anything like it! It's the most beautiful dress in the world! You will look like a princess!"

She handled the dress almost reverently and the entire time she buttoned up the little pearl buttons that went all the way up my back, she kept exclaiming how beautiful the dress was, how well it was sown, and what a pretty bride I was. Rachel helped me to put the veil on and then the metallic flower and leaf headband embedded with crystals over top of the veil to hold it in place. She stepped back and looked at me. Tears welled up in her eyes and she smiled at me.

"Ach, Elise," she said. "You are a *scharmant* bride. You will take John's breath away!"

"Thank you," I said. "Not just for the compliment but I also want to thank you for being my friend, for supporting me, for being my maid of honor, and for helping me today. I am so blessed and happy that today, I not only gain John as my husband but you as my sister."

Rachel hugged me and we both shed some happy tears. Afterwards, I used Ruby's handkerchief to dry my eyes. I smelled a familiar scent. I brought the handkerchief up to my nose and smelled it. It smelled like lilacs. I looked at Rachel and smiled.

"The handkerchief has already proved to be useful," she said, returning my smile.

"Yes it has," I agreed. "It will help us to feel like Ruby is with us today."

The fact that the handkerchief had been made and embroidered by Ruby made it a tangible thing for me to hold, making me feel as if she were with us today. However, it was the scent of the handkerchief that most made me feel that Ruby was with us. As soon as I had smelt the scent of lilacs, my mind transported me back to my dream visit with Ruby. When she had embraced me, she had smelled of lilacs. I knew that Rachel wouldn't understand because I didn't even understand it myself, so I kept the knowledge of the dream visit in my heart.

"It smells just as pretty as it looks," I told Rachel who had been looking at me quizzically as I had just stood there smelling the handkerchief.

"The smell is lilacs," responded Rachel. "Mamm loved the smell of lilacs. We have lilac bushes in our yard and every year when they bloomed, Mamm would collect and dry the blossoms. She would make lilac cachets to put in our dresser drawers. She always kept her handkerchiefs in a small drawer that had multiple lilac cachets in it so that the handkerchiefs would really smell good. Mamm had a weak stomach and bad smells made her sick to her stomach. There is a lady, Lovina, that always sat next to Mamm. Lovina is a sweet lady. She is always helpful to others and willing to give a helping hand, but she doesn't have very good hygiene and to be honest she had terrible body odor. Other people would scooch away from her and made it pretty obvious that they didn't want to sit next to her. Mamm felt sorry for her. So she started standing next to Lovina and walking into church with her; that way when Lovina sat down, Mamm would sit down next to her. No matter how bad Lovina's body odor was—and in the summertime it became really bad—Mamm never scooted away from her. However, she used her handkerchief pretty frequently in order to breathe in the lilac scent. It gave her a little bit of a reprieve from the stench and helped keep her from getting sick. Daett used to tease Mamm about it. He would say, 'Ruby, I noticed that Bishop Troyer's message really affected you today. You were crying and praying into your hankie through the whole sermon!' He would have all of us even Mamm laughing."

Rachel and I chuckled over the odiferous Lovina. I enjoyed hearing stories about John's family. It helped me to understand them and to feel closer to them. Because we would not be part of the Amish, I knew that it was highly likely that we wouldn't be able to be as close to John's family as we would like. But it was my sincere hope that we would have a good relationship with them. For the first time since Poppy and Nana had passed away, I felt like I had a family again. The doorbell rang and since she was closer to the door, Rachel answered it. Nathan stood there smiling broadly.

"Happy wedding day," he said. "Are you ladies ready?"

"Yes, we are," I said as I stepped into the room.

"Wow!" Nathan said when he saw me. "You are a beautiful bride, Elise!"

"Thank you."

Just then, KitKat ran through the living room and jumped up onto the back of the couch and meowed loudly at Nathan as if she were saying hello.

"Look how big you have gotten!" exclaimed Nathan to KitKat. "And beautiful too!"

He reached out and scratched her head and she meowed appreciatively. I slipped into my shoes and then wrapped my cape around me. Nathan opened the door for us and Rachel went out first. I bent down and kissed the top of KitKat's head and scratched her back. She purred in response and gave me slow blinks which is cat speak for "I love you." I slow-blinked back.

"KitKat, I'm going to go marry your pa and bring him home to live with us for the rest of our lives, okay?" I asked her and she meowed back her assent.

Then I smiled at Rachel and Nathan and stepped out of the door. I was ready to go marry my beloved, John.

CHAPTER TWENTY

T he car pulled up at the front door of Fellowship Chapel. Nathan got out of the car and opened the door for Rachel and then for me. Rachel and I went inside the vestibule while Nathan went to park the car. Rachel helped me get out of my cape and to readjust my dress. The florist was there to greet me and to hand me my bouquet. It was a beautiful combination of dark red roses that looked like they were made out of velvet and smelled of summer and blue baby's breath. The stems were bound together with white satin ribbon. I took Ruby's handkerchief and wrapped it around the bouquet; that way, I could hold both of them in the same hand. Rachel noticed what I had done and smiled at me approvingly.

"Nina, you have outdone yourself," I told the florist. "My bouquet is more beautiful than I could've ever imagined."

"Thank you," she said, smiling. "I'm so glad you like it."

She gave Rachel her bouquet and when Nathan came in, she pinned a boutonniere on him. While she was doing that, Ruthie's little face peeked out through the swinging doors leading into the church. When she saw me, her eyes widened and she said, "Wow!"

"Ach, Ruthie, come in here and bring Matthew with you," admonished Rachel. "You two are supposed to enter into the church with us, remember?"

Ruthie's face disappeared and a few seconds later she and Matthew appeared. Like Rachel, Ruthie was wearing a powder-blue Amish dress with a white apron and Kapp. She was carrying a basket full of rose petals. Matthew was wearing a black Amish suit and his hair was neatly combed. Being eight, Matthew had declined carrying a pillow, stating it was too girlish and babyish. He was therefore carrying a black leather Bible with our wedding rings lying on top. Nina arranged the group in order of entry: Rachel was to enter first, followed by Matthew and then Ruthie. I was to come in last.

The music began and the doors swung open wide. Rachel began walking down the aisle. Nathan offered his arm to me and I put my hand through the crook of his arm. He patted my hand and smiled down at me.

"Thank you for walking me down the aisle," I said to him.

"You are very welcome," he responded. "I am very honored."

Matthew walked down the aisle and then Ruthie followed him. She generously and methodically dropped rose petals down the center aisle. We stepped up to the entrance of the church. Nathan squeezed my arm and asked me:

"Ready?"

"Yes," I said emphatically.

Ruthie reached the end of the aisle and stood next to Rachel. Nathan and I stepped into the church and began walking down the aisle. The church looked lovely: there were flowers, candles and beautiful music, and at the end of the aisle was John looking exceedingly handsome and dashing. I felt as though I were stepping into heaven. John's eyes found mine and in his eyes I saw reflected back to me pure, unadulterated love and joy. *This is my beloved*, I thought, *my best friend and today I get to become his wife.*

We reached the end of the aisle. Nathan removed my hand from the crook of his arms, gave it a gentle kiss, and then placed my hand into John's hand. John looked down at me and smiled.

"You are amazingly beautiful," he said softly.

"You are exceedingly handsome," I responded with a smile. "The music for the wedding march was glorious! Thank you for that."

"You are very welcome," John replied. "You were the inspiration for the music."

I stood at the end of the aisle waiting for our wedding to start. For months I had been writing a song without much success. All that I could hear were the opening stanzas and nothing more. I had put it away feeling very frustrated. Most of my songs came to me over the course of minutes or hours at the most. I would have not even bothered with it anymore except for the fact that the melody haunted me. Many times I would be working when the opening notes would began playing in my mind and would not leave me alone. On the night that I had asked Elise to marry me, when she had said yes and we began to kiss, the notes began playing in my mind once again, only this time they did not stop but played on until the ending of the song. That was when I had realized that the song that had haunted me for months was "The Wedding March for Elise" to walk down the aisle to on our wedding day. Elise had trusted me and allowed me to supply the music without her prior approval so that it would be a surprise for her. She had enlisted the help of some of her musician friends who would make up an ensemble and play the wedding march at the wedding for us. I felt a tug on my sleeve and looked over at Sam who was my best man.

"Feeling nervous?" he asked me in sign.

"Just a little," I signed back. "But more excited and happy. Today I marry my beloved, Elise. It is a dream come true."

The music began as the doors at the back of the church opened up. I strained to catch a glimpse of Elise but could not yet see her. Rachel came down the aisle looking beautiful. Then Matthew walked down the aisle stiffly as if he was afraid the rings would fall off the Bible and thus he also kept his eyes staring down at the rings. When he finally reached the end of the aisle without mishap, he gave a sigh of relief. Ruthie was next down the aisle. She was as precious as ever. Whenever Ruthie was concentrating on something, she had a tendency to stick out her tongue slightly. She was doing this now as she carefully dropped flower petals on the aisle. My little sister was absolutely adorable. I looked at Daett and noticed that he was smiling broadly as he watched her progress down the aisle. Then the music changed and became more triumphant. It was time for the bride to walk down the aisle.

Elise stepped into the church and her beauty nearly took my breath away. She looked for me and once her eyes caught mine, she didn't look away for a second. My heart soared with the music. *This is my beloved! She is mine; I am hers and God gave her to me.*

Elise and Nathan reached the end of the aisle and Nathan took Elise's hand, kissed it, and then smiling broadly at me, he placed her hand in mine. As we stood before God and made our vows, I promised Elise and God that I would love her forever and be faithful to her for the rest of our lives. Her beautiful face radiated joy and I knew that when she looked at me, she saw the same happiness radiated back to her.

What makes my beloved more desirable above all others? I have seen her face death and instead of showing fear and a lack of faith, she had been brave and her newly acquired faith in God never wavered. My beloved has stood with me and my family during the worst of times and her love never ceased. In every situation that I have seen her, she has been altogether lovely. I prayed to God for a wife and He gave me Elise. Together we will live a life of praise to Him in everything we do. If God wills it, we will build a family that will raise His kingdom high.

Later that night, we arrived back at the farmhouse. I had not yet learned to drive, so Nathan had been kind enough to drive us back home. He dropped us off and quickly drove away. We stepped up onto the porch and Elise looked down at the welcome mat and gasped. She looked at me in surprise and then back at the envelope on the mat.

"I always look at the mat now," she said. "I got into the habit of looking at it, always hoping for a note and music from you but I didn't really think that you would have left me one tonight! How did you manage it? I know it wasn't there when we left for the church."

"I had a helper named Elias," I answered her. "He snuck away during the reception and put it here for me. Let me get it for you."

I bent down and picked up the envelope and then gave it to Elise.

"I have been researching about Englisher marriage customs and there is one that I found particularly intriguing. It seems that the groom—which is me—is supposed to carry the bride—that's you—across the threshold when we enter our home for the first time as man and wife," I said.

"Well then, you better unlock the door and pick me up, otherwise you are going to miss your chance because I am cold and if you don't hurry up, I'm going inside on my own two legs!" teased Elise.

"All right then, Mrs. Yoder," I said as I unlocked the door. "I live to serve."

I picked her up and carried her into the house, kicking the door shut behind me. I looked down into her lovely face. Holding her in my arms felt so right.

"Are you going to put me down?" she asked.

"Not anytime soon." I smiled at her.

"Well, in that case I might as well open my mail," she said as she opened up the envelope. She pulled out the sheet music and the note paper clipped to it.

Dear Elise,

Since the day that we met, a beautiful melody began playing in my mind. I tried to write the song the melody fit but it never seemed to come. This was unusual for me because as you know, my music generally comes to me by listening to the sounds around me and my composing process is fairly quick. However, this time, I couldn't seem to figure out what place or time of my life where this melody fit. I listened to the sounds of a summer day but the melody did not fit there. I listened to the music of a beautiful fall day but the melody did not fit there either. I listened to the sound of my family laughing and talking and the sounds of home, but my melody did not fit there. Then, when I wasn't even trying, the song came to me.

It was the night I asked you to marry me. When you said yes and we kissed, the melody began playing and this time it played all the way to completion. I was afraid I would lose it by the time I wrote it down on sheet music, but the song stayed with me. Finally the song was written and I knew why the song hadn't come to me before. The song was not written for a particular season or place; this was the song of our love. This is "The Wedding March of Elise."

I love you forever,
John

"I love you, John," she whispered back, her eyes shimmering with tears. "Thank you for the song; thank you for all of the music. Thank you for loving me. You are my beloved, John."

As we kissed, a new melody began to play in my mind. A simple six notes that was all. I smiled because now I knew that this meant God had something wonderful in store for me and Elise that He would reveal to us in His time.

EPILOGUE

His name is Isaac. Other than this and the fact that God has promised us a son with this name, I know nothing about him. I don't know when Isaac will come to us and I don't know what color his hair and eyes will be. He may be short like me or he may be tall like his father, John. All I know is that God has promised Isaac to us and that I already love him with an everlasting love. I long to feel my body change as he grows within me and to feel his movement inside of my womb. My arms ache with the desire to hold him in my arms, to rock my baby asleep, and to hold him close to my breast and to feed him my milk. However, it may be that Isaac will not be born of my body but delivered to me by another. Even if this is true and another woman carries my son within her womb, it will matter not for I will love him the same and this will not change the fact that he will be the much loved and longed for son of both myself and my beloved John.

Who is this child of whom I speak? This child that consumes my thoughts and dreams? His name is Isaac, the Promised.

What will happen in the future for the Lovely Elise and John the Beloved?

Please look for the upcoming books in this trilogy:

Isaac the Promised

&

Rebekah the Betrothed

GLOSSARY

Ach = Oh!

Ausbund = Amish Hymn Book

Es Bobbel = baby

Bobblin = babies

der Bruder = brother

der Bu = boy

Daett = daddy

Dank = thanks

Danki = thank you

Dochder = daughter

Ekschpeckte = expecting, pregnant, with child

Fashrekka = to scare

Faul = rotten, lazy

der Freind = friend

es Gezewwel = children

der Grobaart = old man

die Groossmammi = grandmother

Gut = good, kind

Heichle = hypocrite

Ich liebe dich = I love you

Jah = yes

Es Ketzli = kitten

es Kind = child

Kinner = children

der Liewer = dear, darling

Mamm = mommy

der Mann = husband

es Meedel = girl

Nachtesse = supper, evening meal, night eating

Nee = no

Ordnung = Amish set of rules

die Sau = the pig

Scharmant = elegant, fine, beautiful, very good

der Schatz = sweetheart

Schtuhlgang = discharge of the bowels, discharge, poop

die Schweschder = sister

Sie = she

der soh = son

die Tietschern = female teacher

Vadder = father

der Vorsinger = leader of the choir

Weibsmensch = woman

Wunderbaar = wonderful

CPSIA information can be obtained
at www.ICGtesting.com
Printed in the USA
LVHW031709301219
642060LV00005B/32/P